PRAISE FOR THE OFF-CAMP█████RIES

"Elle has masterfully captured the feelings █████ance and the unbri-
dled sexiness of the New Adult genre wi█████ok! You will swoon
for Garrett!" — Alice Clayton, *New Y███████* bestselling author of
WALLBANGER

"*The Deal* reminds me of all the reasons I love romance" — Jane Litte,
Dear Author

"Elle Kennedy engages your senses from the very first sentence!
Deliciously steamy and heart-achingly tender, *The Deal* is an absolute
winner" — Katy Evans, *New York Times* bestselling author

"I loved this book! Garrett is dreamy. If you love NA, you must read
The Deal!"— Monica Murphy, *New York Times* bestselling author

"Romance. The most adorable couple. The banter - omg the banter.
The romance. The friends. The flirtation. The smiles it gave me." —
Mandi, SmexyBooks

"This was one of the best college romance I've read...I laughed, I
swooned, I couldn't put it down. Highly recommended!!" — Aestas
Book Blog

ALSO AVAILABLE FROM ELLE KENNEDY

Off-Campus

The Deal
The Mistake
The Score
The Goal

After Hours

One Night of Sin
One Night of Scandal
One Night of Trouble

DreamMakers

All Fired Up
Love Is A Battlefleld
Don't Walk Away

A full list of Elle's contemporary and suspense
print titles is available on her website
www.ellekennedy.com

ELLE KENNEDY

NEW YORK TIMES BESTSELLING AUTHOR

THE MISTAKE

OFF-CAMPUS 2

This is a work of fiction. Names, characters, places, and incidents either are the product of the author's imagination or are used fictitiously. Any resemblance to persons, living or dead, business establishments, events, or locales is entirely coincidental.

CHAPTER 1

APRIL

Logan

LUSTING OVER YOUR BEST FRIEND's girlfriend sucks.

First off, there's the awkward factor. As in, it's really fucking awkward. I can't speak for all men, but I'm pretty sure that no guy wants to leave his bedroom and bump into the girl of his dreams after she's just spent the whole night in his best friend's arms.

Then there's the self-loathing element. This one's a given, because it's kind of hard not to hate yourself when you're fantasizing about the love of your best friend's life.

At the moment, the awkwardness is definitely winning out. See, I live in a house with very thin walls, which means I can hear every breathy moan that leaves Hannah's mouth. Every gasp and sigh. Every thump of the headboard smacking the wall as someone else screws the girl I can't stop thinking about.

Fun times.

I'm on my bed, flat on my back and staring up at the ceiling. I'm not even pretending to scroll through my iPod library anymore. I popped the ear buds in with the intention of drowning out the sounds of Garrett and Hannah in the other room, but I still haven't pressed *play*. I guess I'm in the mood to torture myself tonight.

Look, I'm not an idiot. I *know* she's in love with Garrett. I see the way she looks at him, and I see how they are together. They've been a couple for six months now, and not even I, the worst friend on the planet, can deny they're perfect for each other.

And hell, Garrett deserves to be happy. He plays it off like he's a cocky sonofabitch, but truth is, he's a goddamn saint. The best center I've ever skated with and the best person I've ever known, and I'm comfortable enough with my hetero status to say that if I did play for the other team? I wouldn't just fuck Garrett Graham, I'd *marry* him.

That's what makes this a trillion times harder. I can't even hate the dude who's tapping the chick I want. No revenge fantasies to be had, because I don't hate Garrett, not in the slightest.

A door creaks open and footsteps echo in the hallway, and I pray to God that Garrett or Hannah doesn't knock on my door. Or open their mouths, for that matter, because hearing either of their voices right now will only bum me out even more.

Luckily, the loud knock that rattles my doorframe comes from my other roommate, Dean, who waltzes inside without waiting for an invitation. "Party at Omega Phi tonight. You down?"

I dive off my bed faster than you can say *pathetic*, because a party sounds like a fan-fucking-tastic idea right about now. Getting wasted is a surefire way to stop myself from thinking about Hannah. Actually, no—I want to get wasted *and* screw someone's brains out. That way if one of those activities doesn't help me with my don't-think-about-Hannah goal, the other can serve as backup.

"Hell yeah," I answer, already fumbling around for a shirt.

I slip a clean T-shirt over my head and ignore the twinge of pain in my left arm, which is still sore as shit from the bone-jarring body check I took at the championship game last week. But the hit was totally worth it—for the third consecutive year, Briar's hockey team secured another Frozen Four victory. I guess you can call it the ultimate hat trick, and all the players, myself included, are still reaping the rewards of being three-time national champions.

Dean, one of my fellow defensemen, calls it the Three P's of Victory: parties, praise and pussy.

It's a pretty fair assessment of the situation, because I've been on the receiving end of all three since our big win.

"You gonna be the DD?" I ask as I throw a black hoodie over my T-shirt and zip it up.

My buddy snorts. "Did you really just ask me that?"

I roll my eyes. "Right. What ever was I thinking?"

The last time Dean Heyward-Di Laurentis was sober at a party was *never*. Dude drinks like a fish or gets higher than a kite every time he leaves the house, and if you think that affects his performance on the ice in any way, then think again. He's one of those rare creatures who can party like past-day Robert Downey Jr. and somehow be as successful and revered as *present*-day Robert Downey Jr.

"Don't worry, Tuck's the DD," Dean tells me, referring to our other roommate, Tucker. "The pussy's still hung-over from last night. Said he needs a break."

Yeah, I don't exactly blame him. Off-season training doesn't start for another couple weeks, and we've all been enjoying the time off a little too much. But that's what happens when you're riding a Frozen Four high. Last year after we won, I was drunk for two weeks straight.

I'm not looking forward to the off-season. Strength and conditioning and all the hard work it takes to stay in shape are exhausting, but it's even more exhausting when you're working ten-hour shifts at the same time. It's not like I have a choice, though. The workouts are necessary prep for the upcoming season, and the work, well, I made a promise to my brother, and no matter how sick to my stomach it makes me, I can't renege on it. Jeff will skin me alive if I don't fulfill my end of the deal.

Our designated driver waits at the front door when Dean and I come downstairs. A reddish-brown beard devours Tucker's entire face, giving him a werewolf vibe, but he's been determined to try out this new look ever since a chick he met at a party last week told him he had a baby face.

"You know that Yeti-beard doesn't make you look more manly, right?" Dean says cheerfully as we walk out the door.

Tuck shrugs. "I was going for rugged, actually."

I snicker. "Well, it's not that, cither, Babyface. You look like a mad scientist."

He flips up his middle finger as he heads for the driver's side of my truck. I settle in the passenger seat while Dean climbs into the pickup bed, saying he wants some fresh air. I think he just wants the wind to mess up his hair in that tousled, sexed-up way girls drop their panties for. FYI—Dean is nauseatingly vain. But he also looks like a male model, so maybe he's allowed to be vain.

Tucker starts the engine, and I drum my fingers against my thighs, itching to get going. A lot of students in the Greek system piss me off with their elitist attitudes, but I'm willing to overlook that because… well, hell, because if party-throwing was an Olympic sport? Every frat and sorority house at Briar would be a gold medalist.

As Tuck reverses out of the driveway, my gaze rests on Garrett's black Jeep, all shiny in its parking space while its owner spends the night with the coolest girl on the planet and—

And *enough*. This obsession with Hannah Wells is really starting to mess with my head.

I need to get laid. ASAP.

Tucker is noticeably quiet during the drive to Omega Phi. He might also be frowning, but it's hard to tell considering someone shaved off all of Hugh Jackman's body hair and pasted it on Tuck's face.

"What's with the silent treatment?" I ask lightly.

His gaze shifts toward me to offer a sour look, then shifts right back to the road.

"Oh, come on. Is this about all the shit we're giving you about the beard?" Exasperation shoots through me. "Because that's like the first chapter of *Beards for Dummies*, bro—if you grow a mountain man beard, your friends will make fun of you. End of chapter."

"It's not about the beard," he mutters.

I wrinkle my forehead. "Okay. But you *are* pissed about something." When he doesn't respond, I push a little harder. "What's going on with you?"

His annoyed eyes meet mine. "With me? Nothing. With *you*? So much I don't even know where to start." He curses softly. "You need to stop this shit, man."

Now I'm genuinely confused, because as far as I can tell, all I've done in the past ten minutes is look forward to a party.

Tucker notices the confusion on my face and clarifies in a grim tone. "This thing with Hannah."

Although my shoulders stiffen, I try to keep my expression vague. "I have no idea what you're talking about."

Yup, I've chosen to lie. Which is nothing new for me, actually. It seems like all I've done since I came to Briar is lie.

I'm totally destined for the NHL. Going pro all the way!

I love spending my summer as a grease monkey in my dad's shop. It's great pocket money!

I'm not lusting over Hannah. She's dating my best friend!

Lies, lies and more lies, because in every one of those instances, the truth is a total bummer, and the last thing I want is for my friends and teammates to feel sorry for me.

"Save that bullshit for G," Tucker retorts. "And by the way? You're lucky he's distracted with all this lovey-dovey stuff, because if he wasn't? He'd definitely notice the way you're acting."

"Yeah, and what way is that?" I can't stop the edge in my voice or the defensive set of my jaw. I hate that Tuck knows I have feelings for Hannah. I hate even more that he finally decided to bring up the subject after all these months. Why can't he leave it alone? The situation is already shitty enough without having someone call me on it.

"Seriously? Do you want me to list it off for you? Fine." A dark cloud floats through his eyes as he begins to recite every fucking thing I've felt so guilty about. "You leave the room whenever the two of them enter it. You hide in your bedroom when she stays over. If you guys *are* in the same room, you stare at her when you think nobody is looking. You—"

"Okay," I interrupt. "I get it."

"And don't get me started on your manwhoring," Tucker grumbles. "You've always been a player, but dude, you've hooked up with five chicks this week."

"So?"

"So it's *Thursday*. Five girls in four days. Do the fucking math, John."

Oh shit. He first-named me. Tucker only calls me John when I've *really* pissed him off.

Except now he's pissed *me* off, so I first-name him right back. "What's wrong with that, *John*?"

Yup, we're both John. I guess we should take a blood oath and form a club or something.

"I'm twenty-one years old," I continue irritably. "I'm allowed to hook up. No, I *should* be hooking up, because that's what college is all about. Having fun and getting laid and enjoying the fuck out of yourself before you go out in the real world and your life turns to shit."

"You really want to pretend all these hook-ups are just some rite of passage in the college experience?" Tucker shakes his head, then lets out a breath and softens his tone. "You can't screw her out of your system, man. You could sleep with a hundred women tonight and it still wouldn't make a difference. You need to accept that it's not going to happen with Hannah, and move on."

He's absolutely right. I'm well aware that I've been wallowing in my own bullshit and bagging chicks left and right as a distraction.

And I'm equally aware that I need to stop partying myself into oblivion. That I need to let go of the tiny little sliver of hope that something might happen, and simply accept that it *won't.*

Maybe I'll get started on that tomorrow, though.

Tonight? I'm sticking to my original plan. Get wasted. Get laid. And to hell with everything else.

Grace

I STARTED MY FRESHMAN YEAR of college as a virgin.

I'm beginning to think I'll be ending it as one, too.

Not that there's anything wrong with being a card-carrying member of the V-Club. So what if I'm about to turn nineteen? I'm hardly an old maid, and I'm certainly not going to be tarred and feathered on the street for still having an intact hymen.

Besides, it's not like I haven't had opportunities to lose my virginity this year. Since I came to Briar University, my best friend has dragged me to more parties than I can count. Guys have flirted with me, sure. A few of them straight up tried to seduce me. One even sent me a picture of his penis with the caption "It's all yours, baby." Which was…fine, it was super gross, but I'm sure if I'd truly *liked* him, I might have been, um, flattered by the gesture? Maybe?

But I wasn't attracted to any of those guys. And unfortunately, all the ones who *do* catch my eye never even look my way.

Until tonight.

When Ramona announced we were going to a frat party, I didn't have high hopes for meeting anyone. It seems like every time we go to Greek Row, the frat boys just try to sweet-talk me and Ramona into making out. But tonight I've actually met a guy I kinda sorta like.

His name is Matt, he's cute, and he's not giving off any douchebag vibes. Not only is he somewhat sober, but he also speaks in full sentences and hasn't said the word "broski" even once since we started talking. Or rather, since *he* started talking. I haven't said much, but I'm perfectly content to stand there and listen, because it gives me time to admire his chiseled jawline and the adorable way his blond hair curls under his ears.

To be honest, it's probably better if I don't talk. Cute guys make me nervous. Like tongued-tied total-brain-malfunction nervous. All my filters shut off and suddenly I'm telling them about the time I peed my pants in the third grade during a field trip to the maple syrup factory, or how I'm scared of puppets and have mild OCD that could possibly drive me to tidy up your room the moment you turn your head.

So yeah, it's better if I simply smile and nod and toss out the occasional "oh really?" so they know I'm not a mute. Except sometimes that's not possible, especially when the cute guy in question says something that requires an actual answer.

"Wanna go outside and smoke this?" Matt pulls a joint from the pocket of his button-down and holds it in front of me. "I'd light it up here but Mr. President will kick me out of the frat if I do."

I shift awkwardly. "Ah...no, thanks."

"You don't smoke weed?"

"No. I mean, I have, but I don't do it often. It makes me feel all... loopy."

He smiles, and two gorgeous dimples appear. "That's kinda the point of weed."

"Yeah, I guess. But it makes me really tired, too. Oh, and every time I smoke it I end up thinking about this Power Point presentation my dad forced me to watch when I was thirteen. It had all these statistics about the effects of weed on your brain cells, and how, contrary to popular belief, marijuana actually *is* highly addictive. And after every slide he'd glare at me and say, *do you want to lose your brains cells, Grace? Do you?*"

Matt stares at me, and in my head there's a voice shouting *Abort!* But it's too late. My internal filter has failed me once again and words keep popping out of my mouth.

"But I guess that's not as bad as what my mom did. She tries to be the cool parent, so when I was fifteen, she drove me to this dark parking lot and pulled out a joint and announced that we were going to smoke it together. It was like a scene out of *The Wire*—wait, I've never actually seen *The Wire*. It's about drugs, right? Anyway, I sat there panicking the whole time because I was convinced we were going to get arrested, and meanwhile my mom kept asking me how I was feeling and whether or not I was 'enjoying the pot'."

Miraculously, my lips finally stop moving.

But Matt's eyes have already glazed over.

"Uh, yeah, well." He clumsily waves the joint around. "I'm gonna go smoke this. I'll see you later."

I manage to hold in my sigh until he's gone, then release the heavy breath and give myself a mental slap on the wrist. Damn it. I don't know why I bother trying to talk to guys. I go into every conversation nervous I'm going to embarrass myself, and then I end up embarrassing myself because I'm nervous. Doomed from the start.

With another sigh, I head downstairs and search the main floor for Ramona. The kitchen is full of kegs and frat boys. Ditto for the dining room. The living room is packed with very loud, very drunk guys, and a sea of scantily clad girls. I applaud them for their bravery, because the weather outside is frigid and the front door has been opening and closing all night, causing cold air to circulate through the house. Me, I'm nice and toasty in my skinny jeans and tight sweater.

I don't see my friend anywhere. As hip-hop music blasts out of the speakers at a deafening volume, I fish my phone out of my purse to check the time and discover that it's close to midnight. Even after eight months at Briar, I still experience a teeny sense of glee every time I stay out past eleven, which was my curfew when I lived at home. My dad was a real stickler for curfews. Actually, he's a real stickler for *everything*. I doubt he's ever broken a rule in his life, which makes me wonder how he and

Mom managed to stay married as long as they did. My free-spirit mother is the polar opposite of my stuffy, strict father, but I guess that just proves that the whole opposites-attract theory has some merit.

"Gracie!" a female voice shrieks over the music, and the next thing I know, Ramona appears and throws her arms around me in a tight hug.

When she pulls back, I take one look at her shining eyes and flushed cheeks and know she's drunk. She's also as scantily clad as most of the other girls in the room, her short skirt barely covering her upper thighs, her red halter-top revealing a serious amount of cleavage. And the heels of her leather boots are so high I have no clue how she can walk in them. She looks gorgeous, though, and she's drawing a ton of appreciative stares as she links her arm through mine.

I'm pretty sure that when people see us standing side by side, they're scratching their heads and wondering how on earth we could possibly be friends. Sometimes I wonder the same thing.

In high school, Ramona was the fun-loving badass who smoked cigarettes behind the building, and I was the good girl who edited the school newspaper and organized all the charity events. If we hadn't been next-door neighbors, Ramona and I probably wouldn't have known the other existed, but walking to school together every day had led to a friendship of convenience, which had then turned into a real bond. So real that when we were looking at colleges, we made sure to apply to all the same schools, and when we both got into Briar, we asked my father to speak to the residence office and arrange for us to be roommates.

But even though our friendship started off strong this year, I can't deny that we've drifted apart a little. Ramona has been so obsessed with hooking up and being popular. It's all she ever talks about, and lately I'm finding that she kind of…annoys me.

Crap. Even *thinking* it makes me feel like a shitty friend.

"I saw you go upstairs with Matt!" she hisses in my ear. "Did you guys hook up?"

"No," I say glumly. "I think I scared him off."

"Oh no. You told him about your puppet phobia, didn't you?" she demands, before heaving an exaggerated sigh. "Babe, you've gotta stop revealing all your crazy up front. Seriously. Save all that stuff for later, when you're in a relationship with the guy and it's harder for him to run away."

I can't help but laugh. "Thanks for the advice."

"So are you ready to go or should we stay a while longer?"

I glance around the room again. My gaze lands in the corner, where two girls in jeans and bras are making out while one of the Omega Phi guys films the passionate display with his iPhone.

The sight makes me stifle a groan. Ten bucks says that video will wind up on one of those free porn sites. And the poor girls probably won't find out about it until years from now, when one of them is about to marry a senator and the press digs up all her embarrassing dirt.

"I wouldn't mind going now," I admit.

"Yeah, I guess I'm cool with it too."

I raise my eyebrows. "Since when are you cool with leaving a party before midnight?"

A frown puckers her lips. "Not much point in staying. Someone already beat me to him."

I don't bother asking who she's talking about—it's the same guy she's been talking about since the first day of the semester.

Dean Heyward-Di Laurentis.

Ramona has been obsessed with the gorgeous junior ever since she bumped into him at one of the campus coffee houses. Like seriously obsessed. She's dragged me to almost all the Briar home games just to watch Dean in action. I have to admit, the guy is hot. He's also a major player, according to the gossip mill, but unfortunately for Ramona, Dean doesn't date freshmen. Or sleep with them, which is all she really wants from him anyway. Ramona has never gone out with anybody for more than a week.

The only reason she even wanted to come to this party tonight was because she heard that Dean would be here. But clearly the guy isn't fucking around with that no-freshmen rule. No matter how many times Ramona throws herself at him, he always leaves with somebody else.

"Let me just use the washroom first," I tell her. "Meet you outside?"

"'Kay, but be quick. I told Jasper we're leaving and he's waiting in the car."

She darts off toward the front door, leaving me with a prickle of resentment. Nice that she asked me if I wanted to leave when she'd already made the decision for us.

But I swallow the irritation, reminding myself that Ramona has *always* done that, and that it never bothered me in the past. Honestly, if it wasn't for her making decisions and forcing me to step out of my comfort zone, I probably would've spent my entire high school career in the newspaper office, writing the advice column and offering life tips to students without having ever experienced life myself.

Still…sometimes I wish Ramona would at least *ask* me what I thought about something before deciding that we should do it.

The downstairs bathroom has a long line, so I weave through the crowd and head upstairs to where Matt and I had been talking before. I'm just approaching the bathroom when the door swings open and a pretty blonde saunters out.

She jerks when she spots me, then offers a smug little smile and adjusts the bottom of a dress that can only be described as *indecent*. I can actually see the crotch of her pink panties.

As my cheeks heat up, I avert my gaze in embarrassment, waiting until she's at the stairs before I reach for the doorknob. I barely get my hand on it when the door opens *again* and someone else walks out.

My gaze collides with the most vivid blue eyes I have ever seen. It only takes a second for recognition to dawn on me, and when it does, my face burns hotter.

It's John Logan.

Yep, John Logan. AKA the star defenseman of the hockey team. I know this not just because Ramona has been stalking his friend Dean for months, but because his sexy, chiseled face was on the cover of the school newspaper last week. Since the team's championship win, the paper has run feature interviews with all the players, and I'm not going to lie—Logan's interview was the only one I paid any attention to.

Because the guy is smoking hot.

Like the blonde, he looks startled to find me in the hallway, and like the blonde, he recovers quickly from his surprise and flashes me a grin.

Then he zips up his pants.

Oh my God.

I cannot believe he just did that. My gaze involuntarily drops to his groin, but he doesn't seem bothered by that either. He cocks a brow, shrugs, and then walks away.

Wow. Okay.

That should have icked me out. Forget the very obvious bathroom hook-up. The zipper move alone should have placed him directly in douchebag territory.

Instead, knowing he'd just fooled around with that girl in the bathroom evokes a rush of jealousy I don't expect.

I'm not saying I want to have a random hook-up in a bathroom, but—

Fine, I'm lying. I *totally* want that. At least with John Logan, I do. The thought of his hands and lips all over me unleashes a flurry of hot shivers that shimmy up my spine.

Why *can't* I fool around with guys in bathrooms? I'm in college, damn it. I'm supposed to be having fun and making mistakes and "finding myself", but I haven't done jack shit this year. I've been living vicariously through Ramona, watching my bad girl best friend take risks and try new things, while I, the good girl, stand there clinging to the cautious approach to life that my father drilled into me when I was still in diapers.

Well, I'm tired of being cautious. And I'm tired of being the good girl. The semester is almost over. I have two exams to study for and a Psych paper to write, but who says I can't do all that and still squeeze some actual fun in there?

There are only a few weeks left in my freshman year. And you know what? I plan on making good use of them.

CHAPTER 2

Logan

I've decided to ease back on the partying. And that's not just because I got so trashed last night that Tucker had to haul me over his shoulder and cart me upstairs to my bedroom because I was too dizzy to walk.

Though that *was* a major factor in the decision-making process.

So now it's Friday night, and not only did I turn down a party invite from one of the guys on the team, but I'm still nursing the same glass of whiskey I poured more than an hour ago. I also haven't taken a single hit off the joint Dean keeps shoving in my direction.

We're hanging out at our place tonight, braving the early-April chill as we huddle together in the small backyard. I take a drag of my cigarette while Dean, Tucker and our teammate, Mike Hollis, pass around the joint, and I'm only half-listening to Dean's incredibly raunchy recap of the sex he had last night. My mind keeps wandering back to my own hook-up—the sexy-as-sin sorority sister who'd lured me into one of the upstairs bathrooms and had her way with me.

I might have been drunk and my memory might be a bit hazy, but I definitely remember fingering her until she came all over my hand. And I *absolutely* remember being on the receiving end of a pretty spectacular BJ. I don't plan on telling Tuck about it, though. You know, since apparently he's keeping a tally of my hook-ups. Nosy bastard.

"Wait, back up. You did what?"

Hollis's exclamation jars me back to the present.

"I sent her a dick pic." Dean says this as if it's something he does every day.

Hollis gawks at him. "Really? You sent her a picture of your junk? What, like some kind of fucked-up sex souvenir?"

"Naah. More like an invitation for another round," Dean answers with a grin.

"How the hell will that make her want to sleep with you again?" Hollis sounds doubtful now. "She probably thinks you're a douche."

"No way, dude. Chicks appreciate a nice cock shot. Trust me."

Hollis presses his lips together like he's trying not to laugh. "Uh-huh. Sure."

I flick my ash on the grass and take another drag. "Just out of curiosity, what constitutes a 'nice cock shot'? I mean, is it the lighting? The pose?"

I'm being sarcastic, but Dean responds in a solemn voice. "Well, the trick is, you've gotta keep the balls out of it."

That gets a loud hoot out of Tucker, who chokes mid-sip on his beer.

"Seriously," Dean insists. "Balls aren't photogenic. Women don't want to see them."

Hollis's laughter spills over, his breaths coming out in white puffs that float away in the night air. "You've put a lot of thought into this, man. It's kinda sad."

I laugh too. "Wait, is that what you do when you're in your room with the door locked? Take photos of your cock?"

"Oh, come on, like I'm the only one who's ever taken a dick pic."

"You're the only one," Hollis and I say in unison.

"Bullshit. You guys are liars." Dean suddenly realizes that Tucker hadn't voiced a denial, and wastes no time pouncing on our teammate's silence. "Ha. I *knew* it!"

I arch a brow and glance at Tuck, who may or may not be blushing under the five inches of beard growth on his face. "Really, man? Really?"

He offers a sheepish grin. "Remember that girl I was dating last year? Sheena? Well, she texted me a picture of her tits. Said I had to return the favor."

Dean's jaw falls open. "Dick for tits? Dude, you got played. No way are those even remotely comparable."

"What's the equivalent of tits then?" Hollis asks curiously.

"Balls," Dean declares, before taking a deep pull of the joint. He blows out a ring of smoke as everyone laughs at his remark.

"You just said women don't want to see balls," Hollis points out.

"They don't. But any idiot knows that a dick pic requires a full frontal shot in return." He rolls his eyes. "It's common sense."

Someone clears their throat from the sliding door behind me. Loudly.

I turn around to find Hannah standing there, and my chest squeezes so tight my ribs ache. She's wearing leggings and one of Garrett's practice jerseys. Her dark hair is loose and falling over one shoulder. She looks gorgeous.

And yup, I'm a total asshole friend, because suddenly I'm picturing her in *my* jersey. With *my* number scrawled across it.

So much for accepting and moving on.

"Um…okay," she says slowly. "Just making sure I'm not misunderstanding, but…you guys are talking about sending pictures of your penises to girls?" Amusement dances in her eyes as she glances around the group.

Dean snorts. "We sure are. And don't roll your eyes like that, Wellsy. Are you really gonna stand there and tell us that G hasn't sent you pictures of his cock?"

"I'm not going to dignify that with an answer." She sighs and rests her forearm on the edge of the door. "Garrett and I are ordering pizza. Do you guys want to pitch? Oh, and we're putting on a movie in the living room. It's his turn to pick so it'll probably be some God-awful action movie, if you guys want to watch with us."

Tuck and Dean instantly pipe up with yeses, but Hollis shakes his head regretfully. "Maybe next time. My last final is on Monday so I'm spending the rest of the weekend cramming."

"Eek. Well, good luck." She smiles at him before releasing the doorframe and taking a step back. "If you guys want a say in the pizza toppings, you better come inside now, otherwise I'm going to load it with veggies. Oh, and what the hell, Logan?" Those green eyes narrow at me. "I thought you said you only smoke at parties. Am I going to have to beat you up now?"

"I'd like to see you try, Wellsy." My tone is filled with humor, but the second she ducks back inside, the humor fades.

Being around her is like a punch to the gut. And the thought of sitting in the living room with her and Garrett, eating pizza and watching a movie and seeing them all cuddly and in love…a hundred times *worse* than a gut punch. It's an entire hockey team slamming you into the boards.

"You know what? I think I might go to Danny's thing after all. Can I catch a ride with you to the dorms?" I ask Hollis. "I'd drive over myself but I don't know if I'll end up drinking."

Dean stabs out the joint in the ashtray on top of the closed barbecue lid. "You won't end up drinking, dude. Danny's RA is a total Nazi. He patrols the halls and does random room checks. No joke."

I don't care. All I know is that I can't stay here. I can't hang out with Hannah and Garrett, not until I manage to get a handle on my stupid infatuation with her.

"Then I won't drink. I just need a change of scenery. I've been home all day."

"A change of scenery, huh?" Tucker's cloudy expression tells me he sees right through me.

"Yes," I say coolly. "Got a problem with that?"

Tuck doesn't answer.

Gritting my teeth, I mutter my goodbyes and follow Hollis out to his car.

FIFTEEN MINUTES LATER, I'M IN the second-floor corridor of Fairview House, and it's so eerily quiet that my spirits plummet even lower. Shit. I guess the resident advisor really is a hard-ass. I don't hear a peep from any of the rooms, and I can't even call Danny to find out if the party was canceled, because in my haste to escape my house, I forgot to grab my phone.

I've never been to Danny's dorm before, so I stand in the hallway for a moment, trying to remember the room number he'd texted me earlier. Two-twenty? Or was it two-thirty? I wander past each door checking the numbers, and my dilemma solves itself when I realize there isn't even a room two-thirty.

Two-twenty, it is.

I rap my knuckles against the door. Almost immediately, footsteps sound from behind it. Someone's there, at least. That's a good sign.

Then the door swings open, and I find myself looking at a total stranger. Granted, she's a very pretty stranger, but a stranger nonetheless.

The girl blinks in surprise when she sees me standing there. Her light brown eyes are the same shade as her hair, which hangs in a long braid over her shoulder. She's wearing loose plaid pants and a black sweatshirt with the university logo on the front, and from the utter silence in the room behind her, it's obvious I knocked on the wrong door.

"Hi," I say awkwardly. "So...yeah...I guess this isn't Danny's room?"

"Um, no."

"Shit." I purse my lips. "He said it was room two-twenty."

"One of you must've gotten the number wrong then." She pauses. "For what it's worth, there's no one named Danny on this floor. Is he a freshman?"

"Junior."

"Oh. Well, then he definitely doesn't live here. This is a freshman dorm." As she speaks, she plays with the bottom of her braid and not once does she look me in the eye.

"Shit," I mumble again.

"Are you sure your friend said it was Fairview House?"

I falter. I *was* sure, but now...not so much. Danny and I don't hang out too often, at least not on our own. Usually I see him at post-game parties, or he comes over to my place with our other teammates.

"I have no idea anymore," I answer with a sigh.

"Why don't you call him?" She's still not meeting my gaze. Now she's staring down at her striped wool socks as if they're the most fascinating things she's ever seen.

"I left my phone at home." Fuck. As I mull over my options, I run a hand through my hair. It's growing out and I desperately need to get it buzzed, but I keep forgetting to do it. "Is it cool if I use yours?"

"Um...sure."

Even though she looks hesitant, she opens the door wider and gestures for me to come in. Her room is a typical double with two of everything, but while one side is neat as a pin, the other is slob central. Clearly this girl and her roommate have *very* different philosophies about tidiness.

For some reason, I'm not surprised when she walks over to the tidy side. She definitely seems like she'd be the neat one. She goes to the desk and unplugs a cell phone from its charger, then holds it out to me. "Here."

The second the phone exchanges hands, she creeps back toward the door.

"You don't have to stand all the way over there," I say dryly. "Unless you're debating making a run for it?"

Her cheeks turn pink.

Grinning, I swipe the phone screen and pull up the keypad. "Don't worry, gorgeous. I'm just using your phone. I'm not going to murder you."

"Oh, I know that. Or at least I *think* I know that," she stammers. "I mean, you seem like a decent guy, but then again, lots of serial killers probably seem decent too when you first meet them. Did you know that Ted Bundy was actually really charming?" Her eyes widen. "How messed up is that? Imagine you're walking along one day and you meet this really cute, charming guy, and you're like, oh my God, he's *perfect*, and then you're over at his place and you find a trophy dungeon in the basement with skin suits and Barbie dolls with the eyes ripped out and—"

"Jesus," I cut in. "Did anyone ever tell you that you talk a lot?"

Her cheeks are even redder now. "Sorry. Sometimes I babble when I'm nervous."

I shoot her another grin. "I make you nervous?"

"No. Well, maybe a little. I mean, I don't know you, and…yeah. Stranger danger and all that, though I'm sure you're not dangerous," she adds hastily. "But…you know…"

"Right. Ted Bundy," I supply, fighting hard not to laugh.

She fidgets with her braid again, and her averted gaze gives me the opportunity to study her more closely. Man, she really is pretty. Not drop-dead gorgeous or anything, but she has a fresh-faced, girl-next-door look that's seriously appealing. Freckles on her nose, delicate features, and smooth, creamy skin right out of a makeup commercial.

"Are you going to call?"

I blink, suddenly remembering why I came inside in the first place. I look down at the phone in my hand, and now I'm examining the number pad as intently as I was examining her moments before.

"Here's a tip—you use your fingers to dial, and then you press send."

I lift my head, and her barely restrained grin summons a laugh from my throat. "Great tip," I agree. "But…" I let out a glum breath. "I just realized I don't know his number. It's saved in my phone."

Shit. Is this my punishment for inappropriately fantasizing about Garrett's girlfriend? Getting stranded on a Friday night with no phone or ride home? I guess I deserve it.

"Fuck it. I'll call a cab," I finally decide. Luckily, I know the number for the campus taxi service, so I dial that instead, only to be placed on hold immediately. As elevator music chirps in my ear, I smother a groan.

"You're on hold, huh?"

"Yup." I glance over at her again. "I'm Logan, by the way. Thanks for letting me use your phone."

"No problem." She pauses. "I'm Grace."

A click sounds in my ear, but instead of the dispatcher's voice coming on the line, there's another click followed by another swell of music. I'm not surprised, though. It's Friday night, the busiest night for the campus taxis. Who knows how long I'll have to wait.

I sink down on the edge of one of the beds—the one that's perfectly made—and try to remember the number for the cab service in Hastings, the town where most of the off-campus housing is, including my townhouse. But I'm drawing a blank, so I sigh and endure some more elevator music. My gaze drifts to the open laptop on the other side of the bed, and when I notice what's on the screen, I look at Grace in surprise.

"Are you watching *Die Hard*?"

"*Die Hard Two*, actually." She looks embarrassed. "I'm having a *Die Hard* night. I just finished the first one."

"Do you have a thing for Bruce Willis or something?"

That makes her laugh. "Nope. I just like old action movies. Last weekend I watched the *Lethal Weapon* franchise."

The music in my ear stops again, then starts over, bringing a curse to my lips. I hang up and turn to Grace. "Do you mind if I use your computer to get the number for the taxi service in Hastings? Maybe I'll have better luck there."

"Sure." After a beat of hesitation, she sits next to me and reaches for the laptop. "Let me pull up a browser for you."

When she goes to minimize the video, the movie unpauses, and sound blasts out of the speakers. As the opening fight scene in the airport fills the computer screen, I immediately lean closer to watch it. "Oh shit, this is such a great fight sequence."

"I know, right?" Grace exclaims. "I love it. Actually, I love this whole movie. I don't care what anyone says—it's awesome. Obviously not as good as the first one, but it's really not as bad as people think."

She's about to pause the movie, but I intercept her hand. "Can we finish watching this scene first?"

Her expression fills with surprise. "Um…yeah, okay." She visibly swallows, adding, "If you want, you can stay and watch the whole movie." Her cheeks flush the moment she voices the invitation. "Unless you have somewhere you need to be."

I think it over for a second before shaking my head. "Naah, I have nowhere else to be. I can hang out for a while."

Really, what's the alternative? Go home to watch Hannah and Garrett hand-feed pizza to each other and sneak kisses during the movie?

"Oh. Okay," Grace says warily. "Uh…cool."

I chuckle. "Were you expecting me to say no?"

"Kind of," she admits.

"Why would I? Seriously, what guy turns down *Die Hard*? The only thing that could sweeten this deal is if you offered me some booze."

"I don't have any." She stops to think. "But I've got a whole bag of gummy bears hidden in my desk drawer."

"Marry me," I say instantly.

Laughing, she wanders over to the desk, opens the bottom drawer, and, sure enough, pulls out a huge bag of candy. As I slide up the bed and lean back on the stack of pillows at the head of it, Grace kneels in front of the mini-fridge next to the desk and asks, "Water or Pepsi?"

"Pepsi, please."

She hands me the massive bag of gummy bears and a can of soda, then settles on the bed beside me and positions the laptop on the mattress between us.

I shove a gummy bear in my mouth and focus my gaze on the screen. Okay, then. This definitely wasn't the way I expected this evening to go, but hell, might as well roll with it.

CHAPTER 3

Grace

JOHN LOGAN IS IN MY dorm room.

No, John Logan is on my *bed*.

I am *so* not prepared for this. In fact, I'm tempted to secretly text Ramona with an SOS and beg for advice, because I have no idea what to do or say. On the plus side, we're watching a movie, which means I don't have to do or say anything except stare at the laptop, laugh at the appropriate one-liners, and pretend that the hottest guy at Briar isn't sitting *on my bed*.

And he's not just physically hot. He's also temperature hot. Seriously, his body heat is like a blast from a furnace, and since I'm already hot and tingly from his mere presence, the warmth he's radiating is starting to make me sweat.

Trying to be inconspicuous, I wiggle out of my sweatshirt and tuck it beside me, but the movement causes Logan to turn his head toward me. Those deep blue eyes focus on my tight tank top, resting briefly on my chest.

Oh God. He's checking out my boobs. And even though I'm only rocking a B-cup, the way his expression smolders, you'd think I had a porn star rack.

When he realizes I've caught him staring, he just winks and turns back to the screen.

It's official: I've actually met a guy who can pull off a *wink*.

Paying attention to the movie is impossible. My eyes are on the screen, but my mind is somewhere else. Focused wholly on the guy beside me. He's a lot bigger than I thought. Impossibly broad shoulders, muscular chest, long legs stretching out in front of him. I've seen him play hockey so I know he's aggressively physical on the ice, and having that powerful body inches from mine shoots a thrill up my spine. He looks so much older and more masculine than the freshmen guys I've hung out with all year.

Well, duh. He's a junior.

Right. But…he seems older than that too. He's got this whole manly thing going on that makes me want to rip his clothes off and lick him like an ice cream cone.

I pop a gummy bear in my mouth, hoping the act of chewing will bring some much-needed moisture to my dry throat. On the screen, McClane's wife is on the plane arguing with the pesky news reporter who caused trouble for the McClanes in the first movie, and suddenly Logan glances over at me, curiosity flickering in his expression.

"Hey, do you think you could land a plane if you had no other choice?"

I laugh. "I thought you said you've seen this movie. You know she doesn't have to land the plane, right?"

"No, I know that. But it made me wonder what I'd do if I was on a plane and I was the only one who could land it." He sighs. "I don't think I'd be able to do it."

I'm surprised he's so quick to admit that. Other guys might try to act all macho and scoff about how they could land that thing in their sleep or something.

"Me neither," I confess. "If anything, I see myself making it worse. I'd probably accidently depressurize the cabin by touching the wrong control. Actually, no. I'm scared of heights, so I'm pretty sure I'd pass out the second I stepped into the cockpit and looked out the windshield."

He chuckles, and the husky sound sets off another round of tingles. "I might be able to fly a helicopter," he muses. "That's probably easier than a jet, right?"

"Maybe? Honestly, I know nothing about aviation." It's my turn to sigh. "Don't tell anyone, but sometimes I'm not sure I understand how planes even stay in the air."

He laughs, and then we both focus on the movie again, and I give myself a mental pat on the back. I just had an entire conversation with a cute guy without babbling incoherently. I deserve a frickin' gold star for that.

Don't get me wrong, I'm still nervous as all get out. But something about Logan puts me at ease. He's so laidback, and besides, it's hard to feel intimidated by a guy when he's chomping away on *gummy bears*.

As we watch the movie, my gaze darts toward him every few seconds to admire his chiseled profile. His nose is slightly crooked, as if it's been broken once or twice before. And the sexy curve of his lips is…pure temptation. I want to kiss him so badly I can't think straight.

God, and I'm such a loser, because kissing *me* is probably the last thing on his mind. He stuck around to watch *Die Hard*, not to fool around with a freshman who compared him to Ted frickin' Bundy an hour ago.

I force myself to concentrate on the film, but I'm already dreading the moment it ends, because then Logan will have to leave.

But when the credits scroll up on the screen, he doesn't make a single move to get up. Instead, he looks over and asks, "So what's your deal?"

I furrow my brow. "What do you mean?"

"It's Friday night—how come you're sitting around watching action movies?"

The question makes me bristle. "What's wrong with that?"

"Nothing." He shrugs. "I'm just wondering why you're not out partying or something."

"I was at a party last night." *Don't remind him you saw him, don't remind him you saw him—* "I saw you there, by the way."

He seems startled. "You did?"

"Yeah. At the Omega Phi house."

"Huh. I don't remember seeing you." He gives me a sheepish look. "I don't remember much, actually. I got pretty shitfaced."

It stings a little that he doesn't remember our encounter outside the bathroom, but I quickly chastise myself for feeling insulted. He was drunk, and he'd just hooked up with someone else. Of course I hadn't made an impression on him.

"Did you have fun at the party?" For the first time since he walked into my dorm room, his tone contains an awkward note, as if he's trying to make small talk and isn't comfortable with it.

"Sure, I guess." I pause. "Actually, I take that back. It was fun until I totally humiliated myself in front of this guy."

The discomfort on his face dissolves as he chuckles. "Yeah? What'd you do?"

"I babbled. A lot." I offer a little shrug. "I have a really bad habit of doing that around guys."

"You're not babbling right now," he points out.

"Yeah, *now*. Do you not remember the serial killer rant I gave you two hours ago?"

"Trust me, I remember." His answering grin speeds up my pulse. God, he's got a sexy smile. Slightly crooked, and every time he flashes it, his eyes twinkle playfully. "I don't make you nervous anymore, do I?"

"No." I'm lying. He absolutely makes me nervous. He's John fucking Logan, one of the most popular guys at Briar. And I'm Grace fucking Ivers, one of thousands of girls who are crushing on him.

His gaze travels over me again, a hot, lingering perusal that crackles along my skin like an electric current. This time there's no mistaking the interest in his eyes.

Should I make a move?

I should make a move, right?

Lean closer or something. Kiss him. Or maybe ask him to kiss me? My brain races back to my high school days, trying to pinpoint how all *those* kisses happened, if the guys I locked lips with made the first move, or if it was a mutual yeah-we're-going-to-kiss-now sorta thing. Except none of those kisses were with guys even half as gorgeous as this one.

"Do you want me to go now?"

His gruff voice startles me, and I realize I've been staring at him for almost a full minute without saying a single word.

My mouth is so dry I have to swallow a few times before answering. "No. I mean, you can stay if you want. We can watch something else, or—"

I don't get to finish that sentence, because he slides closer and touches my cheek, and my vocal cords freeze as my heart rate skyrockets.

John Logan is *touching* my *cheek*.

The pads of his fingers are calloused, a rough scrape against my skin, and he smells so good I feel light-headed when I inhale the faint scent of his aftershave.

He lightly strokes my cheekbone and I have to stop myself from purring like an affection-starved cat. "What are you doing?" I whisper.

"Well, you were looking at me like you wanted me to kiss you." His blue eyes become heavy-lidded. "So I was thinking I might do that."

CHAPTER 4

Grace

MY HEARTBEAT IS OUT OF control. A fast drumbeat in my ears, a frantic hammering against my ribs.

Oh my God.

He wants to kiss me?

"Unless I misread the moment?" he prompts.

I gulp, desperately trying to control my careening pulse. Talking is not an option. My throat has clamped shut. Despite the fact that my motor skills aren't operating at full capacity, I manage to shake my head.

His laughter heats the air between us. "Is that a no to misreading the moment, or a no to me kissing you?"

I'm miraculously able to produce an entire sentence in response. "I want you to kiss me."

He's still chuckling as he moves closer, stretching on his side beside me and gently nudging me onto my back. Every muscle in my body tenses with anticipation as he hovers over me, and when he rests one hand on my hip, I tremble hard enough for him to notice.

A smile curves his lips. Lips that are getting closer and closer to *my* lips. Inches away. Millimeters away.

And then his mouth brushes mine, and holy shit, I'm kissing John Logan.

Almost immediately, my mind is flooded with so many thoughts it's hard to focus on just one. I hear my father's endless lectures about respecting myself and behaving properly and not going wild in college.

And then there's my mother's cheery voice, ordering me to have fun and live life to the fullest. And somewhere in between an excited voice is shouting, *You're kissing John Logan! You're kissing John Logan!*

His mouth is warm, his lips firm as he kisses me. Gently at first. A soft, sensual tease that makes me whimper. He licks my bottom lip, nips lightly at it before the tip of his tongue touches the seam of my lips. He tastes like candy, and for some reason that makes me whimper again. When his tongue finally slides inside my mouth, he lets out a raspy groan that vibrates through me and settles in my core.

Kissing Logan is the single most incredible thing I've ever experienced. Forget that family vacation to Egypt when I was nine. The glory of the pyramids and temples and the frickin' Sphinx is nothing compared to the feel of this guy's lips on mine.

Our tongues meet, and he makes another low, husky sound, gliding one hand up my body to cup my left breast. Oh shit. Boob groping alert. I thought we were just going to make out, but now we're *fooling around*.

I'm not wearing a bra under my tank top, so when his thumb brushes the very thin fabric and presses down on my nipple, it sends a bolt of heat from the tips of my breasts right down to my clit. My entire body is hot and achy, tight with excitement. Logan's tongue explores my mouth as he rubs my distended nipple, his hips moving slightly against my hip. His erection is like a hot brand on the side of my thigh, and I'm unbelievably turned on by the knowledge that I'm turning *him* on.

Breathing heavily, he wrenches our mouths apart. "Should I be worried that your roommate is going to walk in on us?"

"No, she's not coming home tonight. She went to some bar in town, and then she's planning on crashing with this girl Caitlin from Kappa Beta. Which I think is a really bad idea because the last time she went out with Caitlin, they almost got arrested for public drunkenness, but then Ramona flirted with the cop and—"

Logan shuts me up with another kiss. "*No* would have sufficed," he murmurs against my lips. Then he reaches for my hand and places it directly on the hard bulge in his pants. In the same breath, he cups my sex over my PJs.

Oh crap. Downstairs action alert.

I'm not worried about my response to *his* hand—one slow glide of his palm is all it takes for a burst of pleasure to erupt inside me. Nope, it's *my* hand that triggers the rush of nervousness. The hand that's currently stroking the erection straining behind Logan's zipper.

I've given handjobs before, plus a few blowjobs that I know were a huge success because…well, semen and all that. But I don't have enough experience to consider myself an expert penis-wrangler or anything. And all those past penis encounters involved *one* guy, my high school boyfriend Brandon, who was equally inexperienced.

If the rumors I've heard about Logan are true, then this guy has slept with half the girls at Briar. Sounds like an insanely high statistic, so I'm sure it's not accurate, but he's definitely hooked up with more people than *I* have.

"Is this okay?" he asks as he strokes between my legs.

I nod and stroke *him* again, and a tortured moan slips out of his mouth.

"Fuck, hold on." He shifts on the mattress, and my heart stops when he unzips his pants. He eases them down just low enough to free his erection from his boxers, then tugs on the waistbands of my PJs and underwear.

A second later, his hand grazes my bare sex, and my hips lift involuntarily, seeking closer contact.

Logan teases the tip of his index finger over my clit. "Better?" he says, his voice thick and raspy.

So much better. And so good it makes my head spin, limiting my response to a breathy mumble of nonsense.

Smiling at my incoherent answer, he leans in and kisses me again. With his free hand, he grasps my right hand and brings it to his erection, gently wrapping my trembling fingers around the shaft. He's long and hard, his smooth, hot flesh sliding easily inside my closed fist.

My body is on fire. Waves of arousal swell in my core, and when he pushes his middle finger inside me, my inner muscles clamp around it, the pressure so intense I forget how to breathe.

We don't stop kissing. Not even to come up for air. We're both panting, our tongues tangling and our hands hard at work. His thumb presses on my clit as his finger moves inside me, and the pleasure spiraling through me gathers in strength, a tight knot of anticipation that causes the movement of my hips to become even more erratic.

Minutes pass. Or maybe hours. I have no idea, because I'm too caught up in the incredible sensations. I stroke his erection, squeezing the blunt head on each upstroke, until his hips start moving too, and a rough command leaves his mouth.

"Faster."

I quicken the pace and he thrusts into my fist with a low groan, his breath tickling my lips as he breaks the kiss. His eyes are closed, his features taut and his teeth digging into his bottom lip.

"I'm gonna come," he mumbles.

Excitement ripples between my legs, and I know he can feel how wet I am because he groans again and his finger plunges deeper, faster. A few seconds later, he sags into me, his forehead resting on my shoulder as his hips flex forward one last time before going still.

As wetness spurts onto my hand, his eyes slowly open and the sleepy pleasure swimming in them takes my breath away. Holy shit. I don't think I've ever seen anything sexier than the sight of John Logan right after he's had an orgasm.

His breathing is still labored as he meets my gaze. "Did you come?"

Crap. Right. His finger is still lodged inside me. No longer moving, but a reminder of the orgasm I'd been about to reach before I got distracted by the way he looked when he was coming, the restless grind of his hips and the sexy sounds he made.

But I'm too embarrassed to admit I didn't finish, and since *he* already did, I feel awkward asking him to keep going.

So I nod and say, "Uh-huh. Of course."

A shadow of doubt passes through his eyes, but before I can blink, he sits up abruptly and says, "I should go."

I ignore the equal doses of disappointment and irritation that tighten my belly. Seriously? He can't even stick around for a few minutes of post-hook-up small talk? What a prince.

It's even more awkward now. He grabs a tissue from the box on the end table and cleans up. I pretend to be cool and composed as I pull up my pants and watch him do the same. I even manage a casual smile as he uses my phone to call a cab. Fortunately, he gets through right away this time, which means the awkwardness doesn't last long.

I walk him to the door, where he hesitates for a beat. "Thanks for having me over," he says gruffly. "I had fun."

"Uh, yeah, sure. Me too."

A moment later, he's gone.

CHAPTER 5

Logan

I WALK INTO MY BEDROOM after my morning shower to hear my phone ringing. And since everyone my age texts instead of calls, I know exactly who it is without having to check the screen.

"Hey, Mom," I greet her, gripping the edge of my towel as I head for the dresser.

"*Mom?* Holy shish kebob. So it's true? I mean, I *thought* I gave birth to a beautiful baby boy twenty-one years ago, but that seems like a distant memory. Because if I did have a son, he'd probably call me more than once a month, right?"

I laugh, despite the needle of guilt pricking my chest. She's right. I've been a crappy son lately, too busy with the post-season and term papers to call her as often as I should.

"I'm sorry," I say with genuine remorse. "It always gets crazy busy at the end of the semester."

"I know. That's why I haven't been bugging you. Are you studying hard for your exams?"

"Sure." Yeah, right. I haven't even cracked open a book yet.

Mom sees right through the noncommittal response. "Don't BS your mother, Johnny."

"Fine, I haven't started yet," I admit. "But you know I work better under pressure. Can you hold on a sec?"

"Yup."

I set the phone down and drop my towel, then yank a pair of sweatpants up my hips. My hair is still wet, sprinkling droplets down my bare chest, so I rub the towel over my head before picking up the phone again.

"Back," I tell her. "So how's work going? How's David?"

"Good, and great."

For the next ten minutes she chats about her job—she's a manager at a restaurant in Boston—then tells me what my stepfather has been up to. David is an accountant, and he's so boring that sometimes it's painful to be around him. But he also loves my mother with all his heart and treats her like the queen she is, so I can't exactly hate the guy.

Eventually she gets around to my summer plans, taking on that guarded tone she always uses when she brings up the subject of my father.

"So I take it you're working with your dad again?"

"Yup." I make an effort to sound relaxed. My brother and I agreed a long time ago to keep the truth from Mom.

She doesn't need to know that Dad is drinking again, and I refuse to dredge up that old bullshit for her. She got out, and she needs to *stay* out. She deserves to be happy now, and boring as he is, David makes her happy.

Ward Logan, on the other hand, made her miserable. He didn't hit her or abuse her verbally, but she was the one who had to clean up his messes. She was the one who had to deal with his drunken tantrums and constant visits to rehab. The one who dragged him off the floor when he came home wasted and passed out in the front hall.

Fuck, I'll never forget the time when I was eight or nine, and Dad called the house at two in the morning. He'd been slurring like a maniac and freaking out because he'd drunk himself stupid at a bar, gotten in the car, and had no idea where he was. It had been the dead of winter, and Mom hadn't wanted to leave my brother and me at home alone, so she'd bundled us up, and the three of us drove for hours searching for him. With only half a street name to go on because the sign had been covered in snow and Dad was too drunk to walk over and wipe it away.

After we'd found him and hauled him into the car, I remember sitting in the backseat feeling something I'd never felt before—pity. I felt *sorry* for my father. And I can't deny I was relieved when Mom shipped him back to rehab the next day.

"I hope he's paying you accordingly, sweetie," Mom says, sounding upset. "You and Jeffrey work such long hours at the garage."

"Of course he's paying us." But accordingly? Fuck no. I make enough to pay for rent and expenses during the school year, but definitely not what I *should* be making for full-time work.

"Good." She pauses. "Can you still take a week off to come visit us?"

"I'm planning on it," I assure her. Jeff and I have already worked out a schedule so that each of us can head to Boston to spend some time with Mom.

We talk for a few more minutes, and then I hang up and wander downstairs to find something to eat. I prepare a bowl of cereal, the no-sugar, all-bran bore-fest that Tuck forces us to eat because for some reason he's against sugar. As I settle at the eat-in counter, my mind instantly travels back to what happened last night.

Leaving Grace's room five seconds after she'd jerked me off had been such an asshole move. I know that. But I had to get out of there. The second I'd recovered from that orgasm, my first thought had been, *what the hell am I doing here?* Seriously. I mean, yeah, Grace was awesome, and sexy, and funny, but have I sunk so low that I'm now randomly finger-banging chicks I don't even know? And I can't even use alcohol as an excuse this time because I was stone-cold sober.

And the worst part? She didn't even fucking come.

I clench my teeth at the reminder. There'd been a lot of moaning, sure, but I'm ninety-nine percent certain that she didn't have an orgasm despite her telling me that she had. Or rather, lying to me that she had. Because when a woman drops a noncommittal "Uh-huh" after you ask if she had an orgasm, then that's called *lying*.

And that half-assed "yeah, sure, me too" she gave me about whether she had fun? Talk about bruising a guy's ego. Not only did she *not* come, but my company didn't do it for her, either?

I don't know how I feel about that. I mean, I'm not an idiot. I don't live in a magical bubble where orgasms fall from the sky and land in a woman's bed every time she has sex. I *know* they fake it sometimes.

But I'm fairly confident I speak for most guys when I say that I like to think they don't fake it with *me*.

Damn it. I should've gotten her number. Why the hell didn't I get her number?

I know the answer to that, though. This past month, I haven't cared enough to ask for a girl's number after a hook-up. Or rather, I've been too wasted before, during and after the hook-up to *remember* to ask.

The thud of footsteps from the corridor snaps me out of my thoughts, and I glance up in time to see Garrett stride into the kitchen.

"Morning," he says.

"Morning." I shove a spoonful of cereal into my mouth and do my best to ignore the instant jolt of discomfort, while at the same time hating myself for even feeling it.

Garrett Graham is my best friend. For chrissake, I'm not supposed to feel *uncomfortable* around him.

"So what'd you end up doing last night?" He grabs a bowl from the cupboard, a spoon from the drawer, and joins me at the counter.

I chew before answering. "I hung out with this girl. Watched a movie."

"Cool. Anyone I know?"

"Naah, I just met her yesterday." *And will probably never see her again because I'm a selfish lover and bad company, apparently.*

Garrett dumps some cereal into his bowl and reaches for the milk carton I left out. "Hey, so did you call that agent yet?"

"No, not yet."

"Why not?"

Because there's no point.

"Because I haven't gotten around to it." My tone is harsher than I mean for it to be, and Garrett's gray eyes flicker with hurt.

"You don't have to bite my head off. It was just a question."

"Sorry. I...sorry." Real articulate. Stifling a sigh, I take another bite of cereal.

A short silence settles between us, until Garrett finally clears his throat. "Look, I get it, okay? You didn't get drafted and it sucks. But it's not like you're out of options. You're a free agent now, and you're not locked in with a team, which means you can sign with anyone if they want you. And they're totally going to want you."

He's right. I'm sure there are lots of teams that would want me to play for them. I'm sure one of them would've even drafted me—*if* I'd entered the draft.

But Garrett doesn't know that. He thinks I've been passed over these past two years, and—have I mentioned what an asshole friend I am?—I've been letting him think it. Because fucked up as it sounds, having my best friend believe I didn't get picked bums me out a helluva lot less than admitting that I'm never going to play for the pros.

See, Garrett had a choice about not opting in. He wanted to earn his degree without the temptation that comes with being drafted. A lot of college players choose to ditch school the moment a team holds the rights to them—it's hard not to when you've got a pro team pulling out all the stops to coax you into leaving college early. But Garrett's a smart guy. He knows he'd lose his NCAA eligibility if he did that, and he also knows that signing a contract with a team doesn't guarantee instant success, or even playing time.

Hell, we both saw what happened to Chris Little, our teammate in freshman year. Dude gets drafted, goes pro, plays for half a season, and then? A career-ending injury takes him out. Permanently. Not only will Little never step foot on the ice again, but he spent every dime of his signing contract on his medical expenses, and last I heard, he went back to school to learn a trade. Welding, or some shit.

So yup, Garrett's playing it smart. Me? I knew from the start I wouldn't be going pro.

"I mean, Gretzky went undrafted, and look at everything he accomplished. The guy's a *legend*. Arguably the best player in hockey history."

Garrett is still talking, still trying to "reassure" me, and I'm torn between snapping at him to shut up, and hugging the living shit out of the guy for being such an amazing friend.

I do neither, choosing to placate him instead. "I'll call the agent on Monday," I lie.

He offers a pleased nod. "Good."

The silence returns. We cart our empty bowls over to the dishwasher.

"Hey, we're going to Malone's tonight," Garrett says. "Me, Wellsy, Tuck and maybe Danny. You in?"

"Can't. I've gotta start studying for exams."

It's sad, but I'm starting to lose count of all the things I'm lying to my best friend about.

Grace

"I'm sorry—can you repeat that?" Ramona stares at me in utter disbelief, her eyes so wide they look like two dark saucers.

I shrug as if what I've just told her is no biggie. "John Logan came over last night."

"John Logan came over last night," she echoes.

"Yes."

"He came to our dorm."

"Yes."

"You were in this room, and he walked in, and then both of you were here. In this room."

"Yes."

"So John Logan showed up at our door, and walked inside, and was here. With you. Here."

Laughter bubbles in my throat. "Yes, Ramona. We've established that he was *here*. In this room."

Her mouth falls open. Then slams shut. Then opens again to release a shriek that's so earsplitting I'm surprised the water in my glass doesn't jiggle Jurassic Park-style.

"Oh my God!" She runs over to my bed and flops down. "Tell me *everything!*"

She's still wearing her party clothes from last night, a teeny minidress that rides up her thighs when she sits, and silver stilettos that she kicks away in an excited blur of legs.

When Ramona had walked into our room, I'd lasted all of three seconds before spilling the news, but now, with her staring excitedly at me, reluctance jams in my throat. I'm suddenly embarrassed to tell her what happened last night, because…well…I'm just going to say it: because it was *underwhelming*.

I had fun watching the movie with him. And I loved fooling around with him—at least until those final moments—but the guy got off and then *left*. Who does that?

No wonder all his hook-ups take place at frat parties. The girls are probably too drunk to notice whether they have an orgasm or not. Too drunk to realize that John Logan is selling nothing but false advertising.

But I already opened my big mouth, so now I have to follow through and give Ramona *something*. As she gawks at me, I explain how Logan showed up at the wrong door and ended up staying to watch a movie.

"You watched a movie? That's it?"

I feel my cheeks warm up. "Well…"

Another screech flies out of her mouth. "Oh my God! Did you *fuck* him?"

"No," I'm quick to answer. "Of course not. I hardly even know him. But…well, we did make out."

I'm hesitant to disclose any more than that, but the revelation is enough to light up Ramona's eyes. She looks like a kid who's just gotten her first bicycle. Or a pony.

"You *made out* with John Logan! Eeccch! That is *so* awesome! Is he good a kisser? Did he take off his shirt? Did he take off his *pants*?"

"Nope," I lie.

My best friend can't sit still anymore. She hops off the bed and bounces around on the balls of her feet. "I can't believe this. I can't believe I wasn't here to witness it."

"You're into voyeurism now?" I ask dryly.

"If I'm voyeur'ing John Logan? Um, *yeah*. I'd watch the two of you make out for *hours*." She gasps suddenly. "Oh my God, text him right now and ask him to send you a dick pic!"

"What? No!"

"Aw, come on, he'll probably be really flattered and—" Another gasp. "No, text him to invite him over tonight! And tell him to bring *Dean*."

I hate to rain on her parade, but considering the way Logan rushed off last night, I have no choice but to dump a bucket of cold water on Ramona's joy. "I couldn't even if I wanted to," I confess. "I didn't get his number."

"What?" She looks devastated. "What is *wrong* with you? Did you at least give him yours?"

I shake my head. "He didn't have his phone on him, and there wasn't an opportunity for me to give him my number."

Ramona goes quiet for a moment. Sharp brown eyes focus on my face, narrowing, probing, as if she's trying to telepathically tunnel into my brain.

I fidget self-consciously. "What?"

"Be honest," she says. "Was he actually here?"

Shock slams into me. "Are you kidding?" When she offers a tiny shrug, my shock turns to horror. "Why would I make that up?"

"I don't know…" She tucks a strand of dark hair behind her ear, her discomfort obvious. "It's just…you know, he's older, and *hot*, and you didn't exchange numbers…"

"So that means I'm *lying*?" I shoot to my feet, beyond insulted.

"No, of course not." She starts to backpedal, but it's too late. I'm already pissed off and heading for the door. "Where are you going?" she wails from behind me. "Aw, come on, Gracie. I believe you. You don't have to storm out."

"I'm not storming out." I toss her a cool look over my shoulder, then grab my purse. "I'm meeting my dad in fifteen minutes. I really do have to go."

"Really?" she says skeptically.

"Yes." I have to force myself not to scowl at her. "But that doesn't mean I'm not super mad at you right now."

She darts over and throws her arms around me before I can stop her, squeezing tight enough to impede the airflow to my lungs. It's one of her trademark Forgive Me hugs, which I've been on the receiving end of more times than I can count.

"Please don't be mad at me," she begs. "I'm sorry I asked that. I know you wouldn't make it up, and when you get back, I want to hear *all* the details, okay?"

"Yeah…okay," I mutter, not because I mean it, but because I want to get out of here before I smack her in the face.

She pulls back, relief etched into her features. "Awesome. Then I'll see you lat—"

I'm out the door before she can finish that sentence.

CHAPTER 6

Grace

My dad hasn't arrived yet when I walk into the Coffee Hut, so I order a green tea at the counter and find us two comfy chairs in the corner of the room. It's Saturday morning, and the coffeehouse is deserted. I have a feeling most people are probably nursing hangovers from Friday night.

As I settle on the plush armchair, the bell over the door chimes and my father enters the room. He's wearing his trademark brown blazer and starched khaki pants, an outfit my mom refers to as his "serious professor" look.

"Hi, honey," he greets me. "Let me grab a coffee."

A minute later, he joins me in the corner, looking more harried than usual. "I'm sorry I'm late. I stopped by the office to pick up some papers and got cornered by a student. She wanted to discuss her term paper."

"It's okay. I just got here." I pop open the lid of my cup and steam rises up to my face. I blow on the hot liquid for a moment, then take a quick sip. "How was your week?"

"Chaotic. I was concerned with the quality of the papers that were being turned in, so I extended office hours for the students who had questions about the exam. I've been on campus until ten o'clock every night."

I frown. "You know you have a TA, right? Can't he help out?"

"He does, but you know I enjoy interacting with my students."

Yep, I do know that, and I'm sure that's why all his students love him so much. Dad teaches graduate-level molecular biology at Briar, a course you wouldn't think would be all that popular, and yet there's actually a *waiting list* to get into his class. I've sat in on a few of his lectures over the years, and I have to admit, he does have a way of making the ridiculously boring material seem interesting.

Dad sips his coffee, eyeing me over the rim. "So, I made reservations at Ferro's for Friday at six-thirty. Does that work for the birthday girl?"

I roll my eyes. I am *so* not a birthday person. I prefer low-key celebrations, or—in a perfect world—no celebrations at all, but my mom is a birthday fiend. Surprise parties, gag gifts, forcing waiters to sing in restaurants…she's all about inflicting the greatest amount of torture possible. I think she gets a kick out of embarrassing her only daughter. But since she moved to Paris three years ago, I haven't been able to spend my birthday with her, so she's recruited my dad into taking over humiliation duties.

"The birthday girl will only agree to go if you can promise nobody will sing to her."

He blanches. "Lord, do you think *I* want to sit through that? No way, honey. We'll have a nice, quiet dinner, and when you talk to your mom about it afterward, you can tell her a mariachi band came over to the table and sang for you."

"Deal."

"Are you sure you're okay that we're not having dinner on your actual birthday? If you want to celebrate on Wednesday night, I can cancel office hours."

"Friday is fine," I assure him.

"All right, then it's a date. Oh, and I spoke to your mom again last night," he adds. "She asked if you've reconsidered changing your flight to May. She'd love to see you for three months instead of two."

I hesitate. I'm excited to visit Mom this summer, but for three months? Even two is pushing it—that's why I insisted on coming back the first week of August, even though the semester doesn't start until the end of the month. Don't get me wrong, I adore my mother. She's fun and spontaneous, and so bubbly and encouraging it's like having your own personal cheerleader following you around waving her pom-poms. But she's also…exhausting. She's a little girl in a grown woman's body, acting on her every whim without stopping to consider the consequences.

"Let me think about it," I answer. "I need to decide if I have the energy to keep up with her."

Dad chuckles. "Well, we both know the answer to that is *no*. Nobody has the energy to keep up with your mom, honey."

He certainly hadn't, but luckily, their divorce had been one hundred percent amicable. I think when Mom told him she wanted out, Dad was more relieved than upset. And when she decided to move to Paris in order to "find herself" and "reconnect with her art", he'd been nothing but supportive.

"I'll let you know this weekend, okay?" I reach for my tea, but my hand freezes when the bell rings again.

A dark-haired guy in a Briar hockey jacket strolls in, and for one heart-stopping moment, I think it's Logan.

But nope. It's someone else. Shorter, bulkier, and not as devastatingly gorgeous.

Disappointment flutters through me, but I force it away. Even if Logan *had* walked through that door, what would I really expect to happen? He'd come over and kiss me? Ask me out?

Riiiight. I made the guy come last night and he didn't even stick around long enough to kiss me goodbye. So yeah, I have to face the facts: I'm just another girl on a long list of John Logan's conquests.

And honestly? I'm totally cool with that. As underwhelming as it may have been, getting, um...*conquered* by Logan is hands-down the highlight of my freshman year.

Logan

"HAS A GIRL EVER FAKED an orgasm with you?" I blurt out. It's eight o'clock on Monday morning, and I nervously tap my fingers on the kitchen counter as I look at my roommate.

Dean, who was on his way to the fridge, stops in his tracks so abruptly that if he'd been on skates, I would be wiping ice shavings off my face right now.

"I'm sorry, didn't hear you. What was that?"

His expression is the epitome of innocence, so it's not until *after* I repeat myself that I realize I'm being played. Dean doubles over, honest-to-God tears streaming down his cheeks as he shudders with laughter.

"I totally heard you the first time," he croaks. "I just wanted to hear you ask it again…oh shit…I think I might piss myself…" Another howl rips out of his throat. "You tapped a girl and she *faked* it?"

I clench my teeth so hard my molars hurt. What on earth had made me think confiding in Dean was a *good* idea?

"No," I mutter.

He's still laughing like a maniac. "How do you know she faked it? Did she tell you afterward? Oh God, please say yes!"

I stare into my coffee cup. "She didn't tell me anything. I just got a feeling, okay?"

Dean opens the fridge and grabs a carton of OJ, still chuckling to himself. "This is priceless. Big stud on campus couldn't make a girl come. You've officially given me enough ammo to rag on you for *years*."

Yup, I sure did. Nobody ever said I was smart.

And why the hell am I even still obsessing about this? All weekend I've fought the temptation to see Grace. I forced myself to study for exams. I played a six-hour *Ice Pro* marathon with Tuck. I even cleaned my room and did laundry.

And then I opened my eyes this morning and couldn't take it anymore.

I've got *moves*, damn it. Women know that when they hook up with John Logan, they're going to leave with a satisfied smile on their faces, and it drives me crazy thinking that Grace might've been unsatisfied. It's been gnawing at me for days. *Days*, damn it.

You know what? Screw it. I might not have her number, but I know where she lives, and there's no way I'll be able to concentrate on a damn thing today until I've rectified this unholy situation.

Leaving a girl wanting isn't just embarrassing. It's unacceptable.

THIRTY MINUTES LATER, I'M STANDING in front of Grace's door.

Showing up at a girl's dorm at eight-thirty in the morning might not be the best way to score points, but since my stupid ego refuses to let me walk away, I take a breath and tap my fist on the door.

Grace opens it a second later.

Wearing nothing but a bathrobe.

Her eyes widen when she sees me, her voice coming out in a squeak. "Hi."

Swallowing, I do my best not to dwell on the fact that she's probably naked under that robe. The white terrycloth hangs to her knees, the belt secured tightly around her waist, but the top parts slightly, giving me a candid view of her cleavage.

"Hi." My voice sounds gravelly, so I clear my throat. "Can I come in?"

"Um. Sure."

She closes the door behind me, then turns around, an uneasy smile playing on her lips. "I don't have much time. My last psych seminar is in an hour, so I need to get dressed and hike all the way across campus."

"That's okay. I don't have a lot of time either. Study group in thirty minutes." I shove my hands in my pockets to stop from fidgeting. I'm nervous and I have no idea why. I've never had a problem talking to chicks before.

"What's up?" She nonchalantly grasps the front of her robe, as if she's realized it's dangerously close to gaping open.

"You didn't finish, did you?" The question flies out before I can stop it.

"Finish what—" She halts, a flush rising in her cheeks as understanding dawns. "Oh. You mean…?"

I grit my teeth and nod.

"Well…no," she confesses. "I didn't."

I struggle to keep my mouth in a neutral, non-frown position. "Why'd you tell me you did?"

"I don't know." She sighs. "You were already done. And I guess I didn't want to damage your ego or anything. I was reading this article the other day about how men are sensitive about that kind of stuff. How it triggers feelings of inadequacy if a woman doesn't reach orgasm. But did you know that something like ten percent of women don't have an orgasm during sexual activity? So going by that statistic, men really shouldn't feel like—"

"You're doing that babbling thing again."

Her expression is sheepish. "Sorry."

"I don't mind it. I'm glad you're worried about my ego." I grin at her. "You should be."

She looks startled. "Why?"

"Because I've been thinking non-stop about how I didn't make you come last time." I shrug. "And how badly I want to change that."

CHAPTER 7

Logan

GRACE'S CHEEKS GO FROM LILY-WHITE to pale-pink in a matter of seconds. She's got the most expressive face I've ever seen, so quick to display everything she's feeling. I appreciate how easy it is to read her, otherwise her prolonged silence to my last remark might've worried me. But the glimmer of intrigue in her eyes confirms I haven't scared her off.

"Really?" She wrinkles her forehead.

"Yeah." My lips curve in a small smile as I take a step toward her. "So are you gonna let me or what?"

Alarm flits across her face. "Let you do what?"

"Make you come."

I'm gratified to see the unease in her expression melt into molten hot excitement. Oh yeah, I'm not scaring her at all. She's turned on.

"Um…" She lets out a strangled laugh. "This is the first time a guy has ever shown up at my door asking me that. You realize how frickin' crazy that sounds, right?"

"You want to talk crazy? I've spent the whole fucking weekend fantasizing about doing this." Frustration rises in my chest. "I'm not usually such an asshole, okay? I might fuck around, but I always make sure the women I'm with have a good time."

She sighs. "I did have a good time."

"You would've had a better time if I didn't blow my load and take off."

Now she laughs again, which makes *me* sigh. "You're killing me here, gorgeous. I'm talking about how much I want to give you a screaming orgasm, and you're laughing at me?" I grin. "Did we not just establish that my ego is fragile?"

Her lips continue to twitch. "I thought you had to go," she reminds me.

"It takes ten minutes to get to the library from here. Which means I have twenty minutes." My smile becomes downright devilish. "If I can't make you come in twenty minutes, then I'm definitely doing something wrong."

Grace toys with a strand of wet, dark hair, visibly nervous. My gaze lowers to her lips, which glisten as her tongue darts out to moisten them. The urge to kiss her hums in my blood, and the anticipation hanging in the air is thick enough to tighten my throat.

I take another step. "So?"

"Um…" Her breath shudders out in a rush. "Sure. If you want to."

A laugh pops out. "Fuck yeah I want to. But do *you* want it?"

"Y-yes." She clears her throat. "Yes."

I move closer and her eyes flare again. She wants me. I want her too, but I order my rapidly hardening cock to behave. *This ain't about us, bro. Only her.*

My dick twitches in response, but there's no way it's getting any action right now. If this was any other girl, I might suggest a quickie, but unless my V-dar is on the fritz, then Grace is most definitely a virgin. Not only do I not have that kind of time on my hands right now, but I'm also not particularly eager to take on the responsibility of being her first.

But this…I reach for the sash of her robe and give it a slow tug… *this* I'm more than capable of doing.

And I plan on doing it right this time.

I don't part the robe fully. I just slip one hand through the gap in the terrycloth and gently stroke the bare flesh of her hip. She shivers the moment I touch her. Her light brown eyes fix intently on my face, and when my palm conducts another featherlight sweep, she moans softly and moves in closer.

"Get on the bed," I rasp, gently nudging her backward.

She sits on the edge of the mattress, but doesn't lie back. Her gaze stays focused on me, as if she's waiting for me to issue another order.

Exhaling a breath, I kneel in front of her and give the robe one final tug, pushing it off her shoulders. The oxygen I'd just released sucks right back into my lungs. Holy fuck. Her naked body makes my cock ache. She's slender, with tiny hips, long, smooth legs, and small-ish tits with the prettiest pink nipples. Saliva floods my mouth as I lean in to flick my tongue over one nipple. I can't help myself. I need to taste her.

"Oh fuck," I groan against the distended bud, before sucking it between my lips.

Grace whimpers, arching her back and pushing her breast deeper into my mouth. Jesus, I want to suck and play with her tits all day long. I've always been a boob man, and the thought of staying right here in this position for all of eternity sends a sizzle of heat to the tip of my cock. But the reckless rocking of Grace's hips reminds me that time is of the essence. And goddamn, I'm not leaving until I make her come.

I release her nipple with a wet sound and place my hands on her thighs. They tremble beneath my fingers, making me chuckle. "You okay?"

She nods wordlessly.

Satisfied that she's still on board, I spread her legs wider, slide lower to the floor, and bring my mouth to her pussy.

Instant hard-on.

Fuck, I love going down on a girl. The first time I did it I was fifteen, and it turned me on so frickin' much I came in my pants. I'm not so quick on the trigger anymore, but I can't deny that the feel of Grace's slick, warm pussy beneath my tongue gets my dick harder than nobody's business.

I lick her clit in a slow, teasing stroke that makes her moan. She falls back on her elbows, and I peer up to find that she's closed her eyes. Her lips are parted, her pulse visibly throbbing at the center of her throat, and that's all the encouragement I need to keep going.

My tongue travels down her slit to her opening. She's soaking wet. *Hell.* Maybe I *should* be worried about repeating the old coming-in-my-pants fiasco, because my balls draw up so tight they damn near disappear.

I clench my ass cheeks to control the wild tingling at the base of my spine and focus on making her feel good. I lick my way back to the swollen bud that's begging for my attention, gently flicking my tongue against it, kissing and sucking and gauging her every response to find out what she likes. Slow and soft, I determine. Her moans are more desperate and her hips rock harder when I tease her.

Except teasing her is teasing *me*, and now my dick is pressed up painfully against my fly. Damn thing will probably bear the impression of my zipper by the time we're through.

I ease the tip of my index finger inside her, and I'm immediately rewarded by a throaty cry.

"Good?" I murmur, gazing up at her.

Her eyelids are droopy. "Mmm-hmmm."

Satisfaction streaks through me, egging me on, making me even more determined to send her toppling over the edge. I resume my task. Sweet, languid strokes to her clit while my finger inches deeper and deeper, until it's finally lodged inside her. She's tight. *Really* tight. And wet. God. *Really* wet.

And if she doesn't come soon, my pants are about to get wet too, because I'm so close to exploding that—

"I'm coming," she moans.

And hell *yes*, she is. Her clit pulses against my tongue as her pussy squeezes my finger like a steel glove. She's not a screamer. Not much of a moaner either, but the breathy sounds that leave her mouth are hotter than any porn star noises I've ever heard.

I ride out the orgasm with her, stroking her inner channel and sucking on her clit as she shudders quietly on the bed. Several seconds later, she starts to laugh, squirming as she tries to move out of my grasp.

"Too sensitive," she chokes out.

I lift my head with a grin. "Sorry."

"Oh my God, you are not allowed to say that right now. Not after…" She sucks in a breath. "That was…amazing." She's slow to sit up, her eyes hazy with pleasure. "I have no idea what else to say. Thank you?"

Laughter bubbles in my throat. "You're welcome?"

My legs feel unusually weak as I stand up. I'm still ridiculously hard, but the alarm clock on the night table reveals I have exactly eleven minutes to trek over to the library. Under any other circumstances, I wouldn't care about being late, but this is the last study group before tomorrow's marketing final, and I can't afford to miss it. I'm already going into the exam with a D in the course, so failing the class is both a scary possibility and an outcome I refuse to let happen. The course is a prerequisite for my degree, and I have no desire to retake it next year.

"I need to go or I'll be late for study group." I meet her eyes. "Can I get your number?"

"Oh. Um…"

Her hesitation sparks a pang of anxiety. One of the rare times I ask for a girl's number and she's uncertain about doling it out? After I rocked her world?

Jesus. Is my game slipping?

I raise a brow, my voice taking on a note of challenge. "Unless you don't want to give it to me?"

"No. I mean, yes, I do." She bites her bottom lip. "Do you want it now?"

I force a laugh that I hope sounds flirty rather than nervous. "Now would be good." I grab my phone from my back pocket and open a new contact page. "Hit me."

She rattles off a series of numbers. So fast I have to make her stop and repeat it. I type in her name and press enter, then tuck the phone away. "Maybe we can hang out again sometime? We could watch the next *Die Hard* in the lineup…"

"Yeah, sure. That sounds great."

Seriously? Another "yeah, sure"?

What the hell does it take to get an "I'D LOVE TO!" from this chick?

"Okay. Cool." I gulp. "I guess I'll call you, then."

She doesn't say anything, and in the ensuing silence, I'm overcome with a wave of discomfort.

Then I dip down and do the stupidest thing ever. Which says a lot, because I've dabbled in my share of stupidity over the years.

I kiss her forehead.

Not her lips. Not her cheek. Her fucking *forehead*.

Real smooth, bro.

She looks up at me in amusement, but I don't give her the chance to comment on my dumbass move.

"I'll call you," I mumble.

And for the second time in three days, I leave Grace's dorm feeling like a jackass.

Grace

MY PSYCHOLOGY LECTURE IS THREE hours long, and I can honestly say I didn't hear a word the professor said. Not one single word.

For one hundred and eighty minutes, all I did was run through every incredible second of every incredible thing Logan did to me this morning.

Can you nominate anyone for sainthood, or are there eligibility requirements?

Can you nominate someone's *tongue* for sainthood? Or maybe there's an orgasm-giving award that the Department of Sexuality hands out?

If so, Logan deserves to win it.

I'm still flummoxed that he showed up at my door and pretty much *demanded* I let him give me an orgasm. I guess his ego is as sensitive as that *Cosmo* article said it would be, but you know what? I found it kind of charming. And oddly satisfying that someone as confident as John Logan was actually doubting his sexual prowess.

It's funny. Less than a week ago I was bemoaning the lack of excitement in my life, and now look at me—sexy hockey players showing up at my door to excite the hell out of me.

Fuck it. I'm giving *myself* the award.

Logan continues to dominate my thoughts as I meet Ramona and the girls for lunch, joining them at our usual table against the back wall of the cavernous dining hall.

Carver Hall is my favorite place on campus. Whoever constructed it must not have paid attention to the rest of the buildings on campus, though, because Carver has a rustic chalet-style feel to it. High ceilings, wood paneled walls, and ornate light fixtures that cast a soft yellow glow over the room instead of the fluorescent lighting you find in the other meal halls. And it's only two minutes from my dorm, which means I get to bask in its splendor on a daily basis.

I set my tray on the table and pop open the tab of my root beer as I sit in an empty chair. "Hey," I greet everyone. "What are we talking about?"

Ramona, Jess, and Maya instantly clam up, their expressions taking on secretive gleams that tell me precisely what they were talking about.

Me.

I narrow my eyes. "What's going on?"

Ramona glances over sheepishly. "Okay, so don't be mad…but I told them about Logan."

Annoyance spirals through me, but it's mostly directed at myself. I don't know why I bother telling Ramona private things anymore. Asking her to keep a secret is like throwing a ball and asking a dog not to chase it. Well, I threw the damn ball, and now Ramona's scampering back with it. And this year she happened to meet and become BFFs with two girls who gossip even more than she does. Jess and Maya spend so much time dissecting other people's lives they should create a website and give Perez Hilton some competition.

"So is it true?" Jess demands. "Did you seriously hook up with him?"

I feel uncomfortable discussing Logan with them, but I know these girls, and they won't let up until I give them something. Trying to appear casual, I twirl some fettuccine around my fork and take a bite. Then I glance at Jess and say, "Yep."

"That's it? *Yep?*" She looks aghast. "That's all you're going to say?"

"I told you guys, she's being super hush-hush about it." Ramona grins. "Obviously we need to remind Grace about the number one rule of friendship. AKA not skimping on details when you made out with the hottest guy on campus."

I chew my pasta. "I don't kiss and tell."

Maya speaks up, a mocking note in her voice. "You know, considering the complete lack of details, one might think it didn't even happen at all."

One might think?

My head swivels toward Ramona. Unbelievable. Is she spreading that around now? Letting people believe I'm some crazy pathological liar?

Ramona is quick to defend herself against my unspoken accusation. "Hey, we cleared that up, remember? I totally believe that you fooled around with him, babe."

"Twice." The confession slips out before I can stop it. Damn it.

Ramona's jaw falls open. "What you mean *twice?*"

I shrug. "He came over again this morning."

That gets me two gasps, followed by two high-pitched squeals—from Jess and Maya. Ramona remains strangely quiet, but when I study her expression, it's impossible to decipher.

"Oh my God. He did?" Jess exclaims.

"When was this?" Ramona asks.

Her tone is way too polite to not raise my hackles. "Right after you left for class. He didn't stay long, though."

Her dark eyes stay shuttered. "Did you at least get his number this time?"

"No," I admit. "But he has mine now."

"So you still have no way of reaching him." It's not a question. It's not even a particularly pleasant statement. There's an edge to her voice, and when I glance across the table, there's no missing the smirk on Maya's face.

They don't believe me.

Ramona can deny it until she's blue in the face and backpedal until she's in another state, but my best friend still thinks I'm making it up. And now she's recruiting our friends into doubting me too.

Our friends?

The scornful voice raises a good point, and as I think it over, I suddenly can't think of a single person I've hung out with this year that Ramona didn't introduce me to. The one time I invited a few girls from my English Lit class to come over, Ramona laughed and chatted with them all night, told them what a fabulous time she had, and then, after they left, informed me they were boring and that I wasn't allowed to bring them over when she was around.

Damn it, why do I let her dictate my life like that? I tolerated it in high school because…hell, I don't even know why I tolerated it. But we're not in high school anymore. This is college, and I should be able to spend time with whoever I want without worrying about what Ramona will think about them.

"No," I answer through clenched teeth. "I have no way of reaching him. But don't worry, I'm sure my imaginary hook-up partner will get in touch with me sooner or later."

She frowns. "Grace—"

"I'm heading back to the dorm to work on my paper." My appetite has disappeared. I pick up my half-eaten dinner tray and rise to my feet. "I'll see you later."

Maybe I'm naive, but I thought college would be different. I thought all the gossiping and backstabbing and bullshit ceased to exist once you left high school, but I guess mean girls can be found at any level of the education system. It's like visiting a farm—if you go there *not* expecting to see piles of cow shit everywhere, then you're in for a rude awakening. And *there's* a good SAT question for you. *SCHOOL is to MEAN GIRLS as FARMS are to* _____.

Shit. The answer to that is *shit*.

Ramona catches up to me the moment I burst outside, her heels clicking on the limestone entrance as she hurries toward me.

"Grace, wait."

My jaw tenses as I turn around. "What now?"

Panic lights her eyes. "Please don't be pissed at me. I *hate* it when you're pissed at me."

"Gee, I'm so sorry you're upset, Ramona. What can I do to make you feel better?"

Her bottom lip quivers. "You don't have to be sarcastic. I came out here to apologize."

For fuck's sake, if she launches into her whole crocodile-tears act, I might actually lose my shit.

"I'm not having this conversation with you again," I say in a cold voice. "I don't care if you think I'm lying. *I* know I'm not, and that's all that matters to me, okay? Just know that I find it incredibly insulting that my best friend since I was *six* years old believes I—"

"I'm jealous," she blurts out.

I stop talking. "What?"

Her face collapses as our gazes lock. She lowers her voice, then repeats herself. "I'm jealous, all right?"

Hell must have frozen over. There's no other explanation for what I'm hearing. Because in thirteen years of friendship, Ramona has never admitted to being *jealous* of me.

"I've been trying to get with Dean all year," she laments. "All fucking year and he doesn't know I exist, and you just hook up with his best friend without even *trying*." An oddly vulnerable look softens her features. "I've been acting like a total bitch and I'm so sorry. I was insecure and I took it out on you and that wasn't fair, but please don't be angry with me. It's your birthday on Wednesday. I want to celebrate with you, and I want us to be good again, and I—"

I interrupt with a sigh. "We're good, Ramona."

"We are?"

The anger that had been flowing so freely through my veins dissipates as I glimpse her hopeful expression. *This* is the Ramona I invested thirteen years of my life for. The girl who listened to me babble for hours about my high school crushes, who brought my assignments home whenever I was sick, who taught me how to put on makeup, and threatened to kick the ass of anyone who so much as *looked* at me the wrong way. She might be self-absorbed and shallow at times, but she's also fiercely loyal and unbelievably kind when she drops that bad girl bitch act.

All the bullshit with Jess and Maya back there still stings, but I can't bring myself to throw away years' worth of friendship over something so trivial.

"We're good," I assure her. "I promise."

A brilliant smile fills her face. "Good." She flings her arms around my waist and bear-hugs the hell out of me. "Now let's go home so you can tell me every dirty thing John Logan did to you this morning. In *explicit* detail."

CHAPTER 8

Logan

I drive to Munsen on Wednesday morning, my enthusiasm level sitting firmly on its usual spot on the super-happy-fun-time scale: zero.

It's rare that I'm forced go home during the school year, but sometimes I have no choice. Usually it happens if the part-time mechanic at my dad's shop can't cover for Jeff when he takes Dad to his doctor's appointments. Today is one of those instances, but I assure myself that I can handle a couple hours of oil changes and tune-ups without losing my mind.

Besides, it'll be a good warm-up for the summer. I tend to forget how much I hate working in the garage, so on that first day back, it's like being sent to the front lines of a war zone. My stomach drops and fear pummels into me, as I realize that *this* will be my life for the next three months. At least if I dip my toes in today, I can get some of the panic out of the way.

Jeff's van is already gone when I park my pickup in front of Logan and Sons Auto Repair. The name is kind of ironic, seeing as the shop was already called that long before my parents ever had kids. My granddad ran the place before my dad took over, and I guess he'd been hoping to sire a lot of strapping male offspring. He only sired one, though, so technically the place should be called Logan and *Son*.

The shop consists of one small, brick building, the interior of which only has room for two lifts. But the meager square footage doesn't really impact the business since it's not exactly booming. L&S does well enough to cover expenses, my dad's bills, and the mortgage on our bungalow, which sits at the back of the property. Growing up, I hated that our house was so close to the shop. We used to get woken up in the middle of the night by customers pounding on our door because their car broke down nearby, or by phone calls from the tow truck company saying they were bringing over a vehicle.

Since my dad's accident, the close proximity has actually become convenient, because it means he can get from home to work in less than a minute.

Not that he spends much time in the garage anymore. Jeff is the one who does all the work, while Dad drinks himself stupid on the living room recliner.

I walk up to the dented metal door, which is shut and locked. A lined piece of paper sticks to it with a jagged strip of duct tape, and I instantly recognize my brother's handwriting.

YOU'RE LATE.

Two words, all caps. Shit, Jeff was pissed.

I use my set of keys to unlock the side door, then step inside and hit the button that sends the huge mechanical door soaring upward. It's still cold out, but I always keep the door open, no matter how frigid the weather is. It's my one requirement for working here. After a while, the overpowering odor of oil and car exhaust makes me want to kill myself.

Jeff has left me a list of tasks, but luckily, it's not too long. The older model Buick parked on the concrete needs an oil change and a headlight replaced. Easy peasy. I throw on a blue jumpsuit with the L&S logo on the back, turn the radio dial to the first metal station I find, and get right to work.

An hour passes before I take my first break. I chug water from the sink in the office, then pop outside for a quick cigarette.

I've just snubbed the butt out beneath my steel-toed boot when the sound of an engine hums in the distance. My chest tightens when I glimpse the front bumper of my brother's white van slicing through the trees that line the long driveway.

Like a coward, I duck back inside and race to the raised hood of the

Buick. I bend over and pretend to give the engine a spot check, while also pretending I'm too focused on my work to notice the car doors slamming and my dad's harsh voice as he snaps something at my brother. I hear two sets of footsteps, one slow and laborious, leading away from the dirt driveway, the other a fast angry thump as Jeff storms into the garage.

"You couldn't come over and say hello to him?" my older brother demands irritably.

I straighten up and close the hood. "Sorry, I was finishing up. I'll stop by the house before I go."

"You better, because he just gave me shit for it, and I'm not even the one who didn't say hello!" Jeff's dark eyebrows draw together in a displeased frown. He looks like he wants to lecture me some more, so I speedily change the subject before he can.

"So what did the doctor say?"

Jeff responds in a flat voice. "He needs to stop drinking or he's going to die."

I can't help but snort. "Fat chance of him stopping."

"Of course he won't stop. He's drinking *to* die." Jeff angrily shakes his head. "Before the accident, it was an addiction. Now I think it's a purpose."

Jesus. I've never heard a more depressing assessment in my life.

I can't argue, though. The accident really was the game-changer—it had pushed my dad right off the wagon and pretty much erased all those years of sobriety. *Good* years, damn it. Three whole years of having a father again.

When I was fourteen, Dad's latest stint in rehab had miraculously stuck. He'd been sober for an entire year before Mom left, which was the only reason she agreed to let us stay with him. During the divorce, we had a choice about which parent to live with, and since Jeff didn't want to change schools and refused to leave his girlfriend, he chose to stay with our dad. And I chose to stay with my older brother. Not only because I idolized him, but because when we were little, the two of us made a promise to always watch each other's backs.

Dad had stayed sober for two more years after that, but I guess the universe decided that the Logan family wasn't allowed to be happy, because when I was sixteen, my father was involved in a massive car accident on his way back from dropping us off in Boston to see our mom.

Both his legs were crushed. And I mean *crushed*—he was lucky to escape without being paralyzed. He was in a shit ton of pain, but the doctors were hesitant to prescribe painkillers to a man with a destructive history of addiction. They said he needed to be monitored twenty-four/seven, so Jeff left college to come home and help me take care of him. Mom's new husband offered to take out a loan in order to hire someone to care for Dad, but we assured David that we could handle it. Because at the time, we honestly believed we could. Dad's legs would heal, and if he went to physical therapy like the doctors had instructed, then he might be able to walk normally one day.

But again, the universe had another *fuck you* for the Logans. Dad was in so much agony that he turned to drinking to numb the pain. He also didn't finish his PT, which means his legs didn't heal the way they were supposed to.

So now he has a bad limp, constant pain, and two sons who have resigned themselves to the fact that they'll be taking care of him until the day he dies.

"What do we do?" I ask grimly.

"Same thing we've always done. We man up and take care of our family."

Frustration twists my gut, tangling with the pretzel of guilt already lodged there. Why is it *our* job to sacrifice everything for him?

Because he's your father and he's sick.

Because your mother had to do it for fourteen years and now it's your turn.

Another thought bubbles to the surface, one I've had before, and which makes me want to throw up every time it enters my mind.

Things would be so much easier if he died.

As bile burns my throat, I banish the selfish, disgusting notion. I don't want him to die. He might be a mess, he might be a drunk and an asshole sometimes, but he's still my father, damn it. He's the man who drove me to hockey practice, rain or shine. Who helped me memorize my multiplication tables and taught me how to tie my shoes.

When he was sober, he was a really good dad, and that just makes this whole situation so much fucking worse. Because I can't hate him. I *don't* hate him.

"Listen, I've been thinking…" I trail off, too afraid of Jeff's reaction. Coughing, I fish another cigarette out of the pack and head for the door. "Let's talk outside for a sec."

A moment later, I take a deep drag of my smoke, hoping the nicotine will bring me a much-needed dose of confidence. Jeff eyes me in disapproval before releasing a defeated sigh.

"Give me one of those."

As he lights up, I exhale a cloud of smoke and force myself to continue. "I've had some interest from an agent in New York. This really big sports agent." I hesitate. "He thinks I'll have no trouble signing with a team if I test out free agency."

Jeff's features instantly harden.

"That could mean a decent signing bonus. And a contract. *Money*, Jeff." Desperation tightens my throat. "We could hire someone else to run the garage, a full-time nurse for Dad. Maybe even pay off the house if the contract is big enough."

My brother barks out a derisive laugh. "How big of a contract do you think you'll actually land, John? Let's be serious here." He shakes his head. "Look, we talked about this. If you wanted to go pro, you should've gone the Major Junior route. But you wanted the college degree. You can't have it both ways."

Yeah, I did choose the degree. Because I knew damn well that if I picked the alternative, I'd never leave the league, and that would mean screwing over my brother. They would've had to pry that hockey stick out of my cold dead hands to stop me from playing.

But now that the time for Jeff and me to trade places is drawing near, I'm terrified.

"It could be a lot of money," I mumble, but my feeble attempt to convince him doesn't work—Jeff is already shaking his head.

"No way, Johnny. We had a deal. Even if you signed with a team, you wouldn't get all that money up front, and it would take time to get everything here in order. I don't have time, okay? The second they slap that diploma in your hand, I'm out of here."

"Oh, come on. You expect me to believe you're just going to skip town at the drop of a hat?"

"Kylie and I are leaving for Europe next May," Jeff says quietly. "We'll be gone the day after your graduation."

Surprise slams into me. "Since when?"

"We've been planning this for a long time. I already told you—we want to travel for a couple of years before we get married. And then we want to spend some time in Boston before we look for a place in Hastings."

My panic intensifies. "But that's still your plan, right? Living in Hastings and working here?"

That was the deal we'd struck after I graduated high school. Jeff mans the fort while I'm in college, and then I take over for a few years before he and his fiancée settle down in this area, at which point he'll run the shop again and I'll be free.

Granted, I'll also be twenty-five by then, and the odds of playing professional hockey won't be as favorable. Yeah, I might land in the AHL somewhere, but I don't know how many NHL teams would be interested in taking me on at that point.

"It's still the plan," he assures me. "Kylie wants to live in a small town and raise our kids here. And I like being a mechanic."

Well, that makes one of us.

"I don't mind taking care of Dad, either. I…" He breathes heavily. "I just need a break, okay?"

My throat has clamped shut, so I settle for a nod. Then I put out my smoke and force a smile, finally finding my voice. "I still need to change that headlight. Better get back to it."

We walk inside, Jeff heading for the office while I wander back to the Buick.

Fifteen minutes later, I hang up my coveralls on one of the hooks on the wall, call out a hasty goodbye, and practically sprint to my pickup.

Hoping like hell my brother doesn't realize I didn't say hello to our father.

CHAPTER 9

Logan

ALL I WANT TO DO tonight is sprawl on the couch and watch the first playoffs game of the season. I don't even care that Boston isn't playing—I'll watch any game you put in front of me during the post-season. Nothing gets your blood going and heart racing more than playoffs hockey.

Dean, however, has other plans. He waits for me in the hall when I leave the bathroom after my shower, his green eyes narrowed in impatience. "Jesus Christ, bro, what the hell were you doing in there? Shaving your legs? Thirteen-year-old girls take shorter showers than that!"

"I was literally in there for *five* minutes."

I brush past him and duck into my bedroom, but he follows me in. No sense of boundaries, this one.

"Hurry up and get dressed. We're going to a movie and I don't want to miss the previews."

I stare at him. "Are you asking me out on a date?"

That gets me a middle finger. "You wish."

"No, *you* wish, apparently." I grab a pair of boxers from the top drawer and shoot him a pointed look. "Do you mind?"

"Seriously? I've seen your cock hundreds of times in the locker room. Get dressed already." He folds his arms over his chest and taps his foot.

"Go away. I'm watching the Red Wings game tonight."

"Aw, come on, you don't even *like* Detroit. And it's half-price ticket night at the theater—I've been waiting like a week to see this Statham movie just so we could go tonight."

Now I'm gaping at him, because is he for real? "Hey, asshole, you're filthy rich. If anyone should be paying full price for movie tickets, it's *you*."

"I was being nice, *asshole*. Waiting for the cheap day so *you'd* be able to afford it." Then he flashes his trademark grin, the one that makes chicks drop their panties and dive onto his dick.

"Don't give me your sex grin. It's creeping me out."

His mouth stays frozen in the sex-grin position. "I'll stop smiling like this if you agree to be my date tonight."

"You're the most annoying pers—"

The grin widens, and he even throws a little wink in there.

Ten minutes later, we're out the door.

THE MOVIE THEATER IN HASTINGS only has three screens and carries one new release a week, which really limits the selection. Luckily for Dean, the Jason Statham movie he's got a hard-on for is playing there. Dean's a *huge* Statham fan. If someone told me he stands in front of his mirror speaking in a British accent and pretends to transport things around his bedroom? I'd buy it.

I'm still not in the mood to see a movie, but after Dean twisted my arm, I realized that getting out of the house might not be the worst idea. Hannah usually comes by after work on Wednesdays, so hopefully she and Garrett will already be asleep by the time Dean and I get home. And yes, I know her work schedule, sad pathetic loser that I am.

On the bright side, I haven't been obsessing over her as much as usual. The person who monopolized my thoughts all weekend was not Hannah, but Grace. Christ, and don't get me started on Monday's oral spectacular. When I jerked off last night, it was to the memory of Grace's firm, creamy thighs and hot, tight—

"Logan. Hey."

I blink in confusion as Grace enters my line of vision. For a second, I wonder if my dirty mind somehow conjured up the image of her, but nope. She's actually here, standing five feet from the box office.

"Hey," I greet her.

She smiles, tucking a strand of hair behind her ear. She's in a tight sweater, black yoga pants, and an unzipped blue windbreaker, looking like she stepped off the pages of an Abercrombie & Fitch catalogue. I kind of like the whole comfy-but-hot look she has going on.

I hear a soft *ahem* and notice there's someone standing beside her. A curvy, raven-haired girl in a brown leather skirt and fuzzy red top. And she's gaping at me. Like, jaw-scraping-the-floor gaping.

Someone pokes me from behind. "Dude," Dean says irritably. "Stick to the plan. You, tickets. Me, popcorn."

I thrust out the twenty-dollar bill in my hand. "Change of plans. I'll grab the snacks."

He rolls his eyes, then spares an admiring glance at Grace's friend's tits before ambling off to grab the tickets.

"What are you guys here to see?" I ask Grace.

She grins. "What do you think?" She holds up two tickets and I chuckle when I glimpse the title of the Statham movie.

Of course. I forgot what an action nut she is.

"That's what we're watching too. We should all sit together."

Her friend makes another squeaky noise. Actually, it's more of a gasp, with a bit of a wheeze thrown in there. There's a lot going on in that one little sound.

Grace gestures to her friend. "This is Ramona. Ramona, this is Logan."

The friend looks me up and down. "I know who he is."

Aw, hell. I've seen that look before. Many, many times, on the faces of many, many women. As if she's picturing me naked and inside her.

Too bad I'm not interested in fulfilling that fantasy. I'm wholly focused on Grace, and the parade of wicked images flashing through my mind. Like the way her eyes glazed over when my tongue first touched her clit. And the breathy noises she made when she came. And—

"It's Grace's birthday," the friend announces.

Grace's features crease in discomfort. "Ramona."

"Shit, it is?" I grin at her. "Happy birthday, gorgeous."

I don't miss the way her friend's jaw slackens again, or how Grace shifts in visible embarrassment.

"Thanks." Her bottom lip juts out glumly. "I'm nineteen today. Go me."

I snicker. "I take it you're not a birthday person?"

"Absolutely not. My mother scarred me for life."

Her friend suddenly snorts. "Hey, remember the year at the spring fair? When your mom crashed the stage during that folk band's set and performed a birthday rap for you?"

"You mean do I remember the day I researched how to emancipate myself from my parents?" Grace replies in a dry voice. "Vividly."

Ramona shoots me a conspiratorial look. "I wanted to invite some people over to the dorm to celebrate, but she threatened to cut off both my arms and feed them to me if I did. So we compromised by going to the movies."

We're interrupted by Dean, who frowns when he sees my empty hands. "For fuck's sake, do I have to do everything?" Then, as if remembering he's in the presence of two very pretty girls, he breaks out in a grin. "Also, are you gonna introduce me or what?"

"This is Grace and—" Shit, I've already forgotten the friend's name.

"Ramona," she supplies, and that hungry gaze fixates on Dean now.

She can ogle him as much as she wants, but I can pretty much guarantee that the moment he finds out she's a freshman, Dean won't be ogling her back.

For all his manwhoring, the guy has a strict rule about not doing freshmen. I'm not sure I blame him, considering our little stalker incident at the start of the year. Dean had hooked up with a freshman, who, after one night of exquisite passion, decided they were madly in love. She then proceeded to show up at our house at all hours of the day and night, sometimes wearing clothes, other times *not* wearing clothes, usually armed with flowers and love letters and—my personal favorite—a framed photo of herself wearing Dean's hockey jersey.

Sometimes when I'm falling asleep, I can still hear her wailing *Deeeeeeeeean* outside my window.

Needless to say, Dean's avoided the young ones ever since. He calls them level ten clingers.

The four of us stop at the concessions counter so Dean can get his popcorn, and a few minutes later, we enter the dark theater, where the previews have just started. The auditorium is *packed*. There's a better chance of Jason Statham himself showing up to offer commentary on the movie than of us finding four seats together. But from where I stand,

I spot several available two-seat blocks.

The girls are walking ahead of us, so I lean closer to Dean and murmur, "Mind if we split up? I want to sit with Grace. It's her birthday."

His gaze rests on Ramona's undeniably great ass. "I can live with that."

Both Grace and Ramona nod in agreement when I suggest sitting separately. Ramona instantly links her arm through Dean's and whispers something in his ear that makes him chuckle, and then they shuffle forward in the dark to look for seats.

Grace and I do the same. We find two empty spots halfway up the auditorium, right on the aisle, and once we're settled, she slides closer to whisper, "Are you sure your friend is okay sitting with Ramona? Because she's absolutely going to hit on him the whole time."

Her lips are practically on my ear, and she smells incredible. I can't name flowery scents to save my life, but hers is sweet and girly, and when she runs a hand through her hair, a whiff of it floats into my nostrils.

"Don't worry. Dean can handle himself," I whisper back with a grin.

We turn to the screen, which is showing a preview that instantly captivates Grace. It's some shoot-em-up explosion porn with big stars and even bigger guns, and her excited expression makes me want to kiss her so fucking bad. Her love for action movies is a major turn-on.

Before I can stop myself, I reach out and take her hand.

She jerks in surprise, then relaxes and looks over with a smile before refocusing her attention on the screen.

I still can't figure her out. She's sweet, but she doesn't come off as naive. She gives off an innocent vibe, but she also seems incredibly secure with herself. She doesn't barrage me with questions or flirt up a storm. Hell, she hasn't even brought up the fact that I play hockey, which is usually the first thing chicks do when I'm around.

It's crazy how I hardly know a thing about her, yet I had my face between her legs a couple days ago and—oh shit, now I'm thinking about her pussy.

Wonderful. And now I have a boner of monstrous proportions.

I clumsily shift in my seat, resisting the urge to slide my hand down my pants and do some discreet rearranging. Or maybe to slide my hand down *her* pants and give her a birthday present to remember.

I do neither. The sounds of crunching popcorn and crinkling candy wrappers echo all around us, a blatant reminder that we're surrounded by people. I try to concentrate on the opening credits flashing on the screen, but ten minutes into the movie, and my boner's still going strong.

How long does an erection have to last before it's considered bad news? Three hours? Four? No way this movie is *that* long, right?

God, I fucking hope not.

CHAPTER 10

Grace

FOR THE FIRST TIME IN forever, I'm not angry with Ramona for persuading me to go out on my birthday. I wanted to avoid all the fanfare by simply staying home, but she'd dangled Jason Statham under my nose like a little British carrot. We've been friends long enough that Ramona knows all my weaknesses—and exploits them at all costs.

But I owe her big for using Statham as a bargaining chip tonight, otherwise I wouldn't be sitting next to Logan right now.

With that said, I'm still not sure how I feel about him. He didn't make the best first impression when he raced out of my dorm that first night, but I can't deny that his second impression was a screaming-orgasm success. So I guess he's got a checkmark in both the pros *and* cons columns at the moment.

Make that *two* checkmarks in the pros department—because halfway through the movie, he kisses me.

Not a peck. Not a lingering caress of his lips. It's a hot, tongue-tangling kiss that makes my heart pound harder and louder than the deafening explosions blasting from the screen. I lose myself in it, in *him*, in the skillful stroke of his tongue and the warmth of his hand as it curls around the side of my neck.

It isn't until I hear chuckles from the guys on the other side of me that I remember where we are. I self-consciously pull away, and Logan's heavy-lidded gaze rests on my mouth, which is wet and swollen from his kisses.

He leans in closer. "On a scale of one to ten, how much would you care if you missed a few minutes of the movie?"

I think it over. "Two?"

"Thank God."

He tugs me to my feet. Since we're on the aisle, we don't have to shuffle past anyone, thus sparing ourselves and everyone around us that awful *'scuse me, so sorry* disruption that moviegoers hate. Still holding hands, we tiptoe down the steps. I spot Dean and Ramona's heads near the front row, but neither of them notices us making our escape.

"Where are we going?" I whisper.

All I get in response is a mischievous smile. He leads me down the dark corridor toward the auditorium doors, but rather than go through them, he veers left and turns the knob of a door I hadn't even realized was there.

We're in a closet. It's pitch black and reeks of cleaning supplies, but suddenly Logan's body presses up against me, and all I can smell is him. I gasp when his mouth covers mine, because I didn't see the kiss coming. I can't see anything actually. But I sure as hell can *feel*. The hard muscles of Logan's chest straining beneath his long-sleeve shirt. The seductive coaxing of his tongue as it slips through my parted lips and fills my mouth.

I wrap my arms around his neck and eagerly return the kiss. In a heartbeat, he backs me into the wall, one muscular thigh thrusting between my legs. The unexpected contact triggers an instant jolt of arousal that spirals to my core.

He kisses me like he can't get enough, sucking on my tongue like it's made of candy. Then he cups my ass and yanks me closer, grinding our lower bodies together.

"I wish I could fuck you right here." He growls the words against my neck before sinking his teeth into it, bringing a sting of pain that he immediately soothes with his tongue.

I hadn't realized my neck possessed so many sensitive nerve endings. I'm on fire, every inch of skin prickling with awareness, tingling each time his lips travel over my feverish flesh.

My clit swells, *aches*, and the tension between my legs grows and grows until I'm shamelessly grinding against his thigh in a desperate attempt to ease the ache. I've never fooled around in public before, and the notion that anyone could walk in and catch us right now is so thrilling that my hips move faster, craving more friction.

"Oh fuck, keep doing that, baby," he mutters. "Rub your pussy against me."

Oh. God.

Dirty talk is…different. And exciting. And I'm so turned on I can no longer formulate coherent thoughts.

He kisses a path back to my mouth, his tongue plunging deep, mimicking the movements of his hips. If someone told me a week ago that John Logan would be dry humping me in a movie theater closet, I would've laughed my fool head off.

But here we are, and it's frickin' *amazing*. My clit throbs every time the seam of his fly presses into it, and either I'm completely misinterpreting the wild tingling in my core, or…I might actually come this way. Fully clothed, with no contact other than his thigh rubbing my…oh God, yep, I'm about to come.

A desperate noise tears out of my mouth, but it's instantly swallowed up by another blistering kiss from Logan, whose hips rock harder, faster, until the knot of pleasure explodes in a rush of pure bliss that sweeps through me, buzzing in my fingers and curling my toes.

Logan's head falls in the crook of my neck and he lets out a low grunt. Breathing hard against my skin as his entire body trembles.

"*Fuck*. That was so hot," he groans a few seconds later.

His arms wrap around me, holding me tight to his rock-hard chest as we both recover, our breathing labored and our heartbeats hammering in unison. A full minute passes before he releases me and takes a step away.

My eyes have adjusted to the darkness, and I see him reach for a stack of paper napkins on a nearby shelf. His hand dips inside his pants before crumpling the napkin and tossing it in the wastebasket by the door.

Then he's back, his voice husky as he brings his mouth to my ear. "Happy birthday."

I start to laugh. I have no idea why, but this entire hook-up was so surreal that I find myself quaking in amusement, which elicits a deep chuckle from him.

"Thank you," I answer between giggles.

His lips graze mine for one fleeting moment, and then he takes my hand and leads me to the door. He pauses in front of it, bowing gallantly before holding it open for me. "After you, gorgeous."

Aw hell. Those three words turn my heart from a solid to a liquid. A warm, gooey pile of mush in my chest.

Well, at least I've figured out how I feel about him.

I think I might be crushing on the guy. *Hard*.

Logan

THE NEXT EVENING, I'M BATTLING Tucker to the death in an intense game of Ice Pro when Dean wanders into the living room, shirtless and barefoot. He rakes a hand through his spiky blond hair before settling on the armchair next to the couch.

"Listen, I need to talk to you about the freshman."

"What freshman?" Tucker voices the question even as his eyes stay glued to the screen.

Mine do too. "You mean Grace?" I say absently.

My team is kicking Tuck's ass, probably because the idiot refuses to play as anyone other than Dallas, who's been eliminated from playoff contention, what, a million years in a row? I, of course, play exclusively as Boston, because that's the team I grew up cheering for and the one I envisioned myself playing for someday.

"Yes, I mean Grace. Unless there's another freshman you took to the movies and sucked face with the whole time?" Dean's remark oozes sarcasm.

I pause the game to take a sip of my Coke. Yup, Coke. I'm still making an effort to dial down the partying. Well, that and my first exam is tomorrow, and I don't want to show up hung-over.

"I didn't take her to the movies," I answer. "We ran into them there, remember?"

"Oh, I remember. I also remember the sucking face part. Seriously, bro, every time I turned around, you were going at it like porn stars."

It's a good thing I haven't told him what we did in the closet. He'd probably have a field day with that one.

"Wait—you're going out with a freshman?" Tuck's expression is unreadable, but I'm pretty sure I hear a chord of relief in his voice.

"Naah, we're not going out."

"Good," Dean says, nodding briskly. "Those younger chicks bring way too much drama to the table."

Tucker snickers. "Drama? Is that what we're calling the Bethany incident now? Because that wasn't drama, dude. It was *stalking*."

"It was a pain in the ass, that's what it was," Dean mutters. "And thanks *so* much for reminding me of it. Now I'm going to have nightmares tonight. Jerk."

I roll my eyes. "Don't worry, Grace isn't like that. No drama whatsoever with her."

Which is one of the reasons I'm so drawn to her. She's the most uncomplicated girl I've ever met. Plus, when I'm with her, I don't think about Hannah at all, which is—

So you're using her to not think about Hannah?

The accusation flies into my head like a hockey team on the offensive.

No. Of course I'm not using her.

Am I?

No. That's crazy. I genuinely like Grace, and I fucking *love* hooking up with her.

But…she does happen to be a great distraction from all this Hannah bullshit.

A great distraction?

Jesus Christ. I'm such a fucking bastard.

As guilt floods my stomach, I suddenly comprehend the irrefutable shittiness of what I've done. And in that moment, I realize I can't see Grace again. How can I when a part of me views her as a *distraction*? When I still experience that awful clench in my gut every time I see Garrett and Wellsy together? When I'm still consumed with envy and anxiety and so much self-loathing?

I'd texted Grace my number earlier and was planning on asking her if she wanted to hang out tomorrow night, but there's no fucking way I can do that now. I might be an asshole for unintentionally using her as a diversion, but now that I'm conscious of my asshole-ness, I refuse to let it continue. It wouldn't be fair to Grace.

"No drama?" Dean echoes, jolting me from my troubled thoughts. "Yeah, sorry to break it to you, but the drama train has already left the station. That's what I came down here to tell you."

I frown. "What are you talking about?"

"You know Piper?"

Tucker snorts. "Did you really just ask that? We *all* know Piper."

My frown deepens, because if Piper Stevens is involved in whatever Dean's about to tell me, then it sure as hell ain't gonna be good. Piper is the puck bunny of all puck bunnies. She's also hot as fuck, which is why half the guys on the team have slept with her. Which, by the way, is an accomplishment she's incredibly proud of and happy to advertise.

I have no problem with that, though. Every time I hear someone refer to her as a slut, I threaten a beat-down, because what the fuck? Most of the dudes I know have screwed their way through college, and nobody bats an eye when *they* do it. So no, I'm not about to judge Piper for her very active sex life.

Nope, what I have a problem with is the fact that she's a total bitch who spreads nasty rumors and gossips more than a Hollywood tabloid.

"I was chilling with Niko this afternoon and he told me Piper's been saying shit about your freshman," Dean says flatly.

My spine stiffens. "What?"

"Yeah, apparently Piper's little sister is friends with Grace, and I guess Grace told her about the two of you hooking up? Except for some reason, the little sister thinks she's making it up?"

"Are you asking me or telling?" I grumble.

"Both? I don't know. I've given up on trying to understand the complexities of women."

"Preaching to the choir," Tuck says solemnly.

Dean makes an exasperated noise in the back of his throat. "All I know is that Piper's spreading it around that some pathetic freshman is lying about doing you, which is obviously bullshit since I had a front row seat to your hook-up last night—you know, when your tongue was bobbing for apples in the back of her throat?"

"The theater was packed with Briar students. If *you* saw us, then I'm sure other people did too."

"Oh, they saw you, dude."

"Then why is anyone even buying Piper's bullshit? I wasn't trying to hide that we were going at it."

"Hey, if you say shit with confidence, people are going to believe it." He shrugs. "Anyway, figured you should know that Piper's being Piper again. She's tweeting about it too, Niko said. She made up some catty hashtag about your girl."

What? I snatch my phone off the coffee table and launch the Twitter app. "What's the hashtag?"

"No idea. I'm sure you can find it if you go on Piper's account."

I quickly type Piper's name in the search box, click on her profile, and proceed to skim the first dozen or so tweets on the page. Each one causes the anger in my gut to burn and bubble and simmer, until finally it boils over and sends me stumbling to my feet in pure outrage.

Oh *hell* no.

CHAPTER 11

Grace

YOU KNOW THOSE ANXIETY DREAMS where you're walking down the hall in high school, or getting up on the stage of an auditorium to give a big speech—and you suddenly realize you're buck naked and everyone is staring at you? And then all those pairs of eyes get bigger and bigger and it feels like hot lasers boring into your skin?

I am currently living that dream. Sure, I'm fully clothed, but despite Ramona's numerous assurances that nobody is staring at me, I *know* I'm not imagining the curious looks and knowing smirks from my fellow students.

Damn Maya Stevens to hell. That bitch did the impossible—she made me afraid of walking into Carver Hall, my favorite place on campus.

It's actually rather impressive that even limited by one hundred and forty characters, Maya's sister managed to spin a beautiful tale of a pitiful, woe-is-me heroine whose fierce yearning for a certain hockey player leads her to fabricate a grand love affair filled with burning loins and endless passion.

In other words, Piper's calling me a fucking liar.

"This is so humiliating," I mutter as I pick at the chicken stir-fry on my plate. "Can we please just go?"

Ramona's chin sticks out in an obstinate pose. "No. You need to show people that you don't give a rat's ass about what Piper is saying."

Easier said than done. My brain knows that I shouldn't care about some asinine Twitter bash fest, but my stomach hasn't received the memo. Every time the words #GracelessLiar flash in my head, my insides twist into a mortified pretzel.

What the hell is the matter with people? It's infuriating how they grant themselves the right to say whatever hurtful poison they want, without giving a shit about the person they're hurting. Actually, you know what? I'm not even pissed at the rumormongers. I'm pissed at whoever invented the Internet and handed the assholes in the world a platform on which to spew their venom.

Fucking Internet.

My best friend treats my silence as an invitation to keep babbling. "Piper's a bitch, okay? You know how possessive she is about the hockey players. She acts like every single one of them belongs to *her*, which is total bullshit. She's probably consumed with jealousy that you managed to land one of the star players, who, by the way—" Ramona lowers her voice to a conspiratorial pitch "—she's been chasing after since freshman year, but he keeps shutting her down."

Sweet mother of Moses. Now we're gossiping about *Piper*? Are there *any* mature adults at this motherfucking university?

"Can we please not talk about her?" I clench my teeth, which makes it difficult to take a bite of the noodles I've just raised to my mouth.

"Fine," she relents. "But know that I've got your back on this, babe. Nobody talks shit about my BFF and lives to tell about it."

I decide not to point out that Piper wouldn't have been talking shit in the first place if *someone* hadn't implied to Maya that I'd made everything up.

"If you want, we can talk about *my* misery," she says glumly. "As in, the fact that Dean didn't ask for my number after the movie last night—"

Ramona stops talking when footsteps sound from behind us. My shoulders tense, then relax when I realize the footsteps belong to Jess. Then they tense all over again, because it's *Jess*. Lovely. Let another round of torture commence.

"Hey," Jess greets me, her eyes awash with sympathy. "I'm so sorry about this Twitter bullshit. Maya shouldn't have said anything to her sister. She's *such* a gossip."

If I had a dictionary on me, I would've opened it to the H's, passed it to Jess, and forced her to read the definition of *HYPOCRITE*.

Luckily, my phone buzzes before I give in and hurl a bitchy retort her way.

When I see Logan's name on the screen, my heart does an involuntary flip. I'm tempted to hop up on the table and wave the phone around to prove to everyone in Carver Hall that contrary to what Piper Stevens has posited, John Logan *is* "aware of my existence." But I resist the urge, because unlike some people, *I* don't need a dictionary reminder—I already know the meaning of *futile*.

Logan's message is short.

Him: Where u at?

I quickly type back, Dining hall.

Him: Which 1?
Me: Carver.

No response. Okay then. I'm not sure what the point of that conversation was, but his consequent silence has a dampening effect on my already flailing self-confidence. I've been dying to talk to him since last night, but he hasn't called, texted, or attempted to make plans. And finally he gets in touch and *this* is the result? Two questions followed by crickets?

I'm horrified to realize I'm on the verge of tears. I'm not sure who I'm even upset with. Logan? Piper? Ramona? Myself? But it doesn't matter. I refuse to cry in the middle of the dining hall, or give anyone the satisfaction of seeing me rush out five minutes after I got here. The girls at the neighboring table haven't stopped smirking since I sat down, and I can still feel them watching me. I can't make out a word of their hushed discussion, but when I glance over, all five of them quickly avert their gazes.

Ignore them.

Although my appetite has disappeared right along with my self-esteem, I force myself to eat my dinner. Every last bite, shoving stir-fry down my throat while pretending to care about Ramona and Jess's conversation, which has blessedly shifted to a topic that doesn't involve me.

Fifteen minutes. That's how long I last before I can no longer take it. My eyes are actually sore from the incessant blinking required to staunch the threatening flow of tears.

I'm about to scrape my chair back and feed my friends an excuse about needing to study when they both fall silent. Jess literally stops talking mid-sentence. The table beside us has gone suspiciously quiet, as well.

Ramona looks like she's fighting a smile as she peers past my shoulders in the direction of the door.

Frowning, I shift in my chair, turn my head—and find Logan standing there.

"Hey," he says easily.

I'm so surprised to see him that all I can manage is a dumbfounded look. With me sitting down and him looming over me, he appears even bigger than usual. A Briar hockey jersey stretches across his massive shoulders, his dark hair windblown and cheeks flushed with exertion, as if he was just out for a run.

Our gazes lock for one heart-stopping moment, and then he does the absolute last thing I expect.

He leans down and kisses me.

On the mouth. With tongue.

Right there in the dining hall.

When he pulls back, I'm gratified to find that Ramona and Jess are slack-jawed—and so are the girls at the next table.

Not feeling so chatty anymore, are you?

I'm still basking in the glow of victory when Logan flashes me that crooked grin I love so much. "Are you ready to go, gorgeous?"

We didn't have plans. He knows that and *I* know that, but I'm not about to let anyone else know it.

So I play along by answering, "Yep." I start to get up. "Let me just bring back this tray."

"Don't worry about it—I'll do it." He plucks the tray out of my hands, says, "Nice to see you again, Ramona," and then plants another kiss on my lips before striding toward the tray return counter.

Every female in the room admires the way his black cargo pants hug his spectacular ass. Myself included.

Snapping out of my butt-leering trance, I turn to my friends, who still look dazed. "Sorry to eat and run, but I have plans tonight."

Logan comes back a moment later, and I paste on the brightest smile I can muster as he takes my hand and leads me out of the dining hall.

THE SECOND I SLIDE INTO the passenger seat of his pickup truck, the dam I've struggled to keep intact all evening shatters to pieces. As the tears spill over, I make a frantic attempt to wipe them away with my sleeves before he notices.

But it's too late.

"Aw, hey, don't cry." He quickly reaches inside the center console and pulls out a travel pack of tissues.

Damn it, I can't believe I'm bawling in front of him. I sniffle as he hands me the pack. "Thank you."

"No prob."

"No, not just for the tissues. Thank you for showing up and rescuing me. This whole day has been so humiliating," I mumble.

He sighs. "I guess you saw that Twitter feed."

My embarrassment triples. "Just so you know, I haven't been going around and telling everyone about us. The only person who knows we hooked up is Ramona."

"Obvs. She was there at the movies." His smile is reassuring. "Don't worry, you didn't strike me as the type to B&B."

I offer a blank stare. "Bed and breakfast?"

He snickers. "No. Bag and brag."

"Bag and brag?" I'm laughing through my tears, because the phrase is so absurd. "I didn't realize that was a thing."

"Trust me, it is. The puck bunnies excel at it." His voice softens. "And just so *you* know, the chick who started the Twitter bullshit? *Huge* puck bunny. And she's still pissed at me because I turned her down last year."

"Why did you do that?" I've met Maya's sister, and she's beautiful.

"Because she's pushy. And kind of annoying, if I'm being honest." He turns the key in the ignition and gives me a sidelong look. "Do you want me to drive you home? Because I was thinking of taking you somewhere else first, if you're interested."

My curiosity is piqued. "Where?"

His blue eyes twinkle mischievously. "It's a surprise."

"A good surprise?"

"Is there any other kind?"

"Um, *yeah*. I can think of a hundred bad surprises off the top of my head."

"Name one," he challenges.

"Okay—you're set up on a blind date, and you show up at the restaurant and Ted Bundy is sitting at the table."

Logan grins at me. "Bundy is your go-to answer for everything, huh?"

"It appears so."

"Fine. Well, point taken. And I promise, it's a good surprise. Or in the very least, it's neutral."

"All right. Surprise away then."

He pulls out of the parking lot and turns onto the road that leads away from campus. As I gaze out the window and watch the trees whiz by, a heavy sigh leaves my chest. "Why are people such assholes sometimes?"

"Because they are," he says simply. "Honestly, it's not worth getting angry over. My advice? Don't waste your time obsessing over the stupid actions of stupid people."

"It's kind of hard not to when they're slandering my good name." But I know he's right. Why bother expending any mental energy on bullies like Piper Stevens? Three years from now, I won't even remember her name.

"Seriously, Grace, don't stress. You know what they say—haters be hating, and bitches be bitching."

I laugh again. "That's going to be my new motto."

"Good. It should be."

We pass the sky-blue sign with the words *"Welcome to Hastings!"* sprawled across it, and I peer out the window again. "I grew up around the corner," I tell him.

He sounds surprised. "You're from Hastings?"

"Yep. My dad's been a professor at Briar for twenty years. I've spent my whole life here."

Rather than head for the downtown core, Logan veers off in the direction of the highway. We don't stay on it for long, though. A few exits pass and then he gets off at the sign for Munsen, the next town over.

An uneasy feeling washes over me. It's so strange how a quaint, middle-class town like Hastings is equal in distance to both the campus of an Ivy League university and a town that my father, a man who doesn't curse if he can help it, refers to as a "shit box."

Munsen consists of shabby buildings in desperate need of repairs, a handful of strip malls, and rundown bungalows with unkempt lawns. The general store we pass boasts a flickering neon sign with half the letters burnt out, and the one building I see that *isn't* dilapidated is a small brick church with a sign of its own—huge block letters that spell out "GOD PUNISHES THE SINNERS."

The people of Munsen really know how to roll out a welcome mat.

"This is where *I* grew up," Logan says gruffly.

My head swivels toward him. "Really? I didn't know you were local, too."

"Yup." He gives me a self-deprecating look before focusing on the pothole-ridden road ahead of us. "It's not much to look at, is it? Trust me, it's even uglier in the daylight."

The pickup bounces as we drive over a particularly deep pothole. Logan slows down, extending a hand toward my side of the windshield. "My dad's shop is one street over. He's a mechanic."

"That's cool. Did he teach you a lot about cars?"

"Yup." He taps the dashboard in pride. "You hear that sexy purr coming out of this baby? I rebuilt the engine myself last summer."

I'm genuinely impressed. And kinda turned on, because I appreciate a man who works with his hands. No, who actually knows *how* to use his hands. Last week, the guy who lives down the hall from me knocked on my door and asked me to help him change a *light bulb*. I'm not saying I'm Handy McHanderson or anything, but I'm capable of changing a frickin' light bulb.

As we drive through a residential area, a burst of apprehension goes off inside me. Is he taking me to his childhood home? Because I'm not sure I'm ready for—

Nope, we're on another dirt road now, driving *away* from town. Another five minutes, and we reach a large clearing. There's a water tower in the distance, with the town name etched on its side, and it seems to glow in the moonlight, a stark white beacon standing out amidst the dark landscape.

Logan parks fifty yards from the tower, and my pulse speeds up when I realize that's where we're going. My hands shake as I follow him toward a steel ladder that starts at the base of the tower and extends upward, so high I can't see where it ends.

"Are we going up there?" I blurt out. "If so…no thank you. I'm terrified of heights."

"Ah, shit. I forgot." He bites his lip for a second, before giving me an earnest look. "Face your fear for me? I promise, it'll be worth it."

I stare at the ladder, and I can feel all the color draining from my face. "Uh…"

"Come on," he coaxes. "You can climb up first. I'll stand down here the whole time and catch you if you fall. Scout's honor."

"Fall?" I screech. "I wasn't even thinking about *falling*. Oh my God, what if I fall?"

He chuckles softly. "You won't. But like I said, I'll be here to catch you on the off, *off* chance it happens." He flexes both arms as if he's a bodybuilder who just won the crown. "Look at these guns, gorgeous. You really think I can't catch all ninety pounds of you?"

"One hundred and twenty pounds, thank you very much."

"Ha. I lift that in my sleep."

My gaze drifts back to the ladder. Some of the rungs are covered with rust, but when I step closer and curl my fingers around one, it seems sturdy enough. I take a calming breath. Okay. It's a water tower, not the Empire State Building. And I *had* promised myself I'd try new things before my freshman year was over.

"Fine," I mutter. "But God help me, if I fall and you don't catch me, and by some miracle I survive and still have the use of my arms? I will *beat you to death*."

His lips twitch. "Deal."

I inhale another wobbly breath, and then I start to climb. One foot after the other. One foot after the other. I can totally do this. It's just a teeny little water tower. Just a—my stomach drops when I make the mistake of peering down when I near the halfway mark. Logan waits patiently below. A shard of moonlight emphasizes the encouragement gleaming in his blue eyes.

"You've got this, Grace. You're doing great."

I keep going. One foot after the other, one foot after the other. When I reach the platform, relief sweeps through me. Holy shit. I'm still alive.

"You good?" he shouts from the ground.

"Yeah," I shout back.

Unlike me, Logan scales the ladder in a matter of seconds. He joins me on the platform, then takes my hand and leads me farther down to where the metal walkway widens, offering a nice—and safe. *Safe!*—place to sit. He flops down and lets his legs dangle over the edge, grinning at my very obvious reluctance to do the same.

"Aw, don't chicken out now. You've already come this far…"

Ignoring the queasy churning of my stomach, I sit beside him and gingerly position my legs like his. As he slings an arm around my shoulder, I desperately nestle closer to him, trying not to look down. Or up. Or anywhere, for that matter.

"You okay?"

"Mmm-hmmm. As long as I keep staring at my hands then I don't have to think about plummeting two hundred feet to my death."

"This tower definitely isn't two hundred feet tall."

"Well, it's tall enough that my head will crack like a watermelon when it hits the ground."

"Jeez. You really need to work on your romance technique."

I gape at him. "This is supposed to be *romantic*? Wait, do you have a fetish for girls throwing up on you?"

He bursts out laughing. "You're not going to throw up." But much to my relief, he tightens his grip around my shoulder.

The warmth of his body is a nice distraction from my current predicament. So is his aftershave. Or is it cologne? His natural scent? Holy Moses, if it's his natural scent, then he needs to bottle that spicy fragrance up, call it Orgasm, and sell it to the masses.

"See that pond over there?" he asks.

"No." I've squeezed my eyes shut, so all I can see is the inside of my eyelids.

He pokes me in the ribs. "It would help if you opened your eyes.

Come on, look."

I pry my eyes open and follow the tip of his finger to where he's pointing. "That's a *pond*? It looks like a mud swamp."

"Yeah, it gets muddy in the spring. But in the summer, there's actually water in there. And in the winter, it freezes over and everyone comes here to skate on it." He pauses. "My friends and I played hockey there when I was a kid."

"Was it safe to skate on?"

"Oh yeah, the ice is solid. Nobody's ever fallen through it, as far as I know." There's another pause, longer, and fraught with tension. "I loved coming here. It's weird, though. It seemed so much bigger when I was a kid. Like I was skating on an ocean. Then when I got older, I realized how fucking small it actually is. I can skate from one end to the other in five seconds. I timed it."

"Things always look bigger to a kid."

"I guess." He shifts so that he can see my face. "Did you have a place like that in Hastings? Somewhere you escaped to when you were younger?"

"Sure. Do you know that park behind the farmer's market? The one with the pretty gazebo?"

He nods.

"I used to go there all the time and read. Or to talk to people, if anyone was around."

"The only people I've ever seen in that park are the old folks from the retirement home around the corner."

I laugh. "Yeah, most of the ones I met were over sixty. They told the coolest stories about the 'olden days.'" I chew on the inside of my cheek as a few not-so-cool stories come to mind. "Actually, sometimes the stories were incredibly sad. They talked a lot about their families never coming to visit."

"That's really depressing."

"Yeah," I murmur.

He lets out a ragged breath. "I'd be one of them."

"You mean, not getting visits from your family? Aw, I don't believe that."

"No, I'd be the family member who doesn't visit," he answers in a strained voice. "Well, that's not entirely true. I'd definitely visit my mom.

But if my dad was in a home? I probably wouldn't step foot in there."

A wave of sadness washes over me. "You guys don't get along?"

"Not really. He gets along better with a case of beer or a bottle of bourbon."

That only makes me sadder. I can't imagine not being close with my parents. As different as their personalities are, I have a strong bond with each of them.

Logan goes quiet again, and I don't feel comfortable pushing for more details. If he wanted to tell me more, he would have done it.

Instead, I fill the awkward void by shifting the subject back to me. "I guess talking to those seniors *was* depressing sometimes, but I didn't mind listening. I think that's all they really wanted, anyway. For someone to listen." I purse my lips. "It was around that time when I decided I wanted to be a therapist. I realized I had a talent for reading people. And listening to them without passing judgment."

"Are you a psych major?"

"I will be. I didn't declare a major this year because I couldn't decide if I wanted to go the psychology route or the psychiatry one. But I decided I don't want to go to med school. Plus, psychology opens up a lot of doors that psychiatry doesn't. I could be a therapist, social worker, guidance counselor. That sounds so much more rewarding than prescribing pills."

I lean my head on his shoulder as we gaze out at the small town that stretches beyond the tower. He's right—Munsen's not much to look at. So I focus on the pond instead, and picture Logan as a little kid. His skates flying across the ice, his blue eyes alight with wonder as he basks in the certainty that the pond is an ocean. That the world is big and bright and teeming with possibility.

His tone becomes thoughtful. "So you have a talent for reading people, huh? Can you read me?"

I smile. "I haven't quite figured you out yet."

His husky laughter warms my cheek. "I haven't quite figured me out yet either."

CHAPTER 12

Grace

"Confidence," Ramona declares.

I'm sporting a dubious look as I watch her roll a sheer black stocking up her thigh. I had just asked her what she thinks the biggest turn-on for guys is when it comes to sex, and rather than the crude response I'd been expecting, she caught me off-guard with her sincerity.

"Really?"

"Oh yeah." She nods rapidly. "Men appreciate a woman who's confident and secure with her sexuality. And a take-charge attitude doesn't hurt, either. They like it when you make the first move."

"I suck at making the first move," I grumble.

She goes to her closet and rummages through the bottom of it, then emerges with a pair of black heels. "Look, you like him, right?"

"Of course."

"And you want to have sex with him?"

This time I'm slower to answer. Do I want to have sex with him? Yes? I'm not against the idea, and it's not like I'm still a virgin because I'm saving myself for the man I'm going to marry, or even the love of my life. I know sex is a monumental milestone for some girls, but personally, I don't think losing my virginity is going to be the most important thing I do in my life.

I'm attracted to Logan, yes, and if we end up having sex tonight, great. If we don't, that's fine, too. After the way we connected at the water tower the other night, I'm more interested in dating him than getting naked.

Though getting naked, or at least partially naked, is definitely on the agenda for tonight.

I texted him an hour ago asking him to come over, and Ramona has already agreed to let me have the room for the night. Despite the fact that she's still hung-over from yesterday, she's promised to stay out until midnight. It's only seven now, which gives Logan and me plenty of time to hang out. And maybe have sex. Or maybe *not* have sex. I've decided to play it by ear.

"Grace?"

I snap out of my thoughts. "Yeah, I guess I want to sleep with him. If the moment is right."

"Then you've got to separate yourself from the crowd."

I wrinkle my forehead. "Meaning what?"

"Oh, come on, do you realize how many girls he's slept with? A frickin' *harem*. And he's John Logan, babe—I bet he's got crazy moves. You don't want to be just another chick he bats those baby-blues at and screws silly. You want to be confident and sexy and take control. Show him he's met his match."

I bite my lip. Confident and sexy isn't my style. And taking control? I've always been more comfortable sitting in the passenger side while someone else takes the wheel.

"Oh, and you need to show him how kinky you are. That you're up for anything."

Nervous laughter tickles my throat. "Uh-huh. How am I supposed to do that?"

"I don't know. Stick your finger in his ass when you're blowing him."

I almost choke on my tongue. "*What?*"

Ramona flashes a cheeky smile. "Oh God, you really *are* a virgin, huh? Ass play can be a lot of fun."

"I don't want anyone near my ass, thank you very much. And I'm pretty sure he doesn't want me near his."

"Ha. You have no idea how hard a guy gets off from a good prostate massage. Seriously, he'll be coming like nobody's business."

"I'm not giving him a prostate massage," I say primly.

We stare at each other for a moment, then burst out laughing, and it feels good to laugh with her again. I don't even care anymore that she planted the seed that Maya and Piper then used to grow a tree of bullshit. Ramona is my best friend, and I've known her since we were six years old. Is she selfish sometimes? Yes. Does she gossip too much? Absolutely. But she's also sweet and loyal, and she's always there for me when I need her.

"All right, don't finger his ass," she relents. "But I'm serious about the confidence thing. It'll drive him wild."

"I'll do my best."

She narrows her eyes, giving my outfit a thorough once-over. "You're changing before he gets here, right?"

I glance at my tight jeans and skimpy white tank top. "What's wrong with what I'm wearing? Actually, don't answer that. I'm comfy, and I'm not going to change the way I dress because of a guy."

"Fine, but ditch the bra." She waggles her eyebrows. "Then he'll be able to see your nips through your shirt and he'll be hot and bothered from the word *go*."

"I'll take that into consideration."

Ramona smacks a kiss on my cheek, then lets out a little squeal. "Oh my God. I can't believe you're going to have sex for the first time tonight."

"*If* the moment is right," I remind her.

"Babe, it's John Logan," she says with a grin. "There's nothing *wrong* about it."

Logan

Come over tonight?

I've been staring at Grace's text message ever since I got out of the shower. Which was, oh, thirty-eight minutes ago. Wait—I look at the alarm clock. Make that thirty-nine minutes.

I really ought to message back. I haven't spoken to her since Thursday. Granted, that isn't an obscene amount of time considering it's Saturday and she had dinner plans with her father yesterday. So technically, I've only been avoiding her for a day and a half.

She doesn't know I'm avoiding her, though. If she did, she wouldn't have invited me over.

The way I see it, I have three options.

Option 1: Ignore the invitation.

And if she texts again, ignore that too. And then keep ignoring her until she gets the message that I'm not interested. Which is a whopping lie, because I *am* interested. I have fun with her, and if I weren't so fucked in the head about this Hannah thing, I'd absolutely keep seeing Grace.

Christ, I shouldn't have allowed Thursday's impromptu date to happen. It's not fair to lead her on like this.

Which brings me to option 2: Message back, decline the invitation, and tell her I can't see her again because of (insert bullshit excuse here).

Except…well, I've been brushed off via text before and it fucking sucks.

So that leaves option 3: Go over there and talk to her in person. That's the mature course of action, the one I should definitely take. But the thought of glimpsing even a shred of hurt or disappointment in her eyes makes me sick to my stomach.

Man up already.

Fuck. I guess it's time to pull up my big boy pants. Be a man, rub some dirt in it and all that shit. After our night at the water tower, Grace deserves a helluva lot more than a text brush-off.

Stifling a sigh, I drop the towel I've been wearing for the last… forty-two minutes now. I grab a pair of clean boxers and jeans, zip up, and throw on a black sweater my mom got me for Christmas. It's tighter than the shirts I normally wear, but it's the first thing I find in my dresser and I'm in too much of a hurry to change.

I swipe my phone off the bed and text Grace.

Me: When?
Her: Now, if you want.

She punctuates that with a smiley face. Shit.

Me: omw.

TEN MINUTES LATER, I KILL the engine in the parking lot behind the dorms and head for Fairview House. When I reach her door, I'm overcome with hesitation. And a major case of nerves. I take a deep breath. Fuck, it's not like I'm breaking up with her. We're not even a couple. I'm simply letting her know that I'm not in a good place to continue things at the moment. Doesn't mean it's forever over. It's just...*right now* over.

Right now over?

Brilliant, man. You're going to awe her with your lyrical prose.

I knock, armed with my very unimpressive parting speech, but when the door swings open, I don't get a chance to open my mouth. Actually, scratch that—I don't get a chance to voice any words. My mouth *is* open, because Grace yanks me into her dark bedroom and kisses me, and if my mouth was closed, then how is her tongue supposed to get inside it?

The kiss is completely unexpected and hotter than anything I've ever experienced in my life. She wraps her arms around my neck and backs me into the still-open door. It closes when my shoulders bump into it, and suddenly I'm pinned between the door and Grace's soft, warm body.

Her lips tease mine until I can't see straight, and then she eases back breathlessly. "I've wanted to do that all day."

She leans in again.

Oh fuck. Don't let her kiss you again. Don't—

My tongue tangles with hers in another hot duel. Damn it. I plant my hands on her hips, intending to gently push her away, but I no longer have control over my own fingers. They slide lower and dig into her firm ass, pulling her closer instead of *away*.

With her mouth still locked with mine, she grabs the bottom of my sweater and tugs it up. Somehow I find the willpower to break the kiss.

"What are you doing?" I croak.

"Taking your clothes off."

Oh shit. Shit, shit, shit.

The only reason I allow her to remove my sweater is because the material is now caught around my chin and neck, and I need my mouth in order to speak to her. In order to *stop* this. But then she tosses the fabric aside and touches my bare chest, and my brain short-circuits. She delicately strokes her fingertips over my abdomen, and makes a breathy sound. Half-moan, half-whimper, and so sexy it sends a sizzle of lust right to my cock. My balls tighten, drawing up painfully when her fingers find my belt buckle.

"Grace, I…" Instead of finishing that sentence, I groan loudly, because holy fucking shit, she doesn't just slide my pants off.

She slides to her knees as she does it.

I'm pretty sure I've just secured myself a place in hell for this. I came over tonight to end it, and instead I'm thrusting my dick into her warm, wet mouth.

Goddamn whoever invented blowjobs. They feel too damn good, and they do terrible things to your mind—AKA drain it of all lucid thought. I can't focus on anything other than the tight suction around the head of my cock. The exploratory path of Grace's tongue as she licks her way up and down my shaft before sucking on the tip again.

One hand instinctively tangles in her hair, trembling as I cup the back of her head to bring her closer. She moans, and the sound vibrates through me, a seductive promise that sends me teetering closer to the edge.

Christ. I have no idea how long she kneels there working me over, but suddenly I'm consumed with the need to touch *her*. To run my hands all over her body and drive her as crazy as she's driving me right now.

With a strangled noise, I pull out of her mouth and haul her to her feet. Then I'm kissing her again, frantically clawing at her clothes until she's naked. Oh, sweet Jesus, she's naked. How the hell, in the span of *five minutes*, did I let this get so out of control?

But I can't fucking stop. I can't stop kissing her. I can't stop squeezing her tits. I can't stop myself from leading her to the bed and lowering my body on top of her. My cock is pinned between our bodies, a heavy weight on her flat stomach, and the base of it grinds against her clit as we kiss so deeply it's like we're trying to swallow each other up.

Stop this, a sharp voice reprimands.

Hell, I *can't*. I want her too much.

Stop. This.

Yup, that voice is my conscience, trying to prevent me from making a serious mistake. So why can't I listen to it? Why can't I—

Grace breaks the kiss and looks up at me with hazy brown eyes, and suddenly all her bravado is gone. The confident, sexy woman who mauled me at the door has transformed into a shy, blushing girl who says, "Um, so…listen…I've never had sex before."

Oh *fuck*.

Those five words crack my heart in two.

Son of a *bitch*. No way. There is absolutely no way I can do this to her.

Fooling around with her when I know I'm going to end it? Reprehensible. But taking her virginity? Unforgivable.

Oh, and my place in hell? Still solidly secured.

Silence stretches between us as I struggle for the right words to say. Which is damn difficult when we're both naked. When my dick's so hard it could cut a diamond in half.

She lets out a shaky breath. "Is that a problem for you?"

I open my mouth.

And say, "Yes."

Grace looks startled. "What?"

"I mean, no. There's nothing wrong with being a virgin. But…we can't do this." I stumble off the bed with as much grace as a newborn foal. Seriously, my legs are wobbling all over the place as I hurriedly scan the room for my pants.

I can feel her watching me. Her eyes boring into me. I don't want to look over because I know she's still naked, but I can't stop myself from sneaking a peek, and her hurt expression rips my chest apart.

"I'm sorry," I say roughly. "I can't do this. This is your first time, and you deserve something—*someone*—so much better than me for your first time."

She doesn't utter a word, but even in the darkness, I can see the deep flush on her cheeks. And she's biting her lower lip as if she's trying not to cry.

Her silence deepens the guilt coursing through my veins. "I'm in such a fucked up place right now. I have a lot of fun with you, but…" I swallow. "I can't give you anything serious."

She finally speaks, her voice tight and laced with embarrassment. "I'm not asking you to marry me, Logan."

"I know. But sex…sex is serious, okay? Especially for a virgin." I trip over the words, feeling like a total asshole. "You don't want to do this with me, Grace. I'm screwed in the head, and I guess I've been trying to distract myself from all the bullshit in my life, and trying to get over someone else, and—"

"Someone else?" she interrupts, and now there's a thread of anger in her tone. "You're interested in someone else?"

"Yes. No," I say quickly. Then I groan. "I thought I was, and maybe I still am. I don't know, okay? All I know is that this girl has had me tied up in knots for months, and it's not fair to you if we…do this…when I…" I trail off, too confused and uncomfortable to go on.

Avoiding my eyes, Grace bolts off the bed and grabs a T-shirt from the back of the desk chair. "You were using me to get over someone else?" She yanks the shirt over her head. "I was your *distraction*?"

"No. I promise, I like you a lot." I cringe at the pleading note in my voice. "I wasn't intentionally using you. You're so fucking amazing, but I—"

"Oh my God, no," she cuts in. "Please…just shut up, Logan. I can't handle the *it's not you, it's me* speech right now." She rakes both hands through her hair, her breathing becoming shallow. "Oh God. This was such a mistake."

"Grace—"

She interrupts again. "Will you do me a favor?"

It's difficult to speak past the massive lump lodged in my throat. "Anything."

"Leave."

The lump damn near chokes me. I inhale deeply, ignoring the burning sensation in my throat, the ache in my chest.

"I mean it, just leave, okay?" She meets my gaze head-on. "I really, really want you to go right now."

I should say something else. Apologize again. Reassure her. Comfort her. But I'm terrified she might slap me—or worse, break down—if I approach her.

Besides, she's already walking to the door and throwing it open. She doesn't look at me as she waits.

Waits for me to *leave*.

Fuck. I screwed up so badly. My heart physically hurts as I stagger to the door. I pause in the threshold, finding the courage to meet her eyes again. "I'm sorry."

"Yeah, you should be."

The last thing I hear as I step out into the hall is the sound of the door slamming behind me.

CHAPTER 13

Logan

I'VE ALWAYS REFUSED TO USE alcohol as a crutch. If I'm sad or upset or hurting, I avoid it at all costs because I'm terrified I might rely too heavily on it one day. That I might become addicted.

But goddamn, I could really use a drink right now.

Fighting the urge, I bypass the liquor cabinet in the living room and sprint to the sliding door in the kitchen. Cigarettes. Equally destructive habit, but it's the lesser of two evils at the moment. I'll just flood my veins with nicotine—maybe that'll help with the huge ball of guilt taking up residence in the pit of my stomach.

"Everything okay?"

Big tough hockey player that I am, I jump three feet in the air at the sound of Hannah's voice.

I spin around and notice her standing at the sink, an empty glass in her hand. I was so out of it I must have flown right past her during my sprint to the door.

Christ, she's the *last* person I want to see at the moment.

And look at that, she's wearing Garrett's jersey again. Just flaunting it in my face now, isn't she?

"Yeah, everything's fine," I mumble, stepping away from the door. Change of plans. Nicotine overdose—no longer needed. Hiding in my bedroom—must get on that.

"Logan." She approaches me with wary strides. "What's going on?"

"Nothing."

"Bullshit. You look upset. Are you okay?"

I flinch when she touches my arm. "I don't want to talk about it, Wellsy. I really don't."

Her green eyes search my face. For so long that I shift in discomfort and break the eye contact. I try to take another step, but she stops me again, blocking my path as she releases a groan of frustration.

"You know what?" she announces. "I can't fucking take this anymore."

I blink in surprise. "What are you talking about?"

Rather than answer, she grabs my arm so hard it's a miracle it stays in its socket. Then she drags me to the kitchen table and forcibly pushes me into a chair. Jeez. She's freakishly strong for someone so tiny.

"Hannah…" I start uneasily.

"No. I'm done tiptoeing around this." She yanks out a chair and sits beside me. "Garrett keeps telling me you'll get over it, but it's only getting worse, and I hate this awkwardness between us. You used to hang out with us and come to Malone's and watch movies, and now you *don't*, and I miss hanging out with you, okay?" She's so upset that her shoulders are visibly shaking. "So let's clear the air, all right? Let's deal with it head-on."

She takes a deep breath, then looks me square in the eye and asks, "Do you have a thing for me?"

Aw, hell.

Why, *why* didn't I go straight up to my room?

Clenching my teeth, I scrape back my chair. "Well, this has been fun, but I think I'll go upstairs and kill myself now."

"Sit down," she says sternly.

My ass hovers over the chair, but the sharpness of her tone reminds me too much of Coach Jensen when he's reaming us out at practice, and my fear of authority wins out. I drop back down and blow out a tired breath.

"What's the point of talking about this, Wellsy? We both know the answer to that question."

"Maybe, but I still want to hear you say it."

Annoyance tightens my throat. "Fine, you want to hear it? Do I have a thing for you? Yes, I think I do."

Shock fills her expression, as if she truly didn't expect me to reply.

Cue: the longest silence ever. Like, *find a rope and tie it around your neck and hang your fucking self* silence, because the longer she remains quiet, the more pathetic I feel.

When she finally speaks, she throws me for a loop. "Why?"

My forehead creases. "Why what?"

"Why are you into me?"

If she thought she was clarifying, she's dead wrong, because I'm still baffled. What kind of question is that?

Hannah shakes her head as if she's also trying to make sense of it. "Dude, I've seen the girls you bring home or flirt with at the bar. You have a type. Tall, skinny, usually blonde. And they're always hanging all over you and showering you with compliments." She snorts. "Whereas I just insult you all the time."

I can't help but grin. Her sarcasm does veer into insult territory more often than not.

"And you gravitate to the ones who are looking for something temporary. You know, a fun time. I'm not a fun-time girl. I *like* serious relationships." She purses her lips thoughtfully. "I never got the sense that you were interested in relationships."

The accusation raises my hackles. "Why? Because I'm a player?" Indignation makes my tone harsher than I intend for it to be. "Have you ever thought that maybe it's because I haven't met the right girl yet? But no, I couldn't *possibly* want someone to cuddle with and watch movies with, someone who wears my jersey and cheers for me at games, and cooks dinner with me the way you and Garrett—"

Her snort of laughter makes me stop short.

I narrow my eyes. "What are you laughing about?"

In a heartbeat, the laughter dies and her tone grows serious. "Logan… during that whole speech? You didn't once say you wanted to do that stuff with me. You said *someone*." She beams. "I just got it."

Well, good for her, because I have no fucking idea what she's babbling about.

"This entire time, I thought you were looking at *me* all longing-like. But you were looking at *us*." She laughs again. "And all those things you listed right now, they're things Garrett and I do together. Dude, you don't want me. You want me and Garrett."

Alarm flits through me. "If you're implying I want to have a threesome with you and my best friend, then I can assure you, I don't."

"No, you just want what we have. You want the connection and the closeness and all the gooey relationship stuff."

My mouth snaps shut.

Is she right?

As her words sink in, my muddled brain quickly runs through the fantasies I've had about Hannah these past few months, and…well, if I'm being honest, most of them haven't been sexual. I mean, a few have, because I'm a guy and she's hot. And she's also around all the time, therefore providing me with readily available images for my spank bank. But aside from a few naked fantasies, I usually picture PG scenarios. Like I'll see her and Garrett snuggling on the couch and wish I was in his place.

But…am I wishing I'm in his place with *her*, or in his place in general?

"Look, I like you, Logan. I really do. You're funny and sweet, and you're a sarcastic jackass, which is a quality I happen to love in a guy. But you don't…" She looks uncomfortable. "…make my heart pound—I guess that's the best way to put it. No, not even that." Her voice takes on a faraway note. "When I'm with Garrett, my whole world comes alive. I'm so full of emotion I feel like my heart will overflow, and I know this is going to sound like an exaggeration or maybe kind of obsessive, but sometimes I think I need him more than I need food or oxygen." She gazes into my eyes. "Do you need me more than oxygen, Logan?"

I gulp.

"Am I the last person you think about when you go to bed and the first one you think about when you wake up?"

I don't answer.

"Am I?" she pushes.

"No." My voice comes out hoarse. "You're not."

Fucking hell.

She might be right. All this time I've been feeling guilty about wanting my best friend's girl, but I think what I really wanted was my best friend's relationship. Someone to spend time with. Someone who turns me on and makes me laugh. Someone who makes me…happy.

Like Grace?

The mocking thought slices into my mind like a damn lightsaber.

Shit.

Yeah, someone like Grace. Someone *exactly* like Grace, with her Ted Bundy rants and her calming presence and—*hello, irony*.

I broke up with her to avoid getting into a serious relationship with her, and now it turns out that's what I wanted all along.

"Damn it. I…screwed up." I rub my eyes, groaning softly.

"That's not true. We're good, Logan. I promise."

"No, I didn't screw up with us. I ended it with a really great girl tonight because I was so messed up in the head about all this."

"Aw, shit." She eyes me sympathetically. "Why don't you call her and tell her you changed your mind?"

"She kicked me out." I groan again. "There's no way she'll pick up the phone if I call."

We're interrupted by Garrett's voice from the hall. "Seriously, Wellsy, how long does it take you to get a glass of water? Do I need to show you how to use the sink, because if so, that's just sad—" He quits talking the second he spots me. "Oh hey, man. I didn't know you were home."

I hastily slide off the chair and hop to my feet, but it does nothing to ease the suspicion in Garrett's eyes. Which triggers a fresh rush of guilt. Jesus, does he think something happened between us? Does he honestly believe I'd ever, *ever* make a move on his girl?

The fact that I'm even wondering that tells me the state of our friendship is even more precarious than I'd thought.

Swallowing hard, I shuffle over to him. "Listen…I'm sorry I've been such a dick lately. I was…distracted."

"Distracted," he echoes skeptically.

I nod.

He keeps staring at me.

"My head's on straight now. Honest."

Garrett peers past me, and although I can't see Hannah's face, whatever passes between them causes his broad shoulders to relax. Then he grins and slaps me on the arm. "Well, thank God. Because I was seriously considering promoting Tuck to the number one best friend slot."

"Are you kidding? Big mistake, G. He's a terrible wingman. Have you seen his beard?"

"I know, right?"

And just like that, we're good again. Seriously, chicks need to take a lesson from dudes when it comes to burying the hatchet. We know our shit.

"Anyway, I need to make a call," I tell him. "Night, guys."

I'm already pulling up Grace's number as I dart out of the kitchen and head for the stairs. Texting isn't an option. I want her to hear my voice. I want her to hear how agonized I am about everything that went down tonight.

To my frustration, the dial tone rings and rings and rings before switching over to voice mail.

The second time I call, it goes straight to voice mail, which tells me she most likely pressed the *ignore* button.

Crap.

With a crushing sense of defeat, I open a new message and shoot her a text asking if we could talk.

Then I go upstairs and wait.

CHAPTER 14

Logan

It's past midnight, and still no word from Grace. I've sent her three texts already, and now I'm lying on top of my bedspread, staring up at the ceiling and valiantly fighting the urge to send a fourth.

Three messages borders on desperation.

Four would just be pathetic.

Fuck, I wish she would text back. Or call. Or *anything*. At this point, I'd be thrilled if a carrier pigeon tapped its beak on my window and delivered a handwritten letter done in perfect calligraphy.

She's not calling you, man. Deal with it.

Yeah, I guess she isn't. I guess I really did blow it. And I guess I fucking deserve it.

I didn't just lead her on—I led her right up to the point where she wanted to lose her *virginity* to me, and then I threw the offer back in her face and told her I was interested in someone else. Hell, I'm surprised I'm not experiencing random aches and pains in my body right now. You know, from the sharp needles Grace is poking into her voodoo doll.

My phone buzzes, and I hurl myself at the night table like an Olympic high jumper. She texted back. Oh, thank fuck. That means she *doesn't* view me as the antichrist—

The message isn't from Grace.

It comes from an unfamiliar number, and it takes me a solid ten seconds before I'm able to register what I'm reading. No, what I'm *seething* over.

Hey, this is Ramona. Just heard what happened with you and Grace. Need me to come over and comfort you? ;)

Winky face. She actually fucking *winky-faced* me.

I drop the phone as if it's a hot coal. As if the message is contagious and the mere act of touching the device it came on will turn me into a person as contemptible as the one who wrote those words.

Why the hell is Grace's best friend hitting on me? Who *does* that?

I'm so pissed off that I grab the phone and forward the message to Grace without stopping to question my actions. I add a caption—*thought you should see this.*

And then, since I'm already in this deep, I send another one that says, *Can we please talk?*

She doesn't respond to either. Not now, and not by the time three in the morning rolls around, which is when I finally drag my pathetic ass under the covers and fall into a restless sleep.

Grace

I WAKE UP AT FIVE-THIRTY in the morning. Not by choice, but because my traitorous mind decides it's time for me to wallow in misery some more and forces me into consciousness.

The humiliation of last night slaps me in the face the moment I open my eyes. The clothes I was wearing are still strewn on the floor. I hadn't bothered to pick them up, and neither had Ramona, who'd come home around midnight.

"Didn't happen. He's into someone else."

That was all the information I gave her last night, and she must have seen the devastation on my face, because for once in her life, she didn't nag me for details. She simply gave me a hug, a sympathetic squeeze on the arm, and climbed into bed.

Now she's sleeping peacefully, her cheek pressed against her pillow, one arm flung across the mattress. Well, at least one of us is going to feel rested today.

Despite my better judgment, I check my phone. Sure enough, there are two unread messages flashing on the screen. Which brings the final tally to five.

Logan must *really* want to talk to me.

I guess guilt turns some guys into real chatterboxes.

A smart person would delete the messages without reading them. No, delete his *number* from the contact list. But I'm not feeling too smart right now. I feel stupid. So fucking stupid. For inviting him over last night. For developing feelings for him.

For reading the messages he keeps sendi—what the *hell?*

I blink. Once. Twice. Three and four and five times, but it doesn't bring clarity to what I'm seeing.

Hey, this is Ramona. Just heard what happened with you and Grace. Need me to come over and comfort you? ;)

My head swings toward Ramona's bed. She's still out like a light. But that is unarguably her phone number next to the time stamp of the text. Twelve-sixteen a.m. Approximately twenty minutes after she'd gotten home last night.

I stare at her sleeping form, waiting for the fury to come. For my insides to clench and my blood to boil with a sense of white-hot betrayal.

But nothing happens. I'm...cold. And numb. And so frickin' exhausted it feels like someone stuffed sand in my eyes.

My fingers tremble as I bring up the next message—Can we please talk?

No, we can't. In fact, I don't want to talk to anyone right now. Not Logan, and certainly not Ramona.

I suck an unsteady breath into my lungs. Then I stand up and creep toward the door. Stepping into the hall, I sag against the wall before sliding down to the floor and drawing my knees up. My phone rests on my knee, and I stare at it for several seconds before turning it over and accessing my contact list.

It might be too early to call my dad, but in Paris, my mom will be wide-awake and probably fixing lunch right now.

The numbness doesn't go away as I dial her number. If anything, it gets worse. I can't even feel my heart beating. Maybe it's not. Maybe every goddamn part of me has shut down.

"Sweetie!" My mother's overjoyed voice fills my ear. "What are you doing up so early?"

I swallow. "Hey, Mom. I...uh, have an early class."

"You have class on Sundays?" She sounds confused.

"Oh. No, I don't. I meant I have a study group."

Crap, my eyes are starting to sting, and not because I'm tired. Damn it. So much for being numb—I'm seconds away from bursting into tears.

"Listen, I wanted to talk to you about my visit." My throat closes up, and I take another breath hoping to loosen it. "I changed my mind about the dates. I want to come earlier."

"You do?" she says in delight. "Oh yay! I'm so happy! But are you sure? You said you might have plans with your friends. I don't want you to come early on my account."

"The plans got canceled. And I want to come sooner, I really do." I blink in rapid succession, trying to stop the tears from spilling over. "The sooner the better."

CHAPTER 15

MAY

Grace

PEOPLE SAY SPRINGTIME IN PARIS is magical.

They're right.

The city has been my home for the past two weeks, and a part of me wishes I could stay here forever. Mom's apartment is in an area referred to as "Old Paris." The neighborhood is gorgeous—narrow, winding roads, old buildings, cute shops and bakeries at every corner. It's also known as the city's gay district, and her upstairs and downstairs neighbors are both gay couples, who've already taken us out for dinner twice since I got here.

The apartment only has one bedroom, but the pullout couch in the living room is pretty comfortable. I love waking up to the sunlight streaming in from the French doors of the small balcony overlooking the building's inner courtyard. The faint traces of oil paint lingering in the room remind me of my childhood, back when my mother spent hours working in her studio. Over the years, she painted less and less, and she's admitted on more than one occasion that the loss of her art was one of the reasons she divorced my father.

She felt like she'd lost touch with who she was. That being a housewife in small-town Massachusetts wasn't what she'd been destined for. A few months after I turned sixteen, she sat me down and posed a serious question—would I rather have a mother who was miserable but close by, or happy and far away?

I told her I wanted her to be happy.

She's happy in Paris, there's no denying that. She laughs all the time, her smiles actually reach her eyes, and the dozens of bright canvases overflowing from the corner nook she's using as her studio prove that she's doing what she loves again.

"Morning!" Mom waltzes out of her bedroom and greets me in a voice that contains the joyous trill of a Disney princess.

"Morning," I say groggily.

The room has an open floor plan, so I can see her every move as she wanders over to the kitchen counter. "Coffee?" she calls out.

"Yes, please."

I sit up and stretch, yawning as I grab my phone from the coffee table to check the time. Mom doesn't keep clocks in the house because she claims time weighs the mind down, but my OCD doesn't allow me to ever relax unless I know what time it is.

Nine-thirty. I have no idea what she has planned for us today, but I hope it doesn't involve too much walking because my feet are still sore from yesterday's five-hour visit to the Louvre.

I'm about to set down the phone when it rings in my hand, and I'm annoyed to see Ramona's name on the screen. It's two-thirty in the morning in Massachusetts—doesn't she have anything better to do than keep harassing me? You know, like *sleeping*.

Gritting my teeth, I drop the cell phone on the bed and let it ring.

Mom eyes me from the counter. "Which one? The boyfriend or the best friend?"

"Ramona," I mutter. "Who, by the way, I don't care to discuss, seeing as she's no longer my best friend, same way Logan isn't my boyfriend."

"And yet they keep calling and texting, which means they both still care about *you*."

Yeah, well, I don't care that they care. Ignoring Logan is a lot easier than ignoring Ramona, though. I knew him for a whopping total of eight days. I've known her for *thirteen* years.

It's almost pathetic the way everything went down. You'd think a decade-plus long friendship would end with a bang, but my showdown with Ramona was nothing more than a whimpering fizzle. Ramona had woken up, seen my face, and realized that Logan had forwarded me her message. Then she'd snapped into damage control mode, but none of her usual tricks had worked on me.

The Forgive Me hug? The crocodile tears? She may as well have been tugging on the emotional heartstrings of a robot. I just stood there like a statue until she'd finally grasped that I wasn't buying the shit she was trying to sell. And the next day, I moved back home, telling my dad that the dorm was too loud and I needed somewhere quiet to study for exams.

I haven't seen Ramona since.

"Why don't you hear her out?" Mom's tone is cautious. "I know you said she didn't have a good explanation before, but maybe that's changed."

An explanation? Gee, how *does* one explain the betrayal of their closest friend?

Oddly enough, Ramona hadn't even offered an excuse. No *I was jealous*, no *I was drunk and wasn't thinking*. All she'd done was sit on the edge of the bed and whisper, "I don't know why I did it, Gracie."

Well, it wasn't good enough for me then, and it sure as hell isn't good enough now.

"I already told you, I'm not interested in hearing her out. Not yet anyway." I slide off the pullout and walk to the counter, reaching for the ceramic mug she hands me. "I don't know if I'll ever be ready to talk to her again."

"Aw, sweetie. Are you really going to throw away so many years of friendship over a boy?"

"It's not about Logan. It's about the fact that she knew I was hurting. She knew I was humiliated over what happened with him, and instead of supporting me, she waited until I was asleep and then *propositioned* him. It's pretty clear she doesn't give a crap about me or my feelings."

Mom sighs. "I can't deny that Ramona has always been a bit... self-absorbed."

I snort. "A bit?"

"But she's also been your biggest supporter," Mom reminds me. "She's always been there for you when you needed her. Remember when that nasty girl was bullying you in fifth grade? What was her name again—Brenda? Brynn?"

"Bryndan."

"*Bryndan*? Lord, what is the matter with parents these days?" Mom shakes her head in amazement. "Anyway, remember when Bryn—nope, I can't even say it, it's that stupid. When that girl was bullying you? Ramona was like a pit bull, snarling and spitting and ready to protect you to her dying breath."

It's my turn to sigh. "I know you're trying to be helpful, but can we please not talk about Ramona anymore?"

"Okay, let's talk about the boy then. Because I think you should call him back, too."

"Agree to disagree."

"Sweetie, he obviously feels bad about what happened, otherwise he wouldn't be trying to contact you. And…well, you were going to, ah… give him your flower—"

I do a literal spit take. Coffee drizzles down my chin and neck, and I quickly grab a napkin to wipe it away before it stains my pajama top. "Oh my God. Mom. Don't *ever* say that again. I beg of you."

"I was trying to be parental," she says primly.

"There's parental, and then there's Victorian England."

"All right. You were going to fuck him—"

"That's not parental either!" A gale of laughter flies out, and it takes a second before I'm able to speak without giggling. "Again, I know you're trying to help, but Logan's off the table too. Yes, I was considering having sex with him. No, it didn't happen. And that's all she wrote."

Distress clouds her expression. "Fine, I won't bug you about it anymore. But with that said, I refuse to let you spend the rest of the summer sulking."

"I haven't been sulking," I protest.

"Not on the outside. But I can see right through you, Grace Elizabeth Ivers. I know when you're smiling for real, and when you're smiling for show, and so far you've given me two weeks of show smiles." She straightens up, a determined set to her shoulders. "I think it's time we make you smile for real. I wanted us to go down to the canal today and walk along the river, but you know what? Emergency itinerary change." She claps her hands. "We need to do something drastic."

Crap. The last time she used the word "drastic" in conjunction with an outing, we went to a salon in Boston and she dyed her hair pink.

"Like what?" I ask warily.

"We're paying a visit to Claudette."

"Who's Claudette?"

"My hairdresser."

Oh God. I'm going to have pink hair. I just *know* it.

Mom beams at me. "Trust me, there's nothing like a good makeover to cheer a girl right up." She grabs the mug from my hand and sets it on the counter. "Get dressed while I make the appointment. We are going to have *so* much fun today!"

CHAPTER 16

JUNE

Logan

I'M THIRTY-THREE DAYS INTO MY torture stint at Logan and Sons when I have my first run-in with my father. I've been waiting for it, in some sick way even looking forward to it, but for the most part, Dad has left me alone since I moved back home.

He hasn't asked me about school or hockey. Hasn't given me the usual guilt trips about how I don't care enough to visit. All he's done is complain about his leg pain and thrust beers in my direction while pleading, "Have a brewsky with your old man, Johnny."

Right. Like that'll ever happen.

I appreciate that he hasn't been on my case, though. Truth is, I'm too exhausted to fight with him right now. I've been following the rigid off-season training program the coaches designed for us, which means getting up at the crack of dawn to work out, toiling in the garage until eight p.m., working out again before bed, and then crashing for the night and doing it all over again the next day.

Once a week I go to Munsen's crappy arena to work on shooting and skating drills with Vic, one of our assistant coaches who drives over from Briar to make sure I stay sharp. I love him for it, and I look forward to the ice time, but unfortunately, today's not a rink day.

The customer I'm dealing with at the moment is the foreman of the sole construction crew in town. His name's Bernie, and he's a decent guy—well, if you overlook his constant attempts to persuade me to join Munsen's summer hockey league, which I have no desire to do.

Bernie showed up five minutes ago with a two-inch nail jammed in the front tire of his pickup, gave me the usual spiel about how I need to join the league, and now we're discussing the options for his repairs.

"Look, I can easily patch you up," I tell him. "I'll pull the nail out, plug it up, and fill up the tire. Which is definitely the cheaper and quicker option. But your tires aren't in the greatest shape, Bern. When was the last time you replaced them?"

He rubs his bushy salt-and-pepper beard. "Five years ago? Maybe six?"

I kneel next to the left front tire and give it another quick examination. "The tread on all four tires is starting to wear. You're not down to one sixteenth of an inch yet, but it's getting damn close. A few more months and they might not be safe to drive on anymore."

"Aw, kid, I don't have the money to replace them right now. Besides, the crew's working a big job over in Brockton." He gives the hood a hearty thump. "I need this baby with me every day this week. Just do the patch for now."

"You sure? Because you'll have to come back again when the tread is gone. I recommend doing it now."

He dismisses the suggestion by waving one meaty hand. "We'll do it next time."

I nod without argument. First rule of service? The customer's always right. Besides, it's not like his tires are going to explode in the next few hours. It'll still be a long while before the tread is completely worn.

"All right. I'll do it now. It should only take about ten minutes, but I've gotta finish the alignment on this Jetta first. So more like thirty. You wanna wait in the office?"

"Naw, I'll walk around and smoke. I have some phone calls to make." He glares at me. "And for the love of God, we need you on the ice Thursday nights, kid. Think about it, okay?"

I nod again, but we both know what my answer will be. Every year, the Munsen Miners extend an invitation, and every year I turn them down. Honestly, it's too depressing to even consider. It's just a reminder that next year I'll be going from a Division I team to the *Munsen Miners*. Yup, I'll be the star player of an amateur league, on a team that's named after an activity this town isn't even known for. There are no mines in Munsen and never have been.

Less than a minute after Bernie wanders outside, my father emerges from the office and limps over to me. His hands are blessedly devoid of any alcoholic containers. At least he has better sense than to drink in front of our customers.

"'The fuck was that?" he demands.

So much for shielding the customers—he's slurring like crazy and swaying on his cane, and suddenly I'm glad he's been holed up in the office all day, out of sight.

I stifle a sigh. "What are you talking about?"

"Where was the upsell?" His cheeks are flushed in outrage, and even though I've been back home for more than a month, I'm still startled by how gaunt he looks. It's as if all the skin from his face, arms and torso decided to move to his gut, forming an incredibly unflattering beer belly that protrudes beneath his threadbare T-shirt. Other than the paunch, he's skinny as a rail, and it makes me sad to see him this way.

I've seen pictures of him when he was younger, and I can't deny he used to be handsome. And I have memories of him when he was sober. When he was quick to smile, always armed with a joke or a laugh. I miss that man. Christ, I really fucking miss him sometimes.

"A thirty-buck patch job instead of four new tires?" he fumes. "Whatha hell is wrong with you?"

I struggle to control my temper. "I recommended new tires. He didn't want them."

"You don't *recommend*. You *push* it on them. You shove it down their fuckin' throats."

I sneak a worried peek in Bernie's direction, but fortunately he's all the way at the front of the driveway, sucking on a cigarette as he talks into his phone. Jesus. What if he'd been in earshot? Would my father have been able to restrain himself from saying this kind of shit in front of a loyal customer? I honestly don't know.

It's only one-thirty in the afternoon and he's staggering on his feet as if he's consumed the entire stock of a liquor store. "Why don't you go back to the house?" I say softly. "You're stumbling a little. Do your legs hurt?"

"I'm not hurt. I'm pissed!"

He says it like "*pithed*." Awesome. He's so drunk he's lisping now.

"Whatcha even doing here if you're gonna throw money away like it grows on trees? You tell 'em the tires are unsafe. You don't stand around and talk about your fuckin' hockey team!"

"We weren't talking about hockey, Dad."

"Bullshit. I heard ya." The man who used to come to all my ninth-grade hockey games and sit behind the home bench cheering his lungs out… he now smirks at me. "Think you're a big hockey star, doncha, Johnny? But naah, you ain't. If you're so good, why didn't anyone draft you?"

My chest tightens.

"Dad…" The quiet warning comes from Jeff, who wipes his grease-covered hands with a rag and marches up to us.

"Stay outta this, Jeffy! I'm talking to your big brother." Dad blinks. "L'il brother, I mean. He's the younger one, right?"

Jeff and I exchange a look. Shit. He's *really* out of it.

Usually one of us monitors him throughout the day, but we've been swamped since the second we opened up shop this morning. I hadn't been too worried because Dad was in the office, but now I curse myself for forgetting an important rule in the alcoholic handbook: always have booze on hand.

He must keep a stash hidden in the office. Same way he hid his alcohol when he and Mom were still together. One time when I was twelve, the toilet was running so I went upstairs to fix it, and when I lifted the lid, I found a mickey of vodka floating around in the tank.

Just another day in the Logan household.

"You look tired," Jeff says, firmly grasping our father's arm. "Why don't you go back to the house and take a nap?"

He blinks again, confusion eclipsing the anger. For a moment, he looks like a lost little boy, and suddenly I feel like bawling. It's times like these when I want to grab his shoulders and shake him, beg him to make me understand why he drinks. My mom says it's genetic, and I know Dad's side of the family has a history of depression as well as alcoholism. And fuck, maybe that's it. Maybe those really are the reasons he can't stop drinking. But a part of me still can't fully accept that. He had a good childhood, damn it. He had a wife who loved him, two sons who did whatever they could to please him. Why couldn't that be enough for him?

I *know* he's an addict. I *know* he's sick. It's just so hard to put myself in that mind frame, in that place where a bottle of booze is the most important thing in your life, so much so that you're willing to throw away everything else for it.

"I guess I'm a l'il tired," Dad mumbles, his blue eyes still cloudy with confusion. "I'll, ah…go to sleep now."

My brother and I watch as he hobbles off, and then Jeff turns to me with a sad look. "Don't listen to him. You *are* good."

"Yeah, sure." I clench my jaw and stalk back to the lift, where the sporty Jetta I've been working on awaits me. "I need to finish up."

"John, he doesn't know what he's talking about—"

"Forget it," I mutter. "I already have."

I CLOSE UP LATER THAN usual. *Much* later than usual, because when eight o'clock rolled around, I couldn't stomach the thought of going to the house for dinner. Jeff popped in around nine to bring me some leftover meatloaf, and quietly informed me that Dad had "sobered up a bit." Which is laughable, because even if he quit cold turkey this very second, there's so much alcohol flowing through his veins that it would take days for it to exit his system.

Now it's ten-fifteen, and I'm hoping Dad will be asleep when I walk through that door. No, I'm *praying*. I don't have the energy to deal with him right now.

I leave the shop through the side door, stopping to drop the keys of the Jetta into the little mailbox nailed to the wall. Its owner, a cute brunette who teaches at Munsen Elementary, is supposed to pick up the car tonight, and I already parked it outside for her in the designated area.

I double-check the padlock on the garage door, then turn toward the path to the house just as headlights slice through the trees and a taxi speeds up the driveway. An older man sits behind the wheel, eyeing me warily as the back door of the cab opens and Tori Howard hops out, her high-heeled boots raising a cloud of dust when they meet the dirt.

She waves when she spots me, then gestures to the driver that it's okay to go. A second later, she sways her curvy hips my way.

Tori is in her mid-twenties and absolutely gorgeous. She moved to Munsen a couple of years ago and brings her car to be serviced a few times a year, and believe me, that car is not the only thing she wants serviced. She hits on me every time I see her, but I haven't taken her up on her very blatant offers because Jeff is usually around when she shows up and I don't want him to think I'm sleeping with the customers.

But tonight it's just the two of us, with no Jeff in sight.

A smile lifts the corners of her mouth as she approaches me. "Hey."

"Hey." I nod at the retreating taillights of the cab. "You should've told me you didn't have a ride. Jeff or I could've picked you up."

"Oh, really? I had no idea this was a full service joint," she teases.

I shrug. "We aim to please."

Her smile widens, and I realize how sleazy that light-hearted comment had sounded. I hadn't been trying to flirt, but her eyes are gleaming seductively now.

I suddenly notice they're almost the same shade of brown as Grace's eyes. Except Grace never looked at me like she wanted to gobble me up and ask for seconds. There'd been something earnest about her gaze. There was heat, sure, but it wasn't as calculated and overt as the way Tori is gazing at me right now.

And shit, I really need to quit thinking about Grace. I can't even count how many times I've called her this summer, but her continued silence tells me everything I need to know. She doesn't want to hear my apologies. She doesn't want to see me again.

Yet I can't fight the hope that maybe she'll change her mind.

"You know, you get better looking every time I see you," Tori drawls.

I doubt it. If anything, I just get more tired. And I'm pretty sure there's a streak of oil on my cheek at the moment, but Tori doesn't seem to mind.

She pouts. "What, you're not going to return the compliment?"

I can't help but grin. "Tori, you're gorgeous and you know it. You don't need me to tell you that."

"No, but sometimes it's nice to hear it."

I'm not sure how I feel about the direction this conversation is going, so I change the subject. "You got my message, right? I explained everything

THE MISTAKE

we did to the car, but I can run through it with you again, if you want."

"No need. It sounds like you were very thorough." She slants her head. "So. Do you have big plans tonight?"

"Nope. Gonna take a shower and crash. It's been a long day, and it'll be an even longer one tomorrow."

"A shower, huh? You know," she says casually, "I just got a second showerhead installed in my shower."—and there's nothing casual about the end of *that* sentence— "I always see it in the movies, these incredible-looking showers with a million showerheads, and I was like, why can't *I* have that? And then I realized, I absolutely can." She grins. "So I called a plumber and he came by last week and installed it. I can't even describe how amazing it is. Water spraying you front and back? It's glorious."

Annnnnd my dick is semi-hard now.

I'm not about to get all self-judgy, though, because one, I haven't had sex in almost three months, and two, when a beautiful woman is talking about her shower, there's something wrong with you if your brain *doesn't* conjure up the image of her in that shower. Naked. With water spraying her—*front and back.*

"You should come over and check it out sometime," she says, and her wink is about as subtle as a slap on the ass.

Hesitation rises in my chest. Any other time, I'd invite myself into her shower in a heartbeat. But I'm still holding on to hope that Grace might…might what? Text me? Accept my apology? Even if she does, that doesn't mean she'll want to go out with me. Hell, why would she? She wanted to fuck me and I rejected her.

As my silence drags, Tori lets out a sigh. "I've heard the rumors about you, Logan, and I've gotta say, I'm disappointed that they're not true."

I narrow my eyes. "What rumors?"

"You know, that you're sex on a stick. Up for anything. Good in bed." She gives me a sassy grin. "Or maybe all of it *is* true, and you're just not into older women. But I'll have you know, I polled some friends and they all concurred that a six-year age difference does *not* make me a cougar."

A laugh pops out. "You're definitely not a cougar, Tori."

"Then I guess I'm not your type."

My gaze wanders over the perky tits beneath her tight shirt and the shapely legs that go on forever. Not my type? Yeah right. She's exactly the kind of woman I'm normally attracted to.

So what the hell is stopping me? Grace? Because after months of radio silence, maybe it's time for me to finally take the hint.

"Naah, that's not true," I say nonchalantly. "You usually catch me when I'm distracted."

"Hmmm. Well, are you distracted now?"

"Nope. In fact…" My gaze lingers on her chest again before meeting her eyes. "I could really go for a shower."

CHAPTER 17

JULY

Logan

GARRETT SURPRISES ME BY SHOWING up at the garage on a Thursday night with pizza and a six-pack. I don't see much of him during the summer, what with me living at home and him working sixty-hour weeks at a construction company in Boston. We text here and there, usually about the NHL playoffs. We get together to watch the Stanley Cup game every year, which we did last month. But for the most part, our friendship goes on hiatus until I head back to Hastings in September.

I'm happy to see him, though. I'd probably be happier if he *hadn't* brought beer, but hey, how is Garrett supposed to know that my father whipped a beer can at my head this morning?

Yup, shit got real today. Dad threw a can and a tantrum, which resulted in me nearly taking a swing at him. Jeff, of course, broke it up and played peacekeeper, before dragging Dad's drunken ass home. When I popped in for lunch, the old man was drinking Bud Lights in the living room and watching infomercials, greeting me with a smile that told me he'd already forgotten what had happened.

"Hey." Garrett strides up to the Hyundai whose brake pads I just replaced and gives me a macho man-hug that involves many a back slap. Then he glances across the room at my brother. "Jeff, my man. Long time."

"G!" Jeff sets down his socket wrench and wanders over to shake Garrett's hand. "Where the hell have you been hiding this summer?"

"Boston. I've spent the past two weeks slaving away on a roof with the sun beating down on my head."

I grin when I notice the sunburn on his nose, neck and shoulders. And because I'm an ass, I lean in and flick the red patch of his skin on his left shoulder.

He winces. "Fuck you. That hurt."

"Poor baby. You should ask Wellsy to rub aloe on your booboos."

He gives a wolfish smile. "Oh, trust me, she has. Which already makes her a way better roommate than you."

Roommate? Oh, right. I totally forgot that Hannah's been staying at our place for the summer. Which reminds me that the guys and I should probably talk about what's going to happen in the fall. If Hannah's planning on moving in officially. I'm totally over her, and yeah, I love her company, but I also love the dynamic we have going, just us guys. Injecting a dose of estrogen into the system might short-circuit it or something.

"Can you take a break?" Garrett asks. "You too, Jeff. There's enough pizza for three."

I hesitate, picturing my dad's reaction if he wanders outside and sees me chilling with my buddy instead of working. Fuck. I'm not in the mood to throw down with him again.

Jeff, however, answers before I can. "Don't worry. John's done for the night."

I look over in surprise.

"Seriously, I've got this," my brother tells me. "I'll finish up here. You take G around back and relax."

"You sure?"

Jeff repeats himself, his tone firm. "I've got this."

I nod in thanks, then strip off my coveralls and leave the garage with Garrett on my tail. We walk down the path leading to the house, but right before we reach the sprawling bungalow, I veer off toward the grassy clearing at the far edge of the property. Years ago, Jeff and I had set up a fire pit out there and surrounded it with a semi-circle of Adirondack chairs. And in the woods beyond the clearing, there's a tree house we built when we were kids, which any housing inspector worth his salt would condemn thanks to its shoddy workmanship and unstable facade.

Garrett sets the pizza box on the rickety wood table between two of the chairs, then picks up the six-pack, tugs a can off the plastic ring, and tosses it at me.

I catch it, but don't open it.

"Right, I forgot," Garrett says dryly. "Beer is for pussies." He rolls his eyes. "There are no chicks around, man. You don't have to pretend to be all sophisticated."

Sophisticated? Ha. My friends know I don't drink beer unless it's the only option available, but I've always claimed my dislike for it stems from the fact that beer is weak and tastes like shit.

The truth? The smell serves as a depressing reminder of my childhood. So does the taste of bourbon, Dad's backup beverage once he runs out of beer.

"Just don't feel like drinking right now." I place the can on the dirt and accept the bacon-loaded pizza slice he hands me. "Thanks."

Garrett flops in the chair and reaches for a slice. "So how crazy is it about Connor? First round pick—that's gotta be good for his ego."

A bittersweet feeling washes over me. The NHL entry draft took place a couple of weeks ago, and I was thrilled to hear that two Briar players made the cut. The Kings snapped up Connor Trayner in the first round, while the Blackhawks drafted one of our D-men, Joe Rogers, in the fourth. I'm damn proud of my guys. They're both sophomores, both talented players who deserve to be in the league.

But at the same time, it's yet another reminder that *I* won't be in the league.

"Connor earned that first-round pick. The kid is faster than lightning."

Garrett chews slowly, a thoughtful glimmer in his eyes. "What about Rogers? Think he'll make the Hawks roster? Or get sent down to the farm team?"

I mull it over. "Farm team," I answer, albeit reluctantly. "I think they'll want to develop him more before they set him loose on the world."

"Yeah, me too. He's not the best stick handler. And too many of his passes don't connect."

We continue talking hockey as we devour the entire pizza, and eventually I crank open the beer, though I only take a sip or two. I'm not looking for a buzz tonight. Actually, I haven't felt like partying at all lately. If I'm being honest, my mood's been in the dumpster since that night with Tori last month.

"So what's Wellsy planning to do in the fall?" I ask him. "Is she moving in or what?"

Garrett is quick to shake his head. "Nope. First off, I would've asked you guys if it was cool before making that kind of decision. But she doesn't want to, anyway. It made sense for the summer because our place is so close to her work, but she and Allie are definitely rooming together again when the semester starts."

"Does she know yet what she wants to do after graduation?"

"No clue. She's got a whole year to figure it out, though." Garrett goes quiet for a beat. "Hey, you know Wellsy's friend Meg?"

I nod, picturing the pretty drama major, who, last I remember, has a boyfriend who's kind of a douche. "Yeah. She's going out with that Jimmy guy, right?"

"Jeremy. And they broke up." Garrett hesitates again. "Hannah asked if maybe you wanted her to set you two up. Meg's fun. You might like her."

I shift in my chair, uncomfortable. "Thanks for the offer, but I'm not interested in a set-up."

He brightens. "Does that mean the freshman you've been obsessing over finally decided to forgive you?"

After the Stanley Cup game, I had confessed to Garrett about the whole Grace situation, the whiskey I'd consumed loosening my tongue and causing me to give him a sordid play-by-play of V-Night, which is what I'm calling that final hook-up. Now I regret telling him, because talking about her brings an ache to my chest.

"She still won't talk to me," I admit. "It's over, man."

"Shit. That sucks. So I assume you're back to drilling anything in a skirt?"

"No." My turn to pause. "I almost slept with this older chick a few weeks ago."

He grins. "How much older?"

"She's…twenty-seven, I think? She's a teacher here in town. Smoking hot."

"Nice. Are you—wait, what do you mean, *almost*?"

I awkwardly sip my beer. "Couldn't go through with it."

He looks startled. "Why not?"

"Because…it was…" I struggle to find the right adjective to describe that disastrous night with Tori. "I don't know. I went back to her place, fully intending to fuck her brains out, but when she tried to kiss me, I just bailed. It felt…empty, I guess."

"Empty," he echoes, sounding bewildered. "What does that mean?"

Fuck if I can explain it. Since I started college, I haven't passed up many opportunities to get laid. The way I saw it, I might as well live in the moment and take all the pleasure I can get, because tomorrow I'm going to be a goddamn mechanic, living a hollow existence in the shithole that is Munsen. But the night I went to Tori's was…equally hollow.

I raise the beer to my lips again, but this time I down half the can. Christ, everything about my life depresses the shit out of me.

Garrett watches me, deep concern etched into his face. "What's going on, man?"

"Nothing."

"Bullshit. You look like your dog just died." He abruptly glances around the clearing. "Oh shit, did your dog die? Do you *have* a dog? I suddenly realized I know nothing about your life here."

He's right. This is only the second time he's been here in the three years I've known him. I've always made sure to keep my home life separate from my school one.

Not that Garrett wouldn't be able to relate. I mean, *his* father isn't exactly a prince, either. A part of me is still shocked that Garrett's father used to hit him. Phil Graham is hockey royalty around these parts, and I used to idolize him when I was growing up, but ever since Garrett told me about the abuse, I can't even hear the man's name without wanting to shove a skate in his chest and twist. Hard.

So yeah, I guess I could have shared my own crappy upbringing when Garrett shared his. I could have told him about my father's drinking. But I hadn't, because it's not something I like to talk about.

But right now? I'm tired of keeping it all inside.

"You want to know about my life here?" I say flatly. "Two words—it sucks."

Garrett rests his beer on his knee and meets my eyes. "How so?"

"My dad's a raging alcoholic, G."

He hisses out a breath. "Are you serious?"

I nod.

"Why didn't you tell me this before?" He shakes his head, looking upset.

"Because it's not a big deal." I shrug. "It's the way things are. He falls on and off the wagon. He makes messes and we clean them up."

"Is that why you and Jeff are practically running his business for him?"

"Yup." I take a breath. Screw it. If it's confession time, then there's no point half-assing it. "I'll be working here full-time next year."

"What do you mean?" Garrett's mouth puckers in a frown. "Wait, because of the draft? I already told you—"

I interrupt him. "I didn't make myself eligible."

Shock and hurt mingle in his eyes to create a dark cloud. "Are you fucking serious?"

I nod.

"Why the hell didn't you say anything?"

"Because I didn't want you trying to change my mind. I knew the day I accepted the scholarship to Briar that I wouldn't be going pro."

"But…" He's sputtering now. "What about all that talk about you and me in Bruins jerseys?"

"Just talk, G." My tone is as miserable as my future. "Jeff and I made a deal. He works here while I'm at school, and then we switch off."

"That's bullshit," Garrett says again. Vehemently this time.

"No, it's life. Jeff did his time, now it's my turn. Someone has to, or else my dad will lose his business, and the house, and—"

"And that's *his* problem," Garrett interjects, his gray eyes blazing. "I don't mean to sound insensitive, but it's true. It's not your responsibility to take care of him."

"Yes, it is. He's my dad." Regret seizes my throat. "He might be a drunk, and a total asshole sometimes, but he's sick, G. And he got in a car accident a few years back and fucked up his legs pretty bad, so now he has chronic pain and can barely walk." I swallow, trying to tamp down the sorrow. "Maybe we'll be able to get him back to rehab one day. Maybe not. Either way, I need to step up and take care of him. It won't be forever."

"How long then?"

"Until Jeff gets the travel bug out of his system," I say weakly. "He and his girlfriend are going to spend a few years trekking through Europe, and then they're coming back and settling in Hastings. Jeff will run the garage again, and I'll be free."

Disbelief drips from Garrett's voice. "So you're putting your life on hold? For *years*?"

"Yes."

The silence that follows only heightens my discomfort. I know Garrett disapproves of my plans, but there's nothing I can do about that. Jeff and I had a deal, and I have no choice but to stick to it.

"You never had any intention of calling that agent."

"No," I confess.

His jaw tightens. Then he lets out a heavy breath that has him sagging forward. He rakes one hand over his scalp. "I wish you told me all this before. If I'd known, I wouldn't have harassed you about the pros all year."

"Tell you that my future is as bleak as a prison sentence? No, that it pretty much *is* a prison sentence? I don't even like to *think* about it, G."

I stare straight ahead at nothing in particular. The sun has already set, but there's still some light in the sky, giving me a perfect view of the property. The outdated bungalow and dandelion-riddled lawn.

The backdrop to the life I'm going to lead after I graduate.

"Is this why you've been partying like there's no tomorrow?" Garrett demands. "Because you believe there literally isn't a tomorrow?"

"Look around, man." I gesture to the sun-browned grass and old tires strewn on the dirt. "This is my tomorrow."

He sighs. "So, what, you knew you weren't going to have the NHL experience so you figured, hey, might as well take advantage of the minor celebrity college status and enjoy this constant stream of easy pussy?" Garrett looks like he's trying not to laugh. "Please don't tell me you've been playing hockey since you could walk for the sole purpose of getting laid."

I scowl at him. "Of course not. That's just a perk."

"A perk, huh? Then what are you doing lusting over a relationship?" He arches a brow. "Yeah, she told me."

"What exactly are we discussing here, G? My sex life? Because I thought we were talking about my future. Which, by the way, is a fucking joke, okay? I don't have a damn thing to look forward to. No hockey, no girls, no choices."

"That's not true." He pauses. "You've got a year."

A crease digs into my forehead. "What?"

"You've got a whole year, John. Your *senior* year. For one more year, you *do* have choices. You have hockey, and your friends, and if you want a girlfriend, you can have that too." He snorts. "But that means keeping your dick out of party girls who have the IQ of a hockey stick."

I bite the inside of my cheek.

"You want my advice?" Sincerity shines in his eyes. "If I knew I had one year left before I—I was about to say *had to*, but I maintain that you don't *have* to do anything. You *choose* to, but whatever, you've made your choice. But if I knew I had to put my life on hold starting next year, I'd make the most of the time I had left. Stop doing things that make you feel empty. Have fun. Make things right with that girl, if that's what'll make you happy. Quit sulking and make the most of your senior year."

"I'm not sulking."

"Yeah, well, you're not doing anything productive, either."

I chew on my cheek until I've drawn blood, but I barely notice the coppery flavor that fills my mouth. I've been treating this upcoming year like a death sentence, but maybe Garrett's right. Maybe I need to start viewing it as an opportunity. One more year to enjoy my freedom. To play the game I love. To hang out with friends I'm lucky to have and probably don't deserve.

Freedom, hockey, and friends. Yup, all those things make the list.

But the number one slot? That's a no-brainer.

I need to make things right with Grace.

CHAPTER 18

AUGUST

Logan

THERE'S ONE MORE WEEK BEFORE the new semester starts, and I'm finally seeing the light at the end of the tunnel. Though if I'm being honest, the tail end of the summer wasn't all that shitty. I spent a week in Boston visiting my mom, didn't have any major run-ins with my dad, and I even ended up calling Bernie and playing a few games with the Miners. Turns out the players are actually pretty decent. Most of them are in their thirties, a few are in their forties, and I, being the only twenty-one-year-old, schooled each and every one of them on the ice. But it felt good to be part of a team again.

The one dark spot on an otherwise mostly-painless summer record is that Grace hadn't called. After my talk with Garrett, I left her a long voice mail apologizing again and asking for another chance. No response.

Still, she can't avoid me forever. I'm bound to run into her on campus, or...I can always speed up the process by flirting with the hot grad student in the housing office to find out which dorm Grace will be in. My last resort would be calling her "friend" Ramona, but I refuse to do that unless I absolutely have to.

But all that can wait. I have the afternoon off today, and my spirits are high as I drive to Hastings. My strength and conditioning program requires increased weight training now, but since I have the worst selection of weights at home, Jeff agreed to cover for me twice a week so I can use the state-of-the-art weight room in our team facilities on campus.

Dean has been tagging along with me, and when I pull up in front of our townhouse, he's waiting for me in the driveway. Mr. GQ is shirtless, wearing low-riding Adidas tear away pants and jogging in place like a moron.

Grinning, I hop out of the truck and walk over to him.

"Hey. Change of plans," he says. "Wellsy got off work early, so we're going running instead."

I wrinkle my nose. "You and me?"

"You, me and Wellsy," he clarifies. "She and I have been running every night. Sometimes G comes if he's not too beat. But she has plans with her folks tonight."

"Nice. Her parents are in town?" I know Hannah doesn't get to see them as often as she'd like, so I imagine she must be thrilled. I also know that the reason she doesn't see them is…her own damn business. Even though she told Garrett it was okay to confide in me about the sexual assault in her past, it feels inappropriate to bring it up. If she wanted to talk about it with me, she would.

"They're staying at the inn on Main," Dean answers. "Anyway, this is the only time she can run today."

As if on cue, Hannah appears on the front stoop, decked out in a baggy T-shirt and spandex pants that go to her knees. Her ponytail flops around as she hurries over to give me a hug. "Logan! I feel like I haven't seen you in months!"

"That's because you haven't." I tweak the end of her ponytail. "How's your summer going?"

"Good. You?"

I shrug. "All right, I guess."

"So you're coming running with us?"

"Apparently I don't have a choice in the matter." I'm already wearing sneakers, track pants and an old T-shirt, so I don't need to change, but I pop into the house to stash my wallet and keys before joining them outside again. Just in time to hear Hannah scolding Dean about his running attire.

"Seriously, dude, put on a shirt."

"Hey, you know what they say," Dean drawls. "If you've got it, flaunt it."

"No, I'm pretty sure they say *put on a shirt when you go for a run, you cocky narcissist.*"

His jaw drops. "Narcissist? More like *realist*. Look at these abs, Wellsy. Actually, touch them. Seriously. It will change your life."

She snorts.

"What, you're too intimidated by all this masculine beauty?" He slaps a hand over his tight six-pack.

"You know what?" she says sweetly. "I would *love* to touch your abs."

In the blink of an eye, Hannah scoots down and grabs something from the planter next to the garage. A handful of dirt. Which she proceeds to smear on him, leaving a line from his belly button to the top of his waistband. And since it's hot as hell outside and Dean is already sweaty, the dirt cakes to his skin like a mud mask.

"Ready?" she chirps.

Dean glowers at her. "I know you think I'll go inside and wipe that off. But guess what—I won't."

"Oh really? You're going to run through town looking like that?" She tips her head in challenge. "No way. You're far too vain."

I snicker, but I happen to know she's not giving Dean enough credit. As much as his ego probably hates that his pristine abs have been soiled, Dean also happens to be a stubborn-as-fuck hockey player who's not going to allow a tiny ballbuster like Hannah get to him.

"Nuh-uh, baby doll. I'm wearing this dirt as a badge of honor."

He stares at her. Gloating.

She stares back. Annoyed.

I clear my throat. "Are we running or what?"

They snap out of their stare-down and the three of us take off in a brisk pace down the sidewalk. "We usually run the same route," Dean tells me. "Down to the park, hit the trail there, then come back the other way."

Knowing they've been running together often enough to have a "route" brings a strange pang of jealousy. I miss my friends, damn it. I hate how isolated I've been in Munsen, with nobody to talk to but Jeff and my perpetually inebriated father.

We've only been running for a few minutes when Hannah starts humming. Softly at first, but eventually it turns into full-on singing. Her voice is beautiful, sweet and melodic with a throaty pitch that Garrett says gives him goose bumps. As she sings Hozier's "Take Me to Church", I can't help but turn to grin at Dean.

"She sings when she's running," he says with a sigh. "Seriously. She does it the whole time. Garrett and I tried explaining that it messes with your breath control, but—"

"I swear to God," she interrupts, "if I have to hear one more lecture about my breath control, I will punch you. All of you. I like to sing when I run. Deal with it."

I actually don't mind it. Her voice is a nice soundtrack to the thuds of our sneakers pounding the pavement, even if her choice of songs is slightly depressing.

When we reach the entrance of the park, I notice the roof of the gazebo peeking through the trees, and I'm suddenly reminded of the night at the water tower with Grace. She'd told me this was her childhood spot.

My shoulders tense, almost as if I'm anticipating to find Grace in the gazebo. Which is stupid, because of course she's not—

Holy shit, she is. I see a girl on the steps. A long braid and... disappointment surges through me. Wait. It's not Grace. It's a blonde in a green sundress, and the afternoon sunlight catches in her golden braid as she bends her head to read the book in her lap.

Then her head lifts, and holy shit again, because I was right the first time—it *is* her.

I stumble to a stop, completely forgetting about Dean and Hannah, who keep running. From her perch on the steps, Grace looks in my direction, and although thirty or so yards separate us, I know she recognizes me.

Our gazes lock, and a frown mars her lips.

Shit, maybe Dean's onto something. Maybe I *shouldn't* be wearing a shirt right now. Chicks are much more amenable when they're looking at a ripped chest, right?

Jesus, and that's just sad, thinking the sight of my bare chest will make her forget everything that went down between us.

"Logan. Yo, what the hell? Keep up, bro."

My friends have finally noticed I'm not with them, and they come jogging back. Hannah follows my gaze, then gasps. "Oh. Is that Grace?"

For a second, I'm surprised she knows her name, until I realize that Garrett must have told her. Shocker.

Beside me, Dean squints at the gazebo to get a better look. "Naah, that's not her. Your freshman is a brunette. And she doesn't have legs that go on and on and—fuck, those legs are hot. 'Scuse me, I think I'll go over there and introduce myself."

I grab his arm before he can take another step. "It's Grace, dumbass. She obviously dyed her hair. And if you looked at her face and not her legs, you'd see it."

He squints again, and then his jaw drops. "Shit. You're right."

Grace lowers her gaze back to her book, but I know she's aware of my presence because her shoulders are stiffer than the posts at the gazebo's entrance. She's probably waiting for me to run off, but that's not going to happen. I'm not running away, not this time.

"You guys go on ahead," I say gruffly. "I'll catch up. Or I might just meet you back at the house."

Dean continues to leer at Grace, until Hannah finally shoves him to force him to follow her. As they head for the path, I move in the other direction, my heart beating faster and faster the closer I get.

It's not only her hair color that's different, I realize. She's also wearing more makeup than I've seen her wear before, smoky green eye shadow that makes her eyes look bigger. Fuck, it's sexy. Especially combined with the freckles that no amount of makeup can cover up.

My chest clenches as something occurs to me. She's wearing a dress. And makeup. On a Thursday afternoon.

Is she waiting for someone?

My palms are clammy as I approach her. I can't take my eyes off her. Jesus. Her legs really are phenomenal. Smooth and tanned and...crap, I'm imagining them wrapped around my waist. Her heels digging into my ass as I fuck the hell out of her.

I clear my throat. "Hi."

"Hi," she answers.

I can't for the life of me read her tone. It's not casual. Not rude. It's... neutral. I guess I can work with that.

"I..." The nerves get the best of me, and I end up blurting the first thing that comes to mind. "You didn't call me back."

She meets my eyes. "No. I didn't."

"Yeah...I don't blame you." I wish my goddamn track pants had pockets, because I'm experiencing that age-old problem actors have—what the fuck do I do with my hands? They're dangling at my sides, and I'm fighting hard not to fidget. "Look, I know you probably don't want to hear a word I have to say, but can we talk? Please?"

Grace sighs. "What's the point? I said everything I needed to say that night. It was a mistake."

I nod in agreement. "Yes, it was. It was a huge mistake, but not for the reason you think."

Irritation clouds her features. She closes her book and stands up. "I have to go."

"Five minutes," I beg. "Just give me five minutes."

Despite her visible reluctance, she doesn't walk away. Doesn't sit down either, but she's still standing in front of me, and five minutes in the life of a hockey player? More than enough time to score a few points.

"I'm sorry about how everything went down," I say quietly. "I shouldn't have ended it like that, and I definitely shouldn't have let us get that close to having sex when I was so screwed up even before I came over. But all that stuff I said about wanting someone else? I was wrong. I didn't realize until I got home that I was already with the person I wanted to be with."

Zero reaction on her face. Zip. Nada. A part of me wonders if she's even listening to me, but I force myself to continue. "The girl I told you about...she's my best friend's girlfriend."

A flicker of surprise crosses her expression. So she *is* listening.

"I convinced myself I had a thing for her, but it turns out it wasn't really her I wanted. I wanted what she and Garrett have. A relationship."

Grace eyes me dubiously. "Uh, yeah. Sorry, but I don't really buy that."

"It's true." My throat is tight with embarrassment. "I was jealous of what they have. And I was stressing about other things too, family stuff, and hockey. I know it sounds like I'm making excuses, but it's the truth. I wasn't in a good place, and I was too confused and bitter about my life to appreciate what I had. I really did like you. *Do* like you," I amend hastily.

God, I feel like a frickin' pre-teen. I wish she'd offer some shred of encouragement, a hint of understanding, but her expression remains blank.

"I've been thinking about you all summer. I keep kicking myself for the way I acted, and wishing I could make it right."

"There's nothing to make right. We barely know each other, Logan. We were just fooling around, and honestly, I'm not interested in starting that up again."

"I don't want to fool around." I exhale in a rush. "I want to take you out on a date."

She looks amused.

Goddamn it. *Amused.* As if I've just told her a humdinger of a joke.

"I mean it," I insist. "Will you go on a date with me?"

Grace is quiet for a moment, then says, "No."

As disappointment clenches in my stomach, she tucks her book in her shoulder bag and takes a step away.

"I have to go. My dad and I are going out for lunch soon, and he's waiting for me at home."

"I'll walk you," I say instantly.

"No, thanks. I can make it there all by my lonesome." She pauses. "It was nice seeing you again."

Oh, hell no. There's no way I'm letting it end this way, all cold and impersonal, as if we're nothing more than acquaintances who bumped into each other on the street.

When I fall in step alongside her, she grumbles in annoyance. "What are you doing? I told you I don't need you to walk me home."

"I'm not walking you home," I answer cheerfully. "I happen to be going in that direction."

She points to the trail. "Your friends went that way."

"Yup. And I'm going *this* way."

Her cheeks hollow as if she's grinding her teeth, and then she mumbles something under her breath. It sounds like, "the *one* day I forget to bring my iPod."

Perfect. That means she can't ignore me by listening to music.

"So you're having lunch with your dad? Is that why you're all dressed up?"

She doesn't answer and promptly picks up her pace.

I lengthen my strides to keep up. "Hey, we're already walking in the same direction. No harm in passing the time by making conversation."

She spares me a cursory glance. "I'm dressed up because my mother spent way too much money on this dress, and my paranoid brain thinks that if I don't wear it she'll somehow be able to sense it, even though she's all the way in Paris."

"Paris, huh?"

She responds in a grudging tone. "I spent the summer there."

"So your mother lives in France? Does that mean your parents are divorced?"

"Yes." Then she scowls at me. "Stop asking me questions."

"No prob. Do you want to ask *me* some?"

"Nope."

"Okeydokey. I'll keep being the question-asker then."

"Did you just say okeydokey?"

"Yup. Was that adorable enough to change your mind about that date?"

Her lips twitch, but the laugh I'm waiting for doesn't come. Instead, she falls silent again. And walks even faster.

We're on a street parallel to Hastings' downtown core, passing several quaint storefronts before the area goes from commercial to residential. I patiently wait for Grace to get tired of the silence and say something, but she's more stubborn than I thought.

"So what's with the hair? Not that I don't like the new color. It suits you."

"Also my mother's doing," Grace mutters. "She decided I needed a makeover."

"Well, you look great." I shoot her a sidelong look. Christ, she looks more than great. I've been walking with a semi since we left the park, unable to stop admiring the way her dress flutters around her thighs with each step she takes.

We reach a stop sign and she veers to the right, her pace quickening as we turn onto a wide street lined with towering oak trees. Damn it. Her house must be close.

"One date," I urge softly. "Please, Grace. Give me a chance to show you I'm not a total dick."

She gazes at me, incredulous. "You humiliated me."

Four months' worth of guilt slams into me. "I know."

"I was ready to have *sex* with you, and you didn't just reject me—you told me you were using me as a distraction. So you wouldn't have to think about the person you *actually* wanted to have sex with!" Her cheeks turn bright red. "Why would I ever want to go out with you after that?"

She's right. There's absolutely no reason for her to give me another chance.

My stomach hurts as she brushes past me. She heads for the front lawn of a pretty house with a white clapboard exterior and wraparound porch, and I feel even queasier when I notice a gray-haired man on the porch. He's sitting on a white wicker chair, a newspaper on his lap as he watches us from behind a pair of wire-rimmed glasses. Shit, that's probably Grace's father. Groveling in front of an audience is bad enough, but doing it in front of her father? Fucking brutal.

"What about everything before that?" I call out after her.

She turns to face me. "What?"

"Before that night." I lower my voice when I catch up to her. "When we went to the movies. And the water tower. I *know* you liked me then."

Grace releases a tired-sounding breath. "Yeah. I did."

"So let's focus on that," I say roughly. "On the good parts. I fucked up, but I promise I'll make it up to you. I don't want anyone else. All I want is another chance."

She doesn't answer, and an ache of desperation seizes my chest. At this point I'd be thrilled to receive a "yeah, sure" from her. The silence wrecks me, chipping away at the confidence boost she gave me when she admitted to liking me before V-Night.

"Sorry, but no," she says, and the last scrap of my confidence takes a nosedive. "Look, if you want forgiveness, then sure, you've got it. That night was embarrassing as hell, but I had the whole summer to get over it. I don't hold grudges, okay? If we bump into each other on campus, I'm not going to run screaming in the other direction. Maybe we'll even grab a coffee one day. But I don't want to go out with you, at least not right now."

Fuck. I really thought she'd say yes.

Defeat crushes down on my chest, followed by a surge of hope, because technically, she didn't say *no*.

She said "not right now."

I can absolutely work with that.

CHAPTER 19

Grace

IT'S THE FIRST SEMESTER OF my sophomore year. Which means I'm Sophomore Grace now. Freshman Grace, God rest her soul, let her best friend make decisions for her and guys walk all over her, but Sophomore Grace? She will do no such thing. She will not be Ramona's doormat or Logan's distraction. Nope. Sophomore Grace is the carefree nineteen-year-old who spent the summer gallivanting around France.

Does it still count as gallivanting when you do it with your mother?

Sure it does, I assure myself. Gallivanting is gallivanting no matter who you're with.

Either way, a new year equals a new me.

Or rather, an improved version of the old me.

At the moment, new/old me is making the bed in my new dorm room and desperately hoping that my roommate won't be a bitch, a psycho, or a psycho-bitch. I tried convincing the woman in the housing office to give me a single, but those are reserved for upperclassmen, so I'm stuck doubling up with someone named Daisy.

When my father helped me move my stuff to Hartford House yesterday, Daisy's side of the room had been empty, but I got back from lunch today to find boxes and suitcases all over the place. So now I'm waiting for her to show up because I want to get the awkward nice-to-meet-you's out of the way.

The fact that I'm getting a new roommate brings an unwelcome pang of sorrow. I haven't spoken to Ramona since April, when I informed her

I was done. Maybe we'll sit down and talk one of these days, but right now, I'm looking forward to starting my sophomore year without her.

As exasperating as my mom's ambush makeovers were, she taught me several valuable lessons this summer. First and foremost—be confident. Second—be spontaneous. Third—the only opinion that matters is your own.

I plan on incorporating Mom's advice into my Sophomore Plan, which involves having fun, making new friends, and going out on dates.

Oh, and not thinking about John Logan. That's a critical component in the plan, because ever since I ran into him at the park last week, I haven't been able to get him off my mind.

I'm proud of myself for standing my ground, though. I was surprisingly anger-free when I saw him, but that doesn't mean I'm willing to trust him again. Besides, I'm Sophomore Grace now. I'm not easily dazzled anymore. If Logan is serious about us going out, I need a lot more than a gruff apology and a crooked grin. He'll have to up his game, that's for sure.

The door swings open, and my back tenses as I turn to face my new roomie for the first time.

She is…adorable. Except I'm fairly certain that not only is "adorable" the *last* word other people would use to describe her, but that if she heard me say it, she'd kick my ass. Nevertheless, it's the first adjective that comes to mind, because she's a tiny pixie of a girl. Well, if pixies had black hair with pink bangs, a multitude of piercings, and wore cute yellow sundresses paired with Doc Martens.

"Hi," she says cheerfully. "So you're Grace, huh?"

"Yep. And you're Daisy…?"

She grins as she closes the door behind her. "I know. The name doesn't suit me. I think when they named me, my parents thought I'd grow up to be a Southern Belle like my mom, but much to their chagrin, they got *this*." She gestures to herself from head to toe, then shrugs.

I do hear a trace of the South in her voice, though, a very subtle drawl that adds to her easygoing attitude. I like her already.

"I hope you don't mind all the boxes. I flew in from Atlanta early this morning and haven't had a chance to unpack yet."

"No worries. Do you need help unpacking?" I offer.

Gratitude fills her eyes. "I'd love that. But it'll have to wait until this evening. I just popped in to grab my iPad, and now I'm heading to the station."

"The station?"

"Campus radio station," she explains. "I host an indie rock show once a week, and produce two other ones. I'm a broadcasting and comm major."

"Oh, that's cool. I was actually going to check if there are any available student jobs there," I confess. "I was thinking of joining the school paper, but the guy I spoke to said their freelancer list is a mile long. And I don't have an athletic or musical bone in my body, so sports and music is out, and all the other clubs I looked into sound insanely boring. Or plain nuts—did you know the environmental activist group on campus spends their weekends chaining themselves up to trees to protest all the townhouse developments that are being built in Hastings? And last year some chick got struck by lightning because she refused to unchain herself during a thunderstorm—" I stop abruptly, feeling my cheeks heat up. "For the sake of full disclosure, you should know I'm a babbler."

Daisy bursts out laughing. "Noted."

"You might find it endearing one day," I say helpfully.

"Don't worry, I'm on board with the babbling. As long as you promise to be on board with my night terrors. Seriously, it's brutal. I wake up screaming my lungs out and—*kidding*, Grace." Her laughter is out of control now. "God, you should have seen the look on your face. I promise, no night terrors. But I have been told I talk in my sleep sometimes."

I snicker. "That's fine. I'll babble during the waking hours, you'll babble in the sleeping hours. Match made in heaven."

Daisy unzips one of the suitcases on her bed and fishes around inside until she pulls out a bright pink iPad case. She tucks it into the khaki-green canvas bag that's slung over her shoulder and glances at me. "Hey, if you're serious about the extra-curricular thing, we actually are looking for people to help out at the station. There are a couple of open hosting slots, but I don't think you'll want them—it's the graveyard shift. And if on-air stuff isn't your style, we also need a producer for one of the talk shows."

"What would I have to do?"

"It's a call-in advice show. Monday evenings and Friday afternoons. You'd be screening calls, doing research for the hosts if they plan on talking about a specific topic, that kind of stuff." She gives me an earnest look. "You know what? Why don't you come with me right now? I'll introduce you to Morris, the station manager, and you guys can talk."

I think it over, but it doesn't take long to reach a decision. Daisy seems cool, and it wouldn't hurt to talk to her station manager. Besides, I wanted to make new friends, right?

Might as well start now.

Logan

IT'S GOOD TO BE HOME. Not to rip off Dorothy or anything, but there really is no place like it. The irony doesn't escape me, though—technically the house I stayed in all summer and just left last night is home. But I was never half as happy in Munsen as I am here in Hastings, in the house I've only been renting for two years.

My first morning back, and I'm in such a terrific mood that I start the day off right by blasting Nappy Roots in the kitchen while I scarf down some cereal. The loud strains of "Good Day" draw the others from their bedrooms, and Garrett is the first to appear, clad in boxers and rubbing his eyes.

"Morning, Sunshine," he mumbles. "Please tell me you made some coffee."

I point to the counter. "Go nuts."

He pours himself a cup and plops down on one of the stools. "Did cartoon chipmunks dress you this morning?" he grumbles. "You're scarily chipper."

"And you're scarily grumpy. Smile, dude. It's our favorite day of the year, remember?"

AKA the first day of open tryouts for freshmen who weren't recruited out of high school. The upperclassmen crash every year to scope out the prospective talent, because sadly, losing talented players is a fact of life when you play Briar hockey. Guys graduate, drop out, go pro. And since the team roster changes each year, we're always eager to check out the incoming freshmen.

Hopefully there'll be some gems on the ice today, because the team's in a world of trouble. We lost three of our best forwards—Birdie and Niko, who graduated, and Connor, who signed with the Kings. Our defense lost Rogers to Chicago, and two of our senior defensemen to graduation, which means Dean and I will likely be playing longer shifts, at least until some of the younger D-men get their shit together.

But the biggest hit we took?

Losing our goalie.

Kenny Simms was…magic. Pure fucking magic in that crease. He was a freshman when Coach named him a starter, despite the fact that two senior goalies were already on the roster—the guy was *that* good. Now that he's graduated, the fate of our team rests in the hands of a senior named Patrick, unless this freshmen crop somehow produces another Kenny Simms.

"We should've bribed Simms' profs to fail him," Garrett says with a sigh, and I realize I'm not the only one worrying about Simms' departure.

"We'll be okay," I answer, rather unconvincingly.

"No, we won't," comes Dean's voice, and then he enters the kitchen and heads for the coffeemaker. "I doubt we'll even make it to the post-season. Not without Kenny."

"Ye of little faith," Tucker chides, waltzing through the doorway.

"Holy shit," I blurt out. "You shaved the beard." I glare at Garrett. "Why didn't you tell me? I would've thrown us a party."

Dean snickers. "You mean thrown *him* a party."

"No, he means us," Garrett replies for me. "We're the ones who had to stare at that ghastly thing for half a year."

I smack Tuck's ass as he breezes past my stool. "Welcome back, Babyface."

"Fuck off," he grumbles.

Yup, it's good to be home.

An hour later, I rest my forearms on my knees, clasp my hands together, and lean forward to analyze the slap shot of a stocky freshman with curly red hair poking out the back of his helmet.

"That one's not bad," I remark.

"Who? Mullet Man?" Hollis calls from the end of the bleacher row we've congregated at. "Naah, he hasn't impressed me yet."

Down on the ice, Coach is running a simple skate-and-shoot drill with the freshman hopefuls, who are decked out in either black or silver practice jerseys. And yeah, I know it's only day one, but so far, I'm not too impressed either.

Two at a time, the guys need to skate past the blue line, take a shot at net, then turn up the outer lane and skate hard through the neutral zone, where one of the ACs releases a pass that the skaters need to connect with. It's not complicated at all, yet I'm seeing way too many dropped passes for my liking.

The goalies are decent, at least. They're not exuding any of that Simms magic, but they stop more pucks than they let in, which is promising.

Beside me, Garrett whistles softly. "Hell yeah, *that's* what I'm talking about."

The next skater in the line takes off, and sweet mother of God, he's *fast*. A dizzying streak of black against a backdrop of white as he tears toward the net. And the shot he releases—perfectly timed, perfectly executed, perfectly *perfect*.

"He could fluke out," Tucker warns, but twenty minutes later, the kid is still rocking the practice like Ozzy fucking Osbourne in a packed amphitheater.

"Who *is* that?" Garrett demands.

Hollis peeks over from the far seat. "No clue."

Pierre, a Canadian who joined us last season, leans in from the row behind us and taps Garrett's shoulder. "Hunter something-or-other. He's a rich kid from Connecticut, big star on his prep school team."

"If he's that good, then why wasn't he recruited?" Tucker asks dubiously. "What's he doing at open tryouts?"

"Half the colleges in the country tried recruiting him," Pierre answers. "But apparently he wanted to quit hockey. Coach twisted his arm and convinced him to practice today, but even if he makes the cut, there's a good chance he won't wanna join the team."

"Oh, he's joining the team," Dean declares. "I don't care if I have to

suck his dick to get him to agree to it."

Laughter breaks out all around him.

"Sucking dick now, are we?" I ask pleasantly.

An evil gleam lights his eyes. "You know what? I won't just suck it," he says slowly. "I'll suck him *off.* You know, give him an orgasm."

The other guys exchange mystified looks, but Dean's mocking look tells me exactly where he's going with this. Jackass.

"I'm not sure if you all know this, but an orgasm is the point of completion in the pleasure process." Dean gives me an innocent smile. "Men and women achieve it in different ways. For example, when a woman reaches completion, she might moan or gasp or—"

"What the *fuck* are you talking about?" Garrett interrupts.

Mr. Innocent bats his baby-greens. "I thought you guys might need a refresher course in orgasms."

"I think we're good," Tuck says with a snort.

"You sure? Nobody has any questions?" He's grinning at me as he voices the question, and when the guys turn their attention back to the ice, I jab him in the ribs. Hard.

"Jeez, John, I'm trying to be helpful. You could learn a lot from me. No woman has ever been able to resist my natural charm."

"You know who else had natural charm?" I retort. "Ted Bundy."

Dean dons a blank look. "Who?"

"The serial killer." Oh Jesus, I've jumped on the Bundy bandwagon. I'm turning into Grace.

Great. And now I'm *thinking* about Grace. I've been forcing myself not to since she shot me down last week, but no matter how hard I try, I can't get her out of my head.

Is it an ego thing? I keep asking myself whether it is, because I honestly can't remember the last time I obsessed this hard over a chick. Am I only interested in her because she's not interested in me? I like to think I'm not that arrogant, but I can't deny the rejection stings.

I want another chance. I want to show her I'm not some heartless asshole who was just using her for a little B&B, but I have no idea how to change her mind. Flowers maybe? A big public groveling?

"Hey, ass-hats!"

We bolt to our feet when Coach Jensen's commanding voice snaps toward the bleachers. Our fearless leader—the only Briar faculty member who can get away with calling students "ass-hats"—glares at us from the ice.

"Is there a reason your lazy asses are up in those seats when you should all be in the weight room?" he booms. "Quit stalking my practice!" Then he turns to scowl at the trio of freshmen who are snickering behind their gloves. "What're you ladies laughing at? Hustle!"

The players speed forward as if the ice behind them is cracking to pieces.

Up in the stands, the guys and I hustle just as fast.

CHAPTER 20

Grace

As THE FIRST WEEK OF the semester comes to an end, I finally hear from Ramona again. And after months of ignoring her, I finally pick up the phone.

It's time to see her in person. I'm not particularly enthusiastic about meeting for coffee, but I can't freeze her out forever. There's too much history between us, too many good memories I can't pretend aren't there. But this meet-up is for clearing-the-air purposes only, I assure myself as I walk across campus. We're not going to be best buds again. I'm not sure we can be after what she did.

It's not about her sext to Logan. It's about what the sext indicates—her blatant disregard for my feelings and her coldhearted dismissal of our friendship. A real friend doesn't proposition the guy who hurt her best friend. A real friend puts her own selfish desires aside and offers her support.

Thirty minutes after we get off the phone, I enter the Coffee Hut and join Ramona at a table near the window.

"Hi." She greets me shyly. Fearfully, almost. She looks exactly the same as the last time I saw her, black hair loose around her shoulders, curvy body wrapped in tight clothing. When she notices my hair, her eyes widen. "You went blonde," she squeaks.

"Yeah. My mom talked me into it." I sink into the chair across from hers. A part of me is tempted to hug her, but I fight the urge.

"That's for you." She gestures to one of the coffees on the table. "I just got here, so it's still hot."

"Thanks." I curl both hands around the cup, the heat of the Styrofoam rippling into my palms. I just hiked across campus in eighty-degree weather, but suddenly I feel cold. Nervous.

An awkward silence stretches between us.

"Grace…" Her throat dips with a visible gulp. "I'm sorry."

I sigh. "I know."

A sliver of hope peeks through the cloud of despair in her eyes. "Does that mean you forgive me?"

"No, it means I know you're sorry." I pop open the plastic lid and take a sip of the coffee, then make a face. She forgot the sugar. It shouldn't bother me as much as it does, and yet it's simply another sign that my best friend is attuned to nothing about me. Not my feelings, not even my coffee preferences.

I grab two sugar packets from the little plastic tray, tear them open, and dump their contents into the cup. As I use the skinny wooden stick to stir the hot liquid, I watch Ramona's expression change from slightly hopeful to decidedly upset.

"I'm a shitty friend," she whispers.

I offer no argument.

"I shouldn't have sent him that message. I don't even know why I did—" She stops abruptly, shame reddening her cheeks. "No, I *do* know why. Because I'm a jealous, insecure bitch."

Again, no argument there.

"You really don't get it, do you?" she blurts out when I remain silent. "Everything comes so easy for you. You get straight A's without even trying, you land the hottest guy on campus without—"

"Easy?" I interrupt, an edge to my voice. "Yeah, I have the grades, but that's because I study my ass off. And guys? Remember high school, Ramona? It's not like I had a booming social calendar back then. Or now, for that matter."

"Because you're as insecure as I am. You let your nerves get the best of you, but even when you're all nervous and babbly, people still like you. They like you from the moment they meet you. That doesn't happen to me." She bites her lower lip. "I have to work so hard for it. The only reason anyone even noticed me in high school was because I was the bad girl. I smoked weed and dressed slutty and guys knew that if they asked me out, they'd make it to at least second base."

"You didn't exactly try to discourage that."

"No. Because I liked the attention." Her teeth dig harder into her lip. "I didn't care if it was good attention or bad attention—I just liked being noticed. And that makes me really fucking pathetic, huh?"

Sorrow climbs up my spine. Or maybe it's pity. Ramona is the most confident person I've ever met, and hearing her rag on herself like this makes me want to cry.

"You're not pathetic."

"Well, I'm not a good friend, either," she says woodenly. "I was so fucking jealous of you, Grace. I've always been the one who goes out with the hotties and asks for *your* advice, and suddenly you're talking to me about having sex with John frickin' Logan, and I was so consumed with jealousy I wanted to scream. And when the Logan thing exploded in your face…" Guilt flashes in her eyes. "It made me feel…relieved. And kind of smug, I guess. And then I got it into my head that if *I* was the one hooking up with him, there's no way he would have rejected *me*, and…yeah, so I messaged him."

Jesus. That last thing I said about her not being *pathetic*? Strike that from the record.

"I was stupid and selfish, and I'm so sorry, Gracie." She implores me with her eyes. "Can you forgive me? Can we please start over?"

I take a long sip of coffee, eyeing her over the rim of my cup. Then I set it down and say, "I can't do that right now."

Distress lines her forehead. "Why not?"

"Because I think we need a break. We've spent every waking hour together since the first grade, Ramona." Frustration clenches inside me. "But we're in university now. We should be branching out and forming connections with new people. And honestly, I can't do that when you're around."

"We can do it together," she protests.

"No, we can't. The only friends I made last year were Jess and Maya, and I don't even *like* them. I just need space, okay? I'm not saying we're never going to talk again. You were a huge part of my life for so long, and

I don't know if I want to throw all that away over a stupid text message. But I also can't go back to the way things used to be."

She goes quiet, chewing so hard on her lip I'm surprised it doesn't start spurting blood. I can tell she wants to argue, to force a reconciliation, push her friendship on me, but for once in her life, Ramona defers to me.

"Can we still…I don't know, text? Have coffee sometime?" She sounds like a little girl who's just been told the cherished family dog has been taken to "the farm."

After a beat, I nod. "I'm okay with that. Starting off slowly."

Her hopeful expression returns in full-force. "How about coffee, then? We can meet here again."

Despite my lingering resistance, I offer another nod.

Relief floods her face. "You won't regret this. I promise you, I'm not going to take you for granted ever again."

I'll believe it when I see it. For now, I've made all the inroads I'm willing to make with her.

We exchange a brief and incredibly awkward hug, and then she leaves, saying she needs to get to class.

I'm too sad to move, so I simply sit there, absently stirring the stick in my coffee. I feel as if I've just broken up with someone. In a sense, I *did*.

But I meant every word—I do need a break from her. She was holding me back last year. Freshman Grace was a confined bird that only got to soar when Ramona decided to let her out of the cage.

Well, Sophomore Grace is going to fly all over the place.

The sadness in my chest disperses, replaced by a twinge of excitement. I already feel like I'm soaring. I love my new roommate, I'm enjoying my classes so far, and I'm looking forward to my new job at the campus radio station. Morris, the junior who runs it, gave me the producing job on the spot when Daisy and I came in at the beginning of the week, and as of next Monday, I'll be working on an advice show hosted by a frat boy/sorority girl team who I've been warned are "dumb as posts." Daisy's words, not mine.

Also, that Morris guy seems pretty fucking cool. *And* he's ridiculously hot—that delicious factoid certainly didn't escape me when I met with him.

The bell over the door dings loudly, and my head involuntarily swivels toward it, then immediately swivels back. I hunch over, hoping my hair will shield my face from view of the newcomers.

The newcomers being Logan and four of his friends.

Crap.

Maybe he won't notice me. Maybe I can sneak out before he does.

I don't want to draw any attention to myself, so I don't get up right away. Logan and his buddies approach the order counter, and every gaze in the coffee house hangs on their every move. Something about these guys changes the air in the room on a molecular level. They're larger than life, and not just because they're all tall, strapping hockey players. It's the confidence with which they walk, the good-natured insults they toss back and forth, the easy grins they flash to people.

I know I should be skulking off, but I can't look away. It's almost criminal how attractive he is. Granted, I'm only looking at the back of his head, but it's a very sexy back of the head. And it's so easy to pick him out as an athlete. The long limbs and toned muscles beneath his cargo pants and snug T-shirt create a drool-worthy package that my fingers itch to unwrap.

Argh. I need to drag my head out of the gutter. Lusting over him is too close to *liking* him, and I'm not ready to open that door yet. If ever.

But common sense comes too late, because Logan is now moving away from the counter and marching in my direction.

"Hey, gorgeous." He slides in the seat across from me and places a chocolate-chip muffin on the table. "I got you a muffin."

Damn it, I guess he'd noticed me right when he'd walked in.

"Why?" I ask in suspicion, and without saying hi.

"'Cause I wanted to get you something, and you already have coffee. Ergo, muffin."

I raise one eyebrow. "Are you trying to buy your way into my good graces?"

"Yup. And excellent pun, by the way."

"I wasn't punning. My name just happens to be a homonym."

His blue eyes gleam as he downright *smolders* at me. "I love it when you talk homonyms to me."

"Uh-huh." I choke back a laugh. "I appreciate the gesture, but do you really think a muffin is going to wow me?"

"Don't worry, I'll buy you an entire meal when we're out on our date."

He winks. "Anything you want off the menu."

Damn him and his seductive winking powers.

"Speaking of that, when should we do it?"

I eye him warily. "Do what?"

"Go out." His head tilts in a thoughtful pose. "I'm free tonight. Or any night, really. My schedule is wide open."

God, this guy is incorrigible. And too damn gorgeous for his own good. His chiseled jaw is covered with scruff, as if he hasn't shaved in a few days, and my tongue tingles with the urge to lick a path along the strong line of his chin. This is the first time I've ever wanted to lick a guy's *stubble*. What is the matter with me?

"Congrats on your wide-open schedule," I grumble. "But I'm not going out with you."

Logan grins. "Tonight, or in general?"

"Both."

We're interrupted by the arrival of one of his friends. "Ready?" the guy asks Logan as he flips the top of his coffee cup.

"Go away, G. I'm wooing."

His friend snickers, then turns to me. "Hey, I'm Garrett."

Right. As if I don't know who he is. Garrett Graham is a legend at this school, for fuck's sake. He's also incredibly good-looking, the kind of good-looking that brings a blush to my cheeks despite the fact I'm not even *interested* in the guy.

"I'm Grace," I answer politely.

"I didn't mean to interrupt." He edges away, a barely restrained smile on his lips. "I'll wait outside so my boy can keep, ah, wooing."

"No need. We're all done here." I scrape my chair back and hop to my feet.

"We most certainly are not," Logan mutters.

Amused, Garrett glances from me to Logan. "I took a mandatory conflict resolution seminar back in high school. Do you guys need a mediator?"

I pick up my coffee. "Well, the stenographer who follows me around is on a lunch break, but I can catch you up no problem. Logan asked me out, and I solved the conflict by respectfully declining. There. I did all the work for you."

Garrett laughs loud enough to attract the attention of everyone around us, including the three hockey players who wander over from the counter.

"What's so funny?" Dean asks curiously. He notices me and offers a delighted smile. "Grace. Long time. I'm loving the hair."

I'm surprised he even remembers my name. "Thanks." I inch closer to the door. "I've gotta go. See you around, Logan. And, uh, you too, Logan's friends."

I'm halfway out the door when I hear him call, "You forgot your muffin."

"No, I didn't," I answer without turning around.

Male laughter tickles my spine as the door closes behind me.

"HERE'S WHAT YOU'RE GONNA DO. Pick up a bottle of wine, invite him over to your place, and make sure some old-school Usher is playing when he walks in. Then, you take off all your clothes and—you know what, baby girl?" Pace Dawson drawls into the microphone on Friday afternoon. "Forget the wine and Usher. Just be naked when he shows up and there's no doubt in my mind that he'll be ready to go to the bone zone."

Pace's co-host, Evelyn Winthrop, pipes up in agreement. "Naked never fails. Guys like it when you're naked."

In the privacy of the producer booth, I do my best not to gag. Through the glass that separates my booth from the main one, I see Pace and Evelyn grinning at each other as if they've just dispensed Dr. Phil-worthy advice to the freshman who'd called in for "seduction" tips.

It's my first week at the station, and the second segment of "Whatcha Need" that I've heard Pace and Evelyn host. So far, I'm not blown away by the caliber of wisdom they're handing out, but according to Daisy, the bi-weekly advice show gets more listeners than all the other student shows combined.

"All right, next caller," Evelyn announces.

Which is my cue to take the caller off hold and put him on the air. One of my other tasks is screening the calls to ensure the people calling in have real questions and/or aren't cuckoo-bananas.

"Hey, caller," Pace says. "Tell us whatcha need."

The sophomore who's been waiting on the line wastes no time getting down to business. "Pace, my man," he greets the host. "I wanted to hear your thoughts about manscaping."

In his plush seat, the rugby-shirt-wearing frat boy snorts. "Dude, totally against it. Downstairs grooming is for chicks and sissies."

Evelyn speaks up as if she's leaving a comment on a blog post. "Strongly disagree."

As the hosts start bickering about the pros and cons of male pubic hair, I choke down laughter and concentrate on monitoring the time. Each caller is allowed five minutes, tops. This one still has four left in the allotted five.

My gaze drifts to the other window in the booth, and I watch as Morris organizes a stack of CDs in front of the massive wall of music. Shelf after shelf holds hundreds and hundreds of albums, which is a strange sight to behold. I can't remember the last time I listened to an actual CD—I figured they were as obsolete as VCRs and cassette tapes by now. But the station is old school and so is Morris. He's already confessed to having a record player *and* a rare Underwood typewriter in his dorm room, and he's also rocking a retro fashion sense I find sexy as hell. Part hipster, part newsie, part punk, part—I could go on forever, actually. There's a little bit of everything in the guy's style.

It suits his quirky personality, though. I've only known him a week, but I'm quickly discovering that Morris can't go an hour without making a dry quip, a dirty joke, or at least one groan-worthy pun.

I'm also fairly certain he has a thing for me, if his constant flirting and readily available compliments are any indication.

I *think* I'd be open to it if he asked me out, but every time I consider it, a part of me raises a protest and encourages me to go out with Logan instead. I won't lie—that muffin stunt had been…charming. Presumptuous, sure, but adorable enough that I couldn't stop smiling during the entire walk back to my dorm.

But that doesn't mean I'm giving him a second chance.

I shift my gaze back to the main booth and force myself to concentrate on the radio show. For the next thirty-five minutes, I fight hard not to laugh as I listen to quite possibly the two dumbest people on the planet give advice. Seriously, if their combined IQ is in the double digits, I'll eat my hat. Proverbial hat, of course, since I can't for the life of me pull off hats. My head refuses to look good in them.

Once the hosts sign off, I switch on the rap mix Morris gave me to use as a placeholder while the next deejay sets up. His name is Kamal, and he's a rabid hip hop fan who plays obscure tracks that almost no one has ever heard of, myself included.

When I leave the booth and step into the main room, Morris wanders over with a lopsided grin. "Were you listening to that manscaping call?"

"How could I not? It was one of the most ridiculous debates I've ever heard." I pause, then grin back. "But I did enjoy when Evelyn said that if she wanted to see foliage, she'd take up hiking or gardening."

He laughs and rakes a hand through his hair, drawing my gaze to those unruly dark strands.

He's got the most interesting appearance. Honeyed skin, jet black hair, golden brown eyes. I honestly have no idea what his background is. Asian maybe? Mixed with...no clue. Like his fashion style, his features are a collection of unique elements that I find incredibly attractive.

"You're staring at me." His lips twitch with humor. "Is there something in my teeth?"

"No." My cheeks warm up. "I was just wondering about your ethnic background. Sorry. You don't have to answer that if you don't want to."

He looks highly amused by the question. "My face is like a melting pot of ethnic goodness, huh? Don't worry, I get asked that all the time. My family is like the United frickin' Nations. My mother was born in Zambia—her mom was black, her dad was a white doctor who ran a clinic there. And my father is half-Japanese, half-Italian."

"Wow, that is a lot of culture."

"What about you?"

"Not as interesting. The Ivers family practically founded Massachusetts, and we've got some Scottish and Irish roots, I think."

A high-pitched giggle sounds from behind us, and we turn to see Pace and Evelyn making out against the wall. On my first day here, I asked Evelyn how long they've been dating, and she looked at me as if I'd just gotten off a spaceship, then informed me that they only make out at the station because "radio is *so* boring."

As Morris and I exchange amused looks, Pace catches sight of us and grins over Evelyn's slender shoulder.

"Yo, Morrison," he calls out, even as the blonde continues to nibble on his neck. "Kegger at Sigma tonight. Fat Ted has a new game he wants you to try to beat. You should come too, Gretchen."

Even if I'd wanted to correct him, Pace is no longer paying attention to us, because his tongue is in Evelyn's mouth again.

"Why does he call you Morrison, and who on earth is Fat Ted?" I inquire in a dry voice.

Morris chuckles. "He calls me Morrison because he thinks that's my name, no matter how many times I tell him it's not. And Fat Ted is one of his frat brothers. He's a hardcore gamer, and we sorta have this competition going on. Whenever one of us gets a new game and beats it, we pass it off to the other one and see if they could do it better. Ted's awesome—you'll meet him at the party tonight."

I have to laugh. "Who says 'Gretchen' is even going to that party?"

"Morrison says so. He's wanted to ask Gretchen out since he met her."

I blush at the impish smile he shoots me. "So this will be a date?" I ask slowly.

"If you want it to be. If not, then it'll be two friends going to a party together. Morrison and Gretchen, taking on the world." He cocks a brow. "Take your pick. Date or friend-hang. The choice is yours."

Logan's face flashes in my head, making me hesitate. Except then it makes me mad, because Logan shouldn't be part of the equation. We're not together. We weren't together before. And Morris is a really cool guy.

"What do you say, Gretch?"

His mischievous voice summons a laugh from me. I meet his twinkling dark eyes and say, "Let's make it a date."

CHAPTER 21

Logan

I'M NOT IN THE MOOD to go to a kegger tonight, but Garrett informs me that if he has to go, then I have to go, because, and I quote, "best friends suffer together or not at all."

I politely pointed out that we could always pick the "not at all" option, which earned me a dark scowl and a menacing *you're going* finger-point.

At least he's the designated driver tonight, so I can slug back a shot or two. But no hooking up. Nope. I have a strict new rule about party hook-ups, and I plan on sticking to it. No more meaningless BJs in bathrooms or hurried fucks in bedrooms that don't belong to me.

John Logan is officially in relationship mode.

"I don't understand why you're in a fraternity when you clearly hate being a member," Hannah remarks. She's in the backseat of Garrett's Jeep, because I don't believe in the automatic-shotgun-for-girlfriends rule and therefore called shotgun before she could. Dean and Tucker caught a ride with Hollis earlier, so the three of us are meeting them at the Sigma house.

I'm with her about the frat thing. Garrett is a member of Sigma Tau, yet he doesn't live in the house, attend the meetings, or chill with a single one of his "brothers." His only contribution to the frat is making appearances at the parties, and even then, he barely stays more than an hour.

"I'm a legacy," he answers, his gray eyes focused on the dark road.

"They were obligated to let me rush, and my father forced me to pledge."

"Wait, so you went through the whole hazing process?" she asks.

"Nope. They wanted me so bad—you know, because I come from hockey royalty—that they pretty much gave me a free pass during pledge week. They'd yell real loud when the other pledges were around, order me to clean the bathroom with a toothbrush or some shit, and then one of them would pull me aside and whisper, *Get outta here, kid. Go get some sleep.*"

Hannah bursts out laughing. "Wow. Corruption in the Greek system. I'm shocked, I tell you."

Garrett turns onto Greek Row, which is jam-packed with cars. We end up parking several houses down from Sigma and walking to the massive frat house, where Dean, Tucker and Hollis wait for us on the lawn, passing around a joint.

Dean hands it to me, and I take a deep hit, filling my lungs then exhaling a cloud into the warm night air.

"Guess who just showed up," Dean murmurs. "Your freshman. Well, I guess she'd be your sophomore now."

My pulse quickens. "Grace is here?"

He nods. "Yeah, but…she's, uh, with someone."

What the fuck? With *who*? And it damn well not be some drunken Sigma oaf whose only goal is to get into her pants.

I had no intention of throwing down tonight, but if some slimy mofo so much as *looks* at Grace wrong, he'll be leaving this party on a stretcher.

But Dean is quick to ease my worries. "Hipster type," he says. "Definitely not Sigma."

I'm suddenly eager to get inside, so I herd my friends toward the front door, which gets me a bemused look from Garrett.

"I take it we're wooing again tonight?" he says wryly.

Damn right we are.

The house is more crowded than our arena during a home game, and I don't spot Grace when I scan the sea of faces. The deafening dubstep blasting from the speakers makes it impossible to carry on a conversation, so I gesture to Garrett that I'm going to look for Grace, and then I'm swallowed up by the mob as I venture deeper into the living room.

Several attractive girls smile as I walk past them, but they're not even on my radar. Grace is nowhere to be found. I wonder if maybe Dean made the whole thing up. Grace on a date at a frat party. It does sound kinda farfetched, the more I think about it.

I pop into the kitchen and search the large group gathered around the granite work island. No Grace. But one of the chicks sipping a Corona near the sink separates herself from the pack and slinks my way.

"Logan," she purrs, wrapping her fingers around my bare biceps as she leans in closer.

"Hey, Piper," I mutter, and I'm tempted to shove her away before her lips can graze my cheek.

Piper Stevens is undeniably beautiful, but that Twitter smear campaign she started against Grace has not been forgotten.

The kiss lands on my cheek, and although she pulls away afterward, she's still pressed up against me, her hand stuck to my arm like hockey tape. "So, it's our senior year," she says. "Know what that means?"

I can't even pretend to be interested. I'm busy peering at the kitchen doorway in search of Grace. "What?"

"It means our time is running out."

Warm lips brush the side of my throat, and I flinch and take a step away.

She frowns. "You've been playing hard to get for three years," she accuses. "Isn't it about time you gave us what we wanted?"

A snort slips out before I can stop it. "What *you* want, Piper. I've told you a hundred times, I'm not interested."

Her red-lipsticked mouth forms a pout. "Think about how good it will be. All this pent-up animosity between us?" She stands on her tiptoes and whispers in my ear, her dark hair tickling my chin. "The sex would be fucking *explosive*."

I uncurl her fingers from my arm. "Tempting," I lie. "But I'll pass. Hey, if you're hard up, we've got some new meat on the team. This kid Hunter might be right up your alley."

Her eyes blaze. "Fuck you. Don't try to pimp me out to your teammates."

"I'm not pimping you out, babe. Simply giving you a heads up. See you around, Piper."

I can feel her glaring daggers into my back as I leave the kitchen, but I don't give a fuck. I'm sick of her constant come-ons and total disregard for the fact that *I'm not fucking interested.*

I wander through the main floor again, checking every room twice before giving up. Maybe she's outside. It's crazy-humid tonight, so the party is both an indoor and outdoor affair, which means it's time to widen my perimeter.

I decide to start out front. When I step into the parlor, triumph shoots through me, because I catch a glimpse of Grace on the winding staircase.

She's alone, and my pulse accelerates as I admire how the stretchy fabric of her black skirt hugs her ass. Her long hair flows down her back, rippling like a golden curtain with each step she takes. Shit, she's on the move.

She reaches the second-floor landing and disappears around the corner, and the loss of visual contact spurs me to action.

Without missing a beat, I stride toward the stairs and hurry after her.

Grace

IN THE UPSTAIRS POWDER ROOM, I wash my hands, then dry them with a New England Patriots towel that makes me grin. Sports merchandising has always seemed like such a lucrative industry to me. Slap a team logo on any old item and millions of people will buy it no matter what it is.

I check my reflection in the mirror, satisfied to find that thanks to my heavy-duty frizz-control cream, my hair survived the stifling humidity it endured on the walk to Greek Row. Morris had picked me up at my dorm, and although we talked non-stop all the way here, we haven't spoken much since we came inside. The music is too loud, and Morris is too engrossed in the first-person shooting game they're playing in the den. The moment we arrived, Fat Ted ordered Morris to plant his ass on the couch and slapped a game controller in his hand.

I don't mind, though. I've been having fun watching Morris beat Ted's record on every level. Each time he does it, the frat boys cheer as if they're witnessing the final touchdown in the Super Bowl and heckle Fat Ted about getting his ass beat. Fat Ted, by the way? Not fat.

Sometimes I really don't understand nicknames.

When I step out into the hall, I experience the most acute sense of déjà vu. Except this time, instead of Logan walking out of a bathroom and me waiting in the hall, it's the other way around.

A surprised noise squeaks out of my throat when I spot him. I haven't seen or spoken to him in three days, not since the muffin incident.

"Evening, gorgeous." He grins at me. "I'm totally digging that skirt."

His blue eyes conduct a slow sweep of my bare legs, and I curse Daisy for convincing me to wear a short skirt tonight. I then curse *myself* for allowing his sultry gaze to unleash a flurry of hot tingles, most of which scurry downward and congregate between my legs.

I sigh. "What are you doing here?"

"Attending a party." He rolls his eyes. "Why? What brings *you* here?"

I answer through clenched teeth. "I'm on a date."

The confession doesn't faze him in the slightest. "Yeah? Where's your date at? You should introduce me."

"Not gonna happen."

Logan steps closer, and his spicy scent surrounds me like a thick haze. His big frame dominates my personal space. Broad shoulders and long legs and a chest that's so ripped I can see each individual muscle straining beneath his T-shirt. I want to slide my hands beneath his shirt and run my hands over every hard ridge. And then slide them in the opposite direction, slip them inside his pants and wrap my fingers around his—

Snap out of it.

I try to regulate my breathing, but it's coming out in shallow bursts. From the way *his* breath hitches, I know Logan senses the change in my body, the quickening of my pulse. The sexual awareness heating the air between us.

"How long are you going to keep fighting it?" His voice is husky. Laced with desire.

"I'm not fighting anything." It's a miracle how composed I sound when my heart is thumping harder than the bass line of the dance track downstairs. "I already made it clear I'm not interested in going out with you. And I don't want to rekindle last year's hook-ups, either. We had some fun and now we're done."

"Solid rhymes, Dr. Seuss." Still undeterred, he eliminates two more inches of space, standing so close I can feel the heat of his body. "So you're not attracted to me at all anymore?"

I don't answer. I can't answer. Desire has clogged my throat.

"Because I'm still attracted to *you*." Heavy-lidded eyes rake over my body. "If anything, I think I want you even more."

I know what he means. The attraction seems a thousand times stronger. It's hot and fierce and I can feel it pulsing deep in my sex. My gaze is glued to his mouth, to the sensual curve of his lower lip. I miss kissing him. I miss the greedy thrust of his tongue, and the way he groaned when it swirled against mine.

Distance. I need to back away, steel myself against his palpable sex appeal and—my butt bumps the wall. Crap. Nowhere to go. No way to run from the awareness incinerating all the oxygen around us.

"Kiss me." His raspy command is barely audible over the pounding of my heart.

His head bends, his mouth inches from mine. I'm mesmerized by it. By the beard growth shadowing his jaw and the way his tongue darts out to moisten his top lip. One kiss wouldn't be the end of the world, right? I can just get it out of my system. Get *him* out of my system.

He lifts his hand to my face, and rough fingertips skim my cheek. I shiver.

"Kiss me," he murmurs again, and my control snaps.

I grab the back of his head and bring his mouth to mine, kissing him as if possessed. When he groans against my lips, I feel the strangled sound in my clit. Oh God. I can't breathe. Can't concentrate on anything but his hungry tongue in my mouth and the rapid beating of my heart.

He reaches down and cups my ass, pressing my lower body to his and rotating his hips. "I've been fantasizing about this all summer." His agonized whisper heats my neck before his mouth latches on, sucking hard enough to make me moan.

I cling to his broad shoulders. Helpless to stop this. He kisses a path back to my lips, teases the seam with his tongue before plunging inside again. His hips keep rocking. So do mine. I'm aching for him and he knows it. He growls softly, then slips one hand under my skirt, his fingers tickling my thigh, gliding higher, moving closer to the spot that's begging for his touch. Millimeters. That's how close he is. I want to scream for him to touch me already, but he's taking his time. Rubbing my inner thigh with his thumb. Slowly. Too damn slow.

He breaks the kiss and stares into my eyes, while his hand eases closer to the crotch of my panties. His fingers tremble. His breathing grows labored.

And then he yanks his hand away, his expression so tortured you'd think he'd been water-boarded for three days straight.

"No, goddamn it," he croaks. "This wasn't what I wanted."

"W-what?" I'm stuttering, still dazed from those mind-melting kisses.

"I just wanted a kiss. Not a hook-up." He draws a deep breath. "I meant what I said the other day. I want to take you on a date."

"Logan…" I trail off warily.

Footsteps echo from the stairs, and Logan quickly steps back, his gaze shifting to the landing.

When Morris rounds the corner, my heart jumps to my throat.

Oh shit.

Morris. I totally forgot about Morris.

"There you are," he says, his smile uneasy. "I was worried you might've gotten lost on your way to the bathroom."

I inhale deeply, willing my heart rate to stabilize. Praying that my expression doesn't look too guilty. Or worse, aroused.

"No, I found it," I answer. "I ran into…a friend on my way out."

Logan's nostrils flare.

"This is Logan," I add, then gesture to him as if Morris couldn't figure it out for himself.

My date nods at the guy I was just making out with. "Nice to meet you." He glances at me. "Ready to rejoin the party?"

No.

Yes.

I don't even know anymore.

What I do know is that I came to this party with Morris, who happens to be a terrific person, and I'm not about to ditch him for another guy, no matter how tempted I may be.

"Sure." I make only the briefest amount of eye contact with Logan as I murmur, "I'll see you around." Then I follow Morris downstairs and force myself not to look over my shoulder.

But I can feel Logan's eyes on me the entire time.

CHAPTER 22

Logan

IT'S A DAMN SHAME THAT duels don't play a role in the modern world anymore. Because right now, I'd totally be down for slapping a leather glove on Morris Ruffolo's cheek and challenging him to one.

What the hell kind of name is that, anyway? *Morris Ruffolo*. I'm highly suspicious of people who have last names for first names. And Ruffolo? Is he Italian? He didn't look it.

And yes, I know the name of the guy Grace came to the party with last night. After she'd deserted me upstairs, I asked around and found out everything I needed to know. His name, his rep, and of course, his dorm. Which happens to be my current location.

I've just knocked on the guy's door, but he's taking his sweet ass time answering. I know there's someone in there, though, because I can hear the muffled sound of a television from inside the room.

I knock a second time, and an aggravated voice calls out, "One sec!"

Good. He's home. I'd like to get this out of the way fast so I can enjoy the rest of my Saturday.

When he opens the door and finds me standing there, a deep scowl twists his mouth. "What do you want?"

Okay then. I was wondering if Grace would tell him about the kiss, and his visible hostility answers *that* question.

"I came here to declare my intentions toward Grace," I announce.

"Gee, how honorable of you." Morris snorts. "But the truly honorable thing would have been to *not* make out with my date last night."

I let out a remorseful sigh. "That's the other reason I'm here. To apologize."

Despite the perma-scowl on his face, he opens the door wider and takes a reluctant step back, an invitation to come in. I follow him inside, sparing a quick look at the clutter-ridden room before getting down to business.

"I'm sorry I moved in on your date. It was a total violation of bro code, and for that, I'm offering you one free swing at me. Just make sure to stay away from my nose, because I've broken that motherfucker way too many times and I'm scared one day it won't heal right."

Disbelief-laced laughter flies out of his mouth. "Dude, you can't be serious."

"Sure I am." I widen my stance. "Go ahead. I promise I won't hit back."

Morris shakes his head, looking both amused and irritated. "No, thanks, I'll pass. Now say whatever else you wanna say, and then get lost."

"Suit yourself. That was a one-time offer, by the way." I shrug. "Okay, next. You should know that as long as you and Grace aren't exclusive, I won't stop trying to win her back." Regret rushes through me, and my voice shakes a little. "We hooked up back in April, and I screwed up pretty badly—"

"Yeah, she told me."

"She did?"

He nods. "On our way home from the party last night. She didn't offer many details, but she made it pretty clear that you messed shit up."

"Yup," I say glumly. "But I'm going to fix it. I know that's probably not what you want to hear, but I figured I should warn you, because you might be seeing a lot more of me. You know, if you go out with Grace again." I cock a brow. "*Are* you going out with her again?"

"Maybe. Maybe not." He cocks *his* brow. "Either way, it's none of your business."

"Fair enough." I shove my hands in my pockets. "Anyway, that's all I wanted to say. I hope there're no hard feelings about last night. I didn't show up planning to kiss her, it just sorta happened and—holy shit, are you playing *Mob Boss*?" My gaze has landed on the frozen image on the TV that's mounted on the wall opposite the bed.

Suspicion darkens his eyes. "You know this game? Nobody I talk to about it has heard of it."

I wander over to the cabinet beneath the TV and pick up the video game case. Yup, I have the identical one at home.

"Dude, I'm all over this game," I tell him. "One of my teammates got me hooked on it, this guy Fitzy. Well, his name's Colin Fitzgerald, but we call him Fitzy. He's a serious gamer, plays a ton of weird shit nobody even knows exists. He actually reviews games for the Briar blog—"

"Are you fucking kidding me?" Morris exclaims. "You actually know F. Gerald? I'm *obsessed* with his reviews. Wait—he's your *teammate?*"

"Yeah, Fitzy uses an alias for the blog. He doesn't want chicks knowing he's a hardcore geek." I grin. "As hockey players, we have a certain reputation to uphold."

Morris shakes his head in amazement. "I can't believe you're friends with F. Gerald. He's a fucking legend in the gaming community..."

He trails off and our surprisingly animated discussion reaches it conclusion, an awkward silence creeping in to take its place. Sighing, I gesture to the screen and advise, "Save the ammo."

His eyes narrow. "What?"

"You keep failing this level, right?"

With utmost weariness, he nods.

"Same thing happened to me. I'd make it all the way to the end, but then I wouldn't be able to kill Don Angelo because I'd be out of ammo and there are no fucking ammo crates in the warehouse." I offer a helpful suggestion. "There's a switchblade on the docks. Grab that and use it on Angelo's enforcers, then bust out the AK when you reach the warehouse. You might die the first few times, but eventually you'll get used to killing with the knife. Trust me."

"The switchblade," he says doubtfully.

"Trust me," I repeat. "Do you want me to pass it for you?"

"Fuck off. I'll pass it myself." He reaches for the controller, then sighs and looks my way. "So where's the knife?"

I flop down beside him. "Okay, it's hidden in the corner of the shipyard, near the dock master's office. Just head that way and I'll show you when you get there."

Morris presses *restart*.

Grace

THE FIRST THING I DO after marching out of the media building on Monday evening is send a very curt text message to one John Logan.

> Me: Are u home?
> Him: Yup.
> Me: Txt me your address. I'm coming over.

It's almost a full minute before he responds.

> Him: What if I don't want any visitors?
> Me: Srsly? After all your "wooing" you're really gonna say no?

His next message pops up in no time at all. It's his address.

Ha. That's what I thought.

My next course of action is to call a taxi. Normally I don't mind the thirty-minute walk to Hastings, but I'm afraid my anger might multiply to a scary level if I allow it thirty whole minutes to fester. Yep, I'm angry. And annoyed. And thoroughly flabbergasted. I knew Morris wasn't thrilled about what happened at the Sigma party, but he hadn't given me any indication that it was a deal-breaker. If anything, he seemed incredibly understanding when I explained my history with Logan on the walk home.

Which makes what just happened a hundred times more perplexing.

I fidget impatiently during the five-minute cab ride, and when we reach our destination, I slap a ten-dollar bill at the driver and open the back door before the car even stops moving. It's my first visit to Logan's house, but I don't give my surroundings more than a perfunctory inspection. Neat lawn, white stoop, and a front door I immediately pound my fist against.

Dean answers the door wearing nothing but a pair of basketball shorts, his blond hair sticking up in all directions. "Hey." He greets me in surprise.

"Hi." I set my jaw. "I'm here to see Logan."

He gestures for me to come in, then points to the staircase on our left. "He's in his room. Second door on the right."

"Thanks."

That's the extent of the conversation. He doesn't inquire as to the reason for my visit, and I don't offer an explanation. I simply march upstairs to Logan's room.

The door is wide open, so I have a clear view of him lying on a double bed, his knees drawn up and an open textbook balanced against them. There's a deep furrow in his strong forehead, as if he's concentrating on what he's reading, but his gaze shoots to the door when he hears my footsteps.

"Shit. You got here fast." He tosses the book aside and hops to his feet.

I stalk inside and close the door behind me, requiring privacy for the tongue-lashing I'm about to give him.

"What is wrong with you?" I say in lieu of greeting. "You went to Morris's dorm and declared your *intentions*?"

He offers a faint smile. "Of course. It was the noble thing to do. I can't be chasing after another guy's girl without his knowledge."

"I'm not his girl," I snap. "We went on one date! And now I'm never going to *be* his girl, because he doesn't want to go out with me again."

"What the hell?" Logan looks startled. "I'm disappointed in him. I thought he had more of a competitive spirit than that."

"Seriously? You're going to pretend to be surprised? He won't see me again because your jackass self told him he *couldn't*."

Astonishment fills his eyes. "No, I didn't."

"Yes, you did."

"Is that what he told you?" Logan demands.

"Not in so many words."

"I see. Well, what words did he actually use?"

I grit my teeth so hard my jaw aches. "He said he's backing off because he doesn't want to get in the middle of something so complicated. I pointed out that there's nothing complicated about it, seeing as you and I are *not together*." My aggravation heightens. "And then he insisted that I need to give you a chance, because you're a—" I angrily air-quote Morris's words "—'stand-up guy who deserves another shot.'"

Logan breaks out in a grin.

I stab the air with my finger. "Don't you dare smile. Obviously you put those words in his mouth. And what the hell was he jabbering about when he told me you and him were 'family'?" All the disbelief I'd felt during my talk with Morris comes spiraling back, making me pace the bedroom in hurried strides. "What did you say to him, Logan? Did you brainwash him or something? How are you guys *family*? You don't even know each other!"

Strangled laughter sounds from Logan's direction. I spin around and level a dark glower at him.

"He's talking about the joint family we created in *Mob Boss*. It's this role-playing game where you're the Don of a mob family and you're fighting a bunch of other mafia bosses for territory and rackets and stuff. We played it when I went over there, and I ended up staying until four in the morning. Seriously, it was intense." He shrugs. "We're the Lorris crime syndicate."

I'm dumbfounded.

Oh my God.

Lorris? As in *Logan* and *Morris*? They fucking Brangelina'd themselves?

"What is happening?" I burst out. "You guys are *best friends* now?"

"He's a cool guy. Actually, he's even cooler in my book now for stepping down like that. I didn't ask him to, but clearly he grasps what you refuse to see."

"Yeah, and what's that?" I mutter.

"That you and I are perfect for each other."

No words. There are no words to accurately convey what I'm feeling right now. Horror maybe? Absolute insanity? I mean, it's not like I'm madly in love with Morris or anything, but if I'd known that kissing Logan at the party would lead to...*this*, I would have strapped on a frickin' chastity gag.

I draw a calming breath. "You *used* me," I remind him.

His features crease with regret. "Unintentionally. And I'm trying to make up for that."

"How? By asking me out? By buying me muffins and kissing me at parties?" I'm so frazzled I can barely think straight. "I'm not even convinced you actually *like* me, Logan. This whole thing feels like it's centered on your ego. The only reason you even saw me again after that first night was because you couldn't handle that I didn't have an orgasm.

And at the party, when you found out I was on a date with someone else, it was like you went out of your way to stake a claim or some shit. Your actions scream ego, not genuine feelings for me."

"That's not true. What about the night I came to the dining hall? How did that benefit my ego?" His voice is gruff. "I like you, Grace."

"Why?" I challenge. "Why do you like me?"

"Because…" He drags a hand through his dark hair. "You're fun to be around. You're smart. Sweet. You make me laugh. Oh, and just the sight of you gets me hard."

I swallow a laugh. "What else?"

Embarrassment colors his cheeks. "I'm not sure. We don't know each other very well, but everything I do know about you, I like. And everything I *don't* know, I want to find out."

He sounds so earnest, but a part of me still doesn't trust him. It's the hurt and humiliated Grace who almost had sex with him in April. Who told him she was a virgin and then watched him scramble off the bed as if it was covered with ants. Who sat there—*naked*—while he said he couldn't sleep with her because he was hung up on somebody else.

As if sensing my doubts, he hurries on in a pleading voice. "Give me another chance. Let me prove to you that I'm not an egocentric ass."

I hesitate.

"Please. Tell me what'll it take for you to go out with me, and I'll do it. I'll do anything."

Well. *That's* interesting.

I'm not the type to play games. I'm really not. But I can't fight this nagging distrust, the cynical voice in my head warning me his intentions might not be pure.

Yet I also can't bring myself to say no again, because another part of me, the one that loves spending time with this guy, wants me to say yes.

God, maybe I do need him to prove it to me. Maybe I need him to show me how serious he is about dating me. An idea niggles at the back of my mind. It's a crazy one. Outrageous, even. But hey, if Logan can't tackle a few simple obstacles, then maybe he doesn't deserve another shot.

"Anything?" I say slowly.

His blue eyes shine with fortitude. "Anything, gorgeous. Absolutely anything."

CHAPTER 23

Logan

"WHAT RHYMES WITH INSENSITIVE?" I tap my pen on the kitchen table, beyond frustrated with my current task. Who knew rhyming was so fucking difficult?

Garrett, who's dicing onions at the counter, glances over. "Sensitive," he says helpfully.

"Yes, G, I'll be sure to rhyme *insensitive* with *sensitive*. Gold star for you."

On the other side of the kitchen, Tucker finishes loading the dishwasher and turns to frown at me. "What the hell are you doing over there, anyway? You've been scribbling on that notepad for the past hour."

"I'm writing a love poem," I answer without thinking. Then I slam my lips together, realizing what I've done.

Dead silence crashes over the kitchen.

Garrett and Tucker exchange a look. An extremely long look. Then, perfectly synchronized, their heads shift in my direction, and they stare at me as if I've just escaped from a mental institution. I may as well have. There's no other reason for why I'm voluntarily writing poetry right now. And that's not even the craziest item on Grace's list.

That's right. I said it. *List*. The little brat texted me not one, not two, but *six* tasks to complete before she agrees to a date. Or maybe *gestures* is a better way to phrase it.

I get it, though. She doesn't think I'm serious about her and she's worried I'll screw it up again. Hell, she probably believes this list of hers will scare me off and we won't even get to the dating part.

But she's wrong. I'm not afraid of six measly romantic gestures. Some of them will be tough, sure, but I'm a resourceful guy. If I can rebuild the engine of a '69 Camaro using only the parts I found in Munsen's crappy junkyard, then I can certainly write a sappy poem and produce "a quality collage showcasing the personality traits of Grace's that I find most bewitching."

"I just have one question," Garrett starts.

"Really?" Tuck says. "Because I have *many*."

Sighing, I put my pen down. "Go ahead. Get it out of your systems."

Garrett crosses his arms. "This is for a chick, right? Because if you're doing it for funsies, then that's just plain weird."

"It's for Grace," I reply through clenched teeth.

My best friend nods solemnly.

Then he keels over. Asshole. I scowl as he clutches his side, his broad back shuddering with each bellowing laugh. And even while racked with laughter, he manages to pull his phone from his pocket and start typing.

"What are you doing?" I demand.

"Texting Wellsy. She needs to know this."

"I hate you."

I'm so busy glaring at Garrett that I don't notice what Tucker's up to until it's too late. He snatches the notepad from the table, studies it, and hoots loudly. "Holy shit. G, he rhymed *jackass* with *Cutlass*."

"Cutlass?" Garrett wheezes. "Like the sword?"

"The car," I mutter. "I was comparing her lips to this cherry-red Cutlass I fixed up when I was a kid. Drawing on my own experience, that kind of thing."

Tucker shakes his head in exasperation. "You should have compared them to *cherries*, dumbass."

He's right. I should have. I'm a terrible poet and I do know it.

"Hey," I say as inspiration strikes. "What if I steal the words to "Amazing Grace"? I can change it to…um…Terrific Grace."

"Yup," Garrett cracks. "Pure gold right there. Terrific Grace."

I ponder the next line. "How sweet…"

"Your ass," Tucker supplies.

Garrett snorts. "Brilliant minds at work. *Terrific Grace, how sweet your ass.*" He types on his phone again.

"Jesus Christ, will you quit dictating this conversation to Hannah?" I grumble. "Bros before hos, dude."

"Call my girlfriend a ho one more time and you won't have a bro."

Tucker chuckles. "Seriously, why are you writing poetry for this chick?"

"Because I'm trying to win her back. This is one of her requirements."

That gets Garrett's attention. He perks up, phone poised in hand as he asks, "What are the other ones?"

"None of your fucking business."

"Golly gee, if you do half as good a job on those as you're doing with this epic poem, then you'll get her back in no time!"

I give him the finger. "Sarcasm not appreciated." Then I swipe the notepad from Tuck's hand and head for the doorway. "PS? Next time either of you need to score points with your ladies? Don't ask me for help. Jackasses."

Their wild laughter follows me all the way upstairs. I duck into my room and kick the door shut, then spend the next hour typing up the sorriest excuse for poetry on my laptop. Jesus, I'm putting more effort into this damn poem than for my actual classes. I still have fifty pages to read for my econ course, and a marketing plan to outline, but am I doing either of those things? Nope.

I reach for my cell and text Grace.

Me: What's your email address?

She answers almost instantly: Grace_Ivers@gmail.com

Me: Incoming.

This time around, she takes her sweet time messaging back. Forty-five minutes to be exact. I'm thirty pages into my reading assignment when my phone buzzes.

Her: Don't quit your day job, Emily Dickinson.
Me: Hey, u didn't say it had to be GOOD.

Her: Touché. D- on the poem. Can't wait to see your collage.
Me: How do u feel about glitter? And dick pics?
Her: If there's a pic of your dick on that collage, I'm photocopying it and passing it around in the student center.
Me: Bad idea. You'll give all the other dudes an inferiority complex.
Her: Or an ego boost.

Smiling, I quickly type another message: I'm getting that date, gorgeous.

There's a long delay, then: Good luck with #6.

She's trying to get in my head. Ha. Well, good fucking luck with that. Grace Ivers has underestimated both my tenacity and my resourcefulness.

But she'll find that out soon enough.

Grace

I'M LAUGHING TO MYSELF AS I sit at my desk rereading the God-awful poem Logan emailed me. His similes crack me up—mostly car or hockey comparisons—and his rhyme scheme is all over the place. Is it ABAB? No, there's a third rhyme in there. ABACB?

God, this is epic-level bad.

And yet my heart won't quit doing happy dolphin flips.

"What's so funny?" Daisy waltzes into our room, back from the one-hour show she hosts at the station. She's in ripped jeans, a teeny tank top, and her trademark Docs, but her bangs are now purple. She must have dyed them when I was in class today, because they were still pink when I left this morning.

"Love the purple," I tell her.

"Thanks. Now show me what you're giggling about." She comes up behind me and peers at the screen. "Is it that baby koala video Morris forwarded everyone earlier? Because that was so adorab—*Ode to Grace?*"

she squawks in dismay. "Oh God. Do I even want to know?"

I suppose a better person would have minimized the window before she could read Logan's poem, but I leave it up. It's too hilarious not to.

Her laughter reverberates through the room as she scans the poem. "Oh wow. This is a disaster. Points for the hockey references, though." Daisy lifts a strand of my hair and scrutinizes it. "Hey, it kinda *is* the same shade as those Bruins throwback jerseys from the sixties."

I gape at her. "How on earth do you know what those look like?"

"My brother has one." She grins. "I used to go to all his high school games, which turned me into a reluctant fan. He plays for North Dakota now. I'm surprised my parents haven't disowned us both—we pretty much rejected everything about the South and moved north the first chance we got." Her gaze shifts back to the screen. "So you have a secret admirer?"

"Admirer, yes. Secret, no. You know that guy I was telling you about? Logan?"

"The hockey player?"

I nod. "I'm making him jump through a few hoops before I go out with him."

Daisy looks intrigued. "What kind of hoops?"

"Well, this poem, for one. And…" I shrug, then grab my phone and pull up the text I sent him last night, the one that contains the most absurd list I've ever written.

She takes the phone. By the time she's done reading, she's laughing even harder. "Oh my God. This is insane. *Blue* roses? Do those even exist?"

I snicker. "Not in nature. And not at the flower shop in Hastings. But he might be able to order some from Boston."

"You're an evil, evil woman," she accuses, a wide grin stretching her mouth. "I love it. How many has he done so far?"

"Just the poem."

"I can't believe he's going along with this." She flops on her bed, then wrinkles her forehead and stares at the mattress. "Did you make my bed?"

"Yes," I say sheepishly, but she doesn't seem pissed. I'd already warned her that my OCD might rear its incredibly tidy head every now and then, and so far she hasn't batted an eye when it happens. The only items on her don't-touch-or-I'll-fuck-you-up list are her shoes and her iTunes music library.

"Wait, but you didn't fold my laundry?" She mock gasps. "What the hell, Grace? I thought we were friends."

I stick out my tongue. "I'm not your maid. Fold your own damn laundry."

Daisy's eyes gleam. "So you're telling me you can look at that basket overflowing with fresh-from-the-dryer clothes—" she gestures to the basket in question "—and you aren't the teensiest bit tempted to fold them? All those shirts…forming wrinkles as we speak. Lonely socks… longing for their pairs—"

"Let's fold your laundry," I blurt out.

A gale of laughter overtakes her small body. "That's what I thought."

CHAPTER 24

Logan

An ENTIRE WEEK PASSES BEFORE I'm able to tick another item off the list. So far, I've completed four out of the six, but these last two are a bitch to acquire. The wheels are in motion regarding #6, but #5 is fucking hard. I've been searching high and low for it, even contemplated buying it online, but those things are a lot more expensive than I thought they'd be.

It's Tuesday afternoon, and I'm with Garrett and our buddy Justin. We're picking up Hannah, Allie, and Justin's girlfriend, Stella, at the drama building, and then the six of us are supposed to drive to the diner in Hastings for lunch. But the moment we enter the cavernous auditorium where the girls told us to meet them, my jaw drops and our plans change.

"Holy shit—is that a red velvet chaise lounge?"

The guys exchange a WTF look. "Um…sure?" Justin says. "Why—"

I'm already sprinting toward the stage. The girls aren't here yet, which means I have to act fast. "For fuck's sake, get over here," I call over my shoulder.

Their footsteps echo behind me, and by the time they climb on the stage, I've already whipped my shirt off and am reaching for my belt buckle. I stop to fish my phone from my back pocket and toss it at Garrett, who catches it without missing a beat.

"What is happening right now?" Justin bursts out.

I drop trou, kick my jeans away, and dive onto the plush chair wearing nothing but my black boxer-briefs. "Quick. Take a picture."

Justin doesn't stop shaking his head. Over and over again, and he's blinking like an owl, as if he can't fathom what he's seeing.

Garrett, on the other hand, knows better than to ask questions. Hell, he and Hannah spent two hours constructing origami hearts with me the other day. His lips twitch uncontrollably as he gets the phone in position.

"Wait." I pause in thought. "What do you think? Double guns, or double thumbs up?"

"*What is happening?*"

We both ignore Justin's baffled exclamation.

"Show me the thumbs up," Garrett says.

I give the camera a wolfish grin and stick up my thumbs.

My best friend's snort bounces off the auditorium walls. "Veto. Do the guns. Definitely the guns."

He takes two shots—one with flash, one without—and just like that, another romantic gesture is in the bag.

As I hastily put my clothes back on, Justin rubs his temples with so much vigor it's as if his brain has imploded. He gapes as I tug my jeans up to my hips. Gapes harder when I walk over to Garrett so I can study the pictures.

I nod in approval. "Damn. I should go into modeling."

"You photograph really well," Garrett agrees in a serious voice. "And dude, your package looks huge."

Fuck, it totally does.

Justin drags both hands through his dark hair. "I swear on all that is holy—if one of you doesn't tell me what the hell just went down here, I'm going to lose my shit."

I chuckle. "My girl wanted me to send her a boudoir shot of me on a red velvet chaise lounge, but you have no idea how hard it is to find a goddamn red velvet chaise lounge."

"You say this as if it's an explanation. It is not." Justin sighs like the weight of the world rests on his shoulders. "You hockey players are fucked up."

"Naah, we're just not pussies like you and your football crowd," Garrett says sweetly. "We *own* our sex appeal, dude."

"Sex appeal? That was the *cheesiest* thing I've ever—no, you know what? I'm not gonna engage," Justin grumbles. "Let's find the girls and grab some lunch."

Grace

OH MY GOD. HE ACTUALLY did it. I stare at my phone, torn between laughing, groaning, and running to the nearest sex shop to buy a vibrator, because hot damn, John Logan has the sexiest body on the planet.

Standing in the middle of the radio station with my tongue hanging out probably isn't appropriate work conduct, but technically I'm not working today. I just came in to meet Morris for lunch. And I don't even care that I'm drooling in public—the picture is *that* delicious. Logan's bare chest taunts me from the phone screen, sleek honey-toned muscles, the dusting of hair between his perfectly formed pecs, his rippled abdomen. Jesus, and his boxer-briefs are so tight against his groin and thighs that I can see the outline of his—

"Well, fuck a duck," comes Morris's delighted voice.

I jerk in surprise, then spin around to glare at him for sneaking up on me from behind. Judging by the amusement dancing in his eyes, it's obvious he peeked over my shoulder and caught a glimpse of the photo I'd been drooling over.

"I was wondering how he'd pull that one off," Morris remarks, still grinning like a fool. "Shouldn't have doubted him, though. That dude is an unstoppable force of nature."

I narrow my eyes. "He told you about the picture?"

"About the whole list, actually. We hung out last night—Lorris is close to taking over Brooklyn, by the way—and he was moaning and groaning about not being able to track down a red velvet couch." Morris shrugs. "I offered to throw a red blanket on the sofa in my common room and take some pictures, but he said you'd consider that cheating and deprive him of your love."

Stifling a sigh, I shove the phone in my purse, then walk over to the mini-fridge across the room and grab a bottle of water. I twist off the cap, doing my best to ignore the sheer enjoyment Morris is getting out of this.

"I wish I was gay," he says ruefully.

A snicker pops out. "Uh-huh. Go on. I'm willing to follow you down this rabbit hole and see where it leads."

"Seriously, Gretch, I love him. I have a boner for him." Morris sighs. "If I'd known he existed, I wouldn't have asked you out in the first place."

"Gee, thanks."

"Oh, shut up. You're awesome, and I'd tap that in a second. But I can't compete with this guy. He's operating on a whole other level when it comes to you."

It's funny—after our brief, ill-fated foray into dating, Morris and I have become even closer friends. Sometimes the lingering guilt about kissing Logan at the Sigma party still arises, but Morris won't let me apologize for it anymore. He insists that one measly date doesn't count as either a relationship, or the committing of adultery, and I think he means it. I also think it's probably better that we didn't start anything up, because I've started noticing the way he looks at Daisy, and I'm pretty sure *she's* the one he really wants to "tap."

As for me? I want that date with Logan more than anything else in this world, and I regret all this hoop jumping, because honestly, he won me over the second he sent me that poem. And clearly he wants this date as much as I do, otherwise he wouldn't have put so much effort into the most kickass collage I've ever seen. And the origami hearts. And soggy, near-death roses that he used food coloring to turn blue.

And now the boudoir photo? His determination is downright inspiring.

"You know what," I say slowly. "I feel bad making him do all this stuff when we both know I'm saying yes to the date. I think I should tell him not to bother with the last item."

"Don't," Morris says instantly.

My forehead furrows. "Why not?"

"Purely selfish reasons." He chuckles. "I'm curious to see what he comes up with."

I press my lips together to fight a laugh. "Honestly? So am I."

Logan

TWO DAYS AFTER FATE DELIVERS the red velvet chaise lounge into my life, I speed off the highway ramp and drive toward Hastings, with Garrett sitting quietly in the passenger seat. Neither of us said much during the one-hour return trip from Wilmington, though we probably have different reasons for our silence. Me, I can't stop thinking about the arena we drove past on our way to the restaurant. It was nothing like the splendor of TD Garden. Just a large, nondescript building, similar to any old arena you might find in New England.

And yet I'd sell my soul to the fucking devil for a chance to wake up every morning and practice there.

I pull into our driveway, but leave the engine running as I glance at Garrett. "Thanks for doing that, man. I owe you big." I pause. "I know you don't like relying on your dad's connections."

He shrugs. "Mikey's my godfather. I was using my own connections." But I know he hated making that call. Godfather or not, NHL legend Mikey Hanson is still Phil Graham's best friend, and Garrett has spent most of his life trying to separate himself from his asshole father's shadow.

"Have you spoken to him lately?" I ask cautiously. "Your dad, I mean?"

"Nope. He calls every few weeks, but I just press ignore. Have you spoken to yours?"

"A couple days ago." I've been making an effort to check in on Dad and Jeff, and Mom and David, because once pre-season starts and our practice schedule becomes more intense, I'll be living in a hockey bubble and will probably forget to call my family.

Garrett goes quiet for a beat, then looks over thoughtfully. "Is she worth all this, bro?"

I don't ask who "she" is. I simply nod.

"It's not just for the sex?"

My smile is rueful. "We haven't had sex yet."

Surprise flickers through his eyes. "For real? I assumed you fucked her back in April."

"Nope."

The corners of his mouth tug upward. Either I'm imagining it, or he actually looks *proud* of me. "Well, then that just answered my question about her being worth it." He thumps me on the shoulder, then reaches for the door handle. "Good luck."

Truth be told, I'm not sure I need luck. Every time I delivered one of my cringingly romantic gifts to Grace's door, I was rewarded with a brilliant smile that lit up her entire face. And either I was imagining it, or she kept staring at my mouth, so damn intently, as if she was dying to kiss me. I didn't make a move, though. Didn't want to push too hard, too fast. But I have a feeling I might be getting that kiss tonight.

I knock on Grace's door twenty minutes later, ordering myself to keep the gloating to a minimum. But damn, I'm feeling pretty fucking gloaty about the way I've successfully fulfilled all of her demands. It really is a shame that people don't grasp what a stubborn motherfucker I am.

Grace doesn't look surprised to see me when she opens the door. Probably because I texted to let her know I was coming by. I didn't tell her *why*, but she takes one look at my face and sucks in a breath. "You didn't…"

I hold out my cell in triumph. "Your celebrity endorsement, my lady."

"Okay, get in here. I *have* to see this." One hand snatches the phone while the other tugs me into the room.

Her roommate Daisy is cross-legged on the bed, and she grins when she spots me. "If it isn't Mr. Romance himself. What have you got for us tonight, big boy?"

I grin back. "Nothing special. Just—"

"Hey, Grace," a voice drawls out of the phone speaker. Grace has loaded the video and pressed play with impressive speed, and her roommate freezes at the sound of the cheerful male greeting.

"Shane Lukov here," the dark-haired guy on the screen continues.

"*Holy shit!*" Daisy screeches. She dives off the bed and races over to Grace, while I stand in front of them smirking the smirk of all smirks.

"Coming to you from Wilmington with an important message," announces the second-year Bruins star. Lukov took the league by storm with his explosive rookie year, and people are salivating to see what he does this upcoming season. The twenty-year-old is already being compared to Sidney Crosby, and honestly, I don't think it's that far off the mark.

"I've known Logan a long time." Lukov winks at the camera. "And by long time, I mean five whole minutes, but what *is* time, really? From what I can tell, he's a good guy. Easy on the eyes. Rumor has it he's a total bruiser on the ice. That's all I really need to know to give him my endorsement. So go out with him, sweetheart." A wide grin fills the screen. "My name is Shane Lukov and I approve this message."

The video ends. Daisy is busy picking her jaw off the floor. Grace is staring at me as if she's never seen me before in her life.

"So." I blink innocently. "What time should I pick you up tomorrow night?"

CHAPTER 25

Grace

HASTINGS HAS SEVERAL NICE RESTAURANTS, but if you're looking for fancy, then Ferro's is the way to go. The Italian bistro is gorgeous—dark oak-paneled walls, secluded booths, blood-red linen tablecloths. And candlelight. Lots and lots of candlelight.

It requires a reservation at least a week in advance, and yet Logan somehow snags a table in less than twenty-four hours. When he told me where we were going, I thought maybe he'd made a reservation last week in anticipation of completing the items on my list, but on the drive over he admits to calling in a favor to get us a table.

Did I mention he's wearing a suit?

He looks *spectacular* in a suit. The crisp black jacket stretches across his wide shoulders, and he decided to forgo a tie, so I have the most delicious view of his strong throat peeking from the open top button of his white dress shirt.

The waiter leads us to our booth, and Logan waits for me to slide in first, then sits right beside me.

"We're same-siding?" I squeak. "That's…" *Intimate.* It's the kind of seating arrangement reserved for super-in-love couples who can't keep their hands off each other.

Logan casually stretches his arm along the back of the booth, his fingers resting on my bare shoulder. He strokes lightly. Teasingly.

"That's…?" he prompts.

"Perfectly fine by me," I finish, and he gives a knowing chuckle.

His thigh is pressed up against mine, a hard slab of flesh that demonstrates how ripped he is. My short black dress has ridden up a bit, and I hope he doesn't notice the goose bumps rising on my bare legs. I'm not cold. Just the opposite, in fact. His nearness, and the heat of his body, makes me feverish.

"Can I ask you something?" he hedges, after the waiter recites the specials and pours us two glasses of sparkling water.

"Sure." I angle my body so we can actually look at each other. This same-side thing was not designed for eye contact.

"How come you don't ask me about hockey?"

I freeze, which he obviously mistakes for discomfort, because he hurries on almost apologetically. "Not that I mind. It's actually kind of refreshing. Most girls ask me about nothing *but* hockey, like they think it's the only topic I'm capable of talking about. It's just strange that you've never brought it up, not even once."

I reach for my water glass and take a very, very long sip. Not the most brilliant stalling tactic, but it's the only one I can think of. I knew this would come up eventually. If anything, I'm surprised it didn't come up sooner. But that doesn't mean I was looking forward to it.

"Well. Um. The thing is…" I inhale, then continue with rapid-fire speed. "*Imnotahockeyfan.*"

A wrinkle appears in his forehead. "What?"

I repeat myself, slowly this time, with actual pauses between each word. "I'm not a hockey fan."

Then I hold my breath and await his reaction.

He blinks. Blinks again. And again. His expression is a mixture of shock and horror. "You don't like hockey?"

I regretfully shake my head.

"Not even a little bit?"

Now I shrug. "I don't mind it as background noise—"

"*Background noise?*"

"—but I won't pay attention to it if it's on." I bite my lip. I'm already in this deep—might as well deliver the final blow. "I come from a football family."

"Football," he says dully.

"Yeah, my dad and I are huge Pats fans. And my grandfather was an offensive lineman for the Bears back in the day."

"Football." He grabs his water and takes a deep swig, as if he needs to rehydrate after that bombshell.

I smother a laugh. "I think it's awesome that you're so good at it, though. And congrats on the Frozen Four win."

Logan stares at me. "You couldn't have told me this *before* I asked you out? What are we even doing here, Grace? I can never marry you now—it would be blasphemous."

His twitching lips make it clear that he's joking, and the laughter I've been fighting spills over. "Hey, don't go canceling the wedding just yet. The success rate for inter-sport marriages is a lot higher than you think. We could be a Pats-Bruins family." I pause. "But no Celtics. I hate basketball."

"Well, at least we have *that* in common." He shuffles closer and presses a kiss to my cheek. "It's all right. We'll work through this, gorgeous. Might need couples counseling at some point, but once I teach you to love hockey, it'll be smooth sailing for us."

"You won't succeed," I warn him. "Ramona spent years trying to force me to like it. Didn't work."

"She gave up too easily then. I, on the other hand, never give up."

No, he certainly doesn't. If he did, we wouldn't be in this incredibly romantic restaurant right now, nestled together on the same side of the booth.

"Hey, speaking of Ramona." His expression darkens slightly. "What's going on with you two?"

Tension trickles down my spine. "You mean since she went behind my back and offered to *comfort* you after V-Day?"

He grins. "You call it V-Day? I've been calling it V-Night."

We burst out laughing, and a part of me finds peculiar solace in that, being able to laugh about a night that left me feeling so humiliated. So rejected. But it's in the past. Logan has gone above and beyond to prove how much he regrets what happened and how sincere he is about starting over. And I wasn't lying that day in the park when I told him I don't hold grudges. Both my parents drilled the importance of forgiveness into me, of expelling the bitterness and anger instead of letting those negative emotions consume me.

"I met up with her the day I saw you at the Coffee Hut," I admit. "We talked, she apologized. I told her I was willing to give the friendship another chance, but that I want to do it at my own pace, and she agreed."

He doesn't say anything.

"What? You don't think I should?"

Logan looks pensive. "I don't know. Hitting on me was a really shitty move on her part. Doesn't exactly put her in the running for Friend of the Year." A frown touches his lips. "I don't like the idea that she might hurt you again."

"Me neither, but cutting her off feels…wrong. I've known her my whole life."

"Yeah? I assumed you two just got assigned to the same dorm."

"Nope. We've been friends since childhood."

I explain how Ramona and I were next-door neighbors, and from there, the conversation shifts to what it was like growing up in Hastings, then to what it was like for him to grow up in Munsen. I'm surprised by the complete lack of awkward silences. There's always at least *one* on a first date, but Logan and I don't seem to have that problem. The only time we stop talking is when the waiter takes our orders, and then again when he delivers the check.

Two hours. I can hardly believe it when I peek at the time on my phone and realize how long we've been here. The food was phenomenal, the conversation entertaining, and the company absolutely incredible. After we polish off our dessert—a piece of decadent tiramisu that Logan insists we share—he doesn't even allow me to *look* at the bill. He simply tucks a wad of cash in the leather case the waiter dropped off, then slides out of the booth and holds out his hand.

I take it, wobbling slightly on my heels as he helps me to my feet. I feel weak-kneed and giddy. I can't stop smiling, but I'm gratified to see that he's sporting the same goofy grin.

"This was nice," he murmurs.

"Yes, it was."

He laces our fingers together and proceeds to keep them like that all the way to the car, where he reluctantly lets go so he can open my door for me. The moment he's in the driver's seat, our fingers intertwine again, and he drives one-handed the entire way back to campus.

It's not until we're standing outside my door that his easygoing demeanor falters. "So how did I do?" he asks gruffly.

I snicker. "You want a detailed performance review of our date?"

He tugs on the collar of his shirt, more nervous than I've ever seen him. "Kind of. I haven't been on a date in…fuck, ages. Since freshman year, I think."

My surprised gaze flies to his. "Really?"

"I mean, I've hung out with girls. Played pool at the bar, talked at parties, but an actual date? Picking her up and having dinner and then walking her to her door?" The most adorable red splotches color his cheeks. "Ah, yeah, haven't done that in a while."

God, I want to throw my arms around him and squeeze all the cuteness out of him. Instead, I pretend to mull it over. "Okay, well, your choice of restaurant? Perfect ten. Chivalry…you opened my car door, so that's a ten too. Conversational prowess…nine."

"Nine?" he blusters.

I flash an impish smile. "I'm taking a point off for the hockey talk. That was rather dreary."

Logan narrows his eyes. "You've gone too far, woman."

I ignore him. "Affection levels? Ten. You had your arm around me and held my hand, which was sweet. Oh, and the last one—goodnight kiss. Yet to be rated, but you should know, you're starting at minus-one because you requested a performance review instead of making your move."

His blue eyes twinkle. "Seriously? I'm being penalized for trying to be a gentleman?"

"Minus-two now," I taunt. "Your opening is getting narrower and narrower, Johnny. Soon you won't—"

His mouth captures mine in a blistering kiss.

Belonging. It's the only way to describe the exquisite rush of sensation that washes over me. His lips *belong* on mine. Heat floods my core as his large hands cup my cheeks, thumbs stroking my jaw as he kisses me with a shocking contrast of tenderness and hunger. His tongue slicks over mine, one sweet stroke, then another, before he eases his mouth away.

"You called me Johnny," he says, his breath tickling my lips.

"Is that not allowed?" I tease.

His thumb softly grazes my bottom lip. "My friends call me John sometimes, but only my family calls me Johnny." His gaze burns with intensity. "I liked it."

My pulse accelerates as his mouth brushes over mine again. The slightest amount of contact, like a feather tickling my lips. He slides both hands down my bare arms, leaving goose bumps in his wake, then rests them on my hip, casual almost, except there's nothing casual about the way his touch makes me feel.

"Will you go out with me again?"

He's so tall, I have to tilt my head to look at him. A part of me is tempted to make him sweat, but there's no stopping the swift, unequivocal answer that escapes my mouth.

"Absolutely."

CHAPTER 26

Grace

ON OUR SECOND DATE, LOGAN and I go to a party, which under normal circumstances, I wouldn't be nervous about. Ramona dragged me to a shit ton of off-campus parties last year, so if anything, I should be an old pro by now. But this party happens to be at Beau Maxwell's house. The frickin' quarterback of Briar's football team.

The football crowd freaks me out. Their parties are rowdy and tend to get shut down by the cops more often than not. And most of the players are loud and cocky and walk around like they're God's gift to the world. Which is ironic, because last year the team put up the worst record Briar has seen in twenty-five years.

The last time I encountered the football crowd, it was at a frat party Ramona and I went to, where I had to break up a fight between my best friend and the football groupie who tried to gouge Ramona's eyes out for making out with one of the offensive linemen. And I had to do it on my own, because the players were no fucking help. They'd just formed a circle around the girls and wailed out "Meow!" the entire time. Dickheads.

"Beau's a nice guy," Logan assures me as we hop out the backseat of the taxi after he pays the driver. "Seriously, babe. He's good people."

"How is he even still at Briar? Wasn't he a senior last year?"

"Technically he's a fifth-year senior. He red-shirted freshman year."

"Good, then that gives him another year to get his shit together," I grumble. "His performance last year was disappointing. Were you there

ELLE KENNEDY

for the game where he threw *five* interceptions and zero TDs? What the hell was that?"

Logan wags his finger at me. "Shame on you, Ms. Football Critic. Ripping on a guy for having an off day? That's harsh."

I sigh. "Fine. I guess I can cut him some slack. I mean, not everyone can be as good as Charlie Carole, right?"

Heat flares in his eyes. "Your knowledge of college quarterbacks is strangely a turn-on."

"I think everything is a turn-on for you," I answer, rolling my eyes.

"Yup. Pretty much."

We reach the front door, and the deafening music vibrating behind it brings a pang of uneasiness. I grab his arm. "If it gets too crazy, promise we can leave?"

"But these are your people, remember? Why would you *ever* want to leave the sweet bosom of your precious football family?"

His smug grin makes me snicker. "Hey. Just because I like watching them play doesn't mean I want them to play *me*."

Logan dips down and plants a kiss on my temple. "Don't worry. Whenever you want to go, say the word and we're gone."

"Thank you."

A moment later, he opens the door without knocking, and we step into the lion's den, where I'm immediately blasted with a wave of body heat. God, there are so many people inside the house that the air is on fire. The scent of beer, perfume, cologne and sweat is so strong it makes my head spin, but Logan doesn't seem bothered by it. He takes my hand and leads me deeper into the mob.

In the corner of the living room, a high-spirited game of beer pong is in progress, and the girls standing on one end of the table are in various states of undress. Okay, make that a high-spirited game of *strip* beer pong. On the other side of the room, the makeshift dance floor is packed with gyrating bodies and surrounded by furniture topped with tipsy, half-naked girls getting their dirty dancing on.

We showed up late because Logan had hockey practice, but still, it's only ten o'clock, which seems way too early for everyone to already be this wasted.

"I'll give you twenty bucks if you get up on one of those tables,"

Logan rasps in my ear.

I punch him in the arm.

He flashes his crooked grin and pretends to rub his sore biceps. "Want a drink?" He raises his voice to be heard over the music.

"Sure," I call back.

We wander into the kitchen, which is equally crowded and equally loud. Logan swipes a rum bottle from the counter, pours two plastic cups, then dumps some Coke in them to sweeten the deal. I sip the drink and make a face. God, his rum-and-Coke recipe needs some work. It's pretty much just rum.

The alcohol burns down my throat and heats my belly, spiking my body temperature even more. I'm wearing a short halter dress, which means I can't even shed any items of clothing to battle the sheen of sweat rising on my skin.

"How are *you* friends with this crowd?" I ask as we leave the kitchen. "My dad told me that the hockey and football players at this university have an age-old rivalry."

"Not anymore. It ended three years ago when the savior arrived at Briar."

"Uh-huh. And who was the savior?"

"Dean," he answers with a snort. "I'm sure you already know this, but he chases anything in a skirt—"

I feign a gasp. "Oh my God. Are you *serious*?"

He chuckles. "Anyway, once he ran out of puck bunnies to screw in freshman year, he had no choice but to dip into the football groupie pool. He wound up at one of Beau's parties, the two of them recognized the man-slut in each other, and they've been friends ever since." Logan slings one arm around me as we walk down a hallway littered with people. "Dean dragged me and the guys to a few parties and we hit it off with the meatheads too. And yeah, the blood feud was put to rest."

I have no clue where we're going, but Logan seems to know the house like the back of his hand. He bypasses several closed doors before leading me through a doorway that opens onto a spacious den. Two massive leather sofas set in an L-shape take up the center of the room, facing an entertainment center that's flashing ESPN highlights. There's a pool table behind the larger couch, and a cue-wielding guy with a bushy beard studies the green felt intently, while his opponent taunts him about how he's going to miss the shot.

I'm surprised by how empty the den is. Only a handful of guys near the pool table, a few couples by the back wall, and two people making out on the couch—Dean and a redhead with huge boobs. Beau Maxwell, who's sprawled in an armchair, watches them with an almost bored expression.

The quarterback lifts his head at our entrance. "Logan," he drawls. "How've you been, man?"

Logan settles on the couch adjacent to Dean's and pulls me into his lap as if it's the most natural thing in the world. As his arms come around my waist, I notice the flicker of interest in Beau's blue eyes. He actually looks a lot like Logan, I realize, now that I'm seeing him up close and not from the stands of the football stadium. They're both huge, with dark hair, blue eyes, and chiseled features. But there's one major difference—Beau doesn't make my heart pound the way Logan does.

Dean and the redhead break apart, their faces flushed as they glance over at us. "Hey," Dean says with a wink. "When'd you guys get here?"

"Just now," Logan answers.

Beau is still eyeing me curiously. "Who's your friend?" he asks Logan.

"This is Grace. My date. Grace, Beau."

The quarterback's gaze does a thorough sweep over my bare legs. And thighs, because the way Logan positioned me in his lap caused my dress to ride up, and Beau has definitely noticed.

"Nice to meet you, sweetheart," Beau says, a smile curving his lips. "Gotta say, this is the first time I've seen Logan show up to a party with a date."

"Get used to it," Logan tosses back. "I don't plan on leaving the house without her anymore." Then he kisses my neck, and a shiver races through me. His hand is a solid weight on my hip, keeping me tight to his body, and…yep, I'm not imagining it—there's another solid weight beneath me. His very noticeable erection against my ass.

Sometimes it still amazes me that *I'm* the one turning him on. My entire freshman year, all I heard was rumor after rumor about John Logan. He sleeps around, he's a great lay, he doesn't do relationships. So what the heck is he doing dating *me*? And by dating, I mean *dating*. We haven't even had sex yet, for God's sake.

As I marvel over the knowledge that somehow I managed to land—or maybe *tame* is the better word?—a guy like Logan, the conversation continues around me. Logan and Beau get into an animated debate about drug testing in college sports, though I'm not quite sure how they reach that topic. I'm too busy enjoying the way Logan's fingers absently stroke my hip over my dress. God, I wish he was touching my bare skin. I wish he'd done more than kiss me the other night. I ache for this guy. All the fucking time.

"There you are." A girl in a slinky green dress and black combat boots saunters into the den and heads Beau's way. "I was looking everywhere for you."

"Too loud out there," he sighs. "I think I'm turning into an old man, S. God, baby, make me feel young again. Please."

She laughs and leans down to brush her lips over his cheek. "My pleasure, big boy."

I make an effort not to stare too hard at her, but it's difficult not to. She's got olive-toned skin, bottomless dark eyes, and thick brown hair that cascades down her back, and she's *stunning*. I don't throw that word around a lot, but there's no other way to describe this girl. Stunning. Not to mention ridiculously seductive. Seriously, she's oozing Scarlett Johansson-level sex appeal, from the way she looks at Beau to the way she moves her hips as she perches on the arm of his chair.

Her expression darkens when she notices Dean on the couch. "Richie," she says coolly.

"Sabrina," Dean answers, a derisive gleam in his green eyes.

"I noticed you actually bothered showing up for class this morning." Sabrina smirks. "You realized the TA is a dude, huh? You poor thing. Can't fuck your way into a passing grade this semester."

"Blow me, Sabrina."

She cocks a brow. "Yeah? Pull it out, big boy."

Dean raises a brow of his own. "I should. Maybe having something in your mouth will finally shut you up."

Sabrina throws her head back and laughs. "Oh, Richie, you really think that'll shut me up?" She winks at Beau. "Tell him the kind of noises I make when your dick is in my mouth."

I have no idea what's happening right now. The animosity between Dean and this Sabrina chick is polluting the air, but it fades the moment Beau hauls the gorgeous brunette to her feet.

"'Scuse us," he says, and the gleam of arousal in his eyes reveals exactly why he's dragging Sabrina away.

Once they're gone, I glance over at Dean with a quizzical look. "Why does she call you Richie?"

"Because she's a fucking bitch," is his answer, which is no answer at all.

"Aw, you look upset," the redhead murmurs to him. "Let me help with that."

In the next breath, they've got their tongues in each other's mouths again.

I turn to Logan. "What just happened?"

"No fucking idea." Grinning, he plants a kiss on my lips, then stands and pulls me up with him. "Come on, let's go mingle. I think I saw Hollis and Fitzy around here somewhere."

We leave the den and reenter the land of the loud and wasted, where Logan introduces me to a few more people before we track down some of his teammates. I'm not having a bad time. Not having a great time, either, but that's not because of anything Logan says or does. It's because as the party unfolds, I start to notice something that makes me feel...prickly.

The girls. Lots and lots of girls.

Lots and lots of girls who have no problem flirting shamelessly with my date.

The attention Logan receives is staggering. And really fucking annoying. It's one thing for someone to come over and say hello to him. But these girls don't stop with *hello*. They rake their manicured fingernails along his bare arm. Bat their mascara-thick eyelashes at him. Call him "baby" and "hon." One even kisses his cheek. Bitch.

I try hard not to let it get to me. I knew going into this that he was popular. I also knew that hooking up had been a sport for him before he'd met me. But that doesn't mean I appreciate having the evidence of his former player days smack me in the face every other second.

By the time the ninth chick—yes, I'm keeping count—sashays up to him and gets her flirt on, I've officially had enough.

"I need to use the ladies room," I snap.

Logan blinks at my sharp tone. "Ah…all right. Use the upstairs one—it's usually less crowded."

The fact that he doesn't ask me if I'm okay or offer to walk me upstairs is a tad grating. Gritting my teeth, I stalk out of the living room.

In the hall, I duck a group of guys, dodge a guy and girl who are screaming insults and accusations at each other, and march up the staircase. I've just reached the top when I hear Logan's voice from behind me.

"Grace. Wait."

I reluctantly turn around. "What is it?"

"You tell me." Concerned blue eyes search my face. "You literally cut Sandy off mid-sentence and stormed off."

"Oh no, poor Sandy," I mutter. "Give her my apologies."

His eyebrows shoot up. "Okay. What the hell is going on?"

"Nothing." I'm hit with a rush of embarrassment, because my eyes are stinging like I might actually cry. I spin on my heel and walk in the direction of the bathroom. Damn it. He's right—what the hell *is* going on? I don't know why I'm so pissed off. It's not like he was flirting back. To his credit, he *was* trying to move away whenever one of those girls came close enough to touch him.

"*Grace*." His hand lands on my shoulder, tugging me around to face him. "Talk to me," he orders. "Why are you upset?"

"Because…" I bite the inside of my cheek. Hesitating. Then I release an aggravated groan. "Have you slept with *every girl at this school*?"

Logan looks stricken. "What?"

"Seriously, John, what the hell? We can't walk two feet without some girl coming up to you and *fondling* you and saying, *ooooh, I had such a good time with you last year, you big stud, we should do that again, wink wink, nudge nudge.*"

His mouth falls open. Then understanding dawns, and a slow smile stretches his mouth. "Wait, this is about you being *jealous*?"

I bristle. "No."

"Nuh-uh. You're jealous."

My jaw sets in a tense line. "I just don't appreciate all these girls hitting on you when I'm standing right fucking beside you. It's rude and disrespectful and—"

"Makes you jealous," he finishes, and I feel like smacking that stupid grin off his face.

"This isn't funny." I attempt to shrug his hand off my arm.

But not only does he hold on tighter, he brings his other hand into play, planting both on my waist as he backs me into the wall. Then I've got six-feet and two-hundred-plus pounds of sexy hockey player pinning me in place.

His lips brush mine in a soft kiss before he gazes into my eyes, earnest, amazed. "You have nothing to be jealous of," he says in a husky voice. "All those girls who came over to us? I don't even remember what they look like. I don't remember half their *names*. You're the only one I see tonight, the only one I see *ever*." Those warm lips touch mine again, firm and reassuring. "PS? I never hooked up with Sandy."

"Liar," I grumble.

"It's true." He grins. "She plays for the other team."

I narrow my eyes. "Really?"

"Oh yeah. She and her girlfriend came to a party at our place last semester and fooled around on the couch the entire time."

"Are you just saying that to make me feel better?"

"Nope. It's true. Dean thought he'd died and gone to heaven."

A laugh pops out. I find myself relaxing, my previously tense muscles now loose and tingly from the feel of his hard body pressed up against mine. God, I didn't like feeling that way downstairs. Prickly and peeved, ready to fight any girl who so much as *looked* at Logan.

"But this is even hotter than watching Sandy and her girl make out all night." A seductive note thickens his voice.

"What's hotter?"

"You. Jealous." Those blue eyes go molten hot. "I've never been with anyone who's gotten all possessive over me. It turns me on."

He's not joking. His erection is poking into my belly, and the feel of it sends a streak of satisfaction through me. I move my hips, just enough for my pelvis to rub that hard ridge, and his eyelids grow heavy.

"That turns me on even more," he mumbles.

I hide a smile. "Yeah?"

"Oh yeah. Trust me, baby, you're the only woman I want. The only one who gets me going."

Raising my eyebrows, I reach up to lock my hands around his neck.

"I don't know… I'm still jealous. I think you might need to reassure me some more."

Chuckling, he tips his head toward the door beside us. "Want me to make you come in the bathroom?" My thighs clench, *noticeably*, and he laughs again. "Is that a yes?"

"God, no." I lean up to nibble on his neck. "It's a *hell yes*."

CHAPTER 27

Logan

FOR THE FOURTH TIME THIS week, I skate off the ice after practice wanting to pound my fist through a wall. The sheer lack of skill and common fucking sense I'm seeing from some of the other defensemen is appalling. I'm willing to cut the freshmen recruits some slack, but there's no excuse for the way the juniors have played this week. Brodowski literally stood motionless in the defensive zone looking for someone to pass to, and Anderson lobbed pass after pass to covered forwards instead of cross-passing to me or carrying the puck so the forwards had time to get open.

The hinge plays we ran were a disaster. The freshmen skated in slow motion. The upperclassmen made stupid mistakes. It's becoming painfully obvious that our roster is weak. So weak that the chances of making it to the post-season are looking slimmer and slimmer—and we haven't even played our first game yet.

As I strip my gear in the locker room, I realize I'm not the only one who's frustrated. Far too many surly faces surround me, and even Garrett is surprisingly silent. As team captain, he tries to offer encouragement after every practice, but he's clearly starting to get discouraged by the dismal state of our team.

The only guy who's actually smiling is the new kid Hunter, who received so much praise from Coach for his performance today that he's going to be shitting out lollipops and kittens for weeks to come. I have no clue how Dean managed to convince the guy to join the team—all I know is that my buddy dragged Hunter to the bar one night after tryouts, and the next morning, the kid was on board. Must've been some night out.

"Logan." Coach appears in front of me. "Come talk to me after your shower."

Shit. I quickly search my brain for anything I could've done wrong on the ice, but I'm not being arrogant when I say I played well. Dean and I were the only ones even *trying* out there.

When I enter Coach's office thirty minutes later, he's at his desk, wearing a somber look that heightens my agitation. Fuck. Was it the dropped pass at the start of practice? No. Can't be. Not even Gretzky himself could have held on to the puck with two hundred pounds of Mike Hollis ramming him into the boards.

"What's up?" I sit down, trying not to reveal how rattled I am.

"Let's cut right to the chase. You know I don't like to waste time on preamble." Coach Jensen leans back in his chair. "I spoke to a friend in the Bruins organization this morning."

Every muscle in my body freezes up. "Oh. Who?"

"The assistant GM."

My eyes nearly bug out of their sockets. I knew Coach had connections—of course he does, he was in Pittsburg for seven seasons, for fuck's sake—but when he said "friend" I assumed he meant a lower-level minion in the head office. Not the *assistant general manager*.

"Look, it's no secret you've been on the radar of every scout since your high school career. And you already know I've had inquiries about you before. Anyway, if you're interested, they want you to come in and practice with the Providence Bruins."

Jesus Christ.

They want me to practice with the development team for the Boston fucking *Bruins*?

I can barely wrap my head around it. All I can do is stare at Coach. "They'd want me for Providence?"

"Maybe. When they're interested in taking a look at you, they don't usually put you on the ice with the big boys. They test you out with the minor team first, see how you do." His voice rings with intensity I rarely hear off the ice. "You're good, John. You're really fucking good. Even if they choose to develop you in Providence first, it won't be long before you're called up and playing on the roster you deserve to be on."

Christ. This can't be happening. I'm in the Garden of fucking Eden, salivating over that goddamn apple. The temptation is so strong I can taste the victory. This isn't just a pro team holding out the apple—it's *the* team. The one I grew up rooting for, the one I've fantasized about playing for since I was seven years old.

Coach studies my face. "With that said, I wanted to check if you've reconsidered your plans after graduation."

My throat goes drier than dust. My heart races. I want to shout *Yes! I've reconsidered!* But I can't. I made a promise to my brother. And as big of an opportunity as this is, it's not big *enough*. Jeff won't be impressed if I announce I'm going to be playing for a farm team. Nothing short of a plum contract with the Bruins will convince him to let me have this, and even then, he'd probably still balk.

"No, I haven't." It kills me to say it. It *kills* me.

From the frustration shadowing Coach's eyes, I can tell he senses that. "Look. John." He speaks in a measured tone. "I understand why you didn't opt in. I really do."

Other than my brother, and now Garrett, Coach is the only other person who knows I didn't enter the draft. In that first eligible year, I pretended I'd missed the deadline to declare, which led to Coach dragging me into this very office and screaming at me for forty-five minutes about what an irresponsible idiot I am and how I'm wasting my God given talents. Once he calmed down, he started muttering about calling in favors to try to make me eligible, at which point I had no choice but to tell him the truth. Well, *some* of the truth. I told him about my dad's accident, but not the drinking.

Since then, he hasn't harassed me about it—until now.

"But this is your future we're talking about," he finishes gruffly. "If you pass this up, you're going to regret it for the rest of your life, kid. I guarantee it."

Yeah, no guarantee needed. I *know* I'll regret it. Hell, I already regret a lot of things. But family comes first, and my word means something. To me, to Jeff. I can't go back on it now, no matter how tempting this is.

"Thanks for letting me know, Coach. And please thank your friend for me." I swallow a lump of despair as I slowly rise to my feet. "But my answer is no."

"Are you sure this is what you want?"

Grace's soft voice and timid expression make my chest ache. I don't know why she bothered asking me that, because obviously this is the last thing I want to do. It's what I *have* to do.

Although I went straight to her dorm after practice and wasted no time telling her about my talk with Coach, now I'm kinda wishing I kept it to myself. I told her about my plans for the future a few days after we started dating, but even though she hasn't said it out loud, I know she disagrees with them.

"I didn't want to say no," I say roughly. "But I have to. My brother expects me to move back home the moment I graduate."

"What about your dad? What does *he* expect?"

I lean my head against the stack of decorative pillows on her bed. They smell like her. Sweet and feminine, a soothing fragrance that relaxes some of the tension wedged in my chest.

"He expects us to help him run his business because he can't do it himself. That's what family does. You pitch in when you're needed. You take care of each other."

She frowns. "At the expense of your dreams?"

"If it comes down to that, yes." This entire conversation is too dismal, so I tug her toward me. "Come on, let's put on the movie. I need some explosions and gunfights to distract me from my misery."

Grace grabs her laptop and gets the movie ready, but when she tries to place the computer between us, I shift it to my lap so there's no barrier to keep her from snuggling beside me. I love holding her. And playing with her hair. And leaning in to kiss her neck whenever the urge strikes.

I haven't been in a relationship since high school, but being with Grace is different than it was with my old girlfriends. It feels...more mature, I guess. Back then we just talked about trivial bullshit, and filled in the silences by fooling around. But Grace and I actually *talk*. We talk about our days and our classes, our childhoods, our futures.

Talking isn't *all* we do, though. I've seen her almost every day since our first date, and we've messed around every single time. Christ, that bathroom hook-up at Beau's party? Out of this fucking world—and she hadn't even touched me. I'd jerked off when I was down on my knees eating her pussy, and sweet Jesus, I can't remember ever coming that hard from my own hand.

But we haven't had sex yet, and I don't even *care*. It used to be all about the quick gratification for me—flirt, fuck, get out. Like a game of ball hockey back in middle school, hurriedly played between the time school let out and when my mother would call me in for supper.

With Grace, it's like three periods of *real* hockey. The anticipation and excitement of the first period, the escalating buildup of the second, and then the sheer intensity of the third that results in that euphoric knowledge of having achieved something. A win, a loss, a tie. Doesn't matter. It's still the most powerful feeling in the world.

If I had to identify it, I'd say we're in the second period now. The buildup. Hot hook-up sessions that leave me aching, but none of the third-period pressure to seal the deal.

Twenty minutes into the film, she turns to me suddenly. "Hey. Question."

I click the track pad to press pause. "Hit me."

"Am I your girlfriend?"

I give her my creepiest leer. "I don't know, baby, do you want to be?"

Amusement dances in her brown eyes. "Well, *now* I don't."

Grinning, I lean over the edge of the bed to set the laptop on the floor, then shift around and pounce on her. She squeals as I get her on her back, my body pressed to her side as I prop up on one elbow and peer down at her.

"Liar," I accuse. "Of course you want to be my girlfriend. And FYI? You are."

Her expression grows pensive for a moment, and then she nods. "I can live with that."

"Aw, how generous of you, baby. We should silkscreen it on matching T-shirts—'I can live with that.'"

Her laughter floats up and tickles my chin. I love her laugh. It's so fucking genuine. *Everything* about her is genuine. I've hooked up with too many chicks who play games, who say one thing and mean another, who lie or manipulate to get what they want. But not Grace. She's open and sincere, and when she's pissed off or annoyed, she *tells* me. I appreciate that.

I dip my head to kiss her, and when our tongues meet, a jolt of pleasure zips down to my cock, which thickens against her leg. I nudge my hips forward, and just that tiny amount of friction makes me groan. God. I want to come. She's gotten me there twice this week. Once jacking me off, the other time using her mouth. On the nights that orgasms weren't on the table, I jerked it in the shower, imagining I was fucking her instead of my fist, but self-gratification is nothing compared to what she's doing right now, when she unzips my pants and wraps her fingers around me.

My eyes roll to the top of my head at that first gentle stroke. "When is Daisy coming home?" I mumble.

"At least not for another hour." She rubs a slow circle around the head of my dick. Precome coats her fingers, making it easy to glide her fist up and down my shaft.

I thrust my hips and kiss her, one hand traveling up her stomach to cup a small, firm breast. She's not wearing a bra, and her nipples strain against the soft cotton of her tank top. I rub my palm over the tight bud, tease it with the pad of my thumb, then press down on it, drawing a breathy noise from her lips.

I'm so hard I can't think straight. It's unbearable, this need for release. My breathing becomes shallow as I let go of her breast and slide my hand lower, inching toward the waistband of her yoga pants.

She breaks the kiss, stiffening beneath my touch. "Uh..." Color stains her cheeks. "I'm closed for business tonight. It's my moon time."

I choke out a laugh. "Your moon time?"

"What?" she says defensively. "It sounds a lot more whimsical than *I'm menstruating.*"

I cringe, instantly transported back to those awkward moments in sex ed class.

"See?" she gloats. "My way is better." Then she swats my hand away from her crotch and plants both hands on my chest, giving me a gentle shove. "Lie back. I want to tease you a little."

Christ. Tease me she does. She drags my shirt up and explores every inch of my chest with her mouth. Soft lips plant fleeting kisses along my collarbone, then dance over my left pec, hovering above my nipple and bringing goose bumps to my flesh. Her tongue darts out for a taste, and I feel that tiny flick on my nipple all the way down in my cock. It throbs painfully, and I'm damn near squirming. I want her mouth on me again. I want her to suck on the tip, just a hint of suction and then the swirl of her tongue. I want—

Jesus, she's kissing her way down my stomach, giving me *exactly* what I want. I swear, this girl can read my mind. Her lips close around me, her tongue executing that sexy swirl I was fantasizing about.

I must have made some kind of noise, because she peers up with a satisfied smile. "You okay up there?"

"Fuck. Yes. I'm more than okay."

"Question," she says, and now I'm smiling too, because I love it when she does that. Announces she's about to ask a question instead of just asking it.

I answer with my standard, "Hit me."

"How do you feel about your ass?"

My brow furrows. "Meaning?"

"Meaning, if I do *this*—" Her finger slides over a spot I was *not* expecting her to touch "—are you going to freak out, or go with it?"

She does it again, and I'm stunned when a shock of pleasure skates up my spine. "Go with it," I croak. "Definitely go with it."

Grace's eyes flicker with equal parts surprise and intrigue. Then she lowers her head and sucks me deep in her mouth, another unexpected move that blurs my vision. Sweet Jesus. I'm completely surrounded by tight, wet heat. My blunt head pokes the back of her throat, and my hips move before I can stop them, retreating an inch, two, before sliding back in.

Her moan reverberates around me. Her finger continues to torment me. Gentle and exploratory, coaxing a strange ache of pleasure I hadn't bargained for.

Jesus, this is fucking intense. And it doesn't stop. She tortures me with her tongue, licking my shaft, slowly, thoroughly, like she's a goddamn cartographer who's planning to map it out later. And that finger. Rubbing, teasing.

My balls tighten, my throat so dry I can barely get a word out. But

I manage two. "I'm close." Then two more. "Really close."

The last time she did this, she didn't stay with me until the end. This time, she clamps her lips around me, her long hair tickling my thighs as her head moves over me. Release is imminent. Pulsing in my blood. But still out of reach, a taunting throb of tension that makes me groan with impatience. I want it. I *need* it. I—she slips her finger inside, and holy shit, I ain't gonna lie. It feels so fucking good. She gives my dick a long, hard suck, pushes her finger deeper, and I go off like a grenade.

I gasp for air, my hips shooting off the bed as I come to the sounds of her moans and my ragged pants. Her throat works as she swallows, each tiny contraction milking more pleasure from my body until I'm nothing but a heaving, mindless mess on the bed.

Grace crawls up and nestles beside me, placing her hand on my stomach, a small, warm anchor that keeps me from floating away.

"That was…" I suck in a breath. "Phenomenal."

Her laughter warms the crook of my neck. "I'll make a note of that. Ass shenanigans, phenomenal. Regular shenanigans…what did you call it last time? Just *amazing*, I think."

"Everything you do to me is both amazing *and* phenomenal," I correct, threading my fingers through her hair. I don't think I've ever felt so content in my life. "Hey. Question."

"Hit me."

I grin at the role reversal, then say, "My first pre-season game is tomorrow night. I know you don't like hockey, but…will you come?"

"Aw, I would if I could," she answers, sounding genuinely regretful. "But I'm meeting up with this guy from my psych class."

I shift to my side and narrow my eyes at her. Something strange and unfamiliar slinks through me.

I'm startled to realize it's jealousy.

"What guy?"

She snickers. "Down, boy. He's just a classmate. We're paired up on an assignment together, this case study thing. I'm going to be seeing him a whole bunch the next couple of weeks."

"A whole bunch, huh?" I pause. "Is he good-looking?"

"He's all right, I guess. Really skinny, but some girls are into that."

Some girls? Or one in particular?

When she notices my expression, she laughs even harder. "Ha. Who's jealous *now*?"

"Not me," I lie.

"You totally are." She inches closer and plants a loud kiss on my lips. "Don't be. I have a boyfriend, remember?"

"Damn right you do."

Fuck, now I know how she felt at the party the other night. The possessive clench in my chest is…new. I don't like it, but I can't stop it, either. I've been playing the field since I started at Briar, but there were a few hook-ups that lasted more than one night. Girls I saw on and off, not seriously, but often enough to develop *some* feelings for them. None of those arrangements were exclusive, though. I was well aware that they were seeing other guys, too. And I didn't care.

This time I do care. The idea of Grace with another guy is unacceptable. I won't go as far as to say she's *mine*, but…well, she's mine. Mine to hold and mine to kiss and mine to laugh with.

Yup, mine.

"What time is it?" she asks. "I'm too lazy to lift my head."

I crane my neck to get a better look at the alarm clock. "Ten thirty-two."

"Should we finish watching the movie?"

"Sure." I lean over to grab the laptop, which chimes loudly the moment I pick it up. "Uh…someone's Skyping you, I think."

She peeks at the screen, then shoots up in a panic. "Oh no. Put your pants on!"

I wrinkle my forehead. "Why?"

"Because that's my mother!"

If I'd still had an erection, it would be deflating like a balloon right now. I hurriedly yank my pants to my hips and zip them up as Grace sets the computer in her lap. Her fingers hover over the track pad, and then she looks over at me. "Move ten inches to the left if you don't want her to see you."

"Do *you* not want her to see me?"

Grace rolls her eyes. "I'm cool if she does. Actually, she knows all about you, so you should totally say hi. But I understand if you don't want to do the whole meet-the-parents thing right now."

I shrug. "I'm cool with it."

"Okay then. Brace yourself. She's about to deafen us both with—"

A shriek of delight. The loudest frickin' shriek on the planet.

Fortunately, her voice lowers to a manageable decibel when she speaks. "Sweetie! Yay! You answered!"

The video chat box fills the screen, revealing a very attractive blonde who seems way too young to be the mother of a nineteen-year-old. Seriously, Grace's mother looks like she's thirty. If that.

"Hey, Mom," Grace says. "Do I even want to know why you're awake at five-thirty in the morning?"

Her mother's answering grin is downright devilish. "Who says I even went to bed?"

Grace told me that her mother is bubbly and impulsive and pretty much acts like a teenager, and I can see now that she hadn't exaggerated.

My girlfriend groans. "Please tell me you stayed up painting and not…doing other things."

"I take the Fifth."

"*Mom.*"

"I'm forty-four years old, sweetie. Do you expect me to live like a monk?"

Forty-four? Wow. Totally doesn't look it. Also, I can't stop the snicker that pops out at her breezy response, which causes her brown eyes to narrow.

"Grace Elizabeth Ivers, is there a *man* sitting beside you? I thought that big lump was your blanket, but that's someone's shoulder!" Her mom gasps. "Identify yourself, sir."

Grinning, I scoot closer so the camera can see my face. "Evening, Mrs. Ivers. Or morning, I guess."

"Mrs. Ivers lives in Florida. Call me Josie."

I swallow a laugh. "Josie. I'm Logan."

Another gasp. "*The* Logan?"

"Yes, Mom. *The* Logan," Grace confirms with a sigh.

Josie looks from me to Grace, then puts on a stern face. "Sweetie, I'd like a moment alone with Mr. Logan. Go take a walk or something."

My alarmed gaze flies to Grace, who looks like she's trying not to laugh. "Hey, you said it was cool," she murmurs. Then she plants a kiss on my cheek. "I've gotta pee, anyway. You two go nuts."

Panic fills my gut as my girlfriend hops off the bed and literally *abandons* me. Leaving me at her mother's mercy. Fucking hell. I should have hid when I had the chance.

The moment Grace leaves the room, Josie says, "Is she gone?"

"Yup." I gulp.

"Good. Don't worry, kid, I'll be quick. And I'm only going to say this once, so you'd better listen carefully. Gracie told me she was giving you another chance, and I fully supported that decision." Josie peers into the camera, her expression glittering with menace. "With that said, if you break my daughter's heart, I will hop on the first plane out of here, show up at your door, and beat you to death with a pillowcase full of soap bars."

Despite the terrified shiver evoked by the threat, I can't stop the laugh that flies out of my throat. Jesus. That's a very specific form of violence.

But when I answer, the humor is gone and my voice is gruff. "I won't break her heart," I promise.

"Good. Glad that's settled."

And I swear, this woman has multiple personalities, because in the blink of an eye she's Suzie Sunshine again. "Now tell me all about yourself, Logan. What's your major? When's your birthday? What's your favorite color?"

Swallowing another wave of laughter, I indulge her random questions, which she spits out in rapid fire. I don't mind, though. Grace's mother is hilarious, and it only takes a few seconds to figure out where Grace got her sense of humor and tendency to babble incoherently.

Three minutes into the chat, Josie's phone rings. She says she needs to take it and promises she'll ping us right back, and then the screen goes black. I'm about to put down the laptop, but when I hear footsteps nearing the door, I suddenly have an idea.

AKA the perfect payback for Grace's desertion.

Just as the door opens, I look intently at the screen and act like I'm still chatting with her mother. "—And she stuck her finger in my ass when she was blowing me, which was fucking incredible. I never thought I'd enjoy having anything up there, but—"

Grace screams in horror.

"Oh my God!" She dives onto the bed and grabs the laptop. "Mom, don't listen to him! He's just joking—" She stops abruptly, blinking at the screen before turning to glare at me. "You are *such* an asshole."

I curl over with laughter, which only makes her angrier, and soon she's batting at me with her teeny fists, as if they'll actually do any damage.

"You're the worst!" she yells, but she's giggling even as she pounds those futile fists at me. "I actually thought you told her that!"

"That was the point." I howl in laughter, then roll us both over so she's on her back and I'm looming over her. "Sorry. Couldn't help myself."

Grace reaches up and flicks my forehead. "Jerk."

My jaw drops. "Did you just flick me?"

She flicks me again.

"Did you just flick me *again*?"

Now she's the one howling, because I'm tickling the shit out of her. And as she squirms on the bed and tries to escape my relentless fingers, I reach several conclusions.

One, I've never had more fun with a girl in my entire life.

Two, I never want this to end.

And three…

I think I might be falling in love with her.

CHAPTER 28

Grace

"HE JUST SHOWED UP IN the middle of your study session?" Ramona looks highly amused as she reaches for her coffee. This is the first time I've seen her since our awkward meet-up at the beginning of the month, and I'm surprised by how comfortable it feels. There haven't been any lags in the conversation, no bitterness on my part, and she seems genuinely interested in what's been going on in my life.

"Yep," I answer. "Pretending he was dropping off coffee for me, but we both knew that was bullshit."

Ramona grins. "So John Logan is the jealous type. Honestly? Not a shocker. Hockey players are wired with aggression. They're these big alpha dudes, going all caveman when someone tries to steal the puck from them."

"Am I the puck in this scenario?"

"Pretty much, yeah."

I roll my eyes. "Well, screw that. If anything, *I'm* the one who should be jealous. Do you realize how many girls throw themselves at him? It happens all the time, even when I'm with him. We did have one incredibly satisfying run-in, though." I pause for effect. "We bumped into Piper at the theater in Hastings."

Ramona gasps. "Oooh. Shit. What did she say?"

Satisfaction surges through me. "At first she was super sweet, but that's probably because she didn't notice I was there. She flirted with him, but it was obvious he wasn't reciprocating, so she started talking about hockey instead, and then suddenly she realized I was *with* him, and not just standing *near* him, and it was like she'd walked into a serial killer's dungeon. Pure horror."

Ramona snickers.

"Logan introduced me as his girlfriend, and I swear she looked ready to murder me." I'm gleefully vindictive as I recount the tale. "Then she huffed off and went to join her friends."

"Who was she with?"

"Some chicks I didn't recognize." I pause. "And Maya. Who, by the way, didn't even say hello to me."

That doesn't seem to surprise Ramona. "Maya thinks you hate her," she admits. "You know, for her role in the whole Twitter thing."

"I don't hate her." Shrugging, I take a bite of my chocolate-banana muffin. "But I have no desire to hang out with her, either. We have nothing in common."

I don't miss the way Ramona winces as if the accusation had been directed at *her*. But that wasn't my intention. The two of us had a lot of fun together. One time in high school, we'd stayed up talking for an entire night. I don't even remember what we talked about, just that it went on forever.

Sorrow twines around my insides. I miss that. Other than Daisy, I haven't made any female friends this semester, and although Daisy and I are close, we're nowhere near as close as Ramona and I used to be.

As if reading my mind, her voice softens. "I miss you, Gracie. I really miss you."

My heart clenches. "I miss you too, but…"

But what? *I don't trust you? I haven't forgiven you?* I'm not sure how I feel about our friendship, and I'm not ready to dissect it yet.

"But I think it's better if we keep doing the slow thing," I finish. Then I paste on an encouraging smile. "So what have you been up to? How are your classes?"

She spends a few minutes telling me about her drama courses and some parties she went to, but there's a shadow in her eyes that concerns me. Her voice lacks the carefree pitch I'm used to hearing, and even her appearance feels a bit…off. Her eye makeup is thicker. Her top is tighter than usual, breasts practically hanging out of it. Awful as it sounds, she looks washed up and trashy. In the past, she could pull off trashy no problem and make it *sexy*, because she had the confidence to back it up. But right now, her swagger is noticeably absent.

The conversation switches to our families, and we end up staying at the Coffee Hut for another forty minutes, catching each other up on what our parents have been up to and laughing about their antics. When I announce I need to get to class, her smile fades, but she simply nods and stands up. We toss our empty cups in the waste bin, hug goodbye, and go our separate ways.

Watching her walk away, with her shoulders hunched and her hands in the pockets of her jeans, tugs at my heart. Am I a shitty friend for continuing to keep her at a distance? I honestly don't know anymore.

I debate the issue as I walk along the cobblestone path toward the lecture hall of the film theory course I'm taking as an elective this semester. I'm climbing the steps of the ivy-covered building when my phone rings. It's Logan.

I stifle a sigh as I press the button to answer, hoping he's not calling to apologize again for yesterday's coffee stunt. I still haven't decided if his showing up during my study session with my psych partner was annoying, cute, or both. He ended up coming back later that night and we had a long talk about trusting each other, and I think we managed to reach an understanding about boundaries.

"Hey, gorgeous. Good, I caught you before you went into class."

The sound of his husky voice makes me smile. "Hey. What's up?"

"I wanted to run something by you. Turns out Dean and Tuck are going to a concert in Boston Saturday night and they decided to make a weekend out of it, getting a hotel room for a couple nights and all that. And Garrett is staying with Hannah until Sunday, so…"

He pauses, and I can practically envision the blush on his cheeks. One thing I never expected? Logan blushes when he's nervous, and it's frickin' adorable.

"I thought maybe you'd want to spend the weekend with me."

Excitement ripples through me. Nerves, too, but not a crazy amount. We've been an "official" couple for almost three weeks, and not once has Logan pushed me to have sex. He hasn't even brought it up, actually, which I find both perplexing and reassuring.

And he's quick to offer that reassurance again, adding, "No expectations, by the way. I'm not inviting you to, like, a three-day fuck fest or anything."

I snort. My boyfriend, ever the wordsmith.

"I'll even throw out all the condoms in the house, if you want. You know, to eliminate temptation."

I choke down a laugh. "That's very thoughtful of you."

His voice thickens. "I just want to fall asleep with you. And wake up with you. And go down on you, if you're in the mood for a John Logan orgasm."

The laugh flies out, and he gives an answering one that slides into my ear and makes me light-headed.

"I would love to stay over this weekend," I say firmly. "Oh. But I just remembered. I'm supposed to have dinner with my dad on Sunday night. Would you be able to drop me off at his house around six?"

"No problem." There's a beat. "You're not going to tell him where you spent the weekend, are you?"

I blanch. "God. Of course not. I don't want to give him a heart attack. He still tries to tie my shoelaces for me sometimes."

Logan chuckles. "I'm hitting up the grocery store tomorrow. Is there anything special you want me to pick up? Snacks? Ice cream?"

"Oooh, yes. Ice cream. Mint chocolate chip."

"Done. Anything else?"

"No, but I'll text you if I think of something." My heart races faster than it should, considering we're just talking about a weekend visit. It's not like we're eloping, for God's sake. Yet my entire body is crackling with anticipation, because three uninterrupted days with Logan sounds like absolute heaven.

"So I'll swing by and grab you after your last class tomorrow? You're done around five, right?"

"Yep."

"'Kay. I'll text when I'm on my way. Later, gorgeous."

"Logan?" I blurt out before he can hang up.

"Yeah?"

I take a deep breath. "Don't throw out the condoms."

CHAPTER 29

Grace

It's Friday night. Logan and I are tangled up together on his living room couch, about to watch a horror movie he chose off the film channel on his TV. When we got back from dinner at the fish and chips place in Hastings, I figured we'd go upstairs and rip each other's clothes off. You know, so I could give him my flower, as my mother would say. Instead, he surprised me by suggesting a movie.

I suspect he's trying not to seem overeager, but the heated glances he keeps casting my way tell me he wants it as much as I do. Still, I'm not against taking it slow. Letting the tension build, the anticipation simmer.

"I can't believe this is what you chose," I complain as the opening credits flash on the screen.

"You told me I could pick," he protests.

"Yeah, because I thought you'd pick something *good*." I glare at the television. "I can already tell this is going to make me angry."

"Wait, angry?" He shoots me a baffled look. "I thought you were bitching because you didn't want to be *scared*."

"Scared? Why would I be scared?"

Laughter bubbles out of his throat. "Because it's a scary movie. A ghost is killing people in gruesome ways, Grace."

I roll my eyes. "Horror movies don't scare me. They piss me off because the characters are always so frickin' stupid. They make the worst decisions possible, and we're supposed to feel sorry for them when they die? No way."

"Maybe these characters will be smart, levelheaded adults who do everything right but still get killed," he points out.

"There's a *ghost* in the house and they choose to stay there. The levelheaded response? *Leave.*"

He tugs on a strand of my hair, his tone taking on a chastising note. "Just you wait—there's going to be a good reason for why they can't leave the house. I'll bet you five bucks."

"You're on."

We settle in for the movie, Logan on his back, and me snuggled up beside him with my head on his chest. He strokes my hair as the first scene fills the screen. It's an incredibly *un*-scary cold open involving a busty blonde, an unseen malevolent force, and a scalding shower. The blonde meets her grisly end by burning alive—the evil spirit, of course, has ghosted the water temperature. Logan tries to give me a high-five after the death scene, which I refuse to reciprocate because I actually feel bad for the girl. Kudos to her—the only decision she makes is to take a shower, and who can fault her for that?

The movie unfolds in the most predictable way. A group of college students conduct paranormal experiments in the ghost house, and then bam—the first one dies.

"Here it comes," I say gleefully. "The *levelheaded* reason for why they stay in the house."

"Watch, the ghost won't let them leave," Logan guesses.

He guesses wrong.

On the screen, the characters argue about whether they should go, and one of the girls announces, "We're doing important work here, guys! We're *proving* the existence of paranormal entities! Science *needs* this. Science needs *us.*"

I burst out laughing, shuddering against Logan's rock-hard chest. "Did you hear that, Johnny? Science needs them."

"I fucking hate you," he grumbles.

"Five bucks…" I say in a singsong voice.

His hand slides down to pinch my butt, making me squeak in surprise. "Go ahead and gloat. You win the battle by getting five bucks out of me, but I win the war."

I sit up. "How do you figure?"

"Because you still have to sit through the rest of this movie, and you're going to hate every second of it. I, on the other hand, am enjoying it immensely."

The jerk is absolutely right.

Unless…

As he refocuses his attention on the movie, I nestle close again, only this time I don't rest my hand on the center of his chest. I plant it lower, mere inches from the waistband of the sweatpants he changed into after dinner. He doesn't seem to notice. He's too engrossed in the movie. Ha. He won't be for long.

With the utmost nonchalance, I drag my hand to where the hem of his white wife-beater has ridden up slightly. Then I sneak my fingers beneath it and lightly stroke the hard plane of his stomach, and his breath hitches. Fighting a smile, I flatten my palm and stop moving it. After a moment, he relaxes.

On the screen, the idiot troupe of paranormal "experts" attempts to record the spirit's voice using a contraption right out of *Ghostbusters*.

I scoot up and kiss Logan's neck.

He tenses, and then a chuckle escapes his lips. Low and mocking. "Won't work, baby…"

"What won't work?" I ask innocently.

"What you're trying to do right now."

"Mmm-hmmm. I'm sure it won't."

I tease him with soft kisses on the side of his neck, angling my body so he'll be sure to feel the heat of my pussy against his thigh. God. *Pussy*. I'm even starting to think like him now. He's corrupted me with the dirty words he whispers when we fool around, and I like it. I like the thrill of being bold and wanton, and I *love* the way his warm flesh quivers when I taste him with my tongue.

His head is turned toward the screen, but I know he's no longer paying attention to the movie. The bulge in his sweatpants grows, hardens into a long, thick ridge that pushes up against the fabric. I kiss his throat, feeling the strong tendons straining, his Adam's apple fluttering beneath my lips.

When he speaks, his voice is so raspy it sends a shiver through me. "Do you want to go upstairs?"

I lift my head and meet his eyes. They're heavy-lidded, hazy. I nod.

He doesn't shut off the movie. He just hops to his feet, pulls me up with him, and leads me upstairs, holding my hand the entire time. His bedroom is a lot tidier than the last time I saw it. The night I showed up to yell at him for that stunt with Morris. God, it feels like a lifetime ago.

We stand two feet apart. He doesn't move. Doesn't touch me. He simply stares, with what can only be described as wonder shining in his eyes.

"You're so beautiful."

Hardly. I'm wearing faded jeans and a loose striped shirt that keeps falling over one shoulder, and my hair is a tousled mess because it was insanely windy outside earlier. I know I don't *look* beautiful, but the way he's gazing at me…I *feel* it.

I reach for the bottom of my shirt, then pull it over my head and let it fall to the ground. His nostrils flare when my skimpy bikini-style bra is revealed. Holding his gaze, I bring my hands behind my back and undo the tiny clasp, and then the bra falls away, too.

Logan sucks in a breath. He's seen my breasts before. He's seen me naked, actually. But the hunger in his eyes, the glittering admiration… it's like he's looking at me for the first time.

I wiggle out of my jeans and panties, and approach him with confidence that startles me. I should be nervous, but I'm not. My hands are steady as I tug his wife-beater off him. God, his bare chest never fails to make me light-headed. It's sculpted. Masculine. So fucking perfect.

He doesn't say a word when I ease his sweatpants down. He's not wearing boxers. His erection juts out, hard and imposing, and when I curl my fingers around it, he makes a desperate noise at the back of his throat.

But he still doesn't touch me. His arms remain plastered to his sides, and he stands completely motionless. I don't think he's even blinking.

"Is there a reason your hands aren't all over me right now?" I tease.

"I'm trying to go slow," he says miserably. "If I touch you, I won't be able to stop, and then I'll be inside you and—"

I shut him up with a firm kiss, locking my hands at the nape of his neck. "That's kind of the point. You getting inside me." Then I nibble on his bottom lip, and just like that, the thread of control he was clinging to snaps like an elastic band.

Growling against my lips, he backs me toward the bed, his strong body pressed tight to mine, his erection trapped between us.

My calves bump the edge of the bedframe, and I tumble backward with a screech, pulling him down with me. We land on the bed with a thud that makes us laugh. The sheets smell like lemon laundry detergent, clean and inviting, and the fragrance, mingled with the heady male scent of him, succeeds in fogging my brain. His body ripples with urgency as he kisses me again. He was right to warn me—he doesn't stop kissing me, not even to come up for air. Doesn't stop touching me. *Everywhere.* He hungrily explores my neck, my breasts, my belly, and then he's between my legs, his tongue slicking over my clit, hot and greedy.

I used to be so self-conscious when my high school boyfriend did this to me. It was always too intimate, made me feel exposed, but with Logan I'm too consumed with pleasure to care how vulnerable this position makes me.

My hips strain to meet him, aching for more, and he chuckles and gives me the contact I crave. He wraps his lips around my clit and sucks, and if I hadn't been lying down, I would have keeled right over. Pleasure shoots up my spine and surges through my bloodstream, and when he pushes one long finger inside me, my mind fragments into a million pieces. I come faster than I expect. Faster than *he* expects, and he groans as I convulse against his face, his tongue and finger working me through the orgasm.

As I crash back to earth, he lifts his head with a soft curse. "I love making you come," he mumbles. "It's so fucking hot." His finger slides out, then in again, and an aftershock of pleasure sizzles through me. "And you're so fucking wet."

I whimper when his finger disappears, but the disappointment is replaced with pulsing excitement, because he's reaching into the top drawer on the night table to grab a condom. Swallowing hard, I watch him roll it down the length of his shaft. Skillfully. God, he's probably rolled on a million condoms in his lifetime. He's pretty much a sexpert.

What if I suck at sex?

My heart gallops at a breakneck speed when he lowers his strong body over mine. His lips brush my temple. Softly. Sweetly. "You sure about this?" he whispers.

I gaze up at him, my worries fading away. "Yes."

His features are taut in concentration as he brings his erection to my opening. He nudges forward, and I tense involuntarily. The intrusion is barely a millimeter deep, but the pressure is intense. His cock is a lot bigger than the one finger he'd just had inside me.

"Are you okay?" His voice is husky, laced with concern.

"Yes," I say again.

Heat unfurls in my core, and my clit pulses in time to my rapid heartbeat. Logan eases in half an inch, where he meets resistance. It's a foreign sensation, but not unpleasant. Beads of sweat dot his forehead, and the tendons of his neck strain, as if he's fighting for control.

Anticipation that borders on dread lodges in my chest. It's probably the worst possible comparison to draw right now, but this reminds me of the first time my mom took me to the salon to get my legs waxed. Lying there while the hot wax was applied to my skin, watching the esthetician grip the corner of the warm strip, anticipating the pain as I waited for her to rip it off.

"I think we need to Band-Aid this," I blurt out. "Forget slow. Just do it fast."

He chokes out a laugh. "I don't want to hurt you." In fact, he's stopped moving altogether, his erection neither plunging nor retreating. Just…there.

"What's the matter, Johnny? Scared?"

Defiance flares in his eyes. "Mocking a guy isn't gonna get you laid, baby."

"Stalling isn't going to, either." I grin up at him. "Come on, *baby*. Deflower me."

Logan keeps one hand on my hip, but lifts the other to my mouth, giving my lower lip a chastising pinch. "Don't rush me, woman." His gaze softens as he sweeps it over my face. "Are you sure?"

"Yes—"

That one measly syllable barely leaves my mouth before he plunges deep. I gasp, the jolt of pain taking me by surprise.

He's all the way inside, and from the tight stretch of his features, I know he's forcing himself to remain still.

"You with me?" he murmurs.

I nod. The pain is already abating. I tentatively move my hips, and his eyes roll to the top of his head. "Jesus Christ," he croaks.

God, why isn't he moving? I feel so completely full, yet oddly empty.

He once again checks in on my mental, emotional and physical state. "How're you doing?"

I roll my eyes. "Great. How about you?"

"I'm dying here." Finally, *finally*, he does something other than lie motionless on top of me. His erection inches out, just slightly, then glides back in.

Pleasure shoots through me. "Oh, do that again."

"You sure? I'm trying to give you time to adjust."

"I'm good. I swear."

His mouth finds mine in a sweet, tender kiss, and then his hips begin to move. Thrusting and retreating in a lazy rhythm that draws a shaky noise from my throat. I hold on tight, digging my fingers into his strong back.

"Wrap your legs around me," he rasps.

I do, and the angle changes immediately, deeper contact, locking our bodies tighter than before. He fills me, over and over again, each long stroke intensifying the ache inside me, until every square inch of skin is hot and tight and screaming for relief. I need more. My clit is swollen, throbbing. I reach between us and rub it, and the extra stimulation is glorious.

Logan's elbows rest on either side of my head as he increases the pace, his hips snapping forward, his lips latched on mine as if he can't bear not kissing me. When he hits a spot deep inside, the tension explodes in an orgasm so intense I don't even make a sound. I arch my spine and slam my eyes shut, my breath stuck in my throat, my lips glued to his.

"Oh *fuck*." He slams in one last time. His back, damp with sweat, trembles beneath my palms as he grunts in release.

His heart hammers against my breasts, and I feel almost smug, because *I* did this to him. I made him curse and groan and wobble as if the world beneath his feet had vanished. I made him come apart.

And he did the same damn thing to me.

AFTERWARD, WE LIE ON OUR sides, facing each other. I'm limp and sated, too lazy to move. But not too lazy to admire the beautiful male body stretched out next to me. He's long and powerful, not a shred of fat on him, just thick muscle stretched tight against bone. His arms are deliciously ripped, his thighs massive.

"You're huge," I remark.

"You calling me pudgy?" he demands, but he's smiling as he says it.

"Don't worry, I like being in bed with a big, manly hockey player." I lazily stroke his biceps. "But seriously, you're huge. Big chest, big legs, big hands—"

"Big dick," he supplies. "Don't forget about the big dick."

"You mean this teeny thing?" My fingers travel to his groin, running over his satin-smooth hardness. I have no idea how he's still hard after what we just did. "Hold on," I tell him. "Let me find a magnifying glass so I can get a better look."

"Shut your mouth, woman." Laughing, he flips me over so I'm pinned under the muscular body I was just admiring. He leans in to kiss my neck—nope, the jerk *doesn't* kiss it. He blows a loud raspberry that makes me shriek in delight. "What were you saying about my dick?"

"Nothing," I squeal. "It's the perfect size for my needs."

He snickers, then rolls over so we're face-to-face again and slips one leg between both of mine. "I haven't done this before," he admits. "You know, lie around naked with a girl, just talking."

"I haven't done the naked part, but my high school boyfriend and I did the lying around talking thing all the time."

"What'd you talk about?"

"Everything. School. Life. TV shows. Whatever came to mind."

"Why'd you guys break up?"

"Brandon got a scholarship to UCLA, I got one to Briar, and we didn't want to have a long-distance relationship. Those never work out."

"They do sometimes," he disagrees.

"I guess. But neither of us wanted to even try, so…" I sigh. "So evidently we didn't have a romance for the ages."

"How come you never had sex?" Logan asks curiously.

"I don't know. Just didn't happen. And it didn't help that we hardly ever got to be alone. My dad had a strict rule about me leaving my bedroom door open, and Brandon's parents were even stricter. We weren't even allowed to hang out upstairs. It had to be in the living room, with his mother spying on us from the kitchen."

He wrinkles his forehead. "I find it hard to believe that you couldn't find some alone time in—how long were you together?"

"Six months. And yeah, obviously there were times, but like I said, it just didn't happen."

One large hand covers my breast, squeezing gently. "Are you saying he seriously never tried to get a piece of this? Maybe he was gay?"

"Trust me, he wasn't. He's actually married now."

Logan's jaw falls open. "Really? Was he older than you?"

"Nope, same age. Apparently he fell head over heels in love with some girl on the first day of college, and they got married this summer. His mother told my dad all about it."

I shiver when the pad of his thumb grazes my nipple, but he doesn't seem to be starting anything up. His cheek rests against the pillow, his features relaxed as he absently caresses me.

"Did you have a girlfriend in high school?" I ask.

He waggles his eyebrows. "I had many."

"Oooh, what a stud."

"There were two serious girlfriends, though. The first one was in freshman year. I lost my virginity to her."

"How old were you? Fifteen?"

"Fourteen." He winks at me. "I started early. That's why I'm so good at it."

I roll my eyes. "And so humble, too." I stop to think about it. "Fourteen seems way too young to be having sex."

"I don't know if you could even call what we did *sex*," he answers with a snort. "The first time lasted about three seconds, if that. Seriously, I got in, came, got out. The times after that, it was ten seconds. If that. I was such a horndog I couldn't control myself when she took her clothes off."

"What about the second girlfriend?"

"That's when I was a junior. We dated for about a year. She was a great girl, kind of spoiled, but I didn't mind because I liked spoiling her." He frowns. "She cheated on me with an older guy. Actually, I think he went to Briar."

"Aw, I'm sorry."

"Broke my fucking heart." He gives an exaggerated groan of pain, then takes my hand and places it on his chest. "I've waited years for someone to show up and put it back together."

I groan, too. From the sheer lameness of that statement. "You should have put that line in your poem."

"I'll write you another one," he promises.

"Oh God. Please don't." A yawn overtakes me, and I twist around to glance at the alarm clock, surprised to find that it's only ten-fifteen. "Why am I so tired?"

"I wore you out, huh?" He smiles smugly. "I was afraid I might've lost my moves during my CS, but I've still got it."

"CS?" His abbreviations drive me nuts sometimes. I'm praying one of these days I'll be able to figure them out on my own.

"Celibacy stretch," he explains.

"It's only been three weeks, horndog."

"Actually, it's been…six months?"

My eyebrows soar. "You haven't had sex in six months?"

"Nope." A sheepish look fills his face. "Not since I met you."

"Bullshit."

Now he looks hurt. "You think I'm lying?"

"No…of course not…" My mind struggles to digest the information. Even before I met the guy, I was well aware of his reputation—I witnessed it firsthand when he stumbled out of that bathroom at the frat party.

And he and I were apart the entire summer. Is he seriously telling me he didn't fool around with someone even *once* during that time? Granted, I didn't either, but I'm not *John Logan*, the manwhore who's slept with half the girls at Briar.

"I almost did," he adds, his features pained. "It was early on in the summer, and you were still ignoring my messages. I went to this chick's place, fully intending to sleep with her, but when she tried to kiss me…I took off. It just didn't feel right."

I'm floored. Utterly floored.

"But *this*…" He leans closer and gently presses his mouth against mine in the sweetest kiss imaginable. "This…" Another kiss. "Feels…" And another one. "Right."

CHAPTER 30

Logan

BEST. WEEKEND. EVER.

I honestly can't remember the last time I smiled this much. Or laughed this much.

Or fucked this much.

Grace and I have been going at it like bunnies since Friday night, and each time is even better than the last. Now it's late Sunday morning, and we're *still* going at it, tangled up in the sheets as my cock plunges into her tight heat. I've been diligent about asking her whether she's sore, but she keeps claiming she's not. And if she *is* sore, then she's powering through it like a champ. Like a hockey player who bandages himself up, throws on his pads, and hits the ice, because the game is *that* important to him.

I guess I'm that important to her. Or maybe she just likes the ridiculous amount of orgasms I've given her. And she's about to get another one. I went down on her for thirty minutes before I couldn't take it anymore, desperately needing to be inside her, and her pussy is still wet and swollen from the ministrations of my tongue. It clutches me like a goddamn vise, while her slender body flexes against mine, her spine arching to meet each hurried thrust.

She's close. I've memorized her responses, the noises she makes and the way her inner muscles ripple around my cock when her orgasm is imminent.

"*Oh.*" She gasps when I rotate my hips, and her eyes glaze over.

"Feels…so… good."

Good doesn't even begin to describe it. It's…fucking *divine*. Pure heaven, right here in this bed. I worship her pussy. I worship *her*.

The base of my spine tingles, pleasure tightening my muscles. I snake my hands beneath her ass and dig my fingers into her firm flesh, locking us tighter, fucking her harder. I come first, my mind scattering, foggy and incoherent. She's right behind me, squeezing the hell out of my dick as she makes a breathy, blissful noise that drives me wild.

Every time after we've had sex this weekend, I've almost blurted out that I love her. And every time, I've clamped my lips together to stop the words from escaping because I'm scared of saying it too soon. I've known her since April, but we weren't dating then. Now we are and it's nearing the one-month mark, but I'm not sure what the etiquette for I-love-you's is. I told my first girlfriend I loved her after two weeks of dating. My second, after five months. So maybe I should split the difference and tell Grace…at the three-month point. Yeah. That seems like an appropriate amount of time.

Once we recover from our respective orgasms, we decide to finally drag ourselves out of bed. It's almost noon and we haven't eaten since we woke up, and my stomach rumbles like the engine of a muscle car. We throw on some clothes, because no matter how many times I try to convince her, Grace refuses to walk around naked in case my roommates come home. I've been teasing her mercilessly about her unwarranted modesty, but I'm quickly discovering that Grace has one incredibly annoying trait—she's always right.

We've just entered the kitchen when footsteps echo from the front hall.

"See!" she gloats at me. "They would have caught us!"

"Trust me, the guys have seen me naked on multiple occasions," I answer dryly.

"Well, they're never going to see *me* naked, not if I can help it."

I suddenly picture Dean ogling her bare tits, and the hot streak of jealousy it triggers makes me realize just how grateful I am that she decided to wear clothes.

But it's not Dean who strides into the kitchen a minute later. It's Garrett, with Hannah on his tail. Although they look startled to find Grace at the counter, they greet her with warm smiles before turning to smirk at me. Smug bastards. I know exactly what's going through their heads—a singsong taunt. *Lo-gan has a girrrrl-friend.*

"Hey." I narrow my eyes. "I thought you guys were crashing at the dorm this weekend."

"I bet you did," Garrett mocks, his gray eyes gleaming.

"Yes, because that's what you told me," I say pointedly.

Hannah walks up to Grace and sticks out her hand. "Hi. We haven't been formally introduced. I'm Hannah."

"I'm Grace."

"I know." Hannah can't seem to wipe the big, stupid smile off her face. "Logan talks about you all the time."

Grace glances at me. "You do?"

"All the livelong day," Garrett confirms, flashing *his* big, stupid smile. "He also writes long, sweeping poems about you and recites them to us in the living room every night."

Hannah snorts.

I give him the finger.

"Oh, I know about the poems," Grace tells my best friend. "I've already submitted the one he sent me to an anthology press in Boston."

I whirl around to glare at her. "You better be kidding about that."

Garrett gives a hoot of laughter. "Doesn't matter if she is. Because now *I'll* be submitting it."

"I feel left out," Hannah announces. "Why am I the only one who hasn't read this poem?"

"I'll email it to you," Grace offers, which brings a *hell-no* growl from my lips.

"So what are we eating?" Garrett marches over to the fridge. "I'm starving, and *someone* didn't want to stop at the diner for brunch."

"I'm there four days a week," his girlfriend protests. "It's the last place I want to go on my days off."

He pulls out two cartons of eggs. "You guys feel like omelets?"

We're all in agreement, so Garrett gets busy cracking eggs while Hannah and Grace chop vegetables at the counter. My job is to set the table, which takes all of thirty seconds. Smirking, I plop down on a stool and watch them work.

"You're doing dishes," Hannah warns as she hands Garrett a cutting board laden with green peppers.

I'm cool with that. I lean my elbows on the counter and ask, "So why'd you guys come back early?"

"Because Allie and Sean are currently engaged in an epic fight." She glances at Grace. "My roommate and her boyfriend."

"Soon-to-be *ex* from the sounds of it," Garrett remarks from the stove. "I don't think I've ever heard two people yell at each other like that before."

Hannah sighs. "Sometimes they really bring out the worst in each other. But on the flip side, they also bring out the best in each other. That's why they keep breaking up and getting back together. I thought for sure it would stick this time, but who knows."

A mouthwatering aroma begins wafting through the kitchen. Garrett's not the greatest cook, but he makes damn good omelets. Ten minutes later, he serves us fluffy, golden goodness loaded with cheese, mushrooms, and peppers, and the four of us settle around the table. It feels like a double date, which is surreal as hell. Up until last year, Garrett wasn't interested in girlfriends, and up until last month, neither was I.

I like it, though. Hannah and Grace are getting along. The conversation's lively. We laugh a lot. I can't remember the last time I felt so at peace, and by the time we finish eating, I don't even care that I'm stuck doing dishes.

Grace takes pity on me and helps me clear the table, then follows me to the sink, where I quickly rinse each plate before loading them in the dishwasher.

"I can see why you wanted her." Her voice is barely audible, but wistful enough that it makes my shoulders go rigid.

When I realize she's gazing at Hannah, guilt pricks my heart, bringing a sharp sting of pain. I hadn't mentioned Hannah's name when I told Grace about her in April, but I *had* admitted to liking my best friend's girlfriend. Clearly Grace has put two and two together.

"She's funny. And really pretty," Grace says awkwardly.

I dry my hands with a dishrag and grasp her chin, drawing her gaze to mine. "I didn't want *her*," I murmur. I nudge Grace's head in the direction of the table again. "I wanted *that*."

Garrett has just tugged Hannah into his lap, one arm wrapping around her as he plants a kiss on the tip of her nose. The fingers of his free hand thread through her dark hair, and she leans closer to whisper something in his ear that makes him chuckle. The way they look at each other…the reverence with which he touches her…they're disgustingly in love, and anyone can see it.

Including Grace, who turns back to me with a smile. "Yeah. Who wouldn't want that?"

Once the kitchen is squeaky clean, we disappear upstairs again, but not to have sex. We've barely slept this weekend thanks to our fuck-a-thon—not complaining, by the way—so we decide to take a nap. I set the alarm to make sure we don't oversleep, because I'm supposed to drive Grace to her dad's house at six.

We climb under the covers and I yank her warm body toward me, spooning her from behind. A contented sigh slips out, but right as I start to drift off, her voice teases me back to a state of alertness.

"John?" she murmurs.

My heart squeezes. I don't know why it does that every time she uses my first name. She calls me Logan too, and Johnny when she's making fun of me, but it's only John that floods my chest with emotion like this.

"Mmmm?"

"Do you want to come for dinner?"

I stiffen, and she doesn't miss the response. She releases a soft laugh and adds, "You're allowed to say no. But…I mean, you've already kind of met my mother, and just so you know, my dad isn't too scary. If anything, you might find him boring. He talks about science a lot."

Right. She'd mentioned that he was a biology professor. That's not what worries me, though. The last time I met a girl's parents, I was in high school, and it wasn't a big deal back then. If anything, it was unavoidable, considering my girlfriend and I lived with our parents.

And yeah, I've already Skyped with Grace's mom, but that hadn't felt like an official meeting or anything. It had been fun and casual, no big deal at all. But meeting Grace's father—in *person*—feels like a big deal.

Says the guy who's in love with her.

Good point. Hell, I ventured into BIG DEAL territory the moment I realized how I feel about her.

"Will he mind if I come?"

"Not at all. Mom already told him I had a boyfriend, so he's actually been bugging me about meeting you," she confesses.

"Okay, then sure." My arm tightens around her. "I'd love to."

Grace

IT'S A PLEASANTLY WARM EVENING, so Dad decides we should eat on the patio. He grills up some steaks on the barbecue, while Logan and I take care of the rest of dinner. I'm in charge of the baked potatoes, Logan's handling the salad. But watching the sheer concentration with which he slices those tomatoes, you'd think he was vying for a slot on Top Chef.

"Relax, Johnny," I tease. "Your salad preparation expertise has no bearing on whether he'll like you or not."

Besides, I think my dad already likes him. He hasn't cross-examined Logan like I expected him to, and I think he was secretly relieved when Logan cracked a joke during their introductions. My father always thought Brandon was completely lacking in personality—yep, Mr. I-teach-molecular-biology actually sat me down one day and informed me that my boyfriend was *boring*. Which was totally not the case. Brandon was shy, not boring. When we were alone, that boy had me doubled over in laughter.

But Dad never got to see that, and there's no denying that Logan possesses far more confidence than Brandon ever had. Within five minutes of meeting him, Logan gave my dad a good-natured reprimand for raising me to "hate" hockey, and Dad brings that up again once we're seated at the glass table on the deck.

"Here's the thing, John," he says as he cuts into his T-bone. "Gracie is smart enough to recognize the shockingly inferior level of skill that hockey demonstrates." His eyes twinkle playfully.

Logan mock gasps. "How dare you, sir."

"Face it, kid. Football requires a whole other level of athleticism."

Looking pensive, my boyfriend chews a bite of his baked potato. "All right, little scenario for you. You take every guy on the Bruins roster, throw football gear on them, and stick them on the field. I *guarantee* you they play a solid four quarters of football and kick some serious ass." He smirks. "Now take the Pats, slap on some skates and pads, and put them on the ice—can you honestly tell me they'd be able to play a full three periods, and do it *well*?"

Dad narrows his eyes. "Well, no. But that's because a lot of them probably don't know how to skate."

Logan's smile is triumphant. "But they're operating on a superior level of athleticism," he reminds my father. "Why can't they skate?"

Dad sighs. "Touché, Mr. Logan. Touché."

I snicker.

The remainder of the dinner goes the same way, animated discussions that end with one or both of them grinning. I can't contain the burst of joy in my heart. Seeing them get along is such a relief. Now I've gotten the nod of approval from *both* my parents, whose opinions matter deeply to me.

Dad brings up my mother as the three of us clear the table. "Your mom's thinking of coming to Hastings for Thanksgiving."

"Really?" I'm excited by the news. "Will she stay at the inn, or here at the house?"

"Here, of course. No sense spending money on a hotel room when she has her pick of bedrooms here." Dad balances his plate and the salad bowl in one hand so he can open the sliding door. "I was thinking of taking a few days off and driving up to Boston with her. There are some mutual friends we were talking about visiting."

Any other child of divorce might have gotten their hopes up hearing their parents might take a road trip together, but that ship sailed a long time ago for me. I know my folks are never getting back together—they're much happier apart—but I love that they're still so close. Best friends, even. It's actually kind of inspiring.

To my surprise, after we've thanked Dad for dinner and climbed into Logan's pickup, my parents' relationship is the first thing Logan comments on.

"It's really cool that your folks remained friends after the divorce."

I nod. "I know, right? I thank my lucky stars for it every day. I'd hate it if they were fighting all the time and using me as a pawn or something." Then I tense, realizing that maybe the aftermath of *his* parents' divorce is exactly what I've just described. Logan doesn't talk about it much, and I haven't pushed for details because it's obvious he prefers not to discuss his family.

Especially his father. But that's one subject I *definitely* don't bring up, not for his sake, but my own. Because I'm terrified of revealing my true feelings on the matter—that I think Logan is making a huge mistake quitting hockey after graduation.

He insists that running the business and taking care of his father is what's best for the family, but I disagree. What's best for Ward Logan is a long stint in rehab followed by extensive addiction therapy, but hey, what do I know? A year of psych classes does not a psychologist make.

"Your dad is awesome." Logan's gaze is glued to the windshield, but there's no missing the sadness in his voice. "He seems like the kind of man who'd always be there for you. You know, like he wouldn't desert you in the hospital if you broke your ankle or something."

His example is so alarmingly specific it makes me frown. "Did...did that happen to you?"

"No." He pauses. "To my mom, though."

The frown deepens. "Your father deserted her in the hospital?"

"No, not really. He—you know what, don't worry about it. Long story."

His hand rests on the gearshift, and I reach over and cover it with mine. "I want to hear it."

"What's the point?" he mumbles. "It's in the past."

"I still want to hear it," I say firmly.

He lets out a weary breath. "It happened when I was seven or eight. I was in school so I didn't see how it went down, but I heard about it from my aunt afterward. Actually, the whole neighborhood heard about it, that's how loud she was screaming when my dad finally dragged his ass home."

"Still not telling me what happened..."

He keeps his eyes on the road. "It was winter, the weather was shit, and Mom slipped on a patch of ice while shoveling the driveway." Bitterness lines his tone. "Dad was inside, not plastered, but he'd had a few. Couldn't even be bothered to do the shoveling, or at least help her. Anyway, she fucked up her ankle real bad, pretty much shattered it, and he heard her yelling for help and ran outside. He didn't want to move her because they weren't sure how bad the damage was, but he did throw a blanket on her while they waited for the ambulance."

Logan's shoulders are set in a tight line, as inflexible as his jaw. I'm not sure I want to hear the rest of the story.

"So the ambulance showed up, but Dad didn't ride with her. He told her he'd follow her in the car, that way he'd be able to pick me and Jeff up from school. And that was the last any of us saw of him for three days."

Logan angrily shakes his head. "He got in the car and took off. I have no idea where he went. All I know is that he didn't go to the hospital, where his wife had to have two surgeries to fix her ankle. And he didn't go to the school, because Jeff and I waited for hours and he didn't show. One of the teachers finally noticed we were still there, made some calls, and took us to the hospital, and my aunt drove down from Boston and stayed with us while Mom was recovering, because Dad had gone AWOL."

I suck in a breath. "Why did he do it?"

"Who fucking knows? I guess he realized he'd have to step up and take care of the kids and the house and *her*, and the pressure freaked him out. He went on a three-day bender and didn't visit her at the hospital once."

Indignation on Logan's behalf seizes my chest and makes my hands tremble. What the hell kind of husband does that? What the hell kind of *father*?

Logan has read my thoughts, because he turns his head with a gentle look. "I know you're hating on him right now, but you need to understand something. He's not a bad man—he's got a disease. And trust me, he hates himself for it. More than you or I could ever hate him." His breath comes out wobbly. "When he was sober, he was actually a really good dad. He taught me how to skate, taught me everything he knows about cars. We fixed up this sweet GTO one summer. Spent hours together in the garage."

"So why did he start drinking again?"

"I don't know. I don't think *he* even knows. It's the kind of thing where…like if you were stressed out, you might have a glass of wine, right? Or a beer, a whiskey, something to calm you down. But he can't have just one. He has two, or three, or ten, and he just can't stop. It's an addiction."

I bite my lip. "I know that. But how long does he get to keep using that addiction as an excuse for his actions? I think there comes a point where you have to stop enabling him."

"We've dragged him to rehab before, Grace. It doesn't stick unless he chooses to do it himself."

"Then maybe you need to cut him off. Let him hit rock bottom so he'll choose to get better."

"And, what, make him homeless?" Logan says softly. "Have bill collectors pounding on his door and repo men showing up at the house? Let his business crash and burn? I know you don't understand it, but we can't write him off. Maybe if he beat the shit out of us or treated us like pieces of garbage, then it might be easier to do that, but he's not abusive, he's self-destructive. We can encourage him to get sober, we can help him keep things afloat, but we won't desert him."

"You're right. I *don't* understand," I admit. "I don't get where this unfailing loyalty is coming from. Especially when you consider the example he set for you—where's *his* loyalty? Where's *his* selflessness?"

Logan flips his palm over and laces his fingers through mine. "That's the other reason I'm doing this. *Because* of the example he set. If I abandon him, then I'm no better than he is. Then *I'm* selfish, and that's something I never want to be. Sometimes I hate him so much I want to kick his teeth in, sometimes I even find myself wishing he'd die, but no matter how frustrating it gets, he's still my father, and I love him." His voice cracks. "I treat him the way I'd want to be treated if I was ever in his position. With patience and support, even when he doesn't deserve it."

Logan falls silent, and my heart constricts, then swells, overflowing with emotion. This guy continues to surprise me. To awe me. He's a better person than I am, better than he gives himself credit for, and if I wasn't sure about it before, then I'm damn well sure of it now.

I love him.

CHAPTER 31

Logan

"BEERS AT MALONE'S?" DEAN ASKS as we leave the arena after what might possibly be the worst game of my entire hockey career.

I grit my teeth. "I have plans with Grace. And even if I didn't, I wouldn't be celebrating at the goddamn bar tonight, man."

He runs a hand through his shower-damp blond hair. "Yeah, it was rough out there. But it's done. Game over. No point in dwelling on it."

Times like these, I wonder why he even plays hockey. For the pussy, maybe? Because from the day he joined the team, Dean has shown a lack of intensity about our sport, which is a damn shame because he happens to be an amazing player. But he has no interest in playing hockey after college, at least not professionally.

"Seriously, dude, quit scowling," Dean orders. "Come to the bar with us. I set the freshman up with a fake ID, so I'm showing him some moves tonight. I could use my wingman."

The "freshman", of course, is Hunter, who Dean has taken under his wing and is well on his way to corrupting.

"Naah, I'll pass. Grace and I are having a movie night."

"Boring. Unless it's naked movie night. Then I approve."

I'm kinda hoping it *is* naked movie night. I desperately need to release all the pent-up tension that's been plaguing me since we lumbered into the locker room after that final buzzer, leaving the sour stench of a 0-5 score in our wake.

Granted, it's just a pre-season game, doesn't count toward our standings, but if we're to take anything from tonight's loss, it's this: we're nowhere near ready—and our first game is next fucking week. Plus, we got shut out by St. Anthony's, which only pisses me off more, because St. A's team has a roster of dickheads and douchebags.

I'm still stewing about the game when I walk through Grace's door a short while later, and she clucks in sympathy when she sees my face.

"Didn't go well, huh?" She comes up and wraps her arms around me, her soft lips brushing a soothing kiss at the base of my throat.

"The team's still not gelling," I answer, aggravated. "Coach keeps rearranging the lines, trying to find a good fit, but he might as well be jamming random puzzle pieces together."

It's frustrating, especially since Dean and I are a well-oiled machine when we play on the same line. But we're also the best D-men on the roster, so Coach split us up in the hopes that we'd help the other lines not suck so hard. I'm paired up with Brodowski now, who needs so much work I'm pretty much manning our defensive zone alone.

"I'm sure it'll get better," she assures me. "And I promise, I'll be cheering for you in the stands next week."

I grin. "Thanks. I know what a big sacrifice it is for you."

Grace sighs. "The biggest." She swipes a T-shirt off the floor and tosses it in the laundry basket. "I just want to finish tidying up, and then we can put on the movie. Is that okay?"

"Sure."

I kick off my shoes and unzip my jacket, watching as she wanders around plucking random items of clothing—all belonging to her roommate, I realize. God, Daisy must love her. Awesome roommate and OCD-ridden maid all rolled into one cute package.

Grace bends over to grab a sock that's wedged between Daisy's desk and bed, and the sight of her round ass jutting out makes me groan.

She glances over her shoulder. "You okay?"

"Oh yeah. Stay in that position for a minute. That *exact* position."

"Perv."

"You're right. How *dare* I enjoy the sight of my girlfriend's sexy ass sticking up in the air?" My throat runs dry. "I want to fuck you just like that tonight."

Her breath catches. "I can live with that."

I chuckle at the teasing response. "Then get on the bed. Naked. Now. Bonus orgasms for speed."

She gets rid of her top, leggings and panties in record time, and I snicker as I reach for my zipper. "Jeez, one would think I haven't been meeting your needs."

Her gaze tracks the movement of my fingers as I drag my fly down. I love the way she looks at me. Hungry and appreciative, like she can't get enough.

A minute later, I'm naked and covered with a condom. No foreplay necessary for me tonight—I'm hard as a rock and raring to go—but that doesn't stop me from playing with *her* for a bit.

I crawl between her legs and kiss her inner thighs. Her skin is baby-smooth, silky beneath my tongue, and when I lick my way up to her clit, her fingers tangle in my hair to trap me there. Chuckling, I give her what she wants. Soft, slow licks and gentle kisses, until she's squirming on the mattress. I don't let her finish, though. Her first orgasm is always the most intense, and I want to feel her squeezing my dick and hear her moan my name when she comes.

I plant one last kiss, then grip her hips and roll her over. "All fours, baby. Bring that sweet ass toward me."

Bring it she does. Her firm bottom bumps my groin as I rise on my knees behind her, and then she rubs it against my shaft, sending a bolt of heat up my spine. Two months together and she's still driving me crazy. Melting my goddamn brain with the pleasure she brings me.

I fist my erection and guide it to the crease of her ass, sliding lower until it nudges her opening. Anticipation heats the air. This is my favorite moment, the hint of suction around my tip, the knowledge that soon she'll be clutching me tight, surrounding me with the warmth of her pussy.

She's so wet I slide right in with my first thrust, filling her to the hilt. I fuck her slowly at first, wanting to prolong it, but each deep stroke scrambles my brain more and more, and soon the slow pace turns into a fast, relentless rhythm that makes me groan with abandon. But for all my talk about screwing her from behind, this position feels too…impersonal. I yank her up so her back is flush against my chest, and I fill my palms with her tits, teasing her nipples as I give an upward thrust.

Her head lolls to the side, and I take advantage of it, pressing my lips to her neck. I breathe her in, sucking on her smooth, fragrant flesh as I drive my cock inside her. Quick, shallow thrusts that make both of us gasp. I skim one hand down her body, grazing her tits, dancing over her belly, until I find her clit and rub it with my index finger, gentle circles that contrast the fast strokes of my cock.

We've gotten good at timing our responses, synchronizing our bodies so that we shudder in release at the same time. We collapse in a sweaty tangle of limbs, breathing hard from the orgasms, kissing frantically even as we come down from the euphoric high.

Afterward, she gets her laptop, and we cuddle under the blanket and start the movie. It's her pick, so naturally we're watching an old Jean-Claude Van Damme cheese fest that's bound to put us in hysterics. We're only five minutes in, however, when Grace's cell phone rings.

She drapes across my chest to check the display, but doesn't answer the call. "It's Ramona," she says when I offer a quizzical look. "Not in the mood to talk to her right now. Let's keep watching."

The phone rings again.

Grace makes a frustrated noise and presses *ignore*.

I'm not sure I blame her. Dean told me he ran into Ramona at the bar a few times, but I haven't seen her since last semester. And I don't particularly want to.

"She probably just wants to hang out," Grace says, then switches the phone to vibrate.

She's about to rest her head on my chest, but she barely makes contact before a loud buzz shakes the mattress. "O-kay then, guess I should've picked silent instead of vibrate." She sits up again, snatches the cell, and freezes.

"What's wrong?" I try to peek at the phone.

She flips it over so I can see the screen. *SOS* is all it says. Sent by— who else?—Ramona.

Maybe I'm a cynical bastard, but this smacks of manipulation to me. Grace wasn't answering, so Ramona decided to *make* her answer.

"I have to call her back."

I smother a sigh. "Babe, she's probably trying to scare you into calling—"

"She's not." Grace's expression is stricken. "We don't abuse the SOS. *Ever.* In all the years we've been friends, we've only SOS'd each other twice. I did it when I thought I was being followed by some creep in Boston this one time, and she did it when she blacked out at a party senior year and woke up with no idea where she was. This is real, Logan."

Even if I'd wanted to argue, she's already hopping off the bed and making the call.

Grace

I'm actually frightened. Palms sweating, heart racing, lungs burning. But I guess that's the appropriate response to finding out your friend is being held against her will by a bunch of thugs. When she had to sneak into the bathroom to call you because the thugs in question tried confiscating her phone after she announced she wanted to leave.

In the passenger side of Logan's truck, I drum my fingers against my thighs in an anxious rhythm. I want to beg him to drive faster, but he's already speeding. And he won't stop barking out questions at me, questions to which I have no fucking answers, because Ramona hung up on me five minutes ago and is no longer picking up her phone.

"What hockey players?" Logan demands for the third time in ten minutes. "Briar guys?"

"For the last time, *I don't know.* I told you everything she told me, Logan, so please stop harassing me."

"Sorry," he mutters.

We're both on edge. Neither of us knows what we'll find when we reach the motel, and as we race toward Hastings, my conversation with Ramona buzzes through my mind like a swarm of bees.

"I thought there would be other people here, but it's just the players. And they won't let me leave, Gracie! They promised to give me a ride home and now they're saying I should crash in their room, and I don't want to, and I don't even have my purse with me! Just my phone! I don't have money for a cab, and nobody will come get me...and..."

At that point she'd started to cry, and fear had flooded my stomach. I've known Ramona a long time. I know the difference between her crocodile tears and her real ones. I know when she's fake-panicking, or freaking the fuck out. I know what she sounds like when she's calm, and what she sounds like when she's terrified.

And right now, she's terrified.

The ride into town is thick with tension. My muscles are coiled so tight, my body actually feels sore by the time we reach the motel. The L-shaped brick building is located on the outskirts of Hastings, and although it's nowhere near as nice as the inn on Main Street, it's not a fleabag shithole either.

When Logan pulls into the parking lot, his blue eyes immediately darken. I follow his gaze and notice the shiny red bus parked on the pavement.

"That's the St. Anthony's bus," he says in a curt voice. "They're playing Boston College tomorrow, so I guess it makes sense for them to crash here for the night."

"Wait, this is the team you played against tonight?"

He nods. "They're assholes, each and every one of them, coaching staff included."

My concern escalates. I've heard Logan trash-talk opponents before, but even when he does it, I can tell there's a level of respect there. Like the rivalry with Harvard—Logan will bitch about it, but you'll never catch him saying the Harvard players are hacks, or attacking their character the way he just did with these St. Anthony's guys.

"Are they really that bad?" I ask.

He kills the engine and unbuckles his seatbelt. "Their old captain was suspended last season for breaking a Briar player's arm. Our guy didn't even have the puck when Braxton smashed into him. Their new captain is an entitled shithead from Connecticut who spit on the guys on our bench tonight every time he skated by them. Disrespectful POS."

We hop out of the pickup and march right up to Room 33, which was one of the few details I'd managed to pry out of Ramona while she'd been sobbing. Logan grasps my arm and moves me behind him in a protective gesture.

"Let me handle this," he orders.

The deadly gleam in his eyes is too terrifying to argue with.

He pounds his fist on the door, so hard he rattles the doorframe. Loud music blares inside the room, along with raucous male laughter that turns my veins to ice. It sounds like they're having a raging party in there.

A moment later, a tall guy with dark hair and a goatee appears in the threshold. He takes one look at Logan's Briar jacket and curls his lips into a sneer. "What the fuck do you want?"

"I'm here to pick up Ramona," Logan snaps.

Rap music blasts from the open door, the bass line vibrating beneath my sneakers. I peek from behind Logan's broad shoulders, trying to see what's happening inside the room. All I can make out is a wall of big, bulky bodies. Four, maybe five of them. Horror eddies in my belly. Oh God. Where's Ramona? And why the *hell* did she think it was a good idea to party with these guys—*alone?*

"Go home, asshole." The St. Anthony's player smirks. "She just got here. She doesn't need a ride."

Logan's jaw turns to stone. "Get out of my way, Keswick."

The music dies abruptly, replaced by a beat of silence, then the menacing thump of heavy footsteps as Keswick's teammates come up behind him.

A blond behemoth with ice-blue eyes gives Logan a mocking smile. "Awww, how sweet. You crashing our after-party, Logan? Yeah, I get it. You want a taste of what it's like to be a champion, huh?"

Logan's answering laugh is humorless. "Yeah, I'm *so* fucking jealous of you for winning a pre-season game, Gordon. Now move aside so I can make sure Ramona is all right, or God help me, I'll—"

"You'll what?" another player jeers. "Beat us down? Go ahead and try, buddy. Not even a bruiser like you can take on five dudes at once."

"Unless it's in the ass," someone pipes up. "I bet he likes it up the ass."

The other players snicker loudly, but Logan is unfazed. He flashes a pleasant smile and says, "As tempting as it is to beat the shit out of you—*all* of you—I think I'd rather stay out of jail tonight. But I'm happy to knock on every goddamn door in this place until I find Coach Harrison's room, and then I'm going to blow the whistle on this little sausage party you're having and let *him* deal with you."

Keswick is smug. "He'll probably join us. Coach doesn't give a shit if we get wasted after a game."

"Yeah? Well, I'm sure he'll give a shit about what you're shoving up your nose."

Logan takes a step forward, and I instinctively tense, expecting him to throw a punch. But what he does is tap Keswick on the side of his nose. Drawing my attention to the white specks that are caked under Keswick's nostrils.

Logan bares his teeth in a harsh smile. "Your coke is showing, asshole. Now get the *fuck* out of my way. Stay out here, Grace."

He charges into the room, and I'm left outside, forced into a stare-down with four very pissed off hockey players. Who, apparently, are all hopped up on cocaine. Panic scampers up and down my spine, fast and incessant, and it doesn't ease until Logan reappears less than a minute later.

To my overwhelming relief, Ramona is at his side. Her cheeks are whiter than the coke on Keswick's face, her eyes redder than the bus parked behind us, and she runs into my arms the moment she sees me.

"Oh my God," she whimpers, squeezing me to the point of suffocation. "I'm so glad you're here."

"It's okay. You're okay now." I gently stroke her hair. "Come on, let's go."

I try to lead her away, but she halts, her desperate eyes shooting toward the doorway. "My phone," she stammers. "He took it."

She points at the player Logan referred to as Gordon, and a growl rips out of Logan's mouth as he charges back to the door. "You took her goddamn *phone*? Why? So she wouldn't be able to call for help while you motherfuckers *gangbanged* her?"

I've never seen Logan this enraged. His blue eyes are wild, his broad shoulders trembling. "Give me the phone. Now."

The assholes at the door do a little shuffling around before one of them finally pulls Ramona's iPhone from his back pocket. He hurls it at Logan with lightning speed, but my boyfriend has quick reflexes, and he catches the plastic case before it slaps him in the face.

"Get in the car," he tells us without turning around.

I'm apprehensive to leave him, but Ramona is shaking like crazy, so I force myself to walk away. I keep my gaze fixed on the motel room the entire time, watching as Logan moves in closer and hisses something I can't make out. Whatever it is, it causes every St. Anthony's player to glare bloody murder at him, but none of them act on their volatile impulses. They simply stalk back inside and slam the door behind them.

I slide onto the middle seat of the pickup and Ramona settles in beside me, pressing her cheek against my shoulder. "I was so scared," she moans. "They wouldn't let me go home."

I force her to buckle up, then wrap my arm around her shoulders. "Did they hurt you?" I ask quietly. "Force you…?"

She fervently shakes her head. "No. I swear. I was only there for about an hour, and they were too busy snorting coke and drinking vodka straight from the bottle. It wasn't until right before I called you that they started pawing at me and trying to convince me to strip for them. And when I told them I wanted to leave, they locked the door and wouldn't let me out."

Disapproval hardens my jaw. "God, Ramona. What were you even *doing* with these guys? Why would you agree to hang out with them on your own?"

Another sob flies out of her mouth. "I wasn't supposed to be on my own. Jess and I ran into them after the game and they invited us to the motel, but Jess had to meet up with her dealer first, so she gave me some cab money and said she'd meet me there. But five minutes after I got here, she texted to say she wasn't coming."

My upper arm feels wet, and I realize Ramona's tears have soaked through my sleeve.

"She *bailed* on me and left me alone with them. What kind of friend does that?"

A selfish one.

I bite my tongue and rub her shoulder, and a part of me can't help but feel responsible for what happened to her tonight. I know it's stupid to think that, but I also know I could've prevented this if I'd been more of a presence in her life. Ramona and I had a…balance, I guess. She encouraged me to be impulsive and stop second-guessing myself, and I encouraged her to *not* be impulsive and *start* second-guessing herself.

I force myself to banish the guilt. No. I refuse to take responsibility for this near-catastrophe. Ramona is an adult. *She* made the decision to party with those guys, and she's fucking lucky that I still feel some shred of loyalty toward her and came to her rescue.

That last thought gives me pause, as it suddenly occurs to me that what I did tonight is the same thing I've been criticizing Logan for doing—helping someone who might not deserve it. Allowing years of history and lingering loyalty to drive me to do something I didn't necessarily *want* to do, but felt I *had* to.

I jerk when the driver's door flings open, but it's Logan, sliding behind the wheel with a stony look. When he addresses Ramona, however, his tone is infinitely gentle. "Are you okay? They didn't hurt you?"

"No," she says weakly. "I'm fine." She lifts her head, and the look she gives us is swimming with shame. "Thank you for coming to get me. I'm sorry if I ruined your evening."

"You're welcome," Logan answers. "And don't you fucking worry about our evening, Ramona. The only thing that matters right now is that we got you out of there before shit got out of hand."

His gruff words circle my heart and fill it with warmth. God, I love this guy. I know his opinion of Ramona isn't exactly positive, but he still came to her aid tonight in spite of that, and I love him even more for it.

I'm tempted to lean in and whisper it in his ear. Just tell him how much I love him, but courage eludes me.

Truth is, I'm waiting for him to say it first. I don't know, maybe it's leftover insecurities from what happened in April. Logan *rejected* me, and I'm so afraid of it happening again. I'm afraid of being vulnerable, giving him my heart, only to have him throw it back in my face.

So I stay quiet. So do Ramona and Logan, and the drive back to campus is a silent one.

CHAPTER 32

Logan

THREE DAYS BEFORE OUR FIRST game, the team finally clicks. It's like someone flicked a switch from oh-God-we-suck to we-might-have-a-chance. I still don't think we're one hundred percent there yet, but we've shown improvement during our practices this week, and Coach isn't yelling at us as often, so…progress.

Since midterms are in full swing, Grace and I haven't seen each other in a few days, but we're taking a break from studying to have dinner with her dad tonight. And because I had practice, she cabbed it to Hastings with Ramona, who's visiting her own parents. I'm still not sure how I feel about them rekindling their friendship, but Grace keeps insisting that she won't let Ramona get too close again, and I guess I have to accept that. Besides, after Friday night's sexual-assault-waiting-to-happen, I'm feeling a lot more sympathy toward Ramona. Not to mention a lot more rage toward St. Anthony's.

Did I mention we're facing them in the season opener? Coach isn't gonna like it, but I'm fairly certain I'll be spending a lot of time in the sin bin that night.

I check my phone as I leave the arena. There's a message from Grace, saying she got to her dad's okay.

And a message from Jeff, asking me to call him ASAP.

Shit.

Jeff doesn't usually throw around ASAPs unless it's serious, so I don't waste time calling him back. It takes five rings before he answers, and when he does, he sounds agitated.

"Where the hell have you been the last hour?" he demands.

"Practice. Coach doesn't let us bring our phones on the ice. What's up?"

"I need you to go home and check on Dad."

"Why?" I say uneasily.

"Because I'm at the hospital with Kylie, and I can't fucking do it myself."

"The hospital? What happened? Is she okay?"

"She sliced her hand open making dinner." Jeff sounds panicked. "The ER doctor said it's not as bad as it looks—she'll just need some stitches. But Jesus, I've never seen so much blood, Johnny. They took her in now, so I'm out in the waiting room pacing like a crazy person."

"She'll be okay," I assure him. "Trust the doctors, all right?" But I know Jeff won't relax until he and Kylie are walking out of that emergency room. The two of them have been madly in love since they were fifteen years old.

"What does this have to do with Dad?" I ask.

"I was over at Kylie's, and he called when we were leaving for the ER. He was slurring and mumbling and, I don't know, he might have fallen down? I couldn't understand a fucking word he was saying, and I'm only one fucking person, John. I can't deal with two emergencies at once, okay? So please, just go home and make sure he's all right."

Reluctance jams in my throat like a wad of gum. Christ. I don't want to do that. At all. Except there's no way I can pick a fight with Jeff right now, not when he's freaking out about his girlfriend being in the hospital.

"I'll take care of it," I say roughly.

"Thanks." Jeff hangs up without another word.

With a ragged breath, I text Grace to let her know I might be late for dinner, then head for the parking lot.

I tap my fingers on the steering wheel during the entire drive to Munsen. Dread gathers inside me, growing and tangling in my gut until it becomes a tight knot that brings a rush of nausea to my throat. I don't remember the last time I had to clean up one of my dad's messes. High school, I guess. Once I left for Briar, Jeff became the sole cleaner-upper.

I kill the engine outside the bungalow and approach the front porch the way those paranormal experts in that shitty movie approached the ghost house. Wary, slow with trepidation.

Please let him be alive and well.

Yup, for all my selfish prayers about wanting my father to die, I can't stomach the thought of walking into the house and finding his body.

I use my key to unlock the door, then step into the darkened front hall. "Dad?" I call out.

No answer.

Please let him be alive and well.

I inch toward the living room, my heart racing a mile a minute.

Please let him be—

Oh, thank Christ. He's alive.

But he's not well. Not by a longshot.

My chest clenches so hard I'm surprised I don't crack a rib or two. Dad is sprawled on the carpet, face down and shirtless, his cheek resting in a pool of vomit. One arm is flung out to the side, the other is tucked close to him—cradling a fucking bottle of bourbon like it's a newborn baby. Jesus, had he tried to protect his precious alcohol during his drunken tumble to the ground?

I feel nothing as I take in the pitiful scene in front of me. An acrid odor floats toward me. I wrinkle my nose, almost gag when I realize it's urine. Urine and alcohol, the fragrance of my childhood.

A part of me wants to turn on my heel and walk away. Walk away and not look back.

Instead, I shrug out of my jacket, toss it on the armchair, and carefully approach my passed-out father. "Dad."

He stirs, but doesn't answer.

"*Dad.*"

An agonized moan ripples from his throat. Christ, his pants are soaked with piss. And bourbon leaks from the bottle, staining the beige carpet.

"Dad, I need to check if anything's broken." I run my hands over his body, starting from his feet and moving upward, making sure he didn't break any bones when he fell.

My examination jolts him out of his haze. His eyelids pop open, revealing dilated pupils and a forlorn look that fractures a piece of my aching heart, the part of me that remembers idolizing him as a kid.

ELLE KENNEDY

He groans in panic. "Where's your mother? Don't want 'er to see me like this."

Crack. There goes another shard of my heart. At this rate, my chest will be a hollow cavern by the time I leave here.

"She's not home," I assure him. Then I snake my hands under his armpits so I can prop him into a sitting position.

He looks dazed. I honestly don't think he knows where he is or who I am. "She went grocery shopping?" he slurs.

"Yeah," I lie. "She won't be home for hours. Plenty of time to get you cleaned up, okay?"

He's swaying like crazy, and he's not even on his feet. The combined stench of vomit, alcohol and piss makes my eyes water. Or maybe that's not why they're watering. Maybe I'm on the verge of tears because I'm about to haul my own father in a fireman hold and help him take a shower. And then I'm going to dress him as if he's a goddamn toddler and tuck him into bed. Maybe *that's* why my eyes are stinging.

"Don't tell 'er about this, Jeffy. She's gonna be so mad at me. Don't want 'er to be mad at me. Don't wanna wake up Johnny…" He starts mumbling incoherently.

It's hard to breathe as I lift the stinking, blubbering mess that is my father into my arms and carry him to the bathroom at the end of the hall. Only one thought runs through my head.

My brother is a saint.

He's a goddamn saint.

He's been doing this, day in and day out, since I left for Briar. He's been mopping up my dad's vomit, and running the shop, and taking care of shit without a single complaint.

God, what is wrong with me? Fuck the NHL. Jeff deserves the chance to get out for a while. To travel with his girlfriend and live a normal life that doesn't involve stripping his own father naked and lifting him into the shower.

My lungs are burning now, because cold reality has sunk in. Jesus Christ. This is my future. In less than a year, this will be my full-time job.

I've never had a panic attack before. I'm not sure what they involve. Out-of-control heartbeat—is that a symptom? Cold, clammy hands that won't stop shaking? A windpipe that won't let a single burst of air

– 254 –

through? Because all those things are happening to me right now, and it's scaring the shit out of me.

"Johnny?" Dad blinks as the hot water sprays his head, plastering his dark hair to his forehead. "When'd ya get here?" He staggers in the tiled stall, his gaze darting in all directions. "Lemme get you a beer. Have a beer with your old man."

I almost throw up.

Okay, yeah. I think I might be having a panic attack.

I'M THREE HOURS LATE TO pick up Grace.

My phone died when I was in Munsen, and I don't have her number memorized because it's stored in my phone, so I couldn't even call her from the landline to let her know I'd be late.

My panic has subsided. Somewhat. Or maybe I've gone numb. All I know is that I need to see my girlfriend. I need to hold her and draw warmth from her body, because goddamn, I feel like a block of ice right now.

The porch light is on when I park in her father's driveway, but the yellow glow just ignites a spark of guilt. It's past ten o'clock. I'm so fucking late, and she's had to wait around for hours.

Practice, a cynical voice taunts. *For all the times she'll have to do it next year.*

My lungs seize. Jesus. It's true. How many times will something like this happen once I'm in Munsen full-time? How many plans will I be late for or have to cancel altogether?

How long before she dumps my ass for it?

I push aside the fearful notion as I ring the bell. Grace's dad answers the door, a frown puckering his mouth when he sees me.

"Hi." My voice is hoarse, lined with regret. "I'm sorry I couldn't make it to dinner, sir. I would've called, but my phone died and I…" No. No way am I telling him what I was forced to endure tonight. "Anyway, I'm here to take Grace back to campus."

"She already left," Mr. Ivers says ruefully. "Ramona's mother drove them back."

Disappointment crashes into me. "Oh."

"Gracie waited as long as she could for you…" Another frown, a clear rebuke. "But she needed to go home and study."

Shame funnels down my throat. Of course she waited. And of course she left.

"Ah…okay." I swallow. "I guess I'll head home then."

Before I can go, Mr. Ivers asks, "What's going on, John?"

The ache in my chest gets worse. "Nothing. It's nothing, sir. I, uh… had a family emergency."

He looks concerned. "Is everything all right?"

I nod.

Then I shake my head.

Then I nod again.

Christ, make up your fucking mind.

"Everything's fine," I lie.

"No, it's not. You're white as a sheet. And you look exhausted." He softens his tone. "Tell me what's wrong, son. Maybe I can help."

My face collapses. Oh shit. Oh fuck, why'd he have to call me *son*? The sting in my eyes is unbearable. My throat squeezes shut.

I need to get out of here.

"Why don't you come in?" he urges. "We'll sit down. I'll make some coffee." A wry smile lifts his lips. "I'd offer you something stronger, but you're still a minor, and I have a strict rule about giving alcohol to—"

I lose it.

I just. Fucking. Lose it.

Yup, I bawl like an honest-to-God baby, right there in front of Grace's father.

He freezes.

Only for a moment, and then he springs forward and puts his arms around me. He traps me in a hug I can't escape from, a solid wall of comfort I find myself sagging into. I'm so goddamn embarrassed, but I can't fight the tears anymore. I held them back in Munsen, but the panic is back, and so is the fear, and Grace's father called me *son*, and holy hell, I'm a mess.

I'm a total fucking mess.

CHAPTER 33

Grace

THE MOMENT I FINISH WRITING my Abnormal Psychology midterm, I race out of the lecture hall like I'm trying to outrun a forest fire.

My father is not the kind of man who overreacts or dabbles in melodrama. He's incredibly levelheaded and annoyingly straightforward, but he has the infuriating tendency to downplay a crisis instead of admitting when shit has hit the fan. So when he phoned me this morning and casually suggested that I should check in on my boyfriend today, I immediately knew something was wrong.

Actually, I knew it even before the phone call. The apologetic text Logan sent me last night had triggered my concern, but when I'd pushed him, he insisted that everything was okay, claiming he had to stay with his dad longer than he'd anticipated. He'd also made sure to reiterate that he was truly sorry for not making it to dinner or being able to drive me home.

I went to bed unable to fight the gnawing suspicion that something bad had happened, and now, combined with the vague heads up from my father, I'm certain of it. Which is why I opt to cab it to Logan's house instead of walking or taking the bus. I want to see him as soon as possible, before the crushing worry I'm feeling starts flashing worst-case scenarios in my head.

As I settle in the backseat of the taxi, I pull out my phone and text Logan.

Me: I'm on my way to your place.

Nearly a minute goes by before he responds with: Don't know if that's a good idea, babe. I'm in a lousy mood.

Me: Fine. Then I'll cheer u up.
Him: Not sure if u can.
Me: Still gonna try.

I tuck my cell away and bite my lip, wishing I knew what was going on with him. Obviously it has something to do with his visit home last night, but what the hell had happened?

A burst of anger goes off inside me. I'm running out of sympathy for Logan's father. I really am, and it's making me question how good of a therapist I'm going to be. Granted, I don't plan on specializing in addiction issues, but what does it say about me that I can't feel any compassion for Logan's alcoholic father?

Fuck, and now is *not* the time to be second-guessing my career path. I'm only equipped to deal with one crisis at a time.

The cab driver has to stop at the curb in front of Logan's house because the driveway is full. Logan's pickup and Garrett's Jeep are side-by-side, with Dean's sporty something-or-other and Hannah's borrowed Toyota behind them.

When I ring the bell, it isn't Logan who lets me in, but Tucker. A groove of dismay digs into his forehead as he closes the door behind me.

"Are you guys in a fight or something?" he asks in a low voice.

"No." I suddenly feel cold. "Did he say we were?"

"No, but he's been rude and bitchy all morning. Dean thought maybe the two of you were fighting."

"We're not," I say firmly. Then an unnerving thought occurs to me. "Has he been drinking?"

"Of course not. It's one-thirty in the afternoon." Tucker sounds confused. "He's upstairs. Last I checked, he was working on his marketing midterm."

His answer relieves me, but I'm not sure why. Logan has told me on numerous occasions that he doesn't drink when he's upset. I know he's afraid he might have inherited his father's addictive tendencies, and suddenly I feel like a jerk for asking Tucker that question in the first place.

"I'll go up and talk to him. Maybe he'll tell me what's bugging him."

I leave Tucker in the front hall and head up to Logan's room, where I experience another rush of relief.

He *looks* okay. Short dark hair looks the same. Blue eyes are alert. Sexy muscles rippling beneath his sweats and T-shirt. There are no outward signs of injury, but when our gazes lock, there's a world of pain in his expression.

"Hey," I say softly, walking over to give him a kiss. "What's going on?"

His lips brush mine, but the kiss lacks his usual warmth. "Your dad called you, huh?" he says wryly.

"Yep."

A shadow crosses his eyes. "What'd he say?"

"Hardly anything. He told me you stopped by last night, that he got the sense you were upset, and that I should check on you." I search his face. "What happened in Munsen?"

"Nothing."

"Logan."

"It was nothing, babe." He lets out a tired breath. "Or at least, nothing out of the ordinary."

I take his hand. God, it's like ice. Whatever went down last night, he's still exhibiting the effects of it.

"Sit down." I have to forcibly tug his powerful body beside me on the bed, but even after he submits, he stares straight ahead instead of meeting my eyes. "Will you please tell me what happened?"

"Jesus. What does it matter?"

"Because it *matters*, John." I start to feel aggravated. "Clearly you're upset about it, and I think it'll help if you talk about it."

His bitter laughter echoes between us. "Talking about it won't achieve a damn thing. But fine. You want to know what happened last night? I saw my future, that's what happened."

I flinch at the sharpness of his tone. "What do you mean?"

"I mean I saw my fucking future. I traveled forward in time, I got a visit from the Ghost of Christmas Future—how else do you want me to phrase it, Grace?"

My spine stiffens. "You don't have to be sarcastic. I get it."

"No, you don't. You *don't* get it. I have no life after I graduate. No future. But I'm doing it for my brother, because Jeff has dealt with it for almost four years now. And now it's my turn, and I don't fucking like it, but I'm going to suck it up and move back home, because he's my goddamn father and he needs my help."

His hoarse outburst cracks my heart in two.

"I know what it'll do to me," he continues, sounding more and more despondent. "I know it'll make me miserable and I'll probably grow to hate my dad, and I'll eventually lose you—"

"What?" I interrupt in shock. "What makes you think you'll lose me?"

He looks my way, his blue eyes filled with regret. "Because you'll wake up one day and realize you deserve better. Don't you see? Last night was a preview of what it's going to be like. We'll have plans, but I'll end up having to work late, or my dad will get wasted and fall down the stairs, and then I'll have to cancel on you, or worse, keep you waiting like I did last night. How long do you think you'll put up with that?"

Disbelief hurtles through me. "You honestly think I'm going to break up with you because you might be *late* a couple times?"

Logan doesn't respond, but his stony expression tells me that yes, he *does* believe that.

"Doesn't your brother have a girlfriend he's been with forever?" I point out.

"Kylie," he mumbles.

"Well, did Kylie break up with *him*? No, she didn't. Because she loves him, and she's willing to stand by him no matter what." I'm angry now. So angry I shoot to my feet, fighting the urge to smack some sense into him. "So what makes you think I won't stand by *you*?"

His silence irks the living fuck out of me.

"You know what, John? Screw you." I struggle to control my breathing. "Clearly you don't know me *at all* if you think I'm the kind of person who would give up on a relationship the moment it hits a few obstacles."

He finally answers, his voice low and sullen. "Can we please not talk about this anymore?"

Un-fucking-believable.

I gape at him, unable to fathom what I'm hearing. And unable to listen to it for even a second longer.

"You're right. We won't talk about it anymore." I grab my purse from where I dropped it on the floor and sling the strap over my shoulder. "Because I'm leaving."

That gets his attention. Frowning, he slowly rises to his feet. "Grace—"

I cut him off. "No. I'm not listening to this bullshit anymore. I'm going to leave you to your sulking, and maybe when you're finished with your one-man pity party, we can actually have a rational conversation." I'm spitting mad as I march toward the door. "And just in case my reaction to your idiocy didn't make it clear where I stand with us, then let me spell it out for you." I whirl around to scowl at him. "I love you, you stupid jackass."

Then I storm out of his room and slam the door behind me.

Logan

It takes me much, much longer than it should to snap out of the shocked trance I've fallen into. My mouth keeps opening and closing, my eyelids blinking at a rapid pace as I stare at the door Grace just tore out of.

She's absolutely right. I *am* a jackass. And I *did* doubt her commitment to our relationship. And—

Wait. She *loves* me?

My mouth opens again. And stays open. Agape, in fact, because her last words have finally registered in my extremely idiotic brain. She loves me. Even after I indicted her for a hypothetical future break-up and pretty much told her she was going to desert me when the going gets tough, she still told me she loved me.

And I let her walk away.

What the hell is the matter with me?

I bolt out of my room and take the stairs two at a time. There's no way Grace could have called a cab or made it to the bus stop yet, which means she's probably on the front stoop or nearing the end of the street.

Which means I can still catch her.

I skid into the front hall like a goddamn cartoon character, only to freeze when I find Garrett at the door. Then I hear a car engine from outside, and my heart hits the floor like a sack of bricks.

"Hannah's driving her home," Garrett says quietly.

I curse in frustration, flinging open the door in time to see the retreating taillights of Hannah's car. Damn it.

I spin around and hurry back upstairs, where I grab my phone and dial Grace's number. After it goes straight to voice mail, I shoot off a quick text.

Me: Baby, please come back. I'm such an ass. Need to make this right.

There's a long delay. Five seconds. Ten. And then she texts back.

Her: I need some time to digest your stupidity. I'll call u when I'm ready to talk.

Damn it. I drag both hands over my scalp, fighting the urge to strangle myself to death. Why do I always screw up when it comes to this girl?

Footsteps echo in the hallway, and when Garrett appears, I stifle another curse. "I can't deal with a lecture right now, man. I really can't."

"Wasn't gonna lecture you." He shrugs. "Just wanted to see if you're okay."

I sink down on the edge of the bed, slowly shaking my head. "Not in the slightest. I fucked up again."

"Damn right you did." My best friend props his elbow against the wall and sighs. "Wellsy and I heard her reaming you out."

"I think the whole neighborhood heard it," comes Tucker's voice. He enters my room and leans against the dresser. "Except maybe Dean, but that's because he's balls-deep in a puck bunny down in the living room."

I groan. "Seriously? Why can't he ever fuck in his room?"

"Do we really want to discuss that perv's sex life?" Tuck counters. "Because I don't think that should be at the top of your priority list right now."

He makes a good point. At the moment, my only priority is fixing things with Grace.

Christ, I shouldn't have spewed all that bullshit. I hadn't even meant it, at least not the part about her breaking up with me. That was my fear talking. And she's right—I *was* having a pity party. I was so freaked out about everything that happened with my dad last night, not to mention everything that happened *afterward*. When I cried in her father's arms.

I *cried* in her *father's arms*.

I let out another groan. "What if I lost her for good this time?"

Garrett and Tucker instantly shake their heads. "You didn't," Garrett assures me.

"How can you be so sure of that?"

"Because she told you she loves you."

"You stupid jackass," Tucker adds with a grin.

I love you, you stupid jackass. Not the words a man wants to hear. The first three, sure. The last three? Pass.

"How do I fix this?" I ask, sighing.

"Quick. Write her another poem," Garrett suggests.

I scowl at him.

"No, I think G's onto something," Tuck says. "I think the only way to save this is to bust out another grand gesture. What else was on her list?"

"Nothing," I moan. "I did everything on the list."

Tucker shrugs. "Then come up with something else."

A grand gesture? I'm a *guy*, damn it. I need direction. "Is Wellsy coming back here?" I ask Garrett.

He smirks at my pleading tone. "Even if she is, I'm not letting you pick her brain. You're gonna have to fix this one all on your own."

There's a pause, and then...

"You stupid jackass," my friends say in unison.

CHAPTER 34

Grace

I'M STILL FUMING AS I walk into the media building several hours after storming out of Logan's house. Normally I don't stay angry for long, but this time I'm having trouble expelling the volatile energy coursing inside me. I can't believe he actually thinks I'll dump him once he's in Munsen full-time. That I'll throw him away like an old busted-up toy and find something shiny and new to play with.

Jerk.

When I burst into the station, I spot Morris in the producer's booth, balancing the telephone handset on his shoulder as he jots something down on a notepad. I frown, noticing that Pace and Evelyn are already in their seats in the other booth. Pace snaps his earphones over the backward baseball cap on his head, while Evelyn bends over a sheet of paper in concentration.

Am I late? I glance at the clock on the far wall. Nope. I'm early, actually. So why is Morris in my booth?

I take a step forward, only to halt when Daisy wanders out of the back corridor. She pushes her bangs off her forehead—they're neon-blue now—and grins sheepishly when she sees me.

"Hey," I greet my roommate. "What are you doing here?" She doesn't usually hang out at the station unless she's supposed to host or produce, and I know for a fact she's scheduled to do neither today.

"Hey." For some reason, she looks almost...guilty. "I just popped in to drop off coffee for everyone."

"Since when are you the station gofer?" I narrow my eyes. "Your shirt is inside out." I pause. "And backwards."

She glances at her tank top, wincing when she notices the tag sticking out from her collarbone. Then her eyes flit toward the producer's booth.

I follow her gaze, gasping when I find Morris grinning at us. "Holy shit. You and Morris are hooking up?"

Daisy sighs. "Maybe."

My anger at Logan is momentarily eclipsed by her news. Our schedules are so hectic that Daisy and I are hardly ever in our room at the same time, which works out great for when I want privacy, but it also means I miss out on girl talk and up-to-date gossip.

"Since when?" I squeal in excitement.

"A couple weeks now?" She shrugs. "I didn't tell you because we've both been so busy. You're cool with it, though, right?"

"Of course. Why wouldn't I be?"

"You know, because you and Morris went out."

I laugh. "Once. And my behaviour didn't exactly warrant a second date. I think this is awesome. You totally just made my day—and trust me, my day has been shit, so it really needed to be made."

"Oh no. What happened?"

My bad mood returns like an unwanted rash. "I got in a fight with Logan. And that's all I'm saying on the subject, because if I talk about it right now, it'll just piss me off again and then I'll be too distracted to produce Dumb and Dumber's show."

We both glance at the main booth, where Evelyn is using the reflection on her water glass to check her makeup, dabbing delicately at her eye shadow. Pace is engrossed with his phone, his chair tipped back so far that I predict a very loud disaster in the near future.

"God, I love them," Daisy says with a snicker. "I don't think I've ever met two more self-absorbed people."

Morris saunters out of the booth and wanders over to us. He notices Daisy's shirt and says, "Sweetheart, we're at work. Show some decorum."

"Says the guy who ripped this shirt off me in the supply closet." Rolling her eyes, she takes a step away. "I'm going to make myself presentable in the bathroom. I'd do it out here, but I'm scared Dumber might take a picture and post it on a porn site."

"Wait, the names Dumb and Dumber actually correspond to each of them?" Morris says in surprise. "I thought it was more of a general thing. Which one is Dumber?"

The second the question leaves his mouth, a muffled crash reverberates from the booth, and we all turn to see Pace tangled up on the floor. Yup, the guy who spent an hour regaling me about his cow-tipping days back in Iowa? Tipped himself right over.

From behind the glass, Pace bounces to his feet, notices us staring, and mouths the words, "I'm okay!"

Morris sighs. "I withdraw the question."

As Daisy leaves to fix her shirt, Morris casually follows me to the booth door. "First caller's already on hold," he tells me. "I screened her and wrote her info on the sheet."

My forehead creases. "Did you open the lines before I got here?"

He wears a sheepish look. "Not on purpose. I was calling my dad and pressed the wrong button, and then the phone rang and I was already in there so I took the caller's info. She's got an urgent G-spot question for Evelyn, so this should be interesting."

"Isn't it always?" I say with a grin.

I take my seat and conduct my pre-show check. The blinking lights on the phone tell me there are more callers waiting to be screened. I chat with the first one, verify his motives, then send him back on hold. I'm about to screen the next one when Pace and Evelyn kick off the show.

"What's up, broskis!" Pace greets the radio audience. "You're listening to Whatcha Need with Pace 'N Evelyn."

Cringing, Evelyn leans into her microphone. "Before we start, I'd like to ask everyone to speak in their indoor voices today, because I am currently sporting a *brutal* hang-over." She glares at her co-host. "I'm talking to you, asswipe."

And so it begins.

"Let's chat with our first caller," Pace says cheerfully. "Who we talking to right now?"

Since I'm not eager to listen to Evelyn talk about G-spots, I lean forward to take another call, only to freeze in my chair when a familiar voice wafts out of the speaker over the door.

"Hey, this is Logan."

My pulse speeds up.

Oh God.

What the hell is he doing?

"Tell us whatcha need, my man."

My boyfriend audibly clears his throat. "Well, here's the thing, Pace. And Evelyn—hey, Evelyn, female opinion definitely appreciated. I'm hoping you guys can give me some advice on how to win my girl back."

Pace chuckles into the mic. "Ooooh boy. Someone found themselves in the dog house?"

"Big-time," Logan confirms.

"What'd you do to piss off your lady? We need the deets before we dispense the wisdom."

Every inch of me tenses as I await Logan's response. God. I can't believe he's about to air our dirty laundry on this stupid campus show.

"Long story short? I projected my own fears and insecurities on her, and made some presumptions that I probably shouldn't—"

"Gonna stop you right there, broski," Pace says, rubbing his scruffy beard growth in dismay. "You just threw around a lot of big words. How 'bout you dumb it down for us—I mean, for peeps who might not be good with the English language. Shout out to all our ESL listeners out there!"

A laugh rips out of my throat. *Oh, Pace. Never change.*

Logan sounds like he's trying not to laugh as he rephrases himself. "Bottom line? I screwed up. I said some stupid shit I didn't mean, it pissed her off, and she stormed off."

Pace sighs. "Bitches be cray."

"Hey, Logan?" Evelyn drawls.

"Yeah?"

"You sound hot. Are you sure you even want this chick? Because I'm free tonight if you're interested."

A strangled cough fills the airwaves. "Um. Uh, thanks for the offer. But yeah, I want her." He pauses. "I'm in love with her."

My heart soars like a kite in the wind. He's *in love* with me?

Then it sinks like a stone. Wait. What if he's only saying it because I said I loved *him*?

"I've been in love with her for a few months now," he continues, and his husky confession re-inflates my heart. "I didn't tell her because I didn't want to scare her off by saying it too soon."

"Dude, you should've told her."

I'm startled by Pace's earnest response. Touched, even. At least until he finishes that sentence.

"If you say it right off the bat, they drop their panties super-fast. Means you don't have to put as much work into bagging them."

"Uh-huh," Logan says as if he's in agreement, but I've known him long enough to be able to pick up on his sarcasm. "Anyway, this girl…she's the love of my life. She's smart and funny and unbelievably compassionate. She forgives people even when they don't deserve it. She—"

"Good lay?" Pace interrupts.

"Oh yeah. The best."

God, my cheeks are on fire now.

"But the sex is just icing," Logan says softly. "It's everything else that matters most."

A shadow crosses my peripheral vision. I turn my head expecting to see Daisy or Morris on the other side of the glass door.

My breath hitches when my gaze locks with Logan's. He's on his cell phone, wearing faded jeans and his hockey jacket, and his blue eyes shine with sincerity.

Our esteemed hosts notice him as well, and a gasp echoes in the air.

"Wait—we've been talking to *John Logan?*" Evelyn shrieks.

"Wait—you're talking about *Gretchen?*" Pace exclaims, his gaze darting like a Ping-Pong ball from me to Logan.

"No, I'm talking about Grace," Logan says, smiling at me through the glass. "Grace Elizabeth Ivers. The woman I love."

I don't know whether to stand up on my chair and shout out "I love you too," or hide under the desk in embarrassment. Big, public displays freak me out. If I owned a cloak of invisibility, I'd wear it every time a birthday or some other major event rolled around, because I hate, hate, *hate* being the center of attention.

But I can't tear my eyes off Logan. I can't breathe, or move, or form a single thought other than *He loves me.*

"Anyway, I'm hanging up now," Logan tells the hosts. "I'm pretty sure I can take it from here."

The line cuts off, and I shoot a panicky glance at the switchboard. Shit. The show is still on the air. I'm supposed to put on the next caller.

To my relief, Morris appears, giving Logan a friendly thump on the arm as he hurries into the producer's booth. "Go," Morris orders. "I'll cover the rest of the show."

"Are you sure?"

He grins. "That was always the plan. Who do you think screened the call, Gretch?" He points to the door. "Go."

I don't need to be told twice.

I hurry out of the booth and throw my arms around Logan's strong shoulders. "I cannot believe you just did that," I blurt out.

As his laughter tickles the top of my head, his arms slide down to my hips, large hands curling around my waist. "I figured nothing short of a grand gesture would convince you how shitty I feel about what happened earlier."

I pull back, tipping my head to meet his gorgeous eyes. "You should feel shitty," I chastise. "I can't believe you said all that stuff. I don't plan on *ever* breaking up with you."

"Good. Because I'm never breaking up with *you*." He brings one hand to my cheek, stroking it with infinite tenderness. "Actually, I think I'm going to marry you one day."

Shock jolts through me. "What?"

"*One day*," he repeats when he sees my expression. "I mean it, Grace, I'm in this for the long haul. You still have two years left at Briar, and I'll be in Munsen during that time, but I promise you, I'll come see you as often as I can. Every available second I have will be yours." His voice thickens. "*I'm* yours."

I swallow a lump of emotion. "Did you really mean what you told Pace just now?"

"You mean…that I love you?"

I nod.

"I meant every damn word, gorgeous." He hesitates. Visibly swallows. "Hannah was trying to describe love to me last semester. She said it feels like your heart is about to overflow, and that when you love someone, you need them more than anything else in the world, more than food or water or air. That's how I feel about you. I *need* you. I can't stand the thought of being without you." He releases a shaky breath. "You're the last person I think about before I go to sleep, and the first person I think about when I open my eyes in the morning. You're it for me, baby."

The heartfelt words unleash a flood of warmth inside me, but despite that, I can't help but gaze at him with profound sorrow. "What about everything you said earlier…about your future, and how you're going to be miserable and hate your life…" I bite my lower lip. "I don't want that to happen, Logan. I don't want you to turn bitter, and hateful, and…" I trail off.

His fingers tremble against my cheek. "I won't. Or at least, I'll try not to. It's going to suck, Grace. We both know that, but I promise not to let it destroy me, or *us*." A crack wobbles his voice. "And it won't be forever, just until Jeff comes back and takes over again. The next few years, it'll probably feel like I'm wandering around in a pitch-black tunnel, but there *is* a light at the end of it. And as long as you're with me, there'll be a light inside of it, too. Without you, it'll just be darkness."

I burst out laughing, and a hurt expression fills his eyes.

"You think that's funny?" he says sadly.

"No, I was thinking it's a damn shame you didn't put everything you just said into the poem you wrote me."

A tentative smile lifts his mouth. "You liked that, huh?"

"I *loved* it." My heart constricts. "I love *you*."

The smile widens. "Even after I acted like a stupid jackass today?"

"Yep."

"Even though I'll probably act like a stupid jackass again? Because I can't promise not to. Apparently I'm hopeless when it comes to relationships."

"No, you're not." I ease up on my tiptoes and kiss the corner of his jaw. "You're a bit inept, sure. But you're also ridiculously talented when it comes to romantic gestures, so if you screw up again, I'm ninety percent sure you'll be able to win me back."

"Only ninety percent?" He looks upset.

"Well, it depends how badly you screw up. I mean, if it's picking a fight with me like you did today, then obviously we'll be able to work through it. But if I'm over at your house and I go down to the basement and find a serial killer lair? No promises."

"Jesus Christ, what is your obsession with serial killers?" He grins. "Hey, that should be your specialty. Profiling killers."

Damn. Not a bad idea.

I decide to put a pin in that, then loop my arms around his neck again. "Question."

His eyes twinkle. "Hit me."

"Can we kiss now, or are you still groveling?"

"Depends on whether my girlfriend requires more groveling."

"Nope. I require *this*." I cup the back of his head and yank his mouth down on mine,

The kiss is…magic. It's always magic when we're together. As our tongues meet in a reckless tangle, my mind spins and my body sings.

"Love you, Johnny," I murmur into his lips.

His laughter warms my face. Then he brushes his mouth over mine and whispers, "Love you too, gorgeous."

CHAPTER 35

Logan

THE NEXT MORNING, I WAKE up with Grace snuggled up beside me, and it's the best fucking feeling in the whole fucking world. She slept at my place last night, and we stayed up until four a.m., alternating between talking, cuddling, and having sex. And not the hollow, meaningless kind I've been indulging in since I started college. Sex with Grace means something. It doesn't make me feel hollow, but full. Brimming with emotions I can't even give labels to.

Grace stirs in my arms, and I absently toy with a strand of her hair, twirling it around my fingers.

"Morning," she says, yawning as she lifts her head.

"Morning."

"What time is it?"

"Ten-thirty."

"Oh no. We slept in? Don't you have practice?"

"Not for a few hours."

"Oh, okay, good. We stayed up way too late last night."

She hops out of bed and starts searching the room for her clothes. I grin, because I'm the one responsible for why her pants are flung on top of the dresser and why her lacy panties are scrunched up in a ball across the room. So sue me. Groveling makes me horny.

"Is it cool if I invite Morris and Daisy to the game tomorrow?" She eases her panties up her smooth, bare legs, and I'm so distracted by the sight that I forget what she asked a nanosecond after she asks it.

My cock hardens beneath the sheets, tenting up as if trying to get Grace's attention. She sighs when she notices the campsite on the bed.

"I swear, you've got sex on the brain every second of the day."

"Pretty much," I agree, then waggle my eyebrows. "Why are you getting dressed? Wouldn't you rather come here and sit on my dick?"

She rolls her eyes. "Sure, if you want me to pee all over you." When I open my mouth, she raises a hand in warning. "And don't you dare say you're into that, because I am *not* incorporating *pee* into our sex life."

I flop onto my side and laugh hysterically. "Relax," I stutter between chuckles. "Golden showers don't get me off."

Grace snickers. "Thank God."

After she ducks into the hall to use the bathroom, I reluctantly drag myself out of bed and track down a pair of sweatpants. I'm thinking of suggesting the diner for breakfast. After last night's strenuous sexcapades, I could really go for a huge greasy platter of bacon and sausage and—and Coach will murder me if I show up to practice sluggish and crashing from a grease high. Frickin' in-season nutrition regimen.

I pace around as I wait for Grace to come out of the bathroom, because now I'm the one who needs to piss like a racehorse. My buzzing phone serves as a distraction from my about-to-explode bladder, but when my brother's number flashes on the screen, my good morning mood fades away.

"Hey," Jeff says after I pick up. "Can you come by today?"

I stifle a groan. "I've got practice at one-thirty, man."

"Come now, then. We'll be done long before that."

"Done what?" I ask warily.

"No idea. Dad says he has something important to tell us, but he won't give me any more details than that. Marty's covering for me in the shop right now, so get your ass over here. It won't take long."

I hang up feeling even warier than before. He has something important to tell us? What the hell could it be? We haven't had a family meeting in…ever. My father has never sat us down for a talk, serious or otherwise.

I'm still frowning when Grace reappears, and concern instantly creases her features. "Everything okay?"

I slowly shake my head. "My dad wants to sit down with me and Jeff today."

"Today? But you have practice."

"He said it won't take long. He just needs to tell us something."

"Tell you what?"

"I don't know."

She goes quiet for a moment. "Do you want me to go with you?"

I'm touched by the offer, but I shake my head again. "I don't think he'll want anyone else there."

"Obviously," she says with a smile. "I figured I could wait in the car. That way if it's something bad, you'll have someone to talk to on the drive back."

I hesitate. I'm not sure I want to take the risk of Grace running into my dad.

But I also don't want to be alone.

"Okay," I answer, releasing a breath. "But only if you stay in the car. I don't know what kind of state he'll be in when we get there."

We're both somber as we leave the house fifteen minutes later, and the weather matches our foreboding expressions. The sky is overcast, the metallic scent in the air hinting at a downpour.

My uneasiness grows the closer we get to Munsen. By the time I reach the end of the long driveway and park in front of the bungalow, my nerves have formed a solid, immovable ball in the pit of my stomach.

"I'll be right back," I tell Grace, leaning in to kiss her cheek.

She shakes her head. "Take your time." Unzipping her canvas bag, she pulls out a psych textbook and holds it up. "I'll be fine out here, I promise. So don't try to rush on my account, okay?"

I exhale shakily. "Okay."

A minute later, I walk through the front door without knocking, flinching when the familiar smell of stale beer fills my nostrils. I swear, it's like the walls in this house are soaked with alcohol, slowly releasing the sour odor into the air.

"John?" My brother's voice drifts through the hall. "We're in the kitchen."

I keep my shoes on, a habit left over from childhood. I've stepped on far too many puddles on the floors and carpets of this house and soaked my socks. Puddles that weren't always of the alcoholic beverage variety.

I know something's up the second I enter the kitchen. Jeff and Dad are at the weathered oak table, sitting across from each other. Jeff is sipping a coffee. My father has a longneck bottle of Bud in front of him, both hands wrapped around the base.

"Johnny. Sit down," Dad says.

The beer isn't a promising sign, but at least he looks and sounds relatively sober. And by sober, I mean not passed out in a pool of his own vomit.

I sink into the nearest chair without a word. Studying my dad's face. Waiting. Studying Jeff's face. Waiting.

"Chad Jensen came to see me yesterday."

My head swings back toward my father. "What? Are you serious?" Why the hell would Coach talk to my father?

Dad nods. "He called ahead, asked if he could stop by for a chat. I said sure, why not, and he came by yesterday evening."

I'm still battling my shock. Coach Jensen drove out to Munsen and met with my father?

"I didn't know about it," Jeff speaks up hastily, obviously misconstruing my expression. "I was over at Kylie's when he stopped by, and Dad only told me about it this morning."

I ignore Jeff's assurances. "What did he want?" I ask suspiciously.

Dad's cheeks hollow as if he's grinding his teeth. "To discuss possible solutions."

"Solutions for what?"

"For next year." His gaze stays locked with mine. "He assured me he wasn't trying to be disrespectful or overstep his boundaries, that he understood the car accident was difficult for me and my family, and why you're needed at the shop after you graduate." My father's hands tighten around the beer bottle. "But he was hoping there might be some way for you to play hockey next year while still helping out your family."

My hands curl into fists, and I press them tight to the table, trying to control my temper. I know Coach meant well, but *what the hell?*

"He also asked me why I didn't go on disability, if my injuries from the accident were bad enough to prevent me from working."

Fucking Jensen. He *absolutely* overstepped his boundaries.

"Your coach has no idea I'm a drunk, does he?" Dad mutters, and now he's no longer looking at me. He's staring at his hands.

"No, he doesn't," I mutter back. "I only told him about the accident.

And that was just because I needed to tell him something so he'd get off my case about not entering the draft."

Dad raises his gaze to mine again. "You should've told me you didn't declare."

"What difference would it have made?"

"A huge one," he snaps. "It's bad enough that I woke up the other morning wearing clean underwear and all tucked into bed like a fucking child, with the knowledge that my twenty-one-year-old son is the one who put me there." His head shifts to Jeff. "And that my other son is running my business because I'm too much of a mess to do it myself. But now you're telling me you're passing up the chance to play for the goddamn *Bruins* so you can take care of my sorry ass?"

He's breathing hard, his hands shaking so wildly the bottle is close to toppling over. He lifts it to his lips and takes a hurried sip before slamming it on the table.

Jeff and I exchange a wary look. Seeing him drink brings identical frowns to our faces, which causes Dad to groan in anguish.

"Goddamn it, don't look at me like that. I have to fucking drink this, because the last time I tried to quit cold turkey I ended up in the hospital with seizures."

I suck in a shocked breath.

So does Jeff.

Dad looks from me to my brother, then addresses us in a voice that rings with despair. "I'm going back to rehab."

The announcement is greeted with silence.

"I'm serious. I spoke to someone at the state facility I went to last time and asked to be put on the waiting list, but they told me a slot opened up five minutes before I called." He snorts. "If that's not divine intervention, I don't know what is."

My brother and I remain quiet. We've heard this speech before. Many times before. And we've learned not to get our hopes up anymore.

Sensing our misgivings, Dad sharpens his tone. "It'll stick this time. I'm going to make sure of it."

There's a beat, and then Jeff clears his throat. "How long is the program?"

"Six months."

My eyebrows fly up. "That long?"

"With my history, they think that would be best."

"In-patient?" Jeff asks.

"Yeah." Dad's features grow pained. "Two weeks for the detox. Christ, I'm not looking forward to that part." Then he shakes his head, as if snapping himself out of it. "But I'll do it. I'll do it, and it'll stick. You know why? Because I'm your *father*."

Shame pours off him in palpable waves. "My kids shouldn't be taking care of me. I should be taking care *you*." He gives me a hard look. "You shouldn't be giving up your dreams because of me." He turns to Jeff. "And neither should you."

"That's all good and well," Jeff says, sounding tired. "But what about the garage? Even if the program sticks, you still won't be able to work because of your legs. You can handle the administrative stuff, sure. But not the labor."

"I'll apply for disability." Dad pauses. "And I'm going to sell the business."

My brother does *not* look pleased about that. Me, I'm still reeling from everything else he's just told us.

"Kylie and I are only traveling for a couple years," Jeff says unhappily. "I want to work here when we get back."

"Then we'll hire someone to run it until you're ready to come back. But that someone won't be your brother, Jeffrey. And it won't be you, if you don't want it to be." He slides his chair back and gingerly gets to his feet, then reaches for the cane leaning against the wall. "I know you boys have heard this before. I know it'll take a lot more than a few promises to prove I'm serious about this."

He's right about that.

"The center is picking me up in an hour," he says brusquely. "I have to go pack."

Jeff and I stare at each other again.

Son of a bitch. He's really going to rehab.

"I don't expect a hug goodbye, but it'd be nice if you boys called me every once in a while, let me know how you're doing." He glances at Jeff. "We'll talk about the shop when I'm done packing. Not sure if we should close up while I'm gone, or if you want to stick around a while longer. If we do close, I'd appreciate it if you could finish up the current work orders for this week."

Looking slightly dazed, my brother manages a nod.

"And you…" My father's bloodshot eyes zero in on me. "You better make it to that Providence practice. Jensen said it's pretty much a tryout, so don't screw it up."

I've been silent for so long it takes me a moment to find my voice. "I won't," I say hoarsely.

"Good. I expect you to tell me about it when I call you in two weeks. You probably won't hear from me before that. Not during the detox." His voice is equally hoarse. "Now get outta here, John. Your brother says you've got shit to do today. Jeffrey, we'll talk shortly."

A moment later, he's gone, and we hear his labored footsteps in the hallway, heading toward his bedroom. Suddenly I feel as dazed as Jeff looks, and once again, we gape at each other for several long moments.

"You think he's for real?" Jeff asks.

"Sure seems like it." Old doubts creep in, bringing a cagey note to my voice. "Think he'll manage to stay on the wagon this time?"

"Fuck. I hope so."

Yeah, me too. But I've been burned by my father too many times in the past. Fooled by his promises and his supposed resolve. The cynic in me thinks we'll be having this same conversation in a year or two or five, and maybe we will. Maybe he'll sober up, come home in six months, and start drinking again. Or maybe not.

Either way, I'm free.

The realization slams into me with the force of a tidal wave, nearly knocking me out of my chair. I won't have to live here in May. Won't have to work here. Dad'll be on disability, the garage will either be sold or managed by someone else until Jeff is ready to take over, and I'll be *free*.

I shoot to my feet, startling my brother. "I have to go. My girlfriend's waiting for me in the car."

He blinks. "You have a girlfriend?"

"Yup. I'll introduce you another time. I've really gotta go."

"John." His voice stops me before I reach the doorway.

"Yeah?"

"You'll give me a signed jersey when you make the team, right?"

A smile stretches across my entire face. "Damn right I will."

I leave the kitchen with the sound of my brother's laughter at my back and sprint out of the house. From the porch, I see Grace in the pickup, her feet raised on the dashboard and her nose buried in her textbook. Her peripheral vision must have caught the front door flying open, because she lifts her head and turns it toward the porch, and I must still be grinning like a fool, because a little smile curves her sexy lips.

I quickly descend the porch steps and make my way to the truck. It's still gloomy out. The trees are swaying ominously. The clouds are a thick, dark mass undulating overhead. The sky is more black than gray.

And yet my future has never looked brighter.

EPILOGUE

TWO YEARS LATER

Grace

MAN, THIS EXECUTIVE SUITE AT TD Garden is fancy-pants. I feel like a queen reigning over her kingdom as I lean forward in my plush leather seat and sweep my gaze over the massive arena. Thousands of screaming hockey fans fill the seats, an endless sea of faces, a blur of black and yellow occasionally broken up by the white and turquoise of the Sharks fans who happen to be in attendance.

"This is *so* intense," Hannah whispers in my ear, and I know she's trying to keep her voice down so the three beer-sipping wives standing five feet away don't tease us again about our novice status. Or mine, at least. This is Logan's first season with Boston—he played in the AHL for a year after college, until the Bruins finally decided he was ready and signed him.

Since Garrett had an amazing rookie season last year, I figured Hannah would be an old pro by now, but when we were being led into the private suite, she confessed that she'd sat in the club seats last year because she'd been too intimidated to sit up here alone.

We haven't stopped marveling since we arrived. Each time the other people milling in the suite turned their heads, the two of us have oohed and aahed about something else. The private bar across the room. The gourmet spread on the granite counter. The seats. The view. No detail has gone un-oohed or un-aahed.

I'm hoping we'll learn to restrain ourselves after we've had a few games under our belts, but I'm not sure I'll ever get used to this kind of luxury.

"A part of me keeps expecting security to show up and throw us out," I whisper back. "I've never felt so out of place."

She laughs softly. "Me too. But I'm sure we'll adjust." Her green eyes focus on the rink below us. The players are still warming up, and I know the moment her gaze lands on Garrett, because her entire face lights up.

I'm pretty sure the same thing happens to me when I look at Logan.

"Do you think they'll get a lot of playing time?"

I think it over. "Logan? Probably not. Garrett? Absolutely. He and Lukov were an unstoppable force of nature last season." Thinking of Shane Lukov brings a smile to my face. When I met him in person for the first time this summer, he spent ten minutes teasing me mercilessly about the "endorsement" he gave, and how he credits himself for my relationship with his new teammate.

"Okay, I need to ask you something, and no bullshitting me." Hannah leans in close again. "Do you *really* love hockey now, or is that just the line you're feeding Logan?"

I press my lips together to keep from laughing. "Well, I don't *hate* it. And I definitely don't find it as boring anymore, but…" I lower my voice "…I'd still rather watch football."

She snorts.

The dark-haired woman who slides into the seat beside me is not as amused. "Shame on you, Grace Ivers," Logan's mother chides. "I thought we'd succeeded in converting you."

"Sorry, Jean, not yet."

She sighs. "Well, I'm encouraged by the 'yet'. Means there's still hope that you'll see the error of your ways."

Hannah and I laugh.

God, I adore Logan's mom. She's sweet and funny and so damn supportive of her sons. Her husband David, on the other hand, is one of the blandest men I've ever met in my life, but he's so good to Jean that I can't help but like him.

And if I'm being honest, Logan's father is growing on me too. He's been sober for nearly two years now, and he seems determined to keep it that way. Though sometimes it's hard to reconcile the charming man I've gotten to know with the drunken mess Logan used to have to scrape off the floor.

Since Jean still refuses to have contact with Ward, Logan's parents have agreed to alternate their visits to his games. Same rule applies to their visits to our apartment, which is located halfway between Hastings and Boston, making it only a thirty-minute commute for each of us. Once I graduate this year, we're planning on finding a place in the city. Garrett and Hannah already live here, in a gorgeous brownstone I helped Hannah decorate.

"It's so funny," Hannah muses. "Garrett told me that he and Logan have talked about the two of them in Bruins jerseys ever since freshman year. And now it's actually happening." She smiles. "I guess some dreams really do come true."

I follow her gaze, a smile touching my lips as I watch the man I love in the uniform *he* loves, flying across the ice to the roar of the crowd.

"Yep," I answer softly. "I guess they do."

ELLE KENNEDY

THE DEAL

She's about to make a deal with the college bad boy...

Hannah Wells has finally found someone who turns her on. But while she might be confident in every other area of her life, she's carting around a full set of baggage when it comes to sex and seduction. If she wants to get her crush's attention, she'll have to step out of her comfort zone and make him take notice...even if it means tutoring the annoying, childish, cocky captain of the hockey team in exchange for a pretend date.

...and it's going to be oh so good

All Garrett Graham has ever wanted is to play professional hockey after graduation, but his plummeting GPA is threatening everything he's worked so hard for. If helping a sarcastic brunette make another guy jealous will help him secure his position on the team, he's all for it. But when one unexpected kiss leads to the wildest sex of both their lives, it doesn't take long for Garrett to realize that pretend isn't going to cut it. Now he just has to convince Hannah that the man she wants looks a lot like him.

THE SCORE

He knows how to score, on and off the ice

Allie Hayes is in crisis mode. With graduation looming, she still doesn't have the first clue about what she's going to do after college. To make matters worse, she's nursing a broken heart thanks to the end of her longtime relationship. Wild rebound sex is definitely not the solution to her problems, but gorgeous hockey star Dean Di Laurentis is impossible to resist. Just once, though, because even if her future is uncertain, it sure as heck won't include the king of one-night stands.

It'll take more than flashy moves to win her over

Dean always gets what he wants. Girls, grades, girls, recognition, girls… he's a ladies man, all right, and he's yet to meet a woman who's immune to his charms. Until Allie. For one night, the feisty blonde rocked his entire world—and now she wants to be friends? Nope. It's not over until he says it's over. Dean is in full-on pursuit, but when life-rocking changes strike, he starts to wonder if maybe it's time to stop focusing on scoring…and shoot for love.

THE GOAL

To be published: September 26, 2016

ACKNOWLEDGMENTS

One of my favorite parts of the writing process is getting to interact with some pretty awesome people. With every book I write, I meet new people and make new friends, and I can't thank them enough for their support, assistance and encouragement:

The Locker Room ladies—Kristen, Sarina, Monica and Cora. Chatting with you guys is the highlight of my day! And I have so much love for all the amazing members in the group for making me laugh, introducing me to new books, and posting pics of super-sexy athletes!

Early readers Viv, Jane, Sarina and Kristen for helping me whip Logan into shape.

Extra thanks to Viv, the bestest bestie a girl could ever have.

The amazing and ridiculously patient Zoe York, for holding my hand through the awful business-y stuff!

Nicole Snyder, friend, assistant and overall lifesaver—you're the absolute best!

The fabulous Ms. Katy Evans, for your endless cheerleading, contagious enthusiasm, and for constantly putting a big smile on my face!

My editor Gwen Hayes and proofreader Sharon Muha—you guys know how much I love you!

My publicist Nina Bocci—I'm not sure how I ever survived before without you.

To all the bloggers and reviewers who helped with cover reveals, posted reviews, and pretty much talked up the series to anyone who would listen—you are amazing.

And to all my readers—your passion and enthusiasm for this series is so darn touching. I love you guys!

ABOUT THE AUTHOR

A *New York Times*, *USA Today* and *Wall Street Journal* bestselling author, Elle Kennedy grew up in the suburbs of Toronto, Ontario, and holds a BA in English from York University. From an early age, she knew she wanted to be a writer and actively began pursuing that dream when she was a teenager. She loves strong heroines and sexy alpha heroes, and just enough heat and danger to keep things interesting!

Elle loves to hear from her readers. Visit her website www.ellekennedy. com or sign up for her newsletter to receive updates about upcoming books and exclusive excerpts. You can also find her on Facebook or follow her on Twitter (@ElleKennedy).

Lightning Source UK Ltd.
Milton Keynes UK
UKHW020821290721
387925UK00009B/1922

9 781775 293941